D0278547

LIMERICK CITY LIBRARY

407510

·kcity.ie/library
@limerickcity.ie

The Granary.
Michael S' ·
Limerick

is issued subject to the Rules of this Lib
must be returned not later than the last
stɑ·n ed belov.

Date

WITHDRAWN FROM STOCK

EMPEROR

TIME'S TAPESTRY: 1

EMPEROR

TIME'S TAPESTRY: 1

Stephen Baxter

GOLLANCZ

LONDON

Copyright © Stephen Baxter 2006
All rights reserved

The right of Stephen Baxter to be identified as the
author of this work has been asserted by him in accordance
with the Copyright, Designs and Patents Act 1988.

First published in Great Britain in 2006 by
Gollancz
An imprint of the Orion Publishing Group
Orion House, 5 Upper St Martin's Lane,
London WC2H 9EA

A CIP catalogue record for this book is
available from the British Library

ISBN 0 57507 432 9 (cased)
ISBN 9 780 57507 432 3 (cased)
ISBN 0 57507 433 7 (trade paperback)
ISBN 9 780 57507 433 0 (trade paperback)

1 3 5 7 9 10 8 6 4 2

Typeset by Deltatype Ltd, Birkenhead, Merseyside
Printed in Great Britain at
Mackays of Chatham plc, Chatham, Kent

The Orion Publishing Group's policy is to use papers
that are natural, renewable and recyclable products and made
from wood grown in sustainable forests. The logging and
manufacturing processes are expected to conform to the
environmental regulations of the country of origin.

www.orionbooks.co.uk

Place names:

Banna, Birdoswald
Caledonia, Scotland
Camulodunum, Colchester
Durovernum, Canterbury
Eburacum, York
Dolaucothi
Londinium, London
Mona, Anglesey
Rutupiae, Richborough

Tamesis, R Thames
Sabrina, R Severn
Tinea, R Tyne
Ituna, R Solway
Cantiaci River, R Medway

Gesoriacum, Boulogne
Massilia, Marseilles

Principal British Nations:

Atrebates
Brigantia
Catuvellauni
Cantiaci
Durotriges
Iceni
Ordovices
Silures

Timeline

55–54BC	Julius Caesar's expeditions to Britain
4BC	Birth of Nectovelin
c.AD38	Death of Cunobelin
AD43	Invasion of Britain by Claudius
AD51	Defeat of Caratacus
AD60–61	Revolt of Boudicca
AD69–71	Brigantian civil war and annexation
AD77–84	Agricola's campaigns in Scotland
AD122	Hadrian in Britain; construction of Wall begins
AD193–197	Britain under the rule of Clodius Albinus
AD208–211	Campaigns of Severus in Scotland
AD259–274	Britain under the rule of the Gallic Emperors
AD287–296	Britain under the rule of Carausias and Allectus
AD296	Invasion of Britain by Constantius Chlorus
AD306	Constantine the Great elevated in Britain
AD312	Constantine's defeat of Maxentius in the west
AD314	Constantine raises troops in Britain for war with the east
AD324	Constantine sole emperor, Constantinople founded
AD337	Death of Constantine
AD350	Magnentius proclaimed emperor in Britain
AD367	The Barbarian Conspiracy
AD378	Roman defeat by Visigoths at Adrianopolis
AD383	Magnus Maximus proclaimed emperor in Britain
AD407	Constantine III proclaimed emperor in Britain
AD409	British Revolution; formal end of Roman rule in Britain
AD418	Excommunication of Pelagius

Note on Measurements

1 Roman foot = 0.96 modern foot = 11.5 modern inches (292 mm)
1 Roman mile = 0.96 modern mile = 1686 modern yards (1.54 km)

Oraculum Nectovelinium
(The Prophecy of Nectovelin, 4BC)

Aulaeum temporum te involvat, puer, at libertas habes:
Cano ad tibi de memoriam atque posteritam,
Omni gentum et omni deorum, imperatori tres erunt.
Nomabitur vir Germanicus cum oculum hyalum;
 Scandabit equos enormes quam domuum dentate quasi gladio.
Tremefacabit caelum, erit filius Romulum potens
Atque graeculus parvus erit. Nascitur deus iuvenus.
Ruabit Roma cervixis islae in laqueui cautei.
Emergabit in Brigantio, exaltabitur in Romae.
Pudor! comprecabit deum servi, sed ispe apparebit deum.
Ecclesiam marmori moribundi fiet complexus imperii.
Reminisce! Habemus has verita et sunt manifesta:
Indico: omnis humanitas factus aequus sunt,
Rebus civicum dati sunt ab architecto magno,
Et sunt vita et libertas et venatus felicitae.
O puer! involvaris in aulaeum temporum, fere!

The Prophecy of Nectovelin
(freely translated with acrostic preserved):

Ah child! Bound in time's tapestry, and yet you are born free
Come, let me sing to you of what there is and what will be,
Of all men and all gods, and of the mighty emperors three.
Named with a German name, a man will come with eyes of glass
Straddling horses large as houses bearing teeth like scimitars.
The trembling skies declare that Rome's great son has come to earth
A little Greek his name will be. Whilst God-as-babe has birth
Roman force will ram the island's neck into a noose of stone.
Emerging first in Brigantia, exalted later then in Rome!
Prostrate before a slavish god, at last he is revealed divine,
Embrace imperial will make dead marble of the Church's shrine.
Remember this: We hold these truths self-evident to be –
I say to you that all men are created equal, free
Rights inalienable assuréd by the Maker's attribute
Endowed with Life and Liberty and Happiness's pursuit.
O child! thou tapestried in time, strike home! Strike at the root!

PROLOGUE
4 BC

I

It was a hard day when Brica's baby, Cunovic's nephew, struggled to be born, a hard, long day of birth and death. And it was the day, Cunovic later believed, when the wintry fingers of the Weaver first began to pluck at the threads of the tapestry of time.

The labour began in the bright light of noon, but the midwinter day was short, and the ordeal dragged on into the dark. Cunovic sat through it with his brother Ban, the child's father, and the rest of his family. In the smoky gloom under the thick thatched roof, Brica's mother Sula and the women of the family clustered in the day half of the house, uttering soothing words and wiping Brica's face with warmed cloths. The watchful faces of the family were like captive moons suspended within the house's round walls, Cunovic thought fancifully. But as the difficult birth continued Ban grew quietly more agitated, and even the children became pensive.

The druidh was the only stranger here, the only one not related by blood ties to the unborn child. The priest was a thin man with a light, sing-song accent, which, according to him, emanated from Mona itself, the western island of prayer and teaching where he claimed to have been born. Now he wandered around the house and chanted steadily, his half-closed eyes flickering. No help to anybody, Cunovic thought sourly.

It was old Nectovelin, Cunovic's grandfather, who lost his patience first. With a growl he got to his feet, a mountain of muscle and fat, and crossed the floor. His heavy leather cloak brushed past Cunovic, smelling of blood and sweat and fat, of dogs, horses and cattle, and he limped, favouring his left leg heavily, an injury said to be a relic of the war against Caesar fifty years ago. He stalked out of the house, shoving aside the leather door flap. The other men, who had been sitting quietly in the house's night half, stood stiffly, and one by one followed Nectovelin out of the door.

When Ban himself got up Cunovic sighed and followed. Nectovelin was old; he would be the great-grandfather of the child being born tonight. But all Cunovic's life it had been Nectovelin with his size and power and legacy of youthful combat who had led the family, and especially since the death of his only son, father of Cunovic and Ban. So it was tonight: where Nectovelin led, others followed.

Outside the night was crisp, cloudless, the stars like shards of bone. The men stood in little groups, talking in low voices, some of them chewing bits of bark. Their breath-steam gathered around their heads like helmets. The dogs, excluded from the house tonight, pulled at their leashes and whined as they tried to get to the men. Even in the frosty cold there was a rich moistness in the air; this was an area of wet moorland.

Cunovic spotted his brother standing a little way away from the others, at the edge of the ditch that ringed the little huddle of houses. Cunovic walked over, frost crackling under the leather soles of his shoes.

The brothers stared out into the stillness. This little community, which was called Banna, stood on a ridge that looked south over a steep-walled wooded valley. There was no moon tonight, but starlight glinted on the waters of the river at the foot of the cliff, and Cunovic could make out the sensuous sweep of the shadowed hills further south. This was the home of the Brigantian nation. In the morning you could see trails of smoke spiralling up from houses studded across a landscape thick with people and their cattle. People had been here a very long time, as you could tell from the worn burial mounds that crowded this cliff edge, amid tangles of ancient trees. But now there was not a light to be seen, for the houses sealed in their light and warmth like closed mouths.

Cunovic waited until his brother was ready to talk. Ban was only twenty, five years younger than Cunovic himself.

'I'm glad you're here,' Ban said at last. 'I could do with the company.'

Cunovic was touched. 'I know I've been away a lot. I thought we were growing apart—'

'Never.'

'And besides, I'm not much use. I have no children of my own. I haven't been through this, not yet.'

'But you're here,' Ban said solemnly. 'As I will be for you. I suppose you miss the comforts of your travels. On a night like this a dip in a pool of steaming water would be welcome.'

Cunovic grunted. 'Don't believe everything you hear. The king of the

4

Catuvellaunians has built himself a bath house. He paid through the nose for a Roman architect to design it for him. But the traders from Gaul say that to them it's no more than a muddy hole where you'd let your pigs wallow. Not that they would say such a thing to the king's face, of course.'

That made Ban laugh, but Cunovic was uncomfortably aware that some of the Latin terms he sprinkled in his conversation, unthinking – *architect*, *design*, even *paid* – meant little to his brother.

Ban said, 'But you got away. You're making a success of your trading. Doesn't it feel strange to come back? You're a grown dog returning to the litter, brother.'

Cunovic looked around at the sleeping landscape. 'No,' he said simply. 'In the south they have fussy little hills and valleys, so jammed in together you can't see past the next brow. The soil is clogged with chalk. The summers are too hot and the winters too muddy. And you don't get nights like this,' and he took a deep, cleansing breath of the ice-laden air.

'Ah.' Ban smiled. 'You miss Coventina.'

Coventina was the goddess of this place. You could see the curves of her body in the swelling of the hills, her sex in the green shadows of the valleys. 'Yes, I miss the old girl,' Cunovic admitted.

He was startled by a loud snort, close by his ear. It was Nectovelin. 'Home you call it. But you weren't around to help with the building of the new house, were you? I think we know where your heart is, Cunovic.'

II

Nectovelin had a way of sneaking up on you. Despite his bulk and his limp he could move stealthily, and he always stayed downwind. He still had a warrior's instincts, Cunovic thought, grooves like wheel ruts cut deep into his personality that told more about Nectovelin's past than all his boasts.

It always hurt Cunovic that this impressive man, his grandfather, seemed to think so little of him. 'You're wrong about me, you know,' he said. 'Maybe I didn't put my back into building the house, but the gifts I sent home helped pay for it, didn't they?'

Nectovelin hawked and spat. 'You talk like that bowel-creasing druidh. But words are as dust. Look at what you are! You wear a woollen tunic like your brother's, but your face is smooth, your hair brushed – even your nostrils and ears plucked, if I'm not mistaken. The house of your body shows what you aspire to be.'

Cunovic took a step closer to the old man, a deliberate challenge, and Nectovelin stiffened subtly. 'And you're a hypocrite,' Cunovic said softly. 'I don't recall you turning down my silver brooches and my amphorae of wine, with which only yesterday you bought five head of cattle from Macha, that other old curmudgeon from the valley. You may not like it, grandfather. It may not be like the old days. But this is the way the world works now.'

Nectovelin glared back, as still as a wolf, his face a mask pooled with shadows.

Ban came to their rescue. He stood between brother and grandfather. 'Not tonight, lads. I've got enough to deal with.'

Nectovelin kept up his unblinking stare a heartbeat more, and Cunovic was willing to be the one to look away first. The three of them moved apart, and the tension eased.

In awkward silence the three of them turned to face the house. One of a dozen surrounded by a straggling ditch, in the dark its conical profile was low, almost shapeless. But you had to understand the detail. Its big support posts came from trees marked out for their purpose since they were saplings, so securely fixed and well balanced that no central prop was needed. That big open inner space was set out, according to ancient custom, to reflect the cycles of days and seasons. The single doorway faced south-east, towards the rising sun at the equinox. As you walked around the house, following the track of the sunlight through the day, you passed from the morning side of the house to the left, where children played, cloth was woven and grain was ground, to the night side, where food was prepared and people slept. Even now Brica lay on her hide pallet just to the left of the doorway, for this was the place of birth, while the oldest of her grandmothers sat at the right of the door, ready to walk out into the deeper cold of death.

In Cunovic's experience, stuck-up southern types trying to ape the Romans imagined that such houses were nothing but great middens, heaped up by men with minds like children. They were quite wrong. Brigantians could build any shape they liked. Most of their barns and grain stores were rectangular, for convenience, and sometimes they built of stone, just like the Romans. But they preferred to build their homes round and of living wood, to reflect their minds, the cycles of their lives, and their embedded goddess.

All this swirled around in Cunovic's head. He was proud of his house and his contribution to it: a Brigantian house of the old style, partly paid for with new money. This place was where he came from; he would always be Brigantian.

But as a trader of dogs, horses and leather he had to deal not just with thuggish southern kings but with sophisticates from the Mediterranean, the very heart of the huge and mysterious Roman world. He'd had to learn to *be* a different way. Nectovelin's was a world of family and loyalty into which you were tied with bonds of iron, from birth to death. Cunovic moved in a much looser world, a world where he could do anything he liked, as long as he made money at it. He had learned to cope with this. But before proud old men like his grandfather, he sometimes felt as if he was being torn in two.

The door flap rustled heavily, leaking a little more torch light, and Cunovic could hear Brica's screams and the obsessive chanting of the druidh.

Ban stamped on the ground, jerky, restless. 'It's going badly. It's been too long.'

'You don't know that,' Cunovic said. 'Leave it to the women.'

Nectovelin growled, 'Maybe it's the prattling of that priest. Who could concentrate with that yammering in your ear, even on pushing out a pup?'

When Cunovic had been a boy the priests were there to advise you on the cycle of the seasons, or on diseases of cattle or wheat – all lore passed down through generations, lore it was said it took a novice no less than twenty years of his life to memorise on Mona. In recent years things had changed. Cunovic had heard that the Romans were expelling the priesthood from Gaul, declaring it a conspiracy against the interests of their empire. So the priests went around stirring up feelings against the Romans. Besides, Nectovelin always said that the druidh with their foreign notions only served to come between the people and their gods. Who needed a priest when the goddess was visible in the landscape all around you?

But Cunovic couldn't resist teasing the old man. 'If he's in the way, grandfather, throw him out. It's your house.'

'You can't do that,' Ban said hastily. 'It's said you'll be cursed if you throw out a druidh.'

'Whether it's true or not,' Nectovelin said, 'enough people believe it to cause upset. Don't worry, grandson. We'll stomach the priest as we stomach that Roman piss-wine your brother brings home. And we'll get on with what's important – caring for your boy.' His scarred face was creased by a grudging smile. 'Brica told me you're planning to call him after me.'

'Well, you're seventy years old to the day, grandfather. What other choice could there be?'

'Then let's hope he grows up like me – strong, and with the chance to break a few of those big Roman noses, for I know he is born to fight.'

Cunovic said, 'And if it's a girl and she's anything like you, Nectovelin, she'll be even more terrifying.'

They laughed together.

Then Brica screamed, a noise that pierced the still night air. And she began to gabble, a high-pitched, rapid speech whose strangeness froze Cunovic's blood.

Ban cried out and ran back to the house. Cunovic ran with him, and Nectovelin lumbered after them both.

III

Inside the house Brica lay on her hide pallet. The circle of women, clearly exhausted themselves after the long labour, sat back, helpless.

The paleness of Brica's face contrasted vividly with the crimson splash between her legs, as if all her life force were draining away there. But Cunovic saw a small head, smeared with grey fluid and still misshapen from its passage through the birth canal. The baby, its body still inside Brica, was supported by the strong hand of Sula, its grandmother. Like its mother it looked very pale, and it had hair, a reddish thatch.

And Brica, her eyes fluttering as the druidh's had done as he prayed, was gabbling out that rapid speech. The women were distressed; some of them covered their ears to keep out the noise. Even the priest had stumbled back into the shadows of the house, his eyes wide.

Cunovic stared, entranced. The speech was indistinct and very fast, an ugly barking – but he could make out words, he was sure.

Sula, cradling her grandson's head, looked up at Ban in weary despair. 'Oh, Ban, the baby is weak, his heart flutters like a bird's, and still he won't come. She's growing too tired to push.' She had to speak up to make herself heard over Brica's noise.

'Then you must cut her,' Ban said.

'We were ready to,' Sula said. 'But then she started this chattering, and we can't think, none of us!'

Nectovelin growled. With two strides he closed on the druidh, grabbed a big handful of the priest's robe and hauled him close. 'You! Is this your doing? Are these curse words she utters?'

'No, no! On my mother's life!' The druidh was thin, pale, balding, perhaps forty, and he trembled in Nectovelin's huge grasp.

'Nectovelin!' Cunovic spoke sharply enough to make his grandfather turn. 'That will do no good. It's nothing to do with him. Let him be.'

'And how do you know that?'

'Because I recognise what she is saying. Those aren't the words of gods – not our gods, anyhow.'

'Then what?'

'*Latin*. She's speaking Latin.'

There was a silence, broken only by Brica's continued chattering.

Nectovelin released the druidh's robe. The druidh slumped to the ground, shamed. Nectovelin said heavily, 'How can this be? Who knows Latin here?'

'Nobody but me,' Cunovic said, 'save for a few words picked up from me or the traders.' And certainly not Brica, who, always a quiet girl, had probably ventured no more than a day's walk from her birthplace her entire life.

'Then what does this mean?'

'I've no idea ...'

Cunovic started to hear what Brica was saying, to make out the words. It was only a few lines, like doggerel poetry, repeated over and over. It occurred to him someone ought to write this down. *He* ought, as the only literate member of the family. He found his bag, dug out a tablet and stylus, and began to scribble. The children watched him, wide-eyed; the letters appearing on the wax must seem like magic to them.

Nectovelin glared and turned on Ban. 'With a birth like this, with his mother gabbling Latin, his life is already blighted. Call him what you want, Ban. He will be no warrior.'

Something seemed to snap in Ban. He yelled, 'You arrogant old man! Must you think of yourself even at a time like this? I have no time for you and your antique war. Caesar is long dead, just as you will be soon, and you and your bragging will be forgotten!'

For a desperate heartbeat Cunovic thought the giant Nectovelin might strike down his grandson, even in this dreadful moment. But Nectovelin merely stared down Ban, contempt hardening his scarred face, and he walked out of the house.

'We must cut her,' Sula said, wearily practical amid the mysteries of Brica's gabbling and the posturing of the men. 'Ban is right. We must free the baby before they both die.' The other women nodded and moved closer.

Sula raised a flint blade. This gift of the earth was the traditional tool for such desperate moments, and its carefully worked edge was sharper than the best Brigantian iron, or even Roman steel, Cunovic knew. As the stone blade bit into her flesh, Brica screamed. Ban bit his lip; he knew the risks of the moment.

But still Brica's flood of Latin continued; still Cunovic scribbled at his tablet. The words were strange, enigmatic, disconnected: *Horses large as houses ... A little Greek ... Dead marble ...*

Cunovic started to understand that this was a description of the future – or *a* future – a description of events that could only occur long after he and Brica and all of them were long dead. Fearfully Cunovic imagined a wizard in some dark cell, somewhere in the past or future, pouring these alien words into the head of the helpless Brica, in this moment when birth and death were in the balance – a wizard, a Weaver of the threads of history, threads that were human lives. *But why?*

Cunovic didn't know if he was serving the cause of good or ill by writing down these words – and yet, once having started, he found he dared not stop. And as the words formed in the wax, words in a language the woman could not possibly know – words in the language of the most powerful empire on earth – Cunovic tried to suppress his own superstitious fear.

I

INVADER
AD 43–70

I

Agrippina and her three companions rode to the strip of dunes that lined the coast.

It was close to midday. The air, drenched with sunlight, tasted sharp, like lightning, and Agrippina felt her skin tighten in the gentle breeze. She could already smell the salt in the air, and she thought she heard the soughing of waves. They had crossed a strip of land, drowned at high tide, to get to this near-island, and so the sea surrounded them.

At the edge of the dunes they turned the horses out to forage. The horse Agrippina had shared with her brother Mandubracius, a patient old gelding she had been riding since she was fifteen years old, would not wander far. She was sure that the same could be said of the heavy-muscled beast Nectovelin had been riding: even a war horse would surely not defy her warrior-cousin. Cunedda's horse, though, was much more flighty, though she had enjoyed the ride to the beach, as had her rider.

They walked across the dunes, carrying packs of food, leather bottles of water, spare clothing. They all wore weapons, knives tucked into their belts. This was the land of the Cantiaci, nominally allies of Cunedda's people the Catuvellaunians, but relationships among these strange southern nations were fluid, and it always paid to be on your guard. Nectovelin lugged the heavy leather tent they would all be sharing, folded and tied up with rope. 'By Coventina's shrivelled dug,' he swore, 'this is heavier than it used to be.'

Agrippina hung back a little, letting Nectovelin stomp ahead, while little Mandubracius, ten years old, scampered after him. That way she won a rare moment alone with Cunedda. She leaned close and let him steal a kiss.

'But a kiss will have to do,' she said, breaking away.

Cunedda laughed and pulled back. 'We'll have time.' His southern language was like her own Brigantian tongue, but not quite the same – exotic enough to be pleasing to the ear.

Cunedda was twenty-four, just a year older than Agrippina. Where she was pale he was dark, his hair rich black, his eyes deep brown. Today he wore a sleeveless woollen tunic, and his flesh was turning a tantalising honey brown in the summer sun, quite different to her own pale skin and streaked strawberry-blonde hair. She thought that Cunedda had something of the look of the Mediterranean about him, of the smooth-spoken boys who had pursued her so hard and so fruitlessly while she grew up in Massilia. And he was a prince of the Catuvellaunian royal line, a grandson of dead king Cunobelin, which made him still more intriguing to her.

She could smell the salt sweat on his bare skin, and she longed to hold him. But she could not; not now. They walked on.

Cunedda said, 'Look at old Nectovelin tramping along. He's like a tree uprooted from the forest.'

'He walks like a warrior,' she said. 'Which is all he's ever been.'

'He has the family colour, that red hair going grey. He really is your cousin?'

'In a way. My grandfather, Cunovic, was brother to his father, Ban.'

'He hardly looks the type for a nice day on the beach!'

Agrippina shrugged. 'It was his idea. Any chance to let him get to know you, Cun! In fact he's in charge today, as much as anybody is ...'

Cunedda was in this part of the world for trade, to promote his pottery business, but also as an envoy to the Cantiaci from the Catuvellaunian court at Camulodunum, north of the great estuary. Brigantian Nectovelin had been appointed as his bodyguard for the day.

It wasn't terribly unusual to find Brigantians here in the south working for the Catuvellaunians, who had been the dominant power in this corner of the island since before the Roman invasion ninety years ago, when long-dead Cassivellaunus had faced down Caesar himself. It was Nectovelin's service for Cunedda's family which had brought Cunedda into Agrippina's life in the first place.

And today, Agrippina hoped, she would be able to make Nectovelin accept that Cunedda was here to stay.

They came over the breast of the dunes and faced the sea, a pale blue blanket under the heavy sun. It looked almost Mediterranean to Agrippina, who had seen that central sea for herself, but this was the Ocean, a tide-swollen beast much feared by the superstitious Romans. A low island lay on the breast of the sea a few miles off-shore.

'That's close enough to the water for us,' Nectovelin growled. 'He dumped the heavy tent on the sand. Agrippina saw how the sweat on his back, trapped by the tent, had turned his tunic black.

Mandubracius whooped. 'Catch me if you can!' He ran to the sea, limbs flashing, an explosion of ten-year-old energy. He was so pale he looked like a ghost, barely part of the world at all.

Nectovelin hardly raised his voice. 'Get back here, boy.'

Mandubracius froze immediately. He turned and jogged back.

Cunedda marvelled. 'He's like a well-trained dog.'

Nectovelin said, 'Oh, I train my dogs better than this.'

Mandubracius trotted up, sweating, panting a little, but not resentful.

Nectovelin pointed. 'Here. Put the tent up.'

'I never put a tent up before.'

'Then you need to learn how.'

Mandubracius plucked at the leather sheet. 'But it's hot. We've walked for ever. And it's heavy. Look, I can't even lift it!'

Nectovelin snorted. 'By Coventina's snot-crusted left nostril, I never heard the like. A Roman legionary would have dug out a whole fort in the time you've been standing there like a whelp. Get on with it. I'm going to bathe my feet.' He walked away.

Cunedda said to Mandubracius, 'I'll help you—'

'When he gets stuck,' Agrippina said gently. 'Let him figure it out for himself first. Come. Walk with me to the sea.'

They followed Nectovelin, while Mandubracius struggled to unfold the stiff leather.

II

Nectovelin loosened his sandals to reveal feet that were a mass of hair and fungus-blighted nails. He stepped into the sea, sighing as the cool wavelets broke over his toes. Agrippina kicked off her own sandals to follow. Cunedda was wearing heavier boots and socks, Roman style, and he sat on the damp sand to loosen them.

Then the three of them stood in the sea, side by side like standing stones, facing east towards the grass-covered island, the calm Ocean, and Europe invisibly far beyond.

Cunedda said cautiously, 'I'm surprised at you, Nectovelin.'

'Why so?'

'You held out a Roman soldier as a model to the boy. Suppose he ever had to face a Roman in combat?'

'I build up the Romans in his head. But when Mandubracius sees them for the dour little runts they really are, he will have no fear.'

Agrippina said, 'But it won't happen. The Romans won't be fighting the Catuvellaunians or the Brigantians or anybody else.'

'Caesar did,' said Nectovelin.

Cunedda said, 'And I've heard Caratacus talk of a massing of Roman troops in Gaul, at a coastal town. He and his brother even gathered a few thousand men on the coast in case the Romans crossed. Of course the Romans never came, and it's too late in the season for campaigning now anyhow, and everybody went home. But still—'

'But still, that's all just rumour. The difference with Caesar's time is that now there is all this trade.' She pointed to a shadow on the horizon, a squat heavy-sailed ship. It was a trader from Gaul, probably, a massive ship of nailed timbers, with iron anchors and rawhide sails. 'In Massilia they say that an invasion of Britain would cost the Romans more than it would be worth, because they make so much from customs duties on the trade across the Ocean.'

'Caesar made war here.'

18

'And the Romans are afraid of the Ocean,' Cunedda said. 'Isn't that so? They would never dare cross the water anyhow.'

'Caesar crossed,' Nectovelin said simply. 'The truth is, nobody wants to believe the legionaries would come again because nowadays everybody sucks on the golden teat of Rome. You're a potter, aren't you, boy?'

'Yes.' Actually Cunedda was much more than that; he ran a thriving business, employing twenty artisans, having made good use of his inheritance.

'And who do you sell your pots to? The Romans?'

'Not just the Romans—'

'Those who ape them. The Trinovantes, the Iceni, the Atrebates. Those who live under their protection. Certainly not to us Brigantians.' Nectovelin jabbed his finger in Cunedda's chest. 'If not for the Romans you wouldn't make a living at all, would you?'

Agrippina said, 'Go easy, old man. Don't forget he's paying your wages.'

Cunedda said, 'Anyway what's wrong with taking money off the Romans? I would have thought you'd approve.'

'Why does it matter to you what I think? You're shagging my cousin, aren't you?'

Cunedda coloured.

Agrippina snapped, 'So you knew all the time?'

Nectovelin tapped his forehead. 'You think I lived to the ripe age of forty-seven without eyes that see, ears that hear? Anyhow Bala told me.'

Agrippina gasped. Bala of the Cantiaci had once been a friend; they had fallen out over Cunedda. 'That malicious bitch, I'll rip her throat out.'

Cunedda laughed. 'Now you do sound like Nectovelin's cousin.'

Nectovelin pinched one nostril and cleared the other, leaving a trail of mucus on his beard that he wiped away with his sleeve. 'And that's why you came to the beach. To get around me.'

Agrippina linked his arm affectionately. 'Oh, don't be difficult, you ridiculous old fraud. You know you've been the nearest thing to a father to me, since my own father died.'

'But you don't need my say-so to spread your legs.'

'Don't be crude! No, but I want you to be part of us, part of our relationship.'

Nectovelin eyed Cunedda. 'There are worse choices you could have made.'

'Thanks,' Cunedda said dryly. 'But I thought you didn't like us Catuvellaunians.'

19

'It's nothing personal. I don't like any of you soft southerners.' He glared around at the sunlit beach. 'This is the arsehole of Britain. And that's why Caesar shoved his Roman sword up it.'

'And if this is an arsehole,' Cunedda said carefully, 'are you the turd that is passing through, old warrior?'

Nectovelin frowned, and for a dreadful moment Agrippina thought he would take offence. But he winked at Agrippina. 'Nice reply. But I was the wittier, wasn't I?'

'Oh, you're a regular Cicero,' Agrippina said dryly. 'You must have a little bit of Roman in you after all—'

'As did Cassivellaunus once Caesar got hold of him.'

They all managed to laugh at that.

Nectovelin said suddenly, 'But if you hurt her—'

'I won't,' Cunedda said.

'Are you afraid of me, boy?'

'Not you,' Cunedda said bravely. 'Her, yes.'

Nectovelin's stern expression broke up into another laugh, and he clapped Cunedda on the shoulder.

Agrippina walked forward, and the deeper water lapped deliciously against her bare legs. 'Look.' With her pointing finger she sketched the line of the coast. 'This bay would make a good harbour. It's sheltered by that island, and by the shingle banks over there to the south.'

Cunedda said, 'Somebody else has thought of that.' He pointed out a heap of nets, a crowd of seagulls squabbling over fish guts on the beach. 'In fact I don't know why this place isn't teeming with ships.'

'Because it's too new,' Nectovelin said. 'There was a great storm here, a few years back. A sand bar was breached. That island didn't even exist when I was born.'

Cunedda nodded. 'Then the harbour wasn't here in Caesar's time?'

'No. And he didn't land anywhere near here.' Nectovelin described how Caesar had made a tough landing beneath the white chalk cliffs of the south coast.

Agrippina reflected, with the faintest unease, on a titbit of information she had picked up from a trader in Durovernum, the main town of the Cantiaci, the local people. Though the Cantiaci didn't have a name for this new harbour, the Romans did: they called it Rutupiae. In their endless obsessive mapping and surveying, and the low-level spying they carried on through their traders, the Romans had spotted the potential of the place, even if the locals hadn't.

Her eye was distracted by another silhouette on the horizon. Perhaps it was another hide-sailed trading ship from Gaul. There seemed to be a lot of traffic today. But the air was misty, and she couldn't quite make it out.

'Look,' Cunedda said, 'Mandubracius is waving. He's got the tent up!'

At that moment the shapeless black mound the boy had erected subsided to the sand.

Nectovelin harrumphed. 'He's done his best. Let's go rescue him.' He led the way out of the sea and up the beach.

III

The four of them spent the day playing games, talking, eating, drinking. It was near midsummer, and the light faded only slowly from the sky. Nectovelin even grudgingly accepted some of the Roman wine Cunedda had brought.

Agrippina was glad Mandubracius was here. He was a good-hearted child, full of affection, who wanted nothing more than for everybody to have a good time. In fact she wondered if, unconsciously, she had planned it this way, to have Mandubracius around when she faced Nectovelin over her relationship with Cunedda, as a way to lighten the mood.

First Mandubracius and then Nectovelin succumbed to tiredness, and retired to the tent.

Cunedda and Agrippina walked a little way away from the light of the fire. They brought some spare clothing to spread out on the cool sand, and lay side by side, peering up at the slow unveiling of the stars, while the sea lapped softly.

Cunedda took her hand. 'Do you think he's really asleep? I've heard that old soldiers never sleep.'

'You make fun of him, but he really is a warrior. After all his birth was attended by a Prophecy!'

'Really? Tell me,' Cunedda said, intrigued.

So Agrippina told him how Nectovelin's mother had supposedly started babbling during her difficult labour. 'Brica never explained how come she spouted Latin, for she died in childbirth – although the baby, Nectovelin, survived.' Her grandfather Cunovic had written out a fair copy of the 'Prophecy' on parchment, and had given it to Nectovelin as he grew older.

'I love stories like this,' Cunedda said. 'What did it say?'

'Well, I don't know for sure. Something about the Romans, something about freedom, a lot that made no sense at all. Cunovic had a theory about it, that it was a scrying of some kind, poured into Nectovelin's mother's head by a god, or perhaps by a wizard of the future meddling with the past. A "Weaver", Cunovic called him. He was rather frightened of the Prophecy, I think. He dared not destroy the copy he had made, but he was happy to pass it on to Nectovelin ... I'm told Nectovelin has carried it around all his life, even though he can't read it!'

'And yet it shaped him.'

'Yes. Because of the Prophecy Nectovelin believes he is destined to be a warrior, destined to fight Romans – just as his own great-grandfather fought Caesar. It probably hasn't helped that that great-grandfather gave him his name too.

'But for most of his life he has been a warrior without a war to fight. In Brigantia there is only a little cattle rustling, and a warrior can't get his teeth into that! And he certainly never fit in as a farmer. He was always moody and aggressive. "Like living with a thunderstorm in the house," my mother used to say. He never had children, you know – lovers, but never children. And so, when he heard that you young Catuvellaunians were becoming adventurous – even though he was in his thirties by then – he came down here for a bit of fighting. Cracking a few Trinovantian skulls suited him. But he's still restless. You can see it in him ...'

Since the days of Cassivellaunus, while the Romans brooded across the Ocean, the Catuvellaunians had been busy building an empire of their own.

The Catuvellaunians still boasted of their 'victory' over Julius Caesar, even though in fact Cassivellaunus had won no more than a stand-off with the overstretched Romans. Before he left Britain for good, Caesar had insisted on the Catuvellaunians respecting their neighbours the Trinovantes, who had been friendly to Caesar. Well, that hadn't worked; before long, with brazen cheek, the Catuvellaunians had actually taken the Trinovantes' base of Camulodunum as their own capital.

Then had followed the decades-long reign of Cassivellaunus's grandson Cunobelin, when the Catuvellaunians had been content to sit on their little empire. Agrippina had the impression that Cunobelin had been a wise and pragmatic ruler, able to balance the competing forces of internal pride within his nation with the constant danger represented by Roman might – and all the while growing rich on lucrative trade with Rome.

But then Cunobelin had died. His empire had devolved to the control of two of his many sons, Caratacus and Togodumnus – both in fact uncles of Cunedda, though they weren't much older than he was. To

23

them Caesar's incursion was beyond living memory. And under them the Catuvellaunians had gone in for aggressive expansion.

During the ensuing raids and petty wars Nectovelin had risen quickly, and found a place in the princes' councils.

As his personal wealth grew Nectovelin brought some of his own family down from Brigantia to help him spend it. But he hadn't always been pleased with the results, such as when Agrippina's mother had accepted an offer to let her young daughter, like two of Cunobelin's younger sons, be educated in the empire. The Romans claimed this strengthened links between the peoples, but harder heads described it as 'hostage taking'. Still, Agrippina's mother had seen the benefits of a Roman education. She had even given her daughter a Roman name.

So Agrippina had spent three years of her life in Massilia on the southern coast of Gaul, cramming Latin, learning to read and write, absorbing rhetoric and grammar and the other elements of a Roman education, and soaking up Mediterranean light. It had left her transformed in every way, she knew. And yet she had had no hesitation in coming home when the time was up.

'I went to Massilia against Nectovelin's wishes,' Agrippina said. 'But I wouldn't have been here in the south without him. I wouldn't have met *you*. And none of it would have come about without the Prophecy.'

Cunedda shook his head. 'A strange story. How dramatic it must have been, that moment – the painful labour, the attending women, the brothers, the brooding grandfather – and then the drama of the spouting Latin words! And that one moment, lost in the past, has echoed throughout Nectovelin's life.'

This romantic musing reminded Agrippina of why she had fallen so firmly in love with Cunedda in the first place. She curled up her fingers and gently scratched the palm of his hand. 'But even though it shaped his life, Nectovelin can't read his own Prophecy.'

'You could read it for him.'

'I offered once. He pretended not to hear. He hates my Roman reading. I may as well have waved an eagle standard in his face.' She suppressed a sigh. She had debated this many times with her cousin. 'Words give you such power. If he could read he would be the equal of any Roman, the equal of the Emperor Claudius himself.'

He looked up at her, the stars reflected in his eyes. 'Dear 'Pina. A head full of words, and dreams!'

'Dreams?'

'We need to speak about the future. Our future.' He hesitated. ''Pina – Claudius Quintus has offered me a position in Gaul.'

This sudden, unexpected news turned her cold. She knew that Quintus was one of Cunedda's principal contacts for his pottery business.

'Quintus is expanding,' Cunedda said, uncertain what she was thinking. 'He likes my work. He'll be a partner in the new concern, but it will be my business, just as here.'

'And you didn't bother to tell me any of this?'

'I wanted to be sure that old Nectovelin wouldn't just keep me away from you anyhow. But he seems to accept me, doesn't he? And now that he does, we have to decide what to do. Think of it, Agrippina. If I go to Gaul the trade routes across the whole empire will be wide open to me. And I won't have to train up another woolly-arsed Briton every time I open up a new line!'

'Now you sound Roman yourself,' she said.

He gazed at her, evidently trying to judge her mood. 'Well, is that so bad? It's you who grew up in Gaul.'

'But I came back,' she said softly.

He frowned. 'Look, if you're unhappy we don't have to do this. I'll find some other way to build on Quintus's faith in me.'

'You'd do that for me?'

'Of course. I want us to share the future, 'Pina. But it must be a future we both want ...'

She sighed, and lay back. That was the trouble, though: what did she want? In Gaul her friends, while kind, had always looked down on her as a barbarian from a place beyond civilisation. But now there seemed to be no room for her in Brigantia either, where nobody could share the sparking in her mind when she read. There were more practical issues too. In Britain a woman could rise to be the equal of a man – or better. Why, the ruler of her own nation was a woman, Cartimandua. In Rome, though, she could never aspire to be more than somebody's wife – and even if that somebody was as delicious as Cunedda, could it ever be enough?

'I've upset you,' Cunedda said softly. 'I'm sorry. We'll talk of this tomorrow.' He cupped her cheek in his warm hand. 'Can you read the sky, Agrippina? Are the stars the same, where you were born? There.' He picked out one bright star. 'That is the star we call the Dog, because when we first see it, early in the mornings, we know it marks the start of the summer. It is the lead dog of the pack, you see. And in the winter we look for that one' – he pointed again – 'for when it rises in the east, we know we must plant the winter wheat. We believe that once a girl was washed up on a beach, perhaps not unlike this one, having swum from a faraway land. In her belly was the seed that would grow to be the first king of the Catuvellaunians. But that first night she was cold and it was dark. She built a fire, and the embers flew up into the air. And that is how the stars were formed.'

'We have similar stories,' she said. 'And we read the sky.'

He ran his hand down her side, thrillingly. 'Tell me about Brigantia.'

She smiled in the dark. 'Brigantia is a huge country that stretches from sea to sea, east to west and north to south. You can ride for days and not come to the end of it. The name means "hilly" in our tongue. I was born in a place called Eburacum, which means "the place of the yew trees". Our holy animal is the boar. And Nectovelin was born in Banna, on a ridge overlooking a river valley that looks as if it has been scooped out with a spoon. It's a beautiful place.'

'And sexy Coventina, this huge goddess Nectovelin jokes about?'

'She is all around, in the landscape. You can see her breasts in the swelling of the hills, her thighs in the deep-cut valleys ...' She moved with the stroking of his hand. 'Oh, Cunedda ...'

On the dark water, an oar splashed.

IV

Agrippina sat up sharply.

Cunedda was startled. 'What's wrong?'

She pressed her finger to his lips. When she stared out to sea she could see nothing at all. But there it was again, the unmistakable slap of a clumsily handled oar, the clunk of wood striking wood – and a muffled curse, a man's voice.

'I heard *that*,' said Cunedda, whispering now. 'You have sharp ears.'

A growl from the dark. 'Keep your yapping down.' Nectovelin was a shadow against the night. Agrippina wondered if he had been awake all the time after all.

Cunedda asked nervously, 'You think they are pirates?'

Agrippina said, 'Who else makes landfall in the dark?'

Nectovelin grunted softly. 'Who indeed?'

'What do you mean?'

Cunedda said, 'Whoever it is, we don't want them to know we're here. We should douse the fire.'

'Already done,' Nectovelin said. 'But they'll smell the smoke—'

'Hello!' The small voice came drifting up from the beach. It was Mandubracius, of course. He was carrying a torch, and as he walked down to the sea he was suspended in a bubble of flickering light, a slight, spectral figure.

For a moment there was utter silence from the water. But now came a reply. '*Hello?*' A man's voice, heavily accented.

Nectovelin cursed colourfully. 'I thought he was still sleeping. My fault, my fault.'

Cunedda tried to rise. 'We should stop him.'

'No.' Nectovelin held his arm. 'They may just let him go. Better to risk it than to reveal ourselves now.'

Agrippina felt as if a leather rope attached her heart to the little boy walking down the beach. 'He's only a child. He's curious, that's all.'

'Hush,' said Nectovelin, not harshly.

Mandubracius reached the edge of the water. Now, indistinctly, by the flickering light of his torch, Agrippina made out the boat that had landed. It was bigger than she had imagined, flat-bottomed, evidently for ease of landing on the beach. She saw men aboard, faces shining like coins in the torch's dim glow. One of them stepped into the water and spoke to Mandubracius. Gruff laughter rippled around the landing craft. Mandubracius seemed to take fright. He threw down the torch and turned to run.

But the man standing in the water drew a short, blunt sword, and with it he cut down Mandubracius.

Immediately Nectovelin's hand clamped over Agrippina's mouth. There was a sharp word from the boat, perhaps of reprimand. Agrippina thought she heard a name: *Marcus Allius*. And then the light died at last.

All this in a heartbeat.

'Listen to me,' Nectovelin said, and Agrippina could hear the grief in his own whisper. 'There must be fifty of them in that boat alone, and there will be more boats, hundreds perhaps, landing all around this harbour. If we try to take them on we will die too. Instead we must stay alive, and tell what we saw.' Still Agrippina struggled, but Nectovelin's grip tightened. 'Believe me, I feel as you do. Worse. *I am responsible.* And I won't rest until I have avenged his death – or given up my life for his. But not now, not tonight.'

Gradually he loosened his grip and uncovered her mouth.

Breathing hard, the sand harsh on her skin, she whispered, 'Very well.'

Cunedda was panting too, eyes wide. He nodded.

'Follow me, then,' Nectovelin said. 'Keep low. Try to leave no track. We'll get the horses, and then – well, we'll see. Come now.'

He began to pick his way across the dune. Agrippina followed, and Cunedda brought up the rear.

Aware of the intense danger they were all in, Agrippina concentrated on following Nectovelin's instructions, trying not to disturb so much as a blade of dry dune grass. But she couldn't rid her head of the images of those few moments when the torch had fallen to the water: the armour that had glistened on the chest of the man with the sword, the helmets of the men arrayed in the boat – and the eagle standard held aloft.

V

From his bench in the rear of the landing craft, Narcissus was able to see the first wave of boats driving onto the beach. Under the stars, there was nothing to be seen of the darkened land beyond, nothing but the swell of a dune or two – that, and what might have been the embers of a solitary fire on the beach.

Around Narcissus the legionaries, stinking of sweat, leather and horses, worked their oars under a centurion's softly spoken commands. The rowers held the boat in its place against the tide, for Vespasian's order had been that the Emperor's secretary was not to be allowed to land until the general judged the beachhead had been made reasonably secure.

The delay was perhaps half an hour – or so it seemed to Narcissus, sitting in the dark and silence. The length of an hour was dependent on the length of a day, twelve hours slicing up the interval from sunrise to sunset. He had read from the memoirs of long-dead Carthaginian explorers that in these northern places the length of the day could be quite different from Rome's, the days longer in summer, shorter in winter. That even time was slippery here added to Narcissus's sense of unreality on this swelling sea, in the dark, surrounded by the grunts of irritably frightened soldiers. He had come a long way from home, he admitted to himself.

Not that he was about to show weakness in front of these men. A lot of them, no more than half-civilised barbarians from Germany and Gaul themselves, were predictably more superstitiously terrified of the Ocean than of anything their half-cousins on the British shore could throw at them. And judging from the retching sounds and the stink of vomit, many of them were having a harder time coping with the sea's gentle swell than Narcissus, who could at least pride himself on a strong stomach.

Narcissus was comforted, too, by a deep sense of being present at a

29

pivotal moment in history. He was sorry, in fact, to be making his own landing in the dark like this, though it had been necessary for him to be present at the very spearpoint of the invasion. Somewhere out there were the flagships, the big triremes. By day these grand forms, looming on the horizon with their oars glittering, would be a marvellous sight, enough to strike fear into the heart of any transoceanic barbarian; he wished he could see them now.

At last a light showed on the shore: a lantern, swung back and forth. The centurion growled, 'That's it, lads. You'll be treading on good dry land before you know it. Work those oars now. One, two. One, two ...'

His rhythmic voice brought unpleasant memories of the ship Narcissus had sailed along the coast of Gaul, with the relentless booming of a timekeeper's drum keeping the banks of enslaved oarsmen in step. Narcissus was a freedman, a former slave. In his position he had had to get used to handling slaves. But to be so close to such extreme servitude, where hundreds of men were used as bits of machinery, had been unsettling.

The shallow-draught landing boat grounded on the sand, and the centurion hopped out into ankle-deep water. With a couple of the lads holding the boat steady the centurion offered the secretary his arm. Thus Narcissus strode onto the British shore, barely wetting his feet.

The general himself was here to greet him. Narcissus expected nothing less than a personal welcome from Titus Flavius Vespasianus, legate of the Second Legion Augusta and commander tonight of the beach-head operations – nothing less, for even if Narcissus's formal title was no more than the Emperor's correspondence secretary, he had the ear of Claudius.

'Secretary. Welcome to Britain. I apologise for keeping you waiting.' Vespasian was a stocky, dark man in his mid-thirties. The son of a farmer in Asia, he had a gruff personal manner and an unfortunate provincial accent, but he looked as if he had been born in his armour. Vespasian led Narcissus a little way up the beach, away from the damp littoral. They were trailed by two of Vespasian's staff officers.

Narcissus said, 'I take it the landing was unopposed.'

'Virtually. It seems our bluffs worked.' As the Roman forces had been drawn up in Gesoriacum in Gaul, rude armies had gathered on the British shore to meet them – but when the Romans hadn't crossed quickly, those farmer-warriors had gone back to their lands. The eventual crossing was being made so late in the campaigning season that the British had evidently given up waiting for them altogether.

But Narcissus asked, '"Virtually" unopposed, legate?'

'A boy came running down the beach to meet the very first landing craft.'

'A boy?'

'Alone, we think. My decurion Marcus Allius dealt with him.'

Narcissus winced. 'Was it necessary to spill an innocent's blood as soon as a Roman boot touched British soil?'

Vespasian said neutrally, 'We found the remains of a fire, a crude leather tent, a few trails. But we believe we are still undetected. Just a boy, camping on the beach – wrong place, wrong time.'

'Wrong for him, indeed.' As he walked, Narcissus drew himself up to his full height and sniffed the salty, night-cool air. 'And did we make a good choice of landing site?'

'It's as good as we expected from the traders' maps,' Vespasian said. 'In future this place, Rutupiae, will no doubt become a significant entry point.' He pointed into the dark. 'I imagine a sea wall over there, perhaps a fort there – ah, but all of it will lie in the shade of the triumphal arch dedicated to Claudius.' Vespasian spoke respectfully enough, but Narcissus knew him well enough to detect a little gentle mockery. Vespasian went on, 'Our purpose tonight is to prepare the beachhead so that the main body of the force can be landed tomorrow—'

Narcissus held up his hand. 'I don't need all the details.'

'Let me summarise, then. During the night we will throw a fortification across this semi-island from coast to coast, multiple ditches and a palisade, and within we will set up a tent camp to process the rest of the landings.

'Then, tomorrow, when the legions are mustered, we will move out. We have landed at the eastern tip of a peninsula. From here we will proceed west, following the south bank of an estuary, the outflow of a tidal river which we call the Tamesis. Once over the river we will proceed north to Camulodunum, which is the centre of the Catuvellaunians.'

'Ah yes, those troublesome princes. This "centre" – is it a city, fortified?'

Vespasian smiled. 'Camulodunum is no Troy, secretary. But the Catuvellaunians are the key power in this corner of the island, and Camulodunum is their capital. Their defeat will go a long way to achieving the Emperor's ambitions.'

'And the timetable for this grand scheme?'

'We are confident of taking Camulodunum in this first campaigning season, truncated though it is.'

'The Emperor himself must take the capital.'

Vespasian inclined his head. 'It is understood.'

'It all seems rather simple, legate.'

Vespasian shrugged. 'Simple schemes are best, Plautius says, and I agree. War has a habit of throwing up complications.'

That word briefly puzzled Narcissus. 'Complications? – ah, you mean the British.' In the mesh of personal, economic and political motivation that had brought them all here, it was easy to forget that this land was not an empty arena for Roman ambition but was actually full of people already.

They reached the line of dunes above the beach itself. Narcissus climbed a shallow bank and looked inland, but he could see nothing of the land he had come to claim for Rome, nothing but more dunes.

He breathed deeply. 'It *smells* different, doesn't it? Britain smells of salt and wind. Now I'm standing here I can see Julius didn't entirely exaggerate the strangeness of the crossing in his memoirs. Are your superstitious soldiers right, Vespasian? Have we really gone beyond the end of the world, have we come to conquer the moon?'

Vespasian grunted. 'If we have, let's hope the moon men pay their taxes on time.' He touched the secretary's shoulder. 'Now I must insist you come down from there and let us get you under cover.'

Narcissus smiled. 'Please do your job, legate.' And he clambered down from the sand dune, awkwardly, in the dark.

CITY OF LIMERICK
51220
PUBLIC LIBRARY

VI

While the legionaries constructed their camp, Vespasian entertained Narcissus in a small tent pitched close enough to the water that the secretary could hear the lapping of the waves, close enough to the landing boats for a fast escape if trouble should unexpectedly appear. They drank wine and ate fruit and watched the sea, talking softly. Some of the guard detail took the chance to bathe their feet in the Ocean, letting its salt cleanse them of fungi and other blights. Soldiers always took care of their feet.

After some hours the camp was ready. As Vespasian escorted him through it, Narcissus was struck by the calm, almost cheerful orderliness of it all. Huddled against the natural cover of a river bank, it was like a little town, an array of leather tents enclosed by neatly cut ditches. Sentries were posted around the perimeter, and Narcissus knew that scouts would be working further out in the countryside, operating a deep defensive system.

Unexpectedly the freedman felt a touch of pride swelling his chest. He dared believe there wasn't so orderly a community on this whole blighted island as this place, though this was just a marching camp and just hours old. You could say what you liked about Roman soldiers, and Narcissus wouldn't have wanted one as a neighbour, but they knew their business.

And the camp was proof that the Romans were serious, that they were here to see through this great project, here to stay. Everybody was here to further his own ambition, of course, from Vespasian and himself down to the lowliest auxiliary. Even the Emperor, already wending his own slow way from Rome, was out for what he could get. But the sum of all their individual ambitions was a dream of empire.

Vespasian brought Narcissus to a tent of his own. A legionary was stationed outside, a brute of a man who seemed suspicious of Narcissus himself. The interior of the leather tent, lugged across the Ocean on the back of some other hairy soldier, was musty, and smelled vaguely of the sea. But it contained a pallet, a bowl of dried meat and fruit, pouches of water and wine, and a small oil lantern that burned fitfully. Vespasian offered Narcissus company, but the secretary declined. It would soon be dawn, and he felt he needed time for sleep and reflection.

At last alone, Narcissus loosened his tunic and lay down on the pallet. He felt tension in his body – the clenched fists, the trembling in his gut. Resorting to a mental discipline taught him in his slave days by a captive brought from beyond the Indus, he allowed his consciousness to float around his body, soothing the tension in each finger, each toe, each muscle.

He tried to focus his mind on the needs of the coming day. He had no doubt that the subjugation of Britain would take months, years perhaps. But in the morning, when Aulus Plautius's exuberant legates refined their plans for the first stage of their campaign, he had to be sharp. These first few hours were crucial to the realisation of the Emperor's schemes – and his own.

It was Caesar who had first brought Britain into the consciousness of the Roman world, but of course Caesar had had his own ambitions to pursue. It was a time when the mechanisms of the Republic were creaking under the pressure of Rome's great expansion of territory, and the Roman world was torn apart by the mutual antipathy of strong men. The invasion of Britain, a place of mystery across the terrifying Ocean, would add hugely to Caesar's lustre.

Caesar struck at Britain twice, penetrating deep inland. But his over-extended supply lines were always vulnerable. And, as every superstitious soldier in Aulus Plautius's four legions knew very well, Caesar's ambitions had foundered when the Ocean's moody weather damaged his ships. After his second withdrawal, Caesar planned to return once again. But in the next campaigning season rebellions in Gaul occupied his energies, and after that he was distracted by the turmoil that overwhelmed the Republic in its final days – turmoil that cost Caesar his own life.

Not that Caesar's achievements were insignificant. He had greatly increased the Romans' knowledge of Britain. He polarised the British, especially those in the south, as pro- or anti-Rome, a division which suited Rome's diplomats and traders very well.

Under the first emperors, however, Britain's isolation continued. Augustus, conservative, consolidating and reforming, did not have ambitions that stretched so far – and the loss of three of his legions in a dark German forest did nothing to spur him on. In the reigns of Augustus's successors peaceful contact between the empire and Britain was assisted by the calming, pragmatic policies of Cunobelin, a local king the Romans called *Cymbelinus*. Even in these times, however, tentative plans for the invasion of Britain had been drawn up. Caligula, though unstable, was certainly no fool, and nor were his generals. He had got as far a building a harbour with a lighthouse at Gesoriacum for the purpose.

But now Cunobelin and Caligula were dead, and a new generation on both sides of the Ocean had new ambitions.

It was only two years ago, in the chaos following the murder of Caligula, that Claudius had been raised to the throne by the Praetorian Guard, bodyguards of the Emperor. Since then, despite proving a surprisingly competent ruler and a fast learner, Claudius had faced opposition from the army, the Senate, equestrians and citizens alike. Military power was the key, as always, and what Claudius needed above all was a military triumph – and all the better if he could be seen to outdo even the exploits of Caesar himself. The predatory antics of the Catuvellaunian princes in Britain gave him the perfect pretext.

As for Narcissus, he would survive only so long as he served his Emperor's ambitions, even while furthering his own.

Narcissus had been born a slave. With time, relying on his wits and his charm, he had made himself so invaluable to a succession of masters that he had been able to work his way into the households of the emperors themselves – and in Claudius, first emperor since Augustus able to recognise a sharp intellect as the most valuable weapon of all, he had found a true patron. It was Claudius who had freed him. Under Claudius, though his title was merely correspondence secretary, *epistula,* Narcissus had been able to use his position between Emperor and subjects to accrue power. He had amassed wealth of his own. He had even become a player in the most dangerous game of all, the domestic politics of the Emperor's household, allying himself with Claudius's latest wife, Messalina, in the endless intrigues of the court.

In Rome Narcissus was a powerful man, then. But now fate had brought him across the Ocean, beyond civilisation altogether. And, worse than that, it had cast him alone among soldiers.

He hated being with soldiers. There was a brutal clarity in their gaze, and he knew that when they looked at him they saw, not the freedman, not the powerful ally of the Emperor, but the former slave. Of course the officers had a duty of protection – and Vespasian especially, who owed Narcissus many favours. But Narcissus knew that in the end he had only himself to rely on – only himself, and the sharp wit which had kept him alive, and raised him so far.

Alone in the alien dark he pressed his eyes tight shut. Even a little sleep would serve him well in the complex hours to come.

VII

It took two long, sleepless days and nights of hard riding for Agrippina, Nectovelin and Cunedda to return to Camulodunum. Agrippina rode the patient old gelding, constantly aware that Mandubracius's warm body was no longer at her back.

She saw nothing of the journey. All she saw, over and again, was the scene on the beach: the laughing men, the glinting sword, the slow fall of the torch to the sea. It was like a line of Latin poetry, perfect and self-contained, echoing in her head.

Cunedda rode silently. He had no words; he clearly had no idea how to deal with the situation, which had so suddenly overwhelmed his and Agrippina's dreams of the future. She realised that by turning inwards she was hurting him. But she wanted to avoid speaking to him, thinking about him, *touching* him, for fear of harming him, and herself.

As for Nectovelin, he rode locked in a grim silence of his own, as unreadable as a lump of flint.

On exhausted horses, they came into Camulodunum on the evening of the second day. As they followed a well-beaten track down a shallow slope, Agrippina saw the town spread across the lowland before her, following the bank of its river. It sprawled for miles, a splash of green and brown in which the conical forms of houses stood proud, smoke seeping from their thatched roofs into the gathering gloom. The three of them worked their way through ditches and ramparts, and when they reached the first houses they dismounted and walked their horses along muddy alleys, stepping over chickens and children. There was a strong scent of wood smoke, of animal dung, of food cooking, and the sharp tang of hot metal.

This was the capital of the Catuvellaunians, who had taken it from the Trinovantes in Cunobelin's subtle conquest some decades ago. It was surely one of the most significant clusters of population in the south-east, indeed in the whole of Britain. There was industry here, smiths and leather-workers, potters and carpenters. Why, there was even a mint here, for Cunobelin, growing rich on his trade with Roman Gaul, had gone so far as to issue his own currency. Agrippina, coming from the more sparsely populated lands of the Brigantians in the north, had been mightily impressed with the place the first time she saw it.

But now she saw Camulodunum as if through the eyes of an invading legionary. There was no sense of planning here, none of the neat grid-system layout of a major Roman town. Green pushed right into the centre of the settlement, fields with wheat growing, or sheep and cattle grazing, as if Camulodunum was one vast farm. To a Roman this would scarcely be a town at all. Even the defences were just straggling lines of dykes and ditches.

But the place was busy today. People moved everywhere, lugging bundles of cloth and wooden chests. Leading her horse through this confusion, Agrippina sensed anxiety.

'The place is stirred up,' Cunedda murmured. 'They have heard about the Romans already.'

Nectovelin walked close to Agrippina. 'News travels fast. We were probably the first to see the Romans, but you can't hide legions.'

Agrippina said, 'They seem to be more busy hiding their treasure than preparing to resist.'

Nectovelin shrugged. 'What did you expect? These are farmers. They have children, stock, corn in the fields.'

Cunedda said nervously, 'My uncles will already have called their war council.'

'Those hot-head princes,' Nectovelin growled. 'Let us hope that wise minds win the argument.'

They reached Cunedda's house. His sister and aunt lived here. At Cunedda's call, two ungainly dogs came bounding around the house's curving wall from the smallholding at the back. Cunedda submitted to leaps and face-licking, clearly relishing the uncomplicated pleasure of the dogs' affection.

Agrippina watched him, her heart twisting. 'The dogs make him happy.'

Nectovelin said softly, 'He has suffered too, Agrippina.'

'If I had not been in Cunedda's arms then I would have been with Mandubracius. I might have stopped him going down to the beach.'

'*If* and *then*. You could not have known, Pina. Even if not for Cunedda the outcome might have been the same. This is hard for you, harder than for any of us. It's not just losing Mandubracius. In a moment you went from admiring Rome, never believing they would come here, to loathing them with a passion. You must not blame yourself, or Cunedda, for any of this. And your love for Cunedda will help you now.'

'Will it? Cousin, I think I hate the Roman who killed Mandubracius, though I have never seen his face, more than I love Cunedda. I hate the Romanness in *me* more than I love him. Does that make sense?'

'Perfect sense. But when has sense ever been a guide? Come. Before we deal with princes we must eat, wash, sleep if we can.'

She passed him her horse's reins. 'Nectovelin – what will happen to us when the Romans come?'

Nectovelin considered. 'That depends on what the princes decide. And, I suppose, how they acquit themselves afterwards. But I know in my heart that in the long run we will win.'

She stared at him. 'How can you know that? … Oh. Your Prophecy.'

'I carry it with me always,' he said, and he rapped his chest with a clenched fist. 'Though it was written down a half-century ago it speaks of the coming of the Romans. But it also speaks of freedom, Agrippina. And that is what guides me.'

She resented the perverse pleasure he was taking in all this. Where Agrippina had been plunged into confusion and misery since the Roman landing, where the people of Camulodunum had been thrown into a state of fear, Nectovelin seemed to have grown in stature, his mind clarified. The Romans had come at last; this was what he had been born for.

But curiosity sparked dimly, even now. 'Your Prophecy – does it really tell of the future? Does it really promise freedom? If only you would let me read it—'

'My throat is drier than Coventina's scabby elbow. I need a drink, and so do you. Then we will talk of the future, and a war with Rome.'

VIII

That night she managed to sleep, too exhausted even for her fretful mind to keep her awake any longer.

Not long after dawn, she rose and followed Cunedda and Nectovelin to the hall still known as Cunobelin's House.

This was a mighty roundhouse, the supports of its vaulting roof cut from hundred-year-old oaks, and large enough to hold half the town. There were few ornate flourishes, some bosses which bore the mask of the war god Camulos or the seal of Cunobelin himself – and, here and there, 'C-A-M', the three Latin letters that the king had used to mark his coins. Agrippina suspected that few people here would understand the letters as any other than a symbol of Cunobelin.

Everything about the great house was a reflection of that clever king. Thanks to his trade with Rome the old bear had grown wealthy enough to have imported Roman architects and masons, and to have built himself a palace of stone had he wished. He did allow himself to refurbish his father's bath house. But, aware of the sensibilities of his people, he had also built this, a house in their own best tradition, with every element correctly placed.

Close to the central hearth, where the night's fire was fitfully burning itself out, perhaps fifty people were huddled. They were the leading Catuvellaunians and their princes, Caratacus and Togodumnus, sons of Cunobelin. Among the crowd were shaven heads, probably druidh. The princes and their warriors wore weapons and brooches, splashes of iron, bronze and silver, and heavy golden torques around their necks. In Camulodunum you showed your power and wealth by wearing it. But there were others with finger rings and plucked facial hair, Roman styles even here in the house of Cunobelin, before the grandsons of Cassivellaunus.

Most people, though, wore work clothes from the farms, as dun-coloured as the earth.

Agrippina and her companions found a place to sit, on a hide blanket thrown on the ground. It was soon clear that the ongoing argument was fractious and unsatisfactory. The discussion had evidently been continuing all night.

Though people deferred to the princes this was a very equal debate in which everybody was entitled to speak – very un-Roman, Agrippina thought, very unlike the grave councils of the Roman generals which must be proceeding even now. But neither Caratacus and Togodumnus had the authority of their father Cunobelin, and none of his subtlety either – and, challenged, they were becoming increasingly angry. They were like men left over from the past, Agrippina thought, men from an age when physical strength and drinking prowess were all it took to be a leader.

Cunobelin had always had trouble with his sons. As was the custom of his people, and indeed Agrippina's Brigantians too, Cunobelin had cheerfully taken many wives, who for twenty years had produced a steady stream of children. Cunobelin had lived to see grandsons grow to adulthood, including Cunedda. But even before his death many of Cunobelin's sons had quarrelled among themselves. And when Cunobelin at last died it was as if the lid had blown off an over-heated pot.

The two sons Cunobelin had sent for education in Rome, Adminius and Cogidubnus, had been driven out – the talk was they had gone all the way back to Rome to seek Claudius's help. And meanwhile the two 'warriors', Togodumnus and Caratacus, cared nothing for Caesar who was long dead, the signing of his treaties beyond living memory.

So the princes started to raid their neighbours. This was when Nectovelin had been drawn to the Catuvellaunians, relishing the chance to swing his sword at their side. The peoples they raided were cowed, not assimilated; theirs was a sullen imperium.

At first all this turbulence appeared to do no harm to the Catuvellaunians' trade with the Romans. But then the princes deposed a ruler, Verica of the Atrebates, a nation whose sprawling holdings covered many south coast ports. Verica, a friend of Rome, fled there. And this time Claudius listened.

All summer, Agrippina learned from the talk, just as Cunedda had told her, traders and spies had been bringing back rumours about a build-up of Roman arms and men in the Gallic coastal town of Gesoriacum. The princes and other local rulers had fitfully prepared for an invasion, drawing up their warrior bands on the coast to fend off Roman landings – only to disperse again, bored and hungry. Perhaps, after ninety years of impunity, nobody had really believed that the Romans would ever come again. Meanwhile the princes had continued their wilful ways with the Catuvellaunians' neighbours.

And now the storm had broken. The Romans had landed after all, late in the season, unopposed, and were already moving out of their beachhead. There was a good deal of argument about whose fault all this was. Had the princes been foolish in their truce-breaking aggression? Should they have prepared better for the invasion, and listened to the warnings of their spies? Agrippina couldn't find it in her heart to blame the princes, who had at least tried to assemble a force in response. Even she, who knew Romans far better than they did, had not believed the invasion would come.

There was no eagerness for a battle. This place was named for a war god, for Camulos. But for all the knives in their belts and the swords they hung on the walls of their wooden houses, for all their myths of themselves as a warrior people, these were farmers. Agrippina could see that even now some of them were growing restless, itching to get away from this purposeless talk and back to work. But their princes, restless as they were blamed for their unpreparedness, were now spoiling for a fight.

At length Nectovelin stood up. Even the princes hushed as the massive warrior waited for silence. 'From what I'm hearing I'm glad I had a good night's sleep instead of enduring all this waffle. The question is not who is to blame but how we are to get rid of the Romans now they're here.'

'The old man is right.' The interruption came from one of the druidh. He was a thin young man in a shapeless black robe, and his accent was of the west country, of the Silures or the Ordovices. 'This land is sacred, and must remain inviolate.'

Nectovelin was irritated. 'Everybody knows your game, priest. The Romans drove your sort out of Gaul, and you fled here because you have nowhere else to go. Now the Romans are coming after you again, and you want to spill our blood to save your own cowardly hides. Isn't that true?'

In fact Agrippina thought Nectovelin was unfair. It was the priests' own laws which made it impossible for them to submit to Roman rule. In their way, the druidh had integrity, even if it was suicidal.

And this young man now proved he wasn't a priest for nothing. He said softly, 'Would you fight Roman legions without your gods at your back?'

Nectovelin roared, 'Who are you to stand between me and my gods, boy?'

'Oh, shut up, you bully.' A burly farmer called Braint got to her feet.

42

Her hair was filthy, like a mass of smoky old thatch. She was an immense woman, as muscular as a man, but Agrippina knew she had raised six children and managed one of the largest farms in the area single-handed since the death of her husband. She said, 'I'm going to say what none of you men has the balls to say in front of these posturing princes. We should sue for peace.'

After a brief, shocked silence, there were muttered replies. 'The Romans make peace only on their terms – it would be surrender!' 'We can't fight them. They have the resources of a continent. We have only a few farms.' 'Surrender? Cassivellaunus kicked Caesar himself back into the sea. We can do the same again! ...'

Cunedda surprised Agrippina by standing. He was one of the youngest here, but his status, as a junior member of Cunobelin's line, won him a moment of silence. 'With respect to Braint, I don't think peace is possible. It's gone too far for that. And we Catuvellaunians are in great danger. The Romans certainly recognise us as their strongest foe, and so we have more to lose than anybody else. Think: if we fight and lose, our power will be destroyed by the Romans.'

Nectovelin growled, 'And if we fight and win?'

'Then the Romans will come back, and their vengeance will be terrible. For they cannot afford to appear weak before their subject peoples.'

Caratacus's lip curled. The prince wore armour, a leather chestplate, and cut his hair short, so the lines of his scalp were revealed. His brother was like him but wore his hair in a long, unruly tangle. Caratacus snapped, 'Then what do you suggest, nephew?'

'That we fight,' Cunedda said simply. 'I am no warrior – my own life will be spent cheaply. But we must fight as Cassivellaunus did. We must fight the Romans to a standstill. And then, with our strength proven, we must come to an honourable peace.' He sat down, trembling.

Agrippina patted his arm. 'Well said,' she whispered.

'If they listen.'

Nectovelin stood again. 'So we must fight,' he said gravely. 'The question is, how?'

Togodumnus called out shrilly, 'The boy said it! Like Cassivellaunus!'

'Yes,' said Nectovelin, 'but the Cassivellaunus who won, not the one who lost.'

'What do you mean?'

'We must use our strengths,' Nectovelin insisted. Nobody knew how many troops the Romans planned to field, he said. Reports claimed that many thousands had already landed, and there were more of their

43

terrifying ships on the horizon. But all those Romans needed to be fed, every day. 'We know the land, they don't. A corn field becomes a weapon if burning it leaves a hundred legionaries hungry. We draw them in, as far as they will come. And we wear them down, bit by bit.'

'Then you are suggesting raids,' said Togodumnus. 'Ambushes.'

Braint nodded. 'Cassivellaunus did that. And he used delaying tactics too. He had his allies send embassies to negotiate for peace. All of it used up Caesar's energy and patience.'

The druidh got to his feet. 'Sneak attacks? Delays? Perhaps you should go back to your own country, Nectovelin, for I hear the Brigantians make a living off stealing each other's cattle.'

Nectovelin glowered.

But Caratacus was immediately on his feet. 'The priest is right. We must fight with devastating force. We must gather an army of our allies and meet the Romans in the field. It will be glorious – and we will push the Romans back into the Ocean!'

That won him a few cheers, but Agrippina saw that the support was only half-hearted.

Nectovelin remained standing. Despite his obvious anger at the priest's insult he spoke carefully. 'But that, prince, is the mistake Cassivellaunus made in the end. When he fought limited skirmishes on grounds of his choosing, he won. When he met Caesar in a pitched battle in the field, he lost. Look around you, man! You have only a few warriors. It will be farmers who would take the field. And this will not be a war against the Trinovantes or the Atrebates, who are like you. Now you will face Roman legionaries, who are trained from boyhood for one thing only, and that is for battle. Even if you were to win a victory or two, what then? Your farmers will come home for the harvest, or to plant the winter wheat. The legionaries have no harvest to gather. They will come on and on, until they crush you.

'You know me, Caratacus. I have fought at your side. I would never flinch from a fight. But I'm urging you to pick a fight you can win.'

But Caratacus would have none of it. He yelled, 'I say the priest is right, you think like a Brigantian cattle thief!'

Nectovelin rested his hand lightly on the hilt of a dagger. The tension in the house was extraordinary.

Agrippina could bear it no more. She pushed her way out of the house into the dusty air of Camulodunum. She could see the logic of Nectovelin's argument, that patient resistance was the way to wear down the Romans. But she was not the person she had been a few days before. Her deep, angry core responded to Caratacus's bold cries of total war; she longed to see Roman blood spilled.

IX

Narcissus came to a ridge of high ground. He broke away from his companions and urged his horse to climb the rise. From here, he looked back at the column.

He would not have admitted it to any of the officers, not even to his ally Vespasian. But the fact was that a Roman army on the march was a stunning sight. The legionaries flowed past, an endless river, their metal armour shining under the watery British sun, the standard bearers identifying each unit. The army was noisy too. The sound of thousands of feet was a low thunder that shook the very landscape, overlaid with the amphitheatre-like murmur of a crowd of male voices, and the clatter of metal on metal, and the brittle peals of signal horns.

The men were heavily laden. As well as his weapons and armour each man carried a complicated kit containing a saw, a basket, a pickaxe, a water bottle, a sickle, a chain, a turf-cutter, a dish and pan, and enough rations for three days. Narcissus had heard the men grumble about this load; they called themselves 'Marius's mules', after Gaius Marius, the great general who had helped define the Roman way of waging war. But this meant that each unit was ready at a command to fight – or to dig out a fort or build a bridge – and the army as a whole was unburdened by a long baggage train.

Away from the main column of the legionaries the auxiliaries walked or rode. The specialist foot soldiers marched like the legionaries, the slingers and javelin-throwers and spearmen, the archers with their chain mail and bows, while cavalry units rode out to the flanks, providing cover for the infantry. Most of the auxiliaries were recruited from the provinces or even the barbarian lands beyond, and in the drab British landscape they made splashes of colour with their exotic helmets and cloaks and tunics. Indeed, many of the legionaries were provincials now too, a major change since Caesar's day, and when the cohorts came close enough Narcissus could hear the jabber of alien tongues.

This Roman army was a vast mixing-up of races drawn from Gaul to Asia, from Germany to Africa, and yet they all worked in harmony under the command of a good Roman.

And the marching men threw up dust that caught the sun, so that a band of light stretched dead straight across the undulating British landscape.

Vespasian came trotting up. 'You shouldn't break away like that, secretary. This is hostile country, remember.'

'Oh, I like to test your vigilance, legate. And what a sight!'

'Quite. The poor little British.' *Brittunculi.* 'The legions will crush them like peppercorns in a grinder.'

'Well, it's a marvel of organisation,' Narcissus said. 'It's like a city on the march.'

'Aulus Plautius is nothing if not meticulous.'

Narcissus said softly, 'His enemies say he is nothing *but* meticulous.'

Vespasian raised his eyebrows. 'Are you testing my loyalty, secretary? I suppose that is your job. I'd rather follow a man like Plautius than a Caesar. What we need is planning and control, not brilliance – dedication to the cause, not to oneself.'

Narcissus mulled that over. He actually knew Aulus Plautius a little better than Vespasian probably suspected. The Plautii had a somewhat tangled relationship with the imperial family. A daughter of Plautius's father's cousin had been the Emperor Claudius's first wife – and *her* mother had been a close friend of Livia, the manipulative and dangerous wife of Augustus. So Aulus Plautius was a good choice personally for this crucial project, and as it happened, with his experience as governor of Pannonia, he was well suited militarily and politically as well. Claudius was wily enough to choose a man whom he could trust – but that hadn't stopped him sending Narcissus along to keep an eye on things.

Meanwhile, as Claudius trusted Aulus Plautius, so Narcissus knew he could trust Vespasian. It had been Narcissus's influence that had secured Vespasian this posting in Britain, his first legionary command. From humble origins, Vespasian had used the influence of his better-connected mother to climb up the social ladder. He had acquitted himself well in his first military post, as an equestrian tribune in Thrace. Narcissus watched constantly for young men like Vespasian, clearly able, eager for advancement yet blocked by their social origin. They were the hungry sort who needed a favour – and, once given it, were forever in your debt.

'Well, it's a marvel, however this adventure turns out,' Narcissus said. 'Look at that band of dust we throw up, right across the country, like a dream of the road that will one day be laid here.'

Vespasian grunted. 'Not "one day", secretary – today.' He pointed to the rear of the column.

In the back of the short baggage train, behind bulky shapes that were the components of prefabricated siege engines, Narcissus made out slower-moving units; he saw the flutter of flags, the flash of surveyors' mirrors. 'They are laying the road already?'

'Why not? We aren't coming this way by chance; for decades to come this route is likely to be a key artery inland from Rutupiae. May as well get it right from the start. Anyhow it keeps the troops busy, and there's no harm in that.'

'And show the natives we intend to stay.'

'Quite so.'

'Ah, but *where* is it we have come to stay?'

Narcissus tugged at his rein, turned his horse away and gazed out on the landscape of southern Britain. He saw a gently rolling land. Forest clumped on hilltops and spilled into the valleys – he thought he saw pigs snuffling at one forest fringe – but most of the land was cleared, and covered by a patchwork of fields. Round houses sat everywhere, squat, dark cones. The place was clearly densely populated – though empty today; evidently when they saw a Roman army approaching the people had sensibly run or hidden.

There were strikingly many circular structures: the houses, ditches and banks, rings of standing stones which for all he knew they might have been forts, or temples, or simply places to keep the sheep. It struck him that as seen from the air, by a curious crow perhaps, Britain would be covered by circles, like a muddy field splashed by rain.

But Romans built in straight lines, and the new military road would cut through this landscape of circles, rude as a sword slash. Roman roads ran straight for long stretches because they were designed to support army marches, and as long as they had a good surface and sound drainage and weren't too steep for a soldier loaded with his kit, the roads could be laid across almost any landscape.

Narcissus knew that such stupendous rectilinearity was itself an oppressive marker of Roman dominance. This was a land beyond the Ocean, a land at the very edge of the Roman mind, beyond which lay madness. But here was the army to impose order on chaos.

That was the theory. But, he reflected, this 'chaos' was a place of neat little fields and farmhouses. He murmured, 'We are here to civilise the moon. But there is a civilisation here already!'

'Peaceful, too,' Vespasian murmured. 'Those low walls are for keeping out sheep, not men.'

'Caesar wrote of waves of invaders from the continent. It's true you

47

see pots from Germany and brooches from Gaul. That doesn't mean the potters and jewellers came over in force! Julius wanted to make Britain seem the wilder place, I suppose, and his own deeds the greater by association. Yet I should have anticipated this,' he said. 'After all it is deliberate policy to cultivate our neighbours.'

In return for high-quality goods from the empire, raw materials were imported from Britain: minerals, wheat, leather, minerals, hunting dogs – and, increasingly in the last few decades, slaves, though as Narcissus could testify from his personal experience Britons made for testy servants. The empire made a fat profit on such trade, trinkets exchanged for huge volumes of raw materials. Narcissus, a thoughtful man, considered this pattern probably inevitable when an advanced culture dealt with a more primitive one. And all of this served the longer term goals of the empire. Roman material culture was an invaluable tool for manipulating local elites, and friendly native rulers provided an inexpensive buffer against more remote barbarians.

'So we have tamed these southern Britons. I just didn't expect to see it had gone this far.' Narcissus felt somehow irritated by the landscape's lack of strangeness.

'Perhaps it has gone further than you think,' Vespasian said. He produced a coin, roughly cut and stamped. 'This was part of a hoard, a tribute for Aulus Plautius from the ruler of a local mud-heap. The coin was issued by the king of the Atrebates, in fact – our friend Verica. Yes, the British strike their own coins! Or at least some of them do.'

Narcissus took the coin. 'It's gold.'

'Yes. Used for tribute, it seems, not for commerce, for it has too high a value. Even these half-civilised Britons don't get the point of a currency, it seems.

'But we still know little of what lies beyond this south-east corner. We believe there are more than twenty tribes out there, of which we have made serious contact with only a handful. No doubt there are plenty of hairy-arsed fellows out there in the hills who have never even heard of a Roman.'

Still Narcissus felt faintly uneasy. 'But this is a land with its own story. You can see that, just by looking from here. And now here we are to wipe it all away. You know, when you occupy a country you take on the responsibility for its people, perhaps millions of them, for all their hopes and dreams. I sometimes wonder if Rome knows the gravity of what it is doing.'

Vespasian looked at Narcissus curiously. 'You aren't feeling a prick of conscience, are you, secretary?'

'Every thoughtful man has a conscience.'

'The Britons are farmers, but nothing more. You can buy a woman with a handful of glass beads, and her husband with a mirror so he can comb his scraggly beard – but he will be frightened by the barbarian looking back out at him! We must be like parents with these child-like people. Firm but fair.'

'Oh, I understand that.' Narcissus shook off his mood, reminding himself it was always a mistake to show the merest chink of weakness – always. He took one last glance back at the landscape. 'By Apollo's eyes I couldn't bear to live in one of those wooden huts. They sit there like huge brown turds. No wonder the Britons are dazzled by a goblet of wine or two!'

Vespasian laughed, and led the way down the slope.

X

Agrippina lay on her belly in the low brush. She had been here since first light. She was stiff, her neck was sore, and she was out of food and low on water. But here she lay, silent and motionless, her face blackened by dirt, for she was spying on the Roman army.

Even she, educated in Gaul, had been stunned to see a Roman army on the march close up. The tens of thousands of men in close order had taken no less than three hours, she estimated, to stream past her position. All that time the noise had been deafening. The Romans awed her, even as she clung to her shard of hatred over Mandubracius, and her longing for revenge.

But she kept her mind clear. She had tried to count the troops and units, baggage carts and animals. She had already sent preliminary information by a runner to the camp Caratacus had established to the west of here, on the bank of the River of the Cantiaci. Despite the princes' warlike bluster, for now they had followed Nectovelin's advice, to watch, to gather information on the Romans, and to strike at them in small corrosive ways. Thus Agrippina was just one of a network of spies across the country.

After the main body of the force passed she kept her station, to see what might follow. She was given a lesson in Roman road engineering.

It had begun even before the first soldiers had come this way. Surveyors, protected by a detachment of cavalry, took up positions on ridges and hills. They had mysterious contraptions of wood and string and lead weights that they held up before their faces. Agrippina imagined this must have something to do with making sure the road ran straight. After that the route was marked out with canes thrust into the ground every few paces, and the surveyors hurried on to their next station.

After the main force of the army had passed along the marked-out route a construction gang followed. The gang themselves seemed to be soldiers; a cart followed with armour and weaponry piled high, though every man kept a knife at his belt.

They worked their way along a track already churned up by forty thousand pairs of boots, tens of thousands of hooves. First they cleared the central track of undergrowth, and then dug out ditches to either side, heaping up the dirt along the spine of the road. They piled large, heavy rocks on top of the ridge of dirt, and then a layer of smaller rocks, and finally gravel was shovelled out and spread crudely. The smaller rocks and gravel were hauled along in carts, but the heavy rocks were scavenged locally – mostly from the dry stone walls of local farms, but there were no farmers around to complain. At last the soldier-engineers walked up and down along the newly laid stretch of the road, ramming down the gravel with heavy posts.

As the soldiers worked, under the pleasantly warm British sun, they sang. Many of their work-songs were in Latin, but Agrippina recognised some Gallic, and even a little Germanic. Rome's soldiers did not only come from Rome these days.

Agrippina had seen Gaul; she knew what the future would hold. From this beginning the roads would spread out across the country like ivy over a wall, bifurcating and firing off their straight-line segments, until every corner of the land was reached. Messages would flash along the roads fast as thought, and the next time the soldiers needed to march this way they would be able to make much faster progress than today, through the mud and dirt. And in the future the young fighters of Britain, who today were preparing raids against the advancing Romans, would be marched away along these roads to go fight in Germany and Thrace and Asia, far from the misty cool of their homeland. Thus the empire absorbed its enemies and used them for its own further expansion—

A hand was clamped over her mouth. Agrippina struggled, but she was pinned to the ground. Her mind flooded with awful memories of that night on the beach. But then the weight shifted off her back, and she was able to twist and see the broad, dirt-streaked face of Braint, the farmer.

'Sorry,' Braint hissed. 'Didn't want you yelling out.'

Agrippina tried to control her anger. 'You shouldn't have done that.'

'Well, *you* should be watching your back,' Braint said. She crawled deeper into the undergrowth, and winced.

For the first time Agrippina noticed that Braint's leg was bleeding. 'What happened? Were you found?'

'Nearly. I gashed my leg on a rock, and lost my knife, but I got away. Dodgy work, this spying. No wonder they gave it to us women.'

'You need to tie up that cut. Do you want to borrow my knife?'

'No need.' Braint cast around on the ground, and turned up a lump of flint. She slammed it down against a rock and cracked it in two, exposing an interior as smooth as cream. She tapped half the rock with a pebble to crack off long thin flakes, selected one shard, and began to saw a strip of cloth from her tunic. All this took only heartbeats. 'So,' she said as she worked, 'you counted the legionaries as they went by? How many?'

'You don't want to know. I even stayed to see the road builders pass.'

'Oh, yes. Those blond young Germans, stripped to the waist. I bet you enjoyed the sight.' She leered and grabbed her own crotch.

Agrippina, still shaken up, couldn't help smiling, for she had had some earthy thoughts as she watched the soldiers work.

Braint said, 'I saw them smashing up a holy place. They pulled down a ring of standing stones and crushed them for rubble, to make their road. They have no respect.'

'But it's a mighty force they've brought, Braint. Even Caratacus is going to be discouraged.'

'I wouldn't count on it,' Braint said gloomily. 'He's too fond of himself for that. Yesterday he led another assault on the Roman line. He burned a cart full of legionaries' socks, and lost three warriors in the process.' She snorted her contempt. 'Perhaps a thousand such flea bites will cause the Romans to falter. But it's beneath Caratacus's dignity, and I can't blame him for that. What's worse, all day the Roman commander has been receiving embassies. One local rich man or petty boss after another, coming to pledge allegiance to the Emperor.'

'We expected that,' Agrippina said.

'Yes, but one of them was the princes' own brother, Cogidubnus.' One of the sons Cunobelin had sent off for education to Rome. 'The word is that Cogidubnus is going to travel the country under Roman guard, negotiating treaties for the Emperor.'

'He would betray his own brothers?'

Braint shrugged. 'I think Cogidubnus would say that with their antics in recent years, Caratacus and Togodumnus have brought this storm down on all our heads. But there's rarely a right or a wrong in family matters, Agrippina, as you know.'

'So what now?'

'Caratacus is impatient. He's giving up the plan – the skirmishing, the ambushes. Soon the Romans will have to ford the Cantiaci River.

Caratacus says that is where he will make his stand.'

'He's going for a pitched battle after all?' Agrippina felt a thrill of conflicting emotions. 'I suppose the whole course of Caratacus's life has led him to this point – him and Togodumnus.'

Braint harrumphed. 'If you use the word "honour" about them I'll smack you. The princes are two spoilt little boys who won't quit until they have it their own way. And they have the druidh whispering in their ear. Anyhow we have no choice but to support them. And, who knows, they might even win.' She cut free her strip of cloth and began to bind up her leg.

Idly, Agrippina picked through the flakes of flint.

After all her travelling she had a sense of the broad patterns of life across the island of Britain. Yes, in the south you had coins and pottery, farms and markets. But further away, where the Romans and their traders and their culture had yet to penetrate, older traditions prevailed. In her own nation of Brigantia you counted your wealth not in coin but by the numbers of cattle you owned. You ate off wooden bowls, not pots. You lived amid immense cairns, relics of the past. And you listened to fireside stories of kings of stone, and emperors of copper and tin, distant ancestors who had once ruled the land, their wealth and their domains utterly vanished with the coming of iron.

When Agrippina had learned to read she had come to doubt the truth of the family tales she had grown up hearing. How could such ancient histories have any truth if they had never been written down? But the stories were told and retold to audiences who knew them as well as the teller, and in their very telling the truth of these stories was preserved, from generation to generation. Thus she had grown up with the true deep history of her nation. Britain was an ancient place, soaked by deep culture. And when Braint had without conscious thought picked up a stone and shaped it into a tool, she was echoing a tradition that was far older than Rome.

But now the Romans were here, their army like an iron axe cutting through the trunk of an ancient tree. Whatever the outcome of the next few days, nothing would be the same, ever again – and Agrippina was here to see it. This wider perspective awed her, even as her lust for revenge still burned.

The sun was going down, the air cooling, and there had been no activity on the gleaming new road for some time.

'Come on, let's get back to the camp.' Braint stretched, and winced as the pain of her wound cut in once more. Agrippina helped her to her feet.

In the gathering twilight the two of them made their way through deserted farms towards Caratacus's camp.

XI

With Vespasian, Narcissus rode away from the dusty chaos of the soldiers' camp-building near the river bank. On the afternoon of this hot day, Narcissus was sweating as heavily as the horse beneath him. But as always it was a relief to get away from the army for a while; after another day on the march tens of thousands of men and their animals produced a tremendous stink.

They headed up to a scrap of higher ground, a ridge. Narcissus's horse picked its way cautiously over chalky earth littered with flints, which Narcissus inspected curiously. He had seen almost identical terrain throughout northern Gaul. It was as if, he mused, Gaul and Britain were in reality a single landscape, severed by a strip of Ocean as a surgeon's blade amputates a limb. It was an intriguing notion, but he had no idea how such huge changes in the structure of the earth could have come about. Perhaps Britain was a relic of Atlantis, he mused, or a bit of builder's debris left over from primordial days when giants constructed the earth.

From the ridge they looked west, to the river, and the soldiers who swarmed near its bank. An overnight fortress had been set out above the ford, constructed in a few hours despite the men's usual grumbling after a day of laden marching – but soldiers always complained, Vespasian said. The fort's rectangular formation was marked out by a ditch and a low bank topped by a palisade of wooden stakes, hastily lopped from a scrap of woodland nearby. In the interior the legionaries' leather tents were being set up in their usual rows. Already cooking smells curled up from a dozen fires, and the digging of latrines was itself a minor industry.

And when Narcissus looked further west, across the shining body of the river, he could see another force massed on the opposite bank. They were the Britons, here to oppose the Roman advance. The Britons, lacking any of the obvious discipline of the Roman troops, looked more like an urban mob, Narcissus thought idly, transplanted from Milan or Rome. Some of them seemed to be enacting some kind of ritual at the edge of the water. Narcissus could swear that they were breaking cups and plates, even weapons, and dumping the remains in the water. Was the barbarian mind really so bewildered that it imagined it was a good idea to smash your weapons and dump them in the river on the eve of battle?

But, disorganised and incomprehensible as they were, there were tens of thousands of them, Narcissus saw uneasily, perhaps even out-numbering the Roman forces. And at the rear of the crowd congregated by the river he saw horses drawing small, rapid, two-wheeled carts to and fro. They were the famous chariots of which Caesar had written so eloquently, rehearsing for war.

Vespasian showed no sign of unease. Indeed the legate seemed rather to be enjoying the spectacle. Vespasian pointed east, back the way they had come. 'You can see the native track we've been following,' he said.

The track had run parallel to the south bank of the estuary of the Tamesis, following a roughly straight line – not paved or properly constructed like a Roman road, but obviously ancient, heavily rut-ted and clearly useful. The army had made a thorough mess of its surface, leaving a band of churned earth that stretched off into the afternoon mist. But somewhere back there teams of road-builders laboured; the next force that came this way would make much faster progress.

'But,' Narcissus said, 'the track has led us to this fording place across the river.'

'Quite,' Vespasian said. 'The scouts say that the river here is an eighth of a mile wide. Not far downstream it widens – look, you can see – to perhaps twice that width. Further upstream it deepens quickly. So this ford is by far the easiest place to cross, and the British know it. This is the first significant obstacle we've faced since Rutupiae, the first pinch point where our formation is constrained. And so this is where the Britons have gathered to greet us. No doubt they intend to slaughter us one by one as we struggle across the ford.'

'But,' Narcissus said, 'the Britons know the land as we do not. Why make a stand at all? They could hide, harry us, try to starve us out.'

Narcissus shrugged. 'They've made some rather half-hearted attempts to do just that. But there doesn't seem a great deal of competence over there, secretary. We suspected as much from the moment we landed unopposed.'

'Unopposed save for a foolish boy who thought we were his friends,'

Narcissus said, a little wistfully. 'Well, I imagine you have no intention of falling into the rather pathetic trap the Britons have set for you. What, then?'

Vespasian eyed him, almost mischievously. 'But that would spoil the fun! Do you really want to know how the plot will unfold even before the actors take the stage?'

Narcissus grumpily turned his horse's head, and led the way down towards the lower ground. 'Suit yourself. In the meantime I'm going to spend the rest of the day with Phoebus.' This was the most senior of the surgeons Aulus Plautius had brought with him – and, like most of the army's best doctors, he was Greek, like Narcissus. 'While you crack barbarian skulls, I may get some civilised conversation for a change. And perhaps I'll help stitch a few wounds or bathe a few broken heads. For I'm quite sure that for all your complacency, Vespasian, the Britons' iron blades will do some damage before this is over.'

Vespasian followed, apparently not offended. 'Yes, but we will prevail. Remember, Narcissus, that to these Britons all this is new. Even their leaders, the buzzing Catuvellaunian princes we hear so much about, have never engaged in a set-piece battle. *We* have been waging wars for centuries. We have preserved the wisdom of great generals like Scipio and Marius, Pompey and Caesar himself – we do not forget our victories, or our mistakes.'

'You are nothing if not systematic,' Narcissus said grudgingly.

Vespasian said, 'You're a hard man to amuse. Secretary, this may be the most significant engagement of the first phase of our campaign. It's hard to imagine the Britons raising such a force again, once we've scattered them. This is the battle of Britain! Aulus Plautius himself insists it is important for you to understand how this battle unfolds: you have the ear of the Emperor after all. Just watch, listen, remember – and tell Claudius what a good job we did for him today.'

XII

Nectovelin stalked through the Catuvellaunian camp on the bank of the Cantiaci River, with Agrippina and Cunedda at his side. The three of them were looking for Caratacus and Togodumnus. Nectovelin hoped to find out what, if any, strategy the princes had in mind. They weren't having much luck. The place was in chaos.

The warriors themselves looked imposing enough. Both Nectovelin and Cunedda, dressed for the fight themselves, wore armour: sword belts, chain mail, leather trousers, iron helmets, and big rectangular shields. Nectovelin's shield was especially handsome, with bronze inlays of angry boars over hardened wood, and it bore the scars of multiple axe blows. Cunedda was tense, though, fingering the hilt of his sword. He had no experience of war, but, he said, honour would not allow him to shirk the fight today. Other warriors worked on their weapons and armour, fixing holes in their chain mail vests, grinding the edges of their swords.

But many of the would-be fighters wore only farmers' work clothes, tunics and trousers and cloaks of wool or leather, and had no weapons save for a club or a scythe.

Agrippina admitted that a good crowd swarmed on this muddy river bank. Caratacus's army was made up of levies from the Catuvellaunians themselves and from the peoples who owed the Catuvellaunians tribute, mostly Trinovantes, Cantiaci, Iceni and Atrebates. Nectovelin constantly grumbled that the disunity of the British nations since Cassivellaunus gave the Romans their clearest advantage. Even before the invasion force had landed some southern rulers had allowed Roman soldiers on their territories, making them protectorates of the empire. So it was a significant feat of leadership for the Catuvellaunian princes even to have assembled this horde of many nations, though Nectovelin growled ominously that he could see no sign of the Dobunni's promised warriors. But it was a scramble, a mix-up, a crowd of many tongues, and it was hard to see who was in charge.

And the fighters had brought their families, even their dogs and goats and sheep. Children swarmed around Agrippina's feet, mock-fighting with bits of wood, excited by the noise. Vendors of broiled meat, pine cones and hazelnuts worked the crowd. With the noise of men shouting, children screaming, dogs barking and chickens clucking, it was more like a huge, disorganised market than an army.

This was the way the Catuvellaunians and their allies and enemies had always fought their wars. But Agrippina glanced uneasily across the river, where the clean straight lines of the legionaries' fort were clearly visible.

Cunedda asked Nectovelin, 'So what do you think?'

Nectovelin grunted. 'What a dog-fight. I wouldn't bring *my* family here, put it that way.'

'I'm your family,' Agrippina pointed out.

'Yes, and I had to stop you putting on armour!'

'There are many women preparing to fight here – Braint among them.'

'Braint is a tough old boot with forearms like Coventina's shuddering thighs.'

'I heard that,' Braint growled, suddenly right behind them. Agrippina was always surprised such a massive woman could move so silently.

Nectovelin sighed. 'My point is, 'Pina, *she* will make the Romans piss their pants – whereas you, child, would only make them laugh, before they performed revolting acts on you and slit your throat. I have a feeling you'll get your chance for revenge,' he said grimly. 'But not today, not here. Not like this.'

'You're looking for Caratacus,' Braint said.

'Since the sun was high.'

'The princes are at the edge of the water. Follow me.'

Nectovelin and Braint led the way down to the river. The ground here, already marshy, was churned up by feet and hooves, and was thick with animal droppings. They had to work their way through hastily assembled defences: heaps of boulders, trenches, stakes thrust into the ground, all intended to deter the anticipated Roman crossing. The crowds grew denser until Agrippina was hemmed in on all sides, and the noise and stink of leather and sweat grew overwhelming. It took some heavy shouldering by Nectovelin and Braint to force a way through.

At last Agrippina found herself facing the languid water. But the river itself was crowded. Warriors stalked up and down in water that lapped up to their knees. Some of them waved swords at the Romans on the far bank, or slapped the water with their blades. Women pulled faces at the invaders, with tongues extended and eyes bulging. Even children were showing their little arses.

A handful of Romans on the far bank, washing their feet in the river, seemed unperturbed. They laughed and catcalled and pointed out to each other particular sights that amused them: a fat old warrior doing a war dance in the water, a dog that gambolled in the spray thinking everybody was playing this sunny afternoon.

Agrippina pointed out a mother duck who serenely swam down the river's centre followed by a line of her young, their formation as orderly as a Roman legion. 'All this nonsense doesn't even frighten the ducklings,' she said dryly.

'Perhaps it makes these big men feel better about themselves,' Braint murmured.

Nectovelin said, 'And Caratacus?'

'There.' Braint pointed.

The two princes stood knee-deep in the water, working their way through a heap of weaponry. They destroyed each item, snapping dagger blades, bending swords in two, smashing shields with axes, before hurling the pieces into the deep water. Agrippina saw a priest close to the princes; the druidh held his hands out wide, as if to embrace the river itself, and he chanted as the princes worked.

Amid the ludicrous spectacle of the posturing warriors, Agrippina found this ceremony dignified, oddly moving. Her own people, farmers, had similar rituals in which you offered the gods household objects like cups, bits of clothing, farm tools like ploughs. You placed them in gaps, like ditches and doorways and river banks – places between worlds, where reality came unstuck. These were sacrifices to the gods, pleas for the continuing cycle of the seasons – and, today, pleas for victory and honour in war. And as he destroyed his iron weapons Caratacus built on a still more ancient ritual yet. It was the closure of a circle of life, for some believed that metal, born in fire, was alive, and that it was fitting that it should at last 'die' in water.

But Agrippina saw that among the gifts being offered to the river were Roman goods: Samian crockery, finely worked Gallic daggers and swords, even coins no doubt adorned with the invading Emperor's head. Even in this most sacred of British rituals, she thought, the Romans had already gained a foothold.

A runner approached Togodumnus, evidently bearing bad news. The prince swore, hurled away the last of his offerings, and stomped out of the water. His brother, Caratacus, continued with his patient ceremony.

Cunedda murmured, 'Togodumnus may pay for that. It doesn't do to turn your back on the gods.'

'Probably he's been told that the Dobunni have laid down their arms to the Romans,' Braint said laconically.

Nectovelin snapped, 'Gods, woman! If you were Greek I'd call you an oracle.'

Braint shrugged. 'I just listen to what people say.'

Cunedda asked Nectovelin, 'If things go badly today, what will become of everybody – the old people, the women and the children?'

Nectovelin grunted. 'The Romans haven't crossed an Ocean to be merciful. They'll be looking to strike a blow that will resound throughout the island. We may still be able to stop them doing that, even without the Dobunni. But it's in the hands of the gods.'

Agrippina asked softly, 'But, Nectovelin, your Prophecy – has it no news of what will happen today?'

He laid his fist over the chain mail covering his chest. 'The parchment is brief,' he said. 'Just a few lines. You can't expect it to list every little thing that will ever happen.'

'This isn't some "little thing", cousin!'

Nectovelin glared at her. 'No bit of parchment is going to help us here. Only iron and blood will shape our future now. Drop it, Agrippina.'

They were interrupted by cries of anger, coming from far off to the rear of the roughly assembled mass of Britons. Caratacus, his boots still wet, went running towards the commotion with a group of his allies, their swords already drawn.

Braint hopped onto a storm-smashed tree stump to see better. 'It's the chariots,' she called. 'Somebody's having a go at the horses.'

Nectovelin yelled, 'The Batavians!'

Agrippina asked, 'Who?'

He drew his sword. ''Pina, find somewhere safe, and stay there. Braint – come on, you old boot, we've a few Roman skulls to crack before supper.' And he ran off, pushing through the jostling crowd of old women, children, goats and sheep.

'So it begins,' Cunedda said. With a last helpless glance back at Agrippina he followed Nectovelin.

XIII

Vespasian found his brother in the dark. The two of them met on horseback in a pocket of forest, close enough to the river for them to hear its murmur. They were alone save for their immediate staff officers, and a few burly legionaries as guards.

And, all around them in the blackness, more than ten thousand men were crossing the water.

'It's good fortune it's so dark,' Sabinus whispered to his brother.

'Yes.' So it was, though it was no accident that the night was moonless; the campaign's planning had taken the lunar phases into account. 'But I'm getting the feeling that even had we attempted the crossing in broad daylight the Britons might still not have spotted us.'

'It's hard to credit, isn't it? Wouldn't you post at least a few spies? It's not as if we've tried to conceal ourselves.'

Vespasian shrugged, his armour rustling as its banded plates scraped. 'I have a feeling these barbarians think it dishonourable to sneak around in the dark.'

'And it is more honourable to waste your life needlessly? Well, by this time tomorrow many of them will be able to debate the point with their gods. Come. Let's see how the crossing is going.'

They turned their horses' heads. A staff officer on foot led Vespasian's horse down the track cut out by the scouts earlier, and Sabinus's followed.

Flavius Sabinus, a few years older than Vespasian, had gone ahead of his brother into the army. His progress had been slower, and at one point Sabinus had actually served as staff officer to Vespasian. It had been a situation fraught with problems of rivalry, even though the brothers had always got along well. Thanks to Vespasian's links with Narcissus, though, Sabinus had now been elevated to an equal rank with his brother, and headed a legion of his own on this British adventure. And, as Vespasian had always known he would, Sabinus was proving effective in the field.

Certainly everything had gone well so far. The British had done nothing but sit on the bank opposite the marching camp, waiting for the Romans to hurl themselves on their rusty iron swords. Aulus Plautius's cold calculations concerning the minds of the British leaders seemed to be working out like a Greek mathematician's theorem, Vespasian thought – a simile he must remember for Narcissus and his letters to Claudius.

Meanwhile all eight of Plautius's cohorts of Batavians had slipped across the river, downstream of the marching camp. The Batavians were among the most useful of auxiliary troops, Vespasian had always thought, for they were specially trained to swim across even major rivers in full battle gear.

And, after shaking themselves dry like dogs, the Batavians had fallen on the rear of the British lines. Their purpose was to disable the British chariots.

The chariots had surprised Caesar when he had come across them a century before. They were terrifyingly fast, and would bear down on you with their occupants screaming and hurling their javelins. Even the noise of their wheels was enough to panic men and horses alike. The enemy could use the chariots as a weapon in themselves, and as a way to deliver his best troops to where they would be most effective. For Caesar the chariots were a nightmare from legends of the Trojan wars, and he had had trouble countering these fluid and mobile forces with his stolid legionaries. Even his cavalry had been put under threat.

But after Caesar's day other histories had been dusted off. It turned out that chariot-fighting had once been quite prevalent across much of northern Gaul and Germany, but it had died out in those lands centuries back. For all its mobility a chariot was vulnerable to toppling or breaking down, and its passengers spent more time riding around than in engaging the enemy. The outcome of a battle lay, as it always did, in the slow grind of infantry work. In this way as so many others, it seemed to Vespasian, the Britons on their island were out of step with developments on the continent – even with the practices of their barbarian neighbours, never mind the Romans.

That said, a chariot assault could be a distraction in the course of a battle. So, it was decided, the best way to deal with the threat was to eliminate it before the engagement even started. Hence the Batavians had been sent over to sort it out, which they had done most effectively.

Now it was the turn of the main body of the force to cross.

Vespasian emerged from the cover of the trees close to the river bank, at the place the scouts had picked out in the daylight. By starlight he could see the river's dappling surface – and a silhouetted line of men working their way down the bank, into the water, and, following a rope laid out by the scouts, wading all the way to the far side. The men had bundles tied to their heads and shoulders, and they whispered to each other as they strode through the silvery water. Like everything the Roman army did, even this cautious mass wading was planned and executed meticulously.

A soldier approached him, grinning, his bare legs muddy. 'Good evening, sir.'

'Marcus Allius, is that you? I'd recognise the stink of those feet even in the pitch dark.'

'Half of us are over already.'

'Good work. And no catastrophes?'

'Oh, I had to make the crossing twice myself before they'd go near the water.' Vespasian saw that Allius had his hob-nailed sandals slung around his neck, and he wore his new helmet, a design ordered by Claudius himself, based on a barbarian model from Germany, with a plate that offered better protection for the neck at the back.

Allius had served with Vespasian for years. Now he was a decurion in the first cohort of Vespasian's own legion – the largest cohort, no less than eight hundred men. Allius was a good, solid, unimaginative man, the backbone of any army. Vespasian had heard he had been the first Roman soldier to step ashore when the invasion had begun – he had even been the first to kill a Briton, even if it had only been an idiot boy who had come wandering out of the dark. Because of this Allius had acquired a certain iconic status of his own, which was why Vespasian had assigned him to this crossing, as a good-luck token.

Now Allius said, 'The men are grumbling, sir.'

'Legionaries always grumble. The leeches in the river will probably put up a tougher fight than those *Brittunculi.*'

It was a weak joke that won Vespasian a laugh from some of the men lining up for their crossing. But he thought he heard a note of concern. After all they were far from home, they had crossed the Ocean, and now they faced a barbarian horde that had fought Caesar himself to a standstill. Legionaries were not cowards, but they were superstitious.

Vespasian dismounted and walked up to the line. 'We're surviving, are we, lads?'

A mumble of assent. 'Seen worse, sir.' That was about as much enthusiasm as you'd get from a legionary.

'You.' Vespasian pointed at random at a man. 'What are your orders for tomorrow?'

'In the morning the Britons will realise we're here on their bank.

64

We're to hold our ground until legate Geta has assembled his legion.'

'All right. But you're outnumbered, and will remain so even when Geta joins you. What do you think about that?' Some uncomfortable shrugs. 'You saw all that posturing by the river. Listen to me. First, even if some huge barbarian savage came at you with a club like a tree trunk, he could not defeat you. Why? Because you aren't alone. Your comrades likewise can't be defeated because they have you at their side.

'And then there is the question of the names. Do you know what these names of theirs mean – Catuvellaunian, Cassivellaunus? That *vellau* means good, the best, perfect. So Cassivellaunus called himself "the perfect man". The Catuvellaunians are "the best warriors".' He grinned. 'If they really were so perfect, would they need to tell themselves? You have no need of pompous names. You are citizens of Rome and the finest soldiers in history. Just remember that.'

That won him a whispered cheer.

Vespasian returned to his horse. 'I thought that went well,' he said to Sabinus. 'I've always believed humour is the best antidote to fear.'

'Maybe,' his brother said to him as they rode away. 'It's just a shame you don't have any good jokes.'

XIV

It had been a bad night for the Catuvellaunian forces. Many of them had been discouraged by the Batavians' assault on the chariots and their horses, and the night had been disturbed by the screams of hamstrung and disembowelled animals.

Then, as the light had gathered, they were disconcerted to see the Roman forces drawn up on the western side of the river – *this* side, the British side. Nobody had had the slightest inkling that the Romans had made the crossing in the dark. Indeed, nobody was even sure how they had done so. But here they were, in the grey dawn.

The Romans were drawn up in the units of a few hundred men each that Nectovelin called 'cohorts', orderly rectangles scattered on high points of the gently undulating ground. They looked like toy blocks thrown down by some immense child, Cunedda thought. By contrast the British were just a single undifferentiated mass, with the warriors roughly drawn up in a line, their families and baggage at the back.

And, before a spear was thrown or a sword raised, the British were already melting away. The princes' coalition had always been an uneasy one.

The morning wore on.

Cunedda, restless, asked Nectovelin, 'Why don't the Romans attack?'

'They are waiting for us to charge,' Nectovelin said. 'And we will, if we are fools. If we are wise, we wait.'

'How long? All day?'

'If necessary, and all night, and another day. This is our country, remember. Let them sit here and starve.'

Cunedda said, 'But this waiting is hard. Even I long to start swinging my sword.'

Nectovelin grimaced. 'That's the British way. You draw up your army to face the other fellow's horde. After a lot of screaming and insulting and arse-showing, you might have a minor punch-up. Sometimes you'll just send in a champion or two to fight on behalf of the rest. Then, when honour is satisfied, you go home to your farm.'

'But that's not the Roman way.'

'Oh, no. The Romans believe in finishing what they start.'

'Can we win today, Nectovelin?'

'Of course we can. There are more of us than them, aren't there? And they are a long way from home. But it's out of our hands, Cunedda. It's up to the princes. I don't doubt their courage. Let's see if either of them has half the wisdom of their father.'

So the two forces faced each other, the disciplined Roman cohorts eerily calm and silent, the braying British mob facing them. As the heat gathered and the last of the morning mist burned off, Cunedda grew hot, thirsty, weary from standing, irritable from the discomfort of his heavy armour. He longed for this to be over one way or another – he longed for something to happen, anything – and it seemed to him that the tension was gathering to breaking point.

At last one man rushed forward from the British line, eyes bulging, waving a gleaming sword and howling. Cunedda had no idea who he was or why he had done this, but it was enough to break the stalemate. In a moment the noise rose to a clamorous roar, so loud Cunedda could barely think, and all around him powerful bodies surged forward with a clatter of swords on spears. Cunedda hesitated, but a shove in the back propelled him forward after the rest.

The whole of the British line hurled itself forward at once, with not a command being given.

Cunedda was swept towards the nearest patch of high ground, and the Roman cohort stationed there. But the Romans stood firm. The legionaries in the front line held their half-cylinder shields lodged in the ground so they made a fence, from behind which spears protruded, metal tips on wooden shafts. They were so still it was as if Cunedda was being pushed towards a stone wall.

And before he reached the shields, to a thin trumpet blast, Roman javelins were raised and hurled into the air.

Under a sky black with a thousand javelins the advancing British stalled. Those in the lead scrambled back and raised their shields, but those charging from behind piled into those ahead, and the mass of warriors closed up into a struggling crowd. Now Cunedda was trapped in a compressed mass, wedged so tightly he could barely breathe, and his feet were swept off the ground. He was overwhelmed by the suddenness of all this after the hours of stasis.

Then the first javelins fell. Not a pace away from Cunedda one stitched a man to the ground, where he floundered, screaming, a frothy pink fluid bubbling out of his splayed rib cage. More javelins came down, piercing heads and limbs and torsos. Battle cries were now laced with screams of pain, and the mood of the mass turned from rage and frustration to panic. But there was nowhere to go, no way to flee, or even to advance. And still the javelins fell.

With a mighty effort Cunedda managed to get his own shield raised over his head – and just as he did so a point of hardened metal pushed through splintering wood, stopping not a fraction from his right eye. He lived, he breathed. But the embedded javelin made his shield impossibly unwieldy. The javelin had bent, he found. The shaft was attached to the tip by some soft metal, and the javelin was hard even to get hold of, let alone to pull out of his shield.

As Cunedda struggled, he saw he wasn't alone. Suddenly the ground was covered by a kind of hedge of smashed shields and protruding javelins, so entangling it was impossible to move in any direction. The javelins were *meant* to bend, he saw, even if they didn't succeed in killing. He felt awed by the cunning. Cunedda had been part of a disorganised mob since the charge had begun; now that mob was tripping, falling, those who could still move fighting with each other for space and air.

There was a steady drumming, and Cunedda looked ahead. The Romans were at last advancing. The blank shield wall of the front rank of troops had broken into wedge formations, which were now pushing down the hill. The Romans carried short, heavy-looking swords with massive hilts that they drummed against their shields as they advanced. And in the last moment the Romans ran.

When they closed, their shields thudding into British bodies, the crowd of Britons reeled back as if suffering a massive punch. From behind their shields the Romans stabbed at the faces of their enemies and clubbed at heads and necks. The blows landed with wet, meaty sounds. Cunedda saw a face split open from brow to upper teeth, a belly slashed so that grey guts poured out onto the ground, another man whose lower jaw was all but severed and left gaping almost comically from a sliver of gristle, but he fought on. Horrors, every way he looked. And everywhere blood spurted, impossibly crimson.

The screaming became focused now, as the men of the British front rank, trapped between the Roman shields and their fellows, began to die in a mass, and the air filled with the stink of shit and piss and blood.

Cunedda had had no idea it would be like this. Numbed, he tried to move forward. He dropped his speared shield, though he knew it left him vulnerable. But he was still so jammed in he couldn't even raise his arms.

And the Romans worked on. Cunedda could clearly see how they were leaning into their shields, pushing the British back even as they thrust with their short swords. For armoured men they moved with remarkable flexibility, bending and twisting as they did their grisly work of slicing into the mass of British flesh ahead of them. Their armour was not mail or solid plate but an arrangement of overlapping steel strips, somehow linked together so the soldiers could bend easily. The legionaries did their work efficiently, without humour or joy or even much interest.

Soon the lead Romans had pushed so far into the crowd they were no more than paces away from Cunedda, and still the grinding slaughter continued. It was going to be a squalid death, Cunedda thought, like an animal trapped in a pen before a slaughterman's knife. The waste of it overwhelmed him, a feeling stronger even than fear. But if he must die he would strike at least one blow first. He struggled to keep his feet on ground becoming slick with blood, and he tried again to raise his sword.

Something hard and heavy smashed into the back of his head. A massive hand grasped his neck and pulled him backward. His vision swam with blood, and he knew no more.

XV

Somehow Nectovelin had dragged Cunedda out of the thick of the fighting. He brought him to the cover of a scrap of wood, on a patch of high ground unoccupied by the Romans.

Nectovelin, his own face a mask of blood, loomed over him. 'I don't want to hear a word about how you have been dishonoured by not being allowed to die. You're smart enough to know that there's no honour in a pointless death. And it would have been pointless, wouldn't it?'

Cunedda struggled to sit up. They were in the shade of the trees, in cool green. His head banged with pain; Nectovelin said a warrior on his own side had managed to clatter him with a club. He was drenched with blood, but little of it was his own.

The roaring of the battle continued, and the air stank of shit and death. He scrambled to the edge of the copse and peered out.

From this bit of high ground he could see the disposition of the Roman army. The Roman units were still hard, compact blocks, red and black and silver. There were ten of them, with four in a front row engaged with the British and two rows of three waiting in reserve behind. Further away was another set of ten cohorts with a similar deployment. Away from the stolid blocks of the legionary cohorts were smaller units, on foot or horseback. They were auxiliaries, he knew, cavalry or specialists such as archers and slingers. They held their positions, not needed yet.

By comparison the shapeless British mob looked like a tide that had swept forward. And wherever British wave crashed against sturdy Roman block there was a bright froth of blood.

Nectovelin, beside him, pointed. 'Look over there.'

Marching from the west, Cunedda made out more compact Roman units, tramping steadily towards the fray.

'I've been counting the cohorts,' Nectovelin said grimly. 'I reckon we face three Roman legions today. Ten cohorts each, see? We've already broken ourselves on two of them. And now here comes the third, to mop us up.'

'How long was I out?'

Nectovelin shrugged. 'Heartbeats. Not long.'

Cunedda glanced up and saw that the sun hadn't moved perceptibly from where it had been when the charge had begun. 'And yet the battle is already lost.'

'Oh, there's plenty of killing to be done. But, yes. In fact we lost it the moment we charged. Look.' He pointed to the rear of the British lines, where the non-combatants, the wives and children and traders, were hastily packing up and fleeing. 'The Roman cavalry will come after them, but the women and children ought to get away. Agrippina has a chance.' He laughed darkly. 'Never did think much of Roman cavalry.'

'What of the princes?'

'Who can say?'

'Nectovelin, in the thick of the fighting – the way the Romans killed – it was relentless.'

'This is the way civilised men kill,' Nectovelin said. 'It is an industry. They kill as they make pots. To leave a man to fight again is, to them' – he waved a hand – 'a waste of effort.'

'Why did you pull me out of there?'

'Because, by Coventina's baggy quim, though the day is lost, Cunedda, the war is long. We'll find Agrippina, and we'll think again.'

They turned from the grinding battle and slipped away.

XVI

Agrippina woke to Cunedda shaking her shoulder.

"Pina! You have to see this.'

Reluctantly Agrippina rolled onto her back. She was hot under her thin woollen blanket, and her head was heavy, her throat dry, her bladder full. The air was still smoky from last night's fire, but strong light poured through chinks in the conical thatched roof. It was late in the day. She had slept too long again, and would suffer from a sore head all day. And yet she did not want to wake up, not to another dismal day in defeated Camulodunum.

The house was empty, save for herself and Cunedda, whose family had fled north, away from the Roman advance. But Cunedda was here, kneeling at her side. Agrippina reached up to stroke his face. He was growing his beard. With the Romans so close he didn't dare indulge in such Mediterranean fashions as shaving; sullen in defeat the Catuvellaunians were turning on each other. The beard, thin, straggling, really didn't suit him at all, but she liked the way it held his scent.

The love between them had not recovered from that terrible moment on the beach. But there was tenderness, and comfort.

'Come back to bed,' she said, still sleepy.

'We can't spend our whole lives in bed, 'Pina. Besides, Nectovelin has something you must see.' His eyes were bright with curiosity. Even after the awful shock of the lost battle he was too interested in the world to just lie down and die.

If that was so, why couldn't she feel the same? Her bitterness burned inside her like a blade fresh from the forge. A Roman, a man with a Roman name, Marcus Allius, had killed her little brother, in a careless, arrogant moment. But the Romans were simply too powerful. It was as if Mandubracius had been struck down by lightning; what use would it be to raise a sword against a thundercloud? What use was anger, even?

She had lost hope, then. And yet her heart beat and her lungs filled. She was still alive. And here was dear Cunedda.

She sighed, rolled over stiffly, and sat up. 'Give me a minute.'

He eyed her mischievously. 'You want any help?'

She snorted. 'Not unless you want to hold the cup for my piss.'

She rummaged through her clothing until she found a loose tunic that didn't smell too bad. For her toilet she dragged her fingers through dirty hair, and wiped a hand over her face. She caught her own breath and was aware of its stink. She really ought to find a bit of willow bark to clean her teeth. She had no idea how she looked, nor did she care. After the battle she had smashed all her mirrors and given the fragments to the river. It wasn't a time for mirrors, or other Roman fashions.

She stepped out of the house. It was close to midday, judging by the position of the sun. It had been a hot, oppressive summer, and though autumn would soon be here the heavy heat still lingered.

She walked with Cunedda across Camulodunum. The town was busy. People were on the move, carts rolled through the lanes, children and animals scurried about as they always did, and spindles of smoke rose up from the smiths' forges. The market was thronged too, as people bartered goods and services, a young pig for a new sickle blade, a basket of strawberries for a dyed wool blanket. All this activity had nothing to do with the Romans but with the seasons. This was a town of farmers and, regardless of the great events of the human world, the sun and moon followed their patient cycles through the sky, and soon it would be time to gather in the harvest.

And yet things weren't the same. People went about their work joylessly. Only a few people dared carry weapons; Cunedda himself didn't. The battle had taken a bite out of the population. There were fewer young men around than there had been at the beginning of the summer. And there were injured, amputees, even among the women, and a few helpless folk who could no longer work at all lay in the shade with wooden bowls or cups before them. But nobody was starving in Camulodunum; if your family could no longer support you, the community would do so.

It had been this way since the defeat at the river, forty days already since that disaster. They had been long days of anxiety and waiting for the final blow to fall, while the humid heat lay like a dome across the landscape.

And all the while the Romans sat in their camp just half a day's ride away from Camulodunum.

Everybody had expected the Romans simply to march straight

into Camulodunum. Who could have stopped them? The townsfolk whispered rumours from Gaul and Germany of Roman atrocities, of towns burned, babies disembowelled and women violated – men too, it was said of these decadent Latins. Certainly the Romans might wish to make an example of the town, the centre of the most significant resistance they were likely to face in the whole of Britain. At times Roman soldiers even came riding into Camulodunum itself, as if to inspect their property, their Latin harsh and unfamiliar, their cheek galling.

But still they did not act, and as the days passed the tension of not knowing what was to come became ever harder to bear.

Agrippina and Cunedda reached Braint's house and pushed inside. Braint herself was out but Nectovelin was here, rummaging through a heap of armour and weaponry.

It was hot enough inside the house for Nectovelin to have stripped to the waist; his tunic and cloak were heaped up against the wall behind him. Agrippina's eye was caught by a slim leather folder among his effects. It looked like the kind of document case she had seen in Gaul carried by lawyers or moneylenders. She could only think of one document a Brigantian warrior like Nectovelin might carry in such a case.

Cunedda had brought her here to see the weaponry, for much of it was Roman. 'We managed to pinch all these pieces from a heap outside their fort. The Romans went out onto the battlefield after they routed us. They stripped the bodies of their fallen before taking them away.'

Nectovelin grunted. 'They reclaim the equipment of their dead for repair and reuse. Nothing if not thrifty, these Romans.'

Cunedda said, 'Look, Agrippina.' He picked up shaped strips of iron.

'A legionary's armour,' Nectovelin growled. 'They call these plates *lorica segmentata*. The most advanced armour anybody knows about – twice as good as chain mail, and half as light.'

'See, it's shaped to your body,' Cunedda said. 'These bits go over your chest, these your shoulders and these over your upper back.' The armour was damaged, and some of it was bloodstained, but Cunedda was able to show her how a legionary would join the strips together with metal hooks to make a flexible covering. 'You can even bend down to clean your toes while wearing it. Even their shields aren't simple.' He picked up a fragment of a broken Roman shield, a section of a half-cylinder. Where it had been broken Agrippina could see layers of thin wood. 'You see? They take the wooden plates, bend them into shape, then glue them together. Not only that, they lay the grain of the layers across each other, to give the whole greater strength.'

'Strength maybe,' Nectovelin said, 'but in the end that didn't protect this shield's owner out on the field.'

Agrippina asked, 'Any news of Caratacus?'

'Only that he flees ever west,' Nectovelin said. 'It's said he's hoping to find refuge among the Silures, or even the Ordovices.'

Agrippina asked sceptically, 'Would strangers of the west fight for a failed prince of the east?'

'It's possible,' Nectovelin snapped. 'At least Caratacus stood up to the Romans. At least he didn't just give up. People admire that, I think.'

Cunedda asked, 'And his brother—'

'As far as we know Togodumnus is dead,' Nectovelin said. 'Although the battle was so confused it's hard to say for sure. There is a rumour the Romans displayed his head.' He shook his head. 'He shouldn't have turned his back on the gods of the river.'

Braint came bustling into the house, laden with two limp chickens, their heads dangling from broken necks. She dumped the chickens near the hearth and slapped her hands to clean them of blood and feathers. 'Still playing soldiers? Look at these men, Agrippina, picking over a dead Roman's armour, while we get on with the business of staying alive. Maybe it will take a woman to really give the legionaries a fight – eh? And as for Togodumnus, if he was alive we'd know about it by now, for we'd have heard his cowardly scuttling as he ran away after his brother. The priests have scarpered too – funny, that!'

Cunedda was enough of a warrior now to be irritated by this. 'I won't have that, Braint. The priests may be able to help Caratacus put together a coalition among the nations in the west. They would be no use here – indeed they would only be meat for the Romans' swords, for the Romans hate druidh. And as for Caratacus and his brother, the princes showed courage on the field. More than those Romans, who just stood there and let us come at them.'

Nectovelin shook his head. 'And you still lack wisdom. Can you not see it takes more courage to hold your position when under attack, until the right moment to strike?'

Cunedda bristled. 'Nectovelin, I know you saved my life. And you may think you're special, armed with your famous Prophecy, which nobody has ever seen. But for all your prowess you're just a man, just like the rest of us.'

Nectovelin stared at him, like a wolf considering whether to teach a whelp a lesson. But the moment passed, and Nectovelin turned away.

The mention of the Prophecy reminded Agrippina of Nectovelin's cloak, and the leather document wallet still sticking out from under it. Curiosity stirred in her, an unfamiliar feeling for her in these dead times.

She heard noise outside, and then the thin peal of a trumpet.

Cunedda asked, 'What's going on out there?'

'More Romans in town,' Braint said. 'Walking around the place as if they own it – which, of course, they almost do.'

'Let's go see what they're up to,' Cunedda said.

Nectovelin said, 'Not me. I've seen enough Romans for one summer.'

Braint stood straight. 'If you're staying here, you miserable old man, you can do something useful for once and pluck these birds.' And she kicked the chickens on the floor over to Nectovelin's feet.

Nectovelin rumbled, 'All right, all right.' He bent to pick up the chickens. He was several paces away from his clothes, with his back turned.

The opportunity wasn't to be resisted. As she walked towards Cunedda she brushed past Nectovelin's clothes, and tucked the wallet into a fold of her tunic.

Cunedda called, ''Pina?'

'Coming.'

XVII

Vespasian and Narcissus walked into the heart of Camulodunum – if you could call it a heart, for unlike the meanest Roman town there seemed to be no real centre to this barbarian heaping of midden-like roundhouses. Everything was mixed up, houses with cesspits and grain stores and animal pens, shrines with cemeteries, pottery and metal-working shops with houses and granaries. It was more like walking through a cluttered farmyard. And yet there was industry here. Peering curiously into the doorways of the houses Narcissus saw a potter at his wheel, a woman working an upright loom with weights and spindles of bone and clay.

Vespasian, decked out in his dress armour with its gold inlays, walked with a boldness suitable for a conquering Roman general. But Narcissus's only armour was his second-best toga, and while Vespasian may have been as fearless as he looked, Narcissus was anything but, despite a palisade of a dozen burly legionaries. After all, for all its rudeness they were walking into the capital of a barbarian people who could scarcely be called subdued.

Vespasian sensed his nervousness. 'Of course there is a slight risk, secretary. But the symbolism is all. The two of us walking here, unimpeded, going as we wish, with only a few men at our side – that will be as crushing for these wretched Britons as another lost battle. And speaking of wretched Britons—' He tapped Marcus Allius's shoulder. 'Decurion, assign a couple of men to rounding up some recruits for the Emperor's showpiece battle.'

Allius nodded and spoke to his men; three of them peeled off and walked through the town, peering at resentful, wary natives.

'Symbolism, yes,' Narcissus said dryly. 'Which brings us to the matter of the Emperor. He is now resting with Aulus Plautius by the Tamesis. Two more days and he will be here.'

'Then we must be ready,' Vespasian murmured. 'I hope Plautius doesn't wear him out.'

'Oh, I doubt that. But if I know the Emperor he will be astute enough to understand the wider significance of his location. The Tamesis drains the south-eastern corner of the island, and so is sure to be a key artery for trade and communications in the future. But the locals have made little of it.'

'In fact there is a small settlement by the river,' Vespasian pointed out. 'It's said to be where Caesar crossed the Tamesis, and so Plautius planted his camp there. It's actually quite charming. Fisherfolk go out onto the river in little round wicker boats. The place is dedicated to the local river god Lud.'

Narcissus smiled. '*Lud*! Sounds like some riverine brute hawking up a fish bone. So in the future will these fisherfolk name their island's greatest city after this soggy deity? ...'

Narcissus had come into Camulodunum to prepare for Claudius's glory. The invasion might have been Plautius's, but the victory had to be Claudius's own. So Plautius had loyally stalled his advance to wait for the Emperor.

The imperial party had been preparing to travel even before the first landing. The logistics of the journey had been largely Narcissus's responsibility, and he liked to complain to Vespasian that it was like mounting another invasion. Unlike his two predecessors this emperor was engagingly free of affectation, gluttony, debauchery and sloth; luxury for him was to be left alone with his library. But an emperor could not be seen to travel without a certain standard of magnificence. Then there were the huge (and hugely expensive) exotic beasts from Africa which Claudius had insisted be brought with him on his conquest of Britain. All this Narcissus had organised: special ships chartered, overnight accommodation set up, a small army of servants and artisans arranged. Much of this was paid for by hapless provincials en route.

At last Claudius had handed over control of Rome to his fellow consul Lucius Vitellius and had set off. He travelled with a section of the Praetorian Guard, and with a number of Romans of high rank, some of them friends and advisers who the Emperor liked to keep close – and, more significantly, enemies whom he needed to keep closer still. He had sailed down the Tiber to Rome's great port of Ostia, then by ship along the coast to Massilia, and through Gaul, partly overland and partly by boat along the rivers. Thanks to military despatches Narcissus had been kept aware of this caravan's progress, including alarming reports of a near shipwreck even before they reached Massilia.

Meanwhile Plautius had not been idle. It was a wise commander who ensured that his emperor's personal victory would be just that. Away from Camulodunum the campaign had been pressing deeper into the island. Vespasian himself had pushed to the west, supported by the fleet tracking his progress along the coast, though the legate had been recalled to take part in the imperial celebrations.

And now it was time to make the final preparations for Claudius's victory.

'He's going to need some kind of audience house straight away,' Narcissus said. 'We have a queue of local kings, eleven of them at last count, come here to pledge obedience.'

'My soldiers are good engineers,' Vespasian said smoothly. 'We are prefabricating a suitable dwelling even now; with enough men we can have it built within a day. But it must not be erected before his arrival—'

'Of course not! You can't very well put up an audience chamber in a town you haven't yet conquered; it would make a mockery of the whole thing.'

They were approaching the grandest of the natives' cowpat-shaped hovels of wood and mud. 'I thought perhaps here,' Vespasian said.

Narcissus was shocked. 'You expect an emperor to reside in this midden?'

'Secretary, this was the, um, "palace" of the great king Cunobelin, and of his sons who followed him. This is how they live here.'

'Well, no Roman does – or Greek, for that matter. Of course if it really is Cunobelin's house we must be close to this dung-hill, but I won't place Claudius inside it.' Narcissus stalked around the big house until he came to a smaller building, more conventional to Mediterranean eyes, a low-roofed wooden hut on a rectangular plan. 'How about this?'

One of the soldiers coughed and looked away; he seemed to be trying not to laugh.

'Secretary, this is a barn, I think. Or a granary. You can't lodge an emperor in a granary.'

Narcissus's pride was pricked. 'A good square plan will be much more to the Emperor's taste. I have decided. Get it cleaned up, legate.'

Vespasian bowed, his face expressionless. 'As you wish. Ah, here is Marcus Allius with the recruits.'

The three soldiers returned with some of the locals, around twenty of them, all men, none older than forty. Surely they could easily have overcome the three legionaries, but they came placidly, herded like sheep. Beyond them more townspeople drifted up to watch the spectacle.

With a few barked words from Allius in the local argot, and a glint of sword steel, the men were soon arranged in a rough line. Vespasian stalked along the row in his glittering armour, his magnificence even more enhanced by contrast with these shabby locals. 'By Jupiter but they're a sorry lot. Well-fed I granted you, but knock-kneed, pot-bellied, slack-jawed.'

Narcissus murmured, intrigued, 'They watch us like cattle. They don't know whether to fear us or to ask us for treats.'

'Well, these will have to do,' Vespasian said. 'We can give them some basic training overnight, shape them up into a semblance of a force. Enough to give the Emperor's chroniclers something to write about. Marcus Allius, do you know their jabber well enough to explain what is required of them? They will be paid for their part, but only if they fight reasonably well. We'll try to minimise injury, and only a few will be killed.'

'Tell them to paint their faces,' Narcissus snapped.

Vespasian pursed his lips. 'We didn't see any painted faces in the field, secretary.'

'Caesar reported painted faces, so painted faces we will have. Blue, if possible.' Narcissus, immersed now in the theatre of the Emperor's victorious arrival, was dissatisfied by the array of specimens before him. 'There were women in the field, weren't there?' He boldly walked to a knot of people, a girl with strawberry-blonde hair who might have been attractive if cleaned up, a dark, defiant-looking boy with a strag-gling beard – and a burly farmer's wife of a woman, aged perhaps forty, whose cheek bore a scar from what might have been a blade. 'This one, for instance. You. What's your name?'

Allius translated hurriedly. The woman replied, 'Braint.'

Narcissus flinched from the raw hostility of her expression, but stood his ground. 'She looks savage enough to me. Decurion, explain what's wanted of her. And find a few more, will you?' He looked the woman up and down. 'Oh, and tell her to bare her tits during the action. It will be a nice detail for the chroniclers.'

He walked away from the woman. But with every step the space between his shoulder blades tingled, as if Braint's gaze were a dagger being plunged there.

XVIII

Sheltered from view behind Braint's broad back, with everybody watching the Romans as they strutted through Camulodunum, Agrippina examined the leather document wallet.

After a lifetime pressed against Nectovelin's chest, it was scuffed, battered, and stank of Nectovelin's sweat and blood. The document within, carefully folded, was only a single page of cheap-looking parchment, yellowed with age. It was stamped with a broken seal. And just sixteen lines of Latin, she counted quickly, had been transcribed in a neat hand. Could this really be the hand of her grandfather Cunovic, was this his seal?

She read the first lines feverishly:

> Ah child! Bound in time's tapestry, and yet you are born free
> Come, let me sing to you of what there is and what will be,
> Of all men and all gods, and of the mighty emperors three.
> Named with a German name, a man will come with eyes of glass
> Straddling horses large as houses bearing teeth like scimitars ...

If these were the words of a god, it was a literate god. The phrasing was elegant, the meter at least functional. She wondered if the transcript contained more information than apparent to a first reading; the Romans were famously fond of word play – compression, acrostics.

But the lines were terse. After the salutation and that mention of 'emperors three', there followed a reference to an emperor who called himself a German, but who had, mysteriously, 'eyes of glass'. The single other detail, about some kind of exotic beast, merely confused her further. Could these opaque hints have something to do with the invasion? After all, what use was a prophecy if it *didn't* refer to such a calamity as this? But if so, what did it mean?

She scanned on quickly. The further lines hinted at a 'noose of stone' – some kind of huge building project? – and the elevation of an emperor in Brigantia. How could that ever be possible? The last few lines seemed to be given over to poetry, clumsy stuff that might have been translated from another language altogether, about freedom and happiness: unarguable, but not much use. That, though, was clearly the passage that had touched Nectovelin's heart—

'They took Braint.' Cunedda was tense beside her, his right hand seeking a sword that he no longer carried.

Hastily Agrippina tucked the document inside her tunic, hoping Cunedda wouldn't notice she had it. 'What's happening?'

'They seem to be recruiting warriors. Some kind of display for the Emperor. Must they humiliate us? And I think I heard them talking about Cunobelin's House.' He pointed. 'During his first night here the Emperor is to stay in the granary.'

Agrippina understood. Of course a Roman would seek a square floor plan, rejecting the native roundhouses as barbaric.

It was hard to concentrate on mere events, when the Prophecy, the future itself, burned in her hand. She longed for time to think about it, to decipher its enigmas.

'Just imagine,' Cunedda said, 'the Emperor himself, the very head of the empire, is to stay here, just paces from where we are standing. And we can't do a thing about it!'

'Maybe we can,' Agrippina said, suddenly thinking fast. Perhaps it was the Prophecy that fired her mind. 'Cunedda. I have an idea. The granary must have underground storage pits.'

He frowned. 'So?'

'Do you think the Romans know about them? They might not realise the building is a granary at all. If we could sneak in there—

He started to see. 'And then hide in the pits. Let the Emperor come. And then—'

And then, Agrippina thought, they might strike a blow that would send shudders across the whole world. Suddenly hope sparked in her breast.

Cunedda too looked fully alive, for the first time since the battle. 'Agrippina, Braint was right. Maybe it will take a woman to fight the Romans!'

She pressed a finger to his lips. 'Hush. We mustn't chance somebody overhearing. Let's go find Nectovelin. We'll need his help.' And she must sneak the Prophecy back in Nectovelin's pile of clothes before he finished plucking those wretched chickens.

Excited, burning with their secret plan, the two of them rushed hand in hand back to Braint's house.

XIX

In the middle of the night it wasn't hard for Agrippina, Nectovelin and Cunedda to sneak into the old granary. As Agrippina had expected there was indeed a storage pit dug into the ground. The three of them clambered down into the pit and fixed planks an arm's length under the floor surface. Once they were safely interred, they had friends of Braint fill in the rest of the hole with dirt, tamp it down, and cover the floor with straw.

It was a ruse that would have been obvious to a Catuvellaunian. But the Romans had not yet inspected the interior of the building and probably knew nothing of Catuvellaunian granaries, and it was a gamble worth taking that when they looked inside and saw an unbroken floor they wouldn't be suspicious.

After that, all Agrippina and her companions had to do was to endure the rest of the night, and the whole of another long late-summer day, stuck in a hole in the ground. It wasn't deep enough for them to sit up properly, and the three of them lay curled around each other, 'like three puppies in a litter', as Nectovelin said. After a few hours even Cunedda's closeness became uncomfortable for Agrippina.

They had brought plenty of water, and as the stifling heat built up in the airless hole they drank much of it. Nectovelin had brought pots to piss in. He had even brought some food – dried bread, stuff that he said wouldn't create a smell that might make some dull-witted Roman soldier suspicious. Agrippina didn't know how he could eat in such a situation, but Nectovelin said he didn't want the rumbling of their stomachs to wake the Romans from their slumber. Nectovelin's gut, however, even while not rumbling, was a bottle of noxious gases, which did nothing to add to their comfort.

So they had nothing to do but lie there and wait, in the increasingly fetid dark. Wait and think.

Agrippina couldn't get the Prophecy out of her head. She longed to discuss it with Cunedda, and with Nectovelin, though she knew it was impossible. But the more she brooded on the meaning of its enigmatic lines, the more she began to wonder what it might be telling her of their chances of victory today – and the more she thought it through, the more dread gathered in her heart. *Emperors three.*

In what must have been the middle of the morning there was a bout of crashes, bangs, hammering and splintering, laced by whistles and cheerful curses in Latin, Germanic and Gallic. The legionaries were fitting out the granary to make it ready for an emperor. Agrippina lay rigid, scared that a cough or sneeze might give her away, and fretted that some fat soldier might come crashing down into their hole. After that came a pause that must have stretched through noon. Agrippina heard only softer talk, the rattles of dice, laughter, the clatter of crockery. Guards stationed in the granary were passing the time.

Then, in the afternoon, there was a more general commotion, people running, the ominous scraping of stabbing swords being drawn from scabbards. Agrippina heard soldiers yelling, and was able to make out Latin words: 'The Emperor! He is coming!'

At last, Claudius had completed his procession from Rome all the way here to Camulodunum. Agrippina heard marching feet and cheers – and then thunderous footsteps, as if some monstrous man were walking into the town, to gasps and muttering in Catuvellaunian. She had no idea what this could be, but she thought uneasily of the strange Prophecy line about 'horses large as houses'.

Then there was a roar, half-hearted, and running footsteps. That must be the 'resistance', a few dozen British rounded up and pressed into putting on a show of defiance. Agrippina heard the smash of sword against shield, thuds that might have been javelins landing – and, ominously, screams of pain. Why should the Roman commander keep his promise that few Britons would be hurt in this shameful game? She imagined Braint out there, angry, defiant, perhaps stripped to the waist as that toga-clad Greek snake had ordered. Braint at least would give the Romans as good as she got.

With the 'resistance' vanquished, there was an interval of clattering wheels, marching, speeches and orderly cheering. This must be the entrance of the Emperor himself into the capital. Some of the triumphal pronouncements were in the Catuvellaunian tongue; the Romans, methodical as always, would ensure that the locals knew exactly what was happening here, why the Romans had come, and what the future would hold for the people of Camulodunum.

After that there was more activity in the granary. She heard booming laughter, the clatter of plates, the splash of what might be wine into goblets, and running footsteps that must be serving slaves working. The Emperor and his entourage were evidently having dinner. The smells of cooked food penetrated the hole in the ground, and as Nectovelin had warned, Agrippina felt her empty stomach growl in response.

Nectovelin pressed a bit of dried meat into her hand. He whispered, 'What are they saying?'

Agrippina tried to follow the conversation. She had learned her Latin in Gaul, itself a backward province; the Emperor and his entourage were sophisticated Romans, and their speech was complex. 'Difficult to tell,' she admitted. 'The invasion. Gaul and Britain. But that's the surface. The Romans like to be clever. They like word games—'

Nectovelin snorted. 'A man should say what he thinks.'

'That's not the Roman way.'

'Then I'm glad I'm no Roman.'

The volume of conversation started to die down. Couches were scraped, drunken words of farewell exchanged. Evidently the dinner was over. At last Agrippina identified the Emperor's own voice. It was thin, and broken by an occasional stutter. Responses came curtly, perhaps from slaves, and from a more cultured voice, strongly accented – the Greek in the toga, perhaps, who had walked so arrogantly through Camulodunum yesterday.

Finally the Emperor ordered everybody out.

Nectovelin listened. Now there were no voices at all, no pacing, only a soft scraping that might have been a pen on parchment, a stylus on a wax tablet. Nectovelin whispered, 'Here's our chance. We'll have to move fast.'

Agrippina's heart pounded, and she grasped the hilt of her dagger.

'On my count,' Nectovelin hissed. 'One, two, three—'

XX

Agrippina rolled, got her legs underneath her body, and pushed up with the others. The wooden planks covering their temporary tomb splintered and fell away, and dirt tumbled in around her. Then she found her shoulders pressing against a dense mass of carpet. They had expected this. Nectovelin drove his sword up into the weave and dragged it backwards to make a broad cut.

They thrust upwards into a soft light of torches and oil lamps. Agrippina blinked; it was the first light she had seen all day.

She took in the scene in a heartbeat. The granary had become a palace, the walls hastily whitewashed, a thick carpet with a richly woven pattern laid over the floor. Oil lamps splashed pools of light. Low couches and tables lay littered around the floor, the remains of the dinner party. Amid these bits of luxury Agrippina, standing in a hole in the floor, felt filthy, stinking, a beast in the world of humans.

And at one end of the granary a desk had been set up, heaped with scrolls and parchments. A man, unassuming, dressed in a plain-looking woollen tunic, was sitting at the desk. He was looking over his shoulder at the intruders. Slowly he got to his feet. He was perhaps thirty feet from Agrippina.

Nectovelin roared, 'Claudius!' And he threw his stabbing sword.

Claudius flinched, but shuffled aside. The sword slammed into the desk top, skewering scrolls. The attack had already gone wrong, Agrippina saw. It was chance that their hole in the ground was at one end of the long granary, Claudius's desk at the other, giving him time to step aside.

Nectovelin bellowed his frustration, drew a dagger and began to run at Claudius. But the Emperor, recovering from his shock, called for his guards: *'Custodiae!'*

The first to respond were the two senior Romans of the day before in Camulodunum, the impressive commander and the Greek – though the commander's armour was half undone, and the Greek wore a nightshirt. The commander, unarmed, unhesitating, hurled himself at Nectovelin's legs and brought him crashing to the ground. Nectovelin struggled but the Roman, younger, just as heavy, was on his back, and in an instant he had taken Nectovelin's own dagger and pressed it to his throat.

More soldiers burst into the room. Agrippina didn't hesitate. She grabbed the Greek, easily twisting an arm behind his back, and cut his cheek with a savage swipe of her knife. The Greek screamed, his voice high, like a distressed sheep's.

The Emperor seemed more concerned for the Greek's fate than his own. He took a step forward. 'Narcissus!'

'Stay back,' Agrippina snapped in Latin. 'Let Nectovelin live. Or this one dies before your eyes.'

The crowded granary had become a tableau – the Emperor, Agrippina with Narcissus, Nectovelin with his own blade cutting into his flesh, and the guards staring wildly, their swords drawn. One of them had Cunedda in a bear-hug.

The Roman on the ground looked up. 'Emperor,' he hissed. 'Let me finish off this fat pig.'

Claudius was a small, middle-aged man. The single step he had taken was uneven, a limp, and his mouth open and closed, gulping like a fish, as he took in the situation. The rumours in Gaul were that Claudius was a weakling, perhaps even deformed, the runt of the imperial litter. He wore thick socks, comically; perhaps he had poor circulation too. But he was an emperor, and after that first moment of shock he stood straight, and his voice was firm. 'Let him up, Vespasian.'

'Sir—'

'Let him up! I am in no danger now.' He glanced at one of the soldiers. 'We will deal with the issue of my personal security later, Rufrius Pollio.' The man, perhaps the commander of the guard, cowered. 'But I would not lose my secretary to these grubby thugs. Let him up, I say.'

The Roman commander, Vespasian, clambered reluctantly off Nectovelin. He hauled the Brigantian to his feet with a massive hand at the scruff of his neck, and he kept a grip on Nectovelin's arm. 'One move out of you, you ugly bastard, and I'll slit your throat no matter what the Emperor says.'

Nectovelin had not taken his eyes off the Emperor. Agrippina kept her knife blade at the throat of the Greek, Narcissus.

Claudius walked forward, his gait uneven but his command now obvious. 'Another warrior woman. You were right about their temperament,

Narcissus. But this one seems rather more presentable, under all that dirt, than the muscular hags you paraded before me today. That rather attractive strawberry hair ...'

Narcissus, breathing hard, a knife at his neck, seemed to be trying to regain command of himself. 'I apologise for my poor taste, Emperor.'

Vespasian growled, 'Sir, we must end this.'

'Now, legate, have patience. I would rather enjoy seeing how this little drama plays out. Quite a cast – a hairy savage, a beautiful girl, and a weakling boy who, from the moon-eyed glances he throws, is more in love than fearful.'

Agrippina hissed, her anger overcoming her fear, 'I understand every word you say, Roman.'

'Yes, you spoke Latin, didn't you?' Claudius peered at her, his small face creased with curiosity. 'But accented. Are you Gallic?'

'I am Brigantian.'

'I don't know what a Brigantian is.'

'An as yet undomesticated strain of British,' Narcissus said tightly.

'I was educated in Gaul,' Agrippina said.

'Then you must know who I am.'

'You are Claudius.'

He smiled. 'Tiberius Claudius Nero Germanicus, to be precise.'

Germanicus. *Named with a German name* ... The recognition shocked her, and her blade at Narcissus's throat faltered. Vespasian saw this; his eyes were hard, waiting for an opportunity to move against her. She summoned her concentration. 'My name is Agrippina.'

Claudius clapped his hands. 'A good Roman name! Your parents had sound instincts, even if you don't share them. How ironic, then, that the logic of your life should lead you to this point.' He turned to Cunedda. 'And you?'

'I am Cunedda.' Despite his uncertain Latin he spoke firmly, and Agrippina was proud of him.

Nectovelin growled in his native Brigantian, 'What are they saying, 'Pina?'

With interest Claudius turned to him. 'Ah, your attack dog speaks too! But this hairy fellow has no Latin, I should imagine. Not very friendly, is he?'

Vespasian growled, 'Emperor—'

'Oh, don't fuss, Vespasian. You,' he snapped at Cunedda. 'Speak to your comrade in his own guttural tongue, if you know it, and relate his words to me.' Claudius turned back to Agrippina. 'So you are here to kill an emperor.'

'That was our plan.'

Nectovelin said darkly, translated by Cunedda, 'And I swear by Coventina's ravaged arsehole that if I get the chance I will do it, little man.'

Claudius nodded, as if this was quite matter-of fact. 'Of course you will. And who sent you?'

'You have invaded the island. Every Briton, from the Brigantians to the Atrebates, is your enemy.'

'Oh, come now! Do you expect me to believe that?' Claudius spoke with the manner of a hectoring parent. 'Out with it! Who put you up to this? Was it Valerius Asiaticus? Or Magnus Vinicius, who was nominated before me to my throne?' He went on, listing senators and equestrians and freedmen with grudges, all of whom he suspected of plotting against him, or of scheming to restore the Republic.

Cunedda spoke up. 'You think so little of us that you imagine we need a Roman to tell us what to do? This was for our own purposes, to rid our lands of you. And even if we fail today, with the men of the west and the druidh at his side, Caratacus will return, and you will pay the price in blood.'

Claudius seemed puzzled. He asked his secretary, 'Caratacus?'

Narcissus said, his voice tremulous, 'A son of Cunobelin.'

'Ah, of course, the useful princes who harassed their neighbours, drove their rival chieftains into the arms of Rome, and made themselves healthy profits from the slaves they took.'

Cunedda frowned. 'Slaves?'

Vespasian said coldly, 'Your princes postured in defiance of Rome. But at the same time their raids on your neighbours won them a healthy flow of slaves to send to the markets of Gaul, in return for Roman gold.'

Claudius was watching Cunedda's face. 'You are actually disappointed, aren't you? Are you British fussy about selling slaves? Was Caratacus a hero for you? But can't you see that this is part of your conquest, that the Roman slave market distorted your politics long before a single soldier set foot here? Caratacus and his brother played two games at once, you see. They were not heroes, little boy. They were hypocrites and fools. And such men can never prevail against Rome.'

Nectovelin was as crestfallen as Cunedda, but he sneered, 'We'll see.'

'How defiant you are! But how do you imagine you could possibly succeed, you or your Caratacus? Rome is a system, you see, a system that works on timescales far longer than a mere human life, even an emperor's. And it feeds on expansion. The acquisition of wealth flows back to pay for the army, which then wins still more territory and wealth – on and on the wheel turns. Rome was always going to come here; it is destiny.' His eyes sparkled; he was fascinated, as if this was all an intellectual game, Agrippina thought. 'But emperors have been assassinated before, and no doubt will be again. Yes, if you had killed me it would have made a mess of things for a bit. Is that what you imagined, you hairy Briton, that history trembled at the point of your sword?'

'You gabble, Roman,' Nectovelin said. 'You speak of destiny. But I have a Prophecy, given to me at the moment of my birth. A Prophecy of victory and freedom. That is why we will win.'

But you are wrong, Agrippina thought, her heart sinking.

XXI

'A prophecy? How very interesting. What prophecy?'

Nectovelin glared.

'Search him, Vespasian.'

Vespasian called a guard to help him. It took only a moment for the leather document wallet to be placed in Claudius's hands.

Claudius fingered the wallet gingerly, his face pinched. 'It smells as if it has been strapped to a horse.' But he loosened its ties, extracted the parchment, and unfolded it. He carried it over to a lamp for better light, and squinted. Then he picked up a little wire frame mounted with two lenses, and held it before his eyes.

Agrippina gasped, thinking of another Prophecy phrase – *a man will come with eyes of glass*. Somehow, was it all coming true?

Nectovelin looked at her suspiciously.

'Well, well,' Claudius said. 'A British prophecy written out in Latin – and quite good Latin at that. Tell me how this came to be.' When Nectovelin did not reply the Emperor took off his 'eyes of glass' and turned on him. 'You do understand that all that is keeping you alive is my curiosity.'

Nectovelin seemed to be shaking with rage. Agrippina understood that to him the Prophecy was an amulet, its magical powers independent of whatever its words actually said – and now, in this moment of ultimate failure, he was having to endure those words being read by a stranger, an enemy. But he made himself recount the story of his birth: the Latin chatter of his mother in labour, how her words had been transcribed by Agrippina's grandfather.

Claudius eyed Agrippina. 'So it's a family matter. And when was this? How old are you, man?'

Nectovelin gave his age: forty-seven summers.

'Forty-seven, forty-seven ...' Claudius went to his desk and began pawing through scrolls. 'Something is in the back of my mind. What else was significant about that date? We Romans are partial to a good prophecy, you know,' he said, lecturing the party of rebel Britons and tense soldiers, while casually facing the other way. 'You can see the appeal. We mortals fumble our way through the mist of events like men in blindfolds. How marvellous it would be to glimpse the future clearly – or even the past! We Romans have our own prophetic books ...'

The Sibylline Books had been a gift to a king of Rome by a sorceress called the Sibyl. The Books foretold the entire future of Rome, so the sorceress said.

'Sadly the Books were destroyed in a fire more than a century ago. But a collection of fresh oracles has since been gathered from shrines around the world, and housed in the temple of Apollo on the Palatine since the time of the deified Augustus. Perhaps this new oracle will find a place in that strange library – what do you think? ...

'Ah, here we are.' He dug out a scroll, unrolled it on his desk and ran his thumb along its surface. 'Um. According to this compendium the year of your birth was unremarkable, hairy man – save for one thing: another birth, of a certain prophet in Judea. The Jews, you know, an excitable people! The villain was crucified in the reign of my uncle Tiberius as I recall, and rightly so. No more than a coincidence, no doubt – though if I were a god composing a prophecy, nothing about it would be coincidental.

'And what is it we actually have here?' He held up the parchment, peering down through his lenses. 'Quite brief, isn't it?'

Agrippina found herself saying, 'Only sixteen lines.'

She saw Nectovelin's shoulders stiffen. In that moment Nectovelin knew for certain she had somehow seen the document herself, against his express wishes. Whatever the outcome today, she feared that she had already destroyed her relationship with a man who had been like a father.

Claudius watched this with interest; he seemed fascinated by the British. 'Sixteen lines, yes. You've evidently read it, girl. But I wonder how well you know it – if your education was only Gallic then perhaps not well at all. There is some subtlety here. Why, there's even an acrostic.' He held up the bit of parchment to Agrippina. 'Look, girl, can you see how the first letters of the lines combine to form a phrase? A – C – O – N ... Perhaps this is the key to the whole thing. The original Sibylline Books featured similar acrostics, as I recall. An intriguing connection.

'There are some specific predictions here, aren't there? Of an emperor with a German name ... And I am Germanicus.' He looked up sharply at Agrippina. 'Interesting. But what's this about a noose of stone around the neck of the island?' He glanced at Vespasian. 'Does this island have a neck, legate?'

'Nobody knows, sir.'

'On we go, cryptic and confusing – baffling, as are all such oracles, or I suppose we wouldn't value them so highly – ah, and at the end, a few lines about freedom and happiness and so forth. Clumsy poetry, nothing more; I'm surprised the gods saw fit to include it.' He turned to Nectovelin. 'You, hairy man – can you read this at all?' Claudius threw back his head and laughed. 'So you have a prophecy, uttered by your own mother, in the language of your conquerors – a language you can neither understand nor read! The gods may or may not know the future, but they certainly have a sense of humour.'

'I don't need to read it,' Nectovelin said. 'I know what it says. That you Romans will be thrown off this island, and I will enjoy doing it.'

Claudius seemed perplexed. 'Actually it says no such thing.' He turned to Agrippina. 'Do *you* believe this is prophetic?'

'Yes,' Agrippina admitted.

'And what does it mean?'

'I think we cannot fight you today,' she said quietly.

'What? What? Speak up, girl!'

She took a deep breath, aware of the harm she was about to do to Nectovelin, whether he lived or died. 'We can't win today. The Prophecy says so.'

Nectovelin rumbled like a bull. Vespasian's grip on his arm tightened. All around the room the soldiers tensed, and Narcissus shivered in Agrippina's grasp.

Claudius whispered, 'Well, in that case, what happens next all depends on you, Agrippina. If you will let me, I will spare you. Not through mercy – because you intrigue me, you and your lover.'

'And if I allow you to let me live, will you spare Nectovelin?' The bargaining sounded strange to Agrippina's own ears.

Nectovelin turned to face Agrippina. 'You've betrayed me once today already, child. Don't do it again.'

Vespasian, too, was outraged. 'Sir, you can't listen to this!'

Claudius was composed. 'How amusing that both captor and captive should reject a peaceful solution!'

Somehow Agrippina was in control of the situation. 'Let Nectovelin go,' she said. And in her own tongue she said to Nectovelin: 'I'm sorry.'

'Disarm him and throw him out, legate.'

'Sir—'

'He's broken already. He's no threat to us. And now we'll have to decide what to do with you two children – if you will first stop giving my secretary that unwelcome shave.'

With Nectovelin ejected, Agrippina released Narcissus. He stumbled away from her with a look of murderous hatred, massaging his throat and fingering his cut cheek.

Cunedda, freed, approached Agrippina. 'How could you do that to Nectovelin?'

'I saved his life.'

'But he lost his honour. And the Prophecy—'

'He never understood the Prophecy. Claudius was right. There are times when being able to read is a great advantage. Cunedda, *the Prophecy talks of three emperors.* Claudius is only the first. So we can't defeat him – not if the Prophecy contains any truth. For the Romans will be here for a long, long time.'

He rubbed his upper arm, bruised from a soldier's grasp. 'And Mandubracius?'

She flinched. 'I haven't forgotten. I will avenge my brother. I'll just have to find another way. There's one thing I've learned today above all else, Cunedda. This is a long game we're playing.'

Rufrius Pollio, commander of the Praetorian Guard, approached them. His sword was sheathed, but his look was venomous – but then he was in significant trouble for allowing assassins to come so close to the Emperor. 'Time to go,' he said in Latin.

Agrippina blurted, 'Emperor—'

Claudius turned.

'I must believe the Prophecy is truthful, for its predictions have come to pass. But there is a detail I don't understand.'

Claudius frowned. 'What detail?'

'That you would come to Britain accompanied by exotic beasts – horses big as houses, teeth like scimitars ...'

Claudius stared at her. Then he turned to the commander of his guard. 'Rufrius Pollio, will you open that curtain?'

The soldier did so, to reveal a rectangle of deep blue evening sky. And, through the window, Agrippina saw a shadow moving by: massive yet graceful, a great head nodding. Perhaps distracted by the light from the tent the head turned, and a startlingly human eye peered at her. A trunk was raised, and tusks flashed.

Claudius said gravely, 'Some of this little poem of yours could be no more than sensible guesswork. Rome was bound to come here under one emperor or another. But it's hard to see who but the gods could have foreseen *them,* isn't it?'

Agrippina felt as if the world had come to pieces, and was reassembling in a different shape entirely.

XXII

When the burly soldiers bundled Nectovelin out into the dark, the commotion disturbed the animals in their hastily erected compound. They stomped back and forth, rumbling, their massive bulks like clouds shifting against the darkling sky.

They weren't happy. They were from different families, for the African traders who had sold them to the Romans had been unconcerned about such niceties. They had not enjoyed the sea crossings and the overland journey through Gaul any more than most of the Emperor's companions had. Now they were confined in this strange, cold place, and, missing their siblings and mothers, they growled and jostled restlessly.

But they had served Claudius's purpose, in striking awe into the people of this island. After all, since the glaciers had sullenly drawn back and the last mammoths died, these were the first elephants to have set foot in Britain in ten thousand years.

XXIII

Claudius left Britain after only sixteen days. And he took Agrippina and Cunedda with him, all the way back to Rome.

On the Palatine Hill, where the emperors since Augustus had been building their palaces, Agrippina and Cunedda wandered in silence under ceilings as tall as the sky, and across floors of marble as flat as lakes, all drenched in dense Mediterranean light. Claudius had talked of Rome as a system that worked on timescales that transcended human lifetimes. For more than half a millennium already the wealth of Europe, Asia and Africa had drained here, as water drains through a funnel. And the result was visible all around them in the marble-plated hills of Rome.

Though they remained under nominal guard, Claudius seemed keen to keep Cunedda and Agrippina within his household. He even assigned them tutors. They were his two *Brittunculi*, he said, apparently without malice. Later Agrippina learned that he had brought Gauls home too, and showed a similar interest in that relatively new province. They were treated like pets, Agrippina thought, but there were worse attitudes for a conqueror.

A month after the Emperor's return to Rome Agrippina was brought to Claudius to find him busily engaged in preparations for his triumph, scheduled for the following year. 'There's so much to do,' he told her, fussing over heaps of correspondence. 'So many details to organise! And it's hard to delegate. Even Narcissus, whom I value dearly, is a Greek, and understands little of the tradition, not to say the archaism, with which Rome runs its affairs.

'And I am also busy composing the dedicatory inscription for my triumphal arches.' He showed her a rough outline. 'You can see half of it is taken up by my own formal names, pah! But I have chosen the words carefully, I think. I mention the formal submission of eleven kings. The invasion was carried out without loss of honour to Rome, for it was a response to the breaking of treaties by British princes – it was, you know! Roman wars are always legal. And here I show that Roman rule is now extended to the barbarians across the sea.' *Barbari Transoceanum.*

'Where will your arches be?'

'The Senate has awarded me three – in Rome, and on the coast of the Ocean, perhaps where Plautius made his first landing, and perhaps one in Cunobelin's capital.'

Agrippina said boldly, 'There will be few celebrations in Britain.'

'Why so?'

'Your invasion was brutal. You care nothing for our culture, our identity. You want only the wealth you can extract.'

Claudius sat back and pursed his lips. 'So we are bandits. Violent robbers. But that is the way of things. On your island, you Britons have fallen behind the march of Europe. We have literacy; we have law; we have records; we have a political system which does not depend on the idiosyncrasies of its leader – at least not entirely. For all the undoubted qualities of your culture, in this new world Britain is an anachronism. And in the collision of an advanced culture with a lesser, only one outcome is possible.

'Times change, Agrippina! Once Rome was a vibrant, ancient Republic, and no one would have believed that democrats would abandon democracy – and yet in the tensions of global power Romans yielded to emperors. But the sun continues to rise and set even so. If we suppress your British identity, good: shed it! The future belongs to Rome – and you are a Roman now.'

She nodded, listening carefully. 'I value your words, sir, but—'

'"But you are a pompous old fool!"' He sat back with a sigh. 'You see, I am such a wise ruler that I can even finish your sentences for you. And what of you two? I saw the bond between you, even in that difficult night in Camulodunum. Is love blossoming here in the sweet light of Rome?'

It paid to tell an emperor what he wanted to hear, but she saw no point in concealing what must be obvious. 'We've grown apart.'

'But you loved Cunedda!'

'I did. But—' But the vast dislocation of the invasion had overwhelmed their petty human plans, and the death of her brother seemed to have aged Agrippina prematurely. 'I think I simply grew out of him.'

He studied her. 'I do understand, I think. But tell me: if you are no longer in love, what are your plans now?'

'Plans?' She frowned. 'You make the plans.'

Claudius looked irritated. 'Well, then, tell me your dreams.'

'Cunedda is a potter, like his father before him. I think he would like to go home. Back to Britain. And to begin building up his family's business once more.'

Claudius nodded. 'A shrewd choice. Believe me, now that you are part of Rome there will be a market for his pots!' He tapped his teeth. 'I see no reason to keep the boy here – not past the triumph next year, anyway. I will talk to Narcissus about it.'

She nodded. 'Thank you.'

'And what of you?'

'I would like to stay here in Rome,' she said firmly. 'As you said I am a Roman now. I believe I have wits. Perhaps I could be a clerk, a chronicler.'

'Oh, you may do better than that. I see promise in you. As a barbarian, indeed as a non-Roman, you will face prejudice; I wouldn't hide that. But you could support a suitable husband in an appropriate profession: a lawyer, perhaps, or a moneylender.'

'Or I might just make my own way,' she said.

He raised his thick eyebrows. 'You are ambitious indeed.'

More than even you know, she thought to herself. After all she had already come far. She had survived the storm of invasion. She had plotted the assassination of an emperor, and survived that too. Now here she was, a woman from the edge of the world at the centre of everything.

And, though her hatred of Rome had become meaningless so complete was its victory over her, she still clutched one dark ambition to her heart.

Claudius was immersed once more in his books and parchments. He had probably already forgotten she was here. With a bow she backed out of his presence and left the room.

XXIV

It was when the Romans began to use their siege weapons in earnest, when a cloud of iron-tipped projectiles came sailing over the burning walls of the hill fort to penetrate the bare skulls of posturing Durotriges warriors, that Nectovelin knew the war was lost, and that Britain would not be rid of Romans in his lifetime. And when a bolt penetrated his leg – he could feel his kneecap shatter like a bit of smashed pottery – he knew his own battle was over.

The legionaries entered the fort. Business-like, they torched its buildings and began to demolish the remains of its defences. And they walked among the wounded. Some they put to the sword immediately. Any who looked worth a ransom were rounded up and made to sit in the dirt under a weighted-down net. Nectovelin was one of those chosen to live; he sat among the groans of injured Durotriges, racked by his own pain.

Vespasian had launched his assault on the west while the Emperor was still in the country. Resistance was expected here, as Caratacus had known, for the Durotriges had been nursing a grievance ever since Caesar had disrupted their trading links with Gaul. And so it had proved. The Durotriges and other nations opposed the Roman advance with a ferocity that put the Catuvellaunians to shame.

But it had not been enough. Not even Nectovelin had anticipated the savagery and relentlessness of Vespasian's charge. The legate had fought more than thirty battles, and taken more than twenty towns. And Nectovelin had not anticipated how effectively the Romans could lay siege. Vespasian had been supported by the Roman fleet which had tracked its way along the south coast; the sight of the great silent ships had struck fear into those who watched from the land.

And now the conquering Romans were destroying this fort.

It was in fact a very ancient place. There was a kind of track extending around the rim of the hill, a rutted ditch. The local people talked of the old days when they would appease their gods by walking around the sacred track, repairing the causeway, making offerings. Children, digging in the dirt on summer afternoons, would often find shaped bits of stone, metalwork in bronze or iron – even, occasionally, a human bone. This hill had been occupied and venerated for a time beyond counting; the fort that topped it was only the latest manifestation.

But now the Romans had come and it was the end. The legionaries pushed the ramparts into the ditches, and levered the big stones out of the tall gateways, ensuring the fort could never be used again. The hill would be abandoned, its purpose forgotten, to become a brooding puzzle for later generations, ancient causeway, ruined ramparts and all. Romans always finished what they had started.

'. . . I know you.' The words were in Latin, but Nectovelin had picked up a little in his years with Agrippina. He looked up dully.

The legate himself stood over him: Vespasian. He didn't wear his dress uniform now, as he had that night in Camulodunum, but scuffed and bloodstained armour plates. Dirt and sweat smeared his forehead. Vespasian had always had a seriousness about him, and Nectovelin sensed that now. Vespasian killed in great numbers; that was his job. But he didn't relish it.

As well as his staff officers, Vespasian was accompanied by a younger man, obviously one of the Durotriges serving as an interpreter. He was clean, his tunic unmarked, and he showed no shame in this burning fortress of his people. The young man asked a question in the tongue of the Durotriges.

Nectovelin answered, 'I am of the Brigantians.' The young man switched easily to that tongue.

'I know you,' Vespasian said again through his interpreter. 'That night in Camulodunum. You were the buffoon who tried to kill the Emperor.'

'And but for bad fortune I would have succeeded.'

Vespasian smiled. 'Bad fortune? But you boasted of your Prophecy. I remember digging into your sweating armpit to find it. Where is your Prophecy now? Did it foresee this?'

Nectovelin thought of the ancient fort, now being kicked apart by Roman legionaries. He thought of the Catuvellaunian farmers who had pulled on their grandfathers' chain mail and had gone into battle expecting a clash of champions, only to be met by a Roman meat-grinder.

'No, it didn't tell of this,' he said. 'But the Prophecy tells of freedom for every human being, long after you are dead, Roman.'

'But not for you.'

'No, not for me. I die for that freedom, and for Coventina's rocky heart.'

And with that Nectovelin thrust his arms through the net. He ripped the skin off one hand, and felt a finger break on the other, but he got his hands through the mesh and around Vespasian's throat, before a staff officer stepped forward with his stabbing sword and skewered his belly.

XXV

On her release from the Emperor Claudius's household, Agrippina, aged twenty-four, found employment as a bookkeeper. She worked for a moneylender, a fat, pleasant man called Marcus Crassus Cerealis, whom she eventually married.

Despite her education in Gaul, Agrippina found life in Rome very strange. It wasn't just the scale and clamouring bustle of this world capital, but the small things. In Eburacum she had grown up amid big extended families, where marriages were fluid and children were the responsibility of everybody in the roundhouse, and women had much the same power as men. Now she was stuck in a set of tiny partitioned-off rooms, with Cerealis who, despite his mild nature, clearly expected her to raise him a family alone.

But this was the life she had chosen, and she stuck to it. In time she bore Cerealis two healthy girls, whom she raised in the Roman manner.

She never left Rome again, but always followed events in her native Britain.

Aulus Plautius served as Britain's first governor for four years. In that time he established a new province, Britannia, across the south-east corner of the island. The old nations became mere administrative units, *civitates*, within the Roman province. Camulodunum, once the capital of a Catuvellaunian empire, was made a colony of veteran troops, the first true Roman town in Britain, and renamed *Colonia Claudia*. The exploitation of the British began immediately, with the systematic extraction of the province's surplus agricultural wealth. There were levies of corn and labour corvées, and soon a formalised tax system was imposed.

Caratacus, remarkably, continued to lead resistance in the west for eight years. As Nectovelin had understood, he became popular among all the nations of Britain as the one man who had not given up before the Romans – even if he never actually won a battle. Agrippina was shamed that his final betrayal was at the hands of her own queen Cartimandua, who was keen to cooperate with the Romans. She saw Caratacus brought to Rome and paraded through the city. The Romans rather liked his defiance, now that he was safely defeated, and they saw in him qualities they believed they had lost. Agrippina was dismayed that Caratacus would survive in memory not for who he was but only as an element in the Romans' own story of themselves. His usefulness over, Caratacus was pardoned and pensioned off, and she never heard of him again.

As time passed, the tapestry of history was woven thread by thread. Secretary Narcissus eventually fell foul of the complicated internal politics of the imperial family. Agrippina, who had always feared the Greek might take revenge for the humiliation of that night in Camulodunum, quietly rejoiced in his fall. She was more saddened by the death of Claudius, said to have been poisoned by his manipulative new wife. She thought it was ironic that the frail Emperor had survived assassination in faraway Britain only to be murdered in his own bed by his family.

The British meanwhile chafed under the rule of their 'two kings', the governor and procurator who jointly managed the new province. When Agrippina was forty the brutal reign of Claudius's stepson Nero provoked a revolt in Britain under an Iceni woman called Boudicca, who burned retired soldiers, lawyers, tax collectors and their families in their new temples. Her name meant 'she who brings victories' – if she had been Roman she might have been called 'Victoria'. Braint had been right, Agrippina thought, that it would take a woman to give the Romans a real fight. Boudicca had no vision beyond destruction, and failed to concentrate her energies on military targets, and in the end she fell – but not before tens of thousands had died, and the Roman hold on Britain trembled, just for a moment.

After Nero the imperial succession was bloody, and a civil war broke out between rival claimants. For Agrippina it was a terrifying time, a throwback to the days of Julius Caesar when strong men backed by private armies had battled for power. Indeed the still-young empire was nearly destroyed in the process. The crisis was resolved when an old acquaintance of Agrippina's, Vespasian, came out of retirement to become the third emperor in a year. With the competence and ruthlessness he had once shown in Britain, he soon restored order in Rome.

Meanwhile under Cartimandua, who seemed to be emulating Cunobelin of the Catuvellaunians, Agrippina's people the Brigantians, still independent of Rome, grew rich on trade with the new province to the south. There was a flowering of culture, she sensed from the letters she received from home, of literacy and music and art and education. But sprawling Brigantia was only ever a loose federation, difficult to control, and when even the queen's husband Venutius grew restive, unease about Cartimandua's Roman policy penetrated even her own bedroom. In the end Cartimandua had a reckless affair with her husband's armour-bearer, and Venutius's fury ignited civil war.

The Romans, under Vespasian's strong governors, rescued Cartimandua, and then moved into Brigantia for good, pinning it down under a network of forts and roads. They established a legionary fortress in Agrippina's old birthplace of Eburacum. After that, a generation after their first landing in south-east Britain, the Romans pushed further north still, into the misty highlands of Caledonia.

Meanwhile Agrippina's family was denuded of males by all this turmoil, and lacked heirs. Aged fifty she found herself bequeathed a majority stake in the family's quarrying business. Agrippina had no interest in overseeing this herself – but Cunedda had had a son, born in Camulodunum. Through an exchange of letters she transferred her holding to him, a last gesture to a long-dead lover.

Under the solemn calm of Vespasian's rule, Agrippina watched over her growing children. She made fitful efforts to recover Nectovelin's Prophecy, which Claudius had lodged in the vault of the Sibylline oracles, but these came to nothing. And she tried, even as she turned them into strong Roman maidens, to tell her daughters something of where their blood came from. She told them long stories from her own childhood of ancestral Brigantians, who had ruled with bronze or stone, in ages when only sheep had ruled Rome's seven hills.

But her body betrayed her. A racking cough grew steadily worse, until she woke one morning to find she had been coughing up blood.

She tried to leave her business affairs in order for the benefit of her bereft, helpless husband. Her children were both in their early twenties, they had grown into proud, strong, well-educated Roman women, and she had few concerns about them. Fifty wasn't a terribly young age to die, she told her daughters. Besides she felt her years had been crowded enough for two lifetimes.

But she had one last piece of unfinished business.

XXVI

Though always favoured by his commander Vespasian, and despite his little bit of notoriety following his time in Britain, Marcus Allius had never risen higher than centurion – nor, if truth be told, had he ever wanted to. He retired from the army as early as he could on a fat veteran's pension, and bought himself a compact little vineyard a day's ride from his native Rome. Just as he had always been a competent but never great soldier, so he proved a prosperous but never rich vintner. He raised a strong son who followed his father into the army.

Aged fifty-five, over a quarter of a century after his British adventure and as healthy as he had ever been, Marcus looked forward to a long retirement.

Then, one day, a slave sought him out bearing a letter.

The note was from one Agrippina, British-born but resident in Rome. She had been present at the Roman landing at Rutupiae too, she wrote, and her letter concerned 'unfinished business'.

She had been able to consult Vespasian's official biographer to find out which legion had been the first to land in Britain, that dark night in Rutupiae thirty years before, and which century had landed first, and which man of that century had been the first to set foot on British soil, whose name she thought she had heard. Agrippina summarised the steps she had taken to ensure that she and she alone took full responsibility for the crime that was about to take place – but she would already be dead by the time Marcus Allius opened the letter.

Marcus looked up at the slave, to ask, 'What crime?'

The blade in the slave's hand was the last thing he saw.

II

BUILDER
AD 122–138

I

Brigonius agreed to meet the women from Rome outside the town of Durovernum Cantiacorum, on the road leading east towards Rutupiae at the coast.

For a Brigantian it was a long way from home. But Brigonius reached the rendezvous early in the morning, well before the appointed hour, and had to wait. He found a milestone to sit on, set his battered old wide-brimmed hat on his head to keep out the sun, and let his horse chew on the tough, dirty grass at the roadside. As the day wore on he grew hot, his face itching under a beard still new enough to be a novelty. He was twenty-two years old.

He was maybe half a mile down the road from the town. He inspected the place curiously. Durovernum was an island of wood and stone, of roofs of bright red tiles. It looked very strange to Brigonius, not at all like his own community of roundhouses at Banna – and nor was it like the Roman military architecture he had grown up with in the north, the endless box-shaped forts and watchtowers, like the one in Banna.

He was used to Roman roads, though. The whole country was carpeted by them. This one ran straight as an arrow's flight off to the east, its hard-packed gravel surface pressed flat. His quarryman's eye noted how it had been resurfaced two or three times, so that it was raised proud of the surrounding farmland. Old or not the road was well kept, its drainage gullies swept clear, and with no sign of subsidence. The Roman soldiers who first built this did their job well, he grudgingly admitted.

But it wasn't soldiers who used the road today. For perhaps an hour in the early morning Brigonius was at peace, just himself, his horse, the road and the songs of the birds. But as the day wore on the road filled up with traffic: people on foot and horseback, or riding carts and wagons and litters. The townsfolk were bright, clean, well-fed, their clothes were brilliantly coloured, and their skins shone with cosmetic oils. Slaves walked beside their masters' carriages, or carried them on litters and chairs. Everybody was streaming east. It was as if somebody had tipped up the town and poured out its inhabitants like oil from a pot, spilling them towards Rutupiae, where the Emperor was due to land today.

Sitting on his stone beside this glittering crowd, Brigonius felt out of place, an ill-formed northern clod. But he had been summoned here, he reminded himself.

He took Severa's letter from his satchel and read it over again. It was written in a blue dye on a small, scraped-thin rectangle of wood, scored down the middle and folded over. His own name was written on the outside, with an address: Vindolanda, the large fort planted square in the middle of Brigantia, with which Brigonius did a lot of business. Inside, the Latin text had been written out in two orderly columns by a neat, somewhat cramped hand. But it opened with a generous greeting – 'From Claudia Severa to her friend Brigonius, greetings' – and signed off with a flourish – 'In the hope that this finds you in as good health and fortune as I and my daughter enjoy, C. Severa' – both in a different hand from the main text, which had presumably been written out under dictation by a scribe.

Brigonius was literate. He needed to be. His father had died two years ago, leaving Brigonius, at just twenty, in sole possession of the family quarrying business. His main customer was the Roman army, who devoured cut stone for their forts and roads, their shrines and bath houses. And the army was a hive of writing, writing, writing; a soldier couldn't fart, it seemed, without some junior officer making a note of it.

So Brigonius was used to letters. But he had never received such a letter as this before. For one thing it had come all the way from Rome: a letter from Rome, addressed to *him*. His correspondent, Claudia Severa, lady of Rome, claimed a family connection to Brigonius, saying that an ancestor of hers had once known an ancestor of his.

And the letter spoke of the Emperor's coming visit to Britain. That was no news; everybody had been talking about it for months. But, Severa said, the visit would give their two families, Brigonius's and Severa's, the chance to grow very rich indeed. How did she know all this? Because of a prophecy, she said.

It was hard to know how to take all this. The mention of profit got his attention, but he recoiled from the talk of family histories and prophecies. The superstitious Romans were obsessed with past and future, with dead ancestors and presagings of time to come. Better to live in the present, he thought, and enjoy the now. As time wore on

110

and he sat on this milestone with the smug Cantiaci citizens bustling past him, he wondered if he was wasting his time.

But then the two women arrived. And within a heartbeat of his first meeting with Severa – or rather her daughter, Lepidina – all his doubts were dispelled.

II

Claudia Severa and her daughter arrived in a small carriage covered by an awning of bright red cloth. A servant, probably a slave, led two docile horses. Severa and Lepidina stepped down from the carriage with unreasonable grace, and walked towards Brigonius. The mother might have been forty, the daughter eighteen or nineteen. The two of them were very alike, both very pale, with strawberry-blonde hair piled high in exotic sculptures.

The older woman wore a stola, a swatch of brilliant white cloth embroidered with purple. Under her loose clothing Severa's figure was shapely, her bust prominent and her hips swaying as she walked. She was sensual, but she looked solid, almost muscular. This was a formidable woman, Brigonius thought immediately.

The daughter, though, was slighter, slimmer, and she walked with a loose-jointed beauty. She wore a long skirt and tunic of pink and silver-grey, the colours somehow blending perfectly together, and she wore a scarf around her neck, some purple-pink fabric as light as mist. She was so delicate, so pale-white, she seemed only loosely attached to reality. Again he felt like a clod with his black hair and dark colouring, a lump of earth compared to this creature of air and fire.

Severa was watching him. 'You must be Brigonius,' she said dryly.

He was staring at the girl, still sitting on his milestone like a child. He clambered to his feet, making dust rise in a cloud. The daughter's eyes widened as he revealed his full height. 'I'm sorry,' he said.

'I am Claudia Severa. My daughter, Lepidina.'

The girl turned away coyly. He tried to fix his attention on Severa. 'How did you know me?'

'You weren't hard to spot,' Severa said. 'I just looked for the beard. The Cantiaci go clean-shaven, you know, like all good Romans!'

'I, ah—'

The girl spoke for the first time. 'You seem fascinated by me, Brigantius.'

'Brigonius. I am a Brigantian. My name is Brigonius—'

'Do you like my scarf?' She touched it. Its colour perfectly complemented the grey of Lepidina's tunic, and it cast reflected sunlight over the soft white flesh of her throat.

He was staring again. 'I've never seen material like it.'

'Well, you wouldn't have. It's silk. It comes from a land far to the east, even beyond the Parthians. Nobody knows how it's made – imagine that!'

He saw now that the scarf was fixed by a small brooch: a crossed-over curve of silver wire, a stylised fish perhaps. 'That's a pretty design. The fish.'

Severa evidently hadn't known the brooch was there. She glared at her daughter. 'Cover that up, you little idiot!'

With bad grace, Lepidina tucked the brooch out of sight.

Severa walked around Brigonius, eyeing him up and down as she might a horse. 'Well, you're evidently a lust-addled fool, like all men. But you're healthy enough, and you seem honest. I think we're going to be able to do business, you and me. But first we've an emperor to greet. Will you ride with us to Rutupiae? We've room.'

Lepidina, girlishly friendly now, linked her arm through his. She was soft and fragrant, like a scented cloud. 'Oh, yes, do. We've got fruit and wine. It will be fun!'

So Brigonius found himself sitting between mother and daughter in the shade of the carriage's awning.

The carriage joined the flow towards Rutupiae, the slave guiding Brigonius's horse. As they rolled across the flat coastal plain, it wasn't long before Brigonius caught the first whiffs of salty sea air – and through the awning he glimpsed the gleaming white shoulders of the monument at Rutupiae, a landmark visible for miles around. Meanwhile the air in the carriage was filled with the tickling scent of cosmetics, and the women plied him with a fine light wine and strawberries dipped in ground pepper.

'We heard of your trouble,' Severa said.

'Trouble?'

'The revolt in Brigantia. News of such things reaches Rome, you know!'

'I'd hardly call it a revolt,' Brigonius said. 'It started with a riot outside Vindolanda. Came from a bit of heavy-handedness by a decurion.' In fact the officer had beaten a Brigantian labourer he accused, falsely, of thievery. 'Next thing you know there was trouble all over the place.

113

Some of the lads took the opportunity for a little petty banditry.'

'I thought it was more serious than that,' Severa said.

'Oh, the army had to deploy.' Once roused from its brothels and bath houses the army had, as usual, stamped down with maximum force on the dissidents. Heads were broken, a few villages burned, a gaggle of wives and children taken off into slavery. 'They cleared up the trouble quickly.'

'I don't understand why people even *want* to fight the army,' Lepidina said. 'I mean, what if they *won*, somehow? Why, without the army ...' She tailed off. Her face was empty, her eyes and mouth wide, like a child's.

Her life had been remarkably sheltered, Brigonius thought. He felt an impulse to protect her – an impulse no doubt deriving from lust, but genuine despite that, he thought.

'Not everybody likes the Romans,' he said gently. 'Their taxes, their forced-labour levies—'

'You must like them,' Lepidina said sharply. 'You sell them your stone.'

'That doesn't mean they're my friends.' He grinned. 'I follow my father. I bleed the Romans white, if I can.'

Severa nodded, apparently approving. 'You learned much from your father?'

'He died a couple of years ago.'

'Yet you still rely on his wisdom, as you wait to accrue your own. A sound strategy. We are all shaped by the past, aren't we, Brigonius? In fact we wouldn't be sitting here now if not for deep historical links we share.'

'In your note you talk of your grandmother, who was a Brigantian but went to Rome.'

'Agrippina, yes. She died before I was born, but my mother told me all about her. Fascinating life! Somebody ought to write it down. And, you see, she knew your great-grandfather, Brigonius, who was called Cunedda—'

'Like my own father.'

'Yes. And his father before him. The story goes that Agrippina and Cunedda knew each other at the time of Claudius's invasion of Britain. Your family were Catuvellaunians, Brigonius. My grandmother's family owned an interest in a quarrying concern. Later in life she passed it to your family – to the son of that first Cunedda. And that is how your family came by their interest in quarrying, and moved to Brigantia to take possession of it. So, you see, in a way you are in my debt, aren't you?'

Brigonius, feeling manipulated, wasn't sure about that.

Lepidina had evidently heard all this before. 'I think they were more than friends,' she said mischievously. 'Agrippina and her Cunedda. Otherwise why make such an extravagant gift? I think they were lovers!' She whispered, her eyes huge, 'What do you think, Brigantius-Brigonius? Does love cross the generations, does love stand outside time?'

She was playing games, of course. But he felt a warm flush inside.

It got noisier. Lepidina ducked and looked out of the awning. 'Rutupiae!' she said. 'We're nearly there.'

III

Soon the carriage could move no further in the crush of traffic. The three passengers clambered out, Brigonius briskly, the women elegantly, and, leaving the unnamed slave with the carriage, they walked.

The air off the sea was fresh, and the sun was bright. The road was packed with people, their vehicles, slaves and animals. Everybody was funnelling towards the coast, where the road ended at the feet of the mighty arch. Children ran excitedly around the legs of the adults, and there was a hum of conversation. Vendors worked the slowly moving crowd, selling bits of meat on skewers, and oysters – a speciality of Rutupiae – and tokens and trinkets to welcome the Emperor, pennants in imperial purple, and miniatures of the grave, bearded face that had become so familiar from his coinage.

With Brigonius and his broad shoulders taking the lead, the three of them made their way through the crush. Brigonius loomed taller than most; perhaps Brigantians ate better than these Roman-owned Cantiaci. His spirits rose to be part of this cheerful mob. He said, 'It feels like a festival.'

'Of course it does,' Severa said. 'That's the whole point. The emperors have always shown themselves to the crowds, at feast days, in the amphitheatres. Now this new Emperor is displaying himself to the provinces – I believe he means to travel from end to end of his empire, as if it were one vast amphitheatre.'

'Why?'

'Well, he comes to unite,' she said. 'Not to conquer like Claudius, or to indulge his vanity like Nero. The consolidator, they call him. Look around, Brigonius. Do you imagine any of these people, even the smallest child, will ever forget the day they saw the Emperor himself in person?'

Brigonius grunted. 'From what I hear, there will be plenty of people who won't forget how much it's costing them to entertain him.'

Severa laughed. 'So young yet so cynical!'

At last they broke out of the crowd. They came to a cordon patrolled by soldiers in dress uniform, with bright red cloaks and colourful plumes on their helmets. Severa spoke to one of the soldiers and passed him a note on a slip of wood; he glanced at it and hurried off to find a superior officer.

From here Brigonius could make out Rutupiae itself. It was a major port, in fact quite a large town. Blocky buildings of stone and wood sprawled around a harbour, and the tiled roof of a very grand *mansio*, there to host particularly distinguished visitors, gleamed, polished. On the sea ships floated at anchor, perhaps the ships that had transported the Emperor across the ocean from Gaul. Heavy and complex, their sails furled, they looked as if they had been painted on the blue sky.

And in the foreground, dominating everything, that quadruple triumphal arch loomed over the arrow-straight road from the west, its four columns like the legs of a giant. Clad in white marble imported from Italy, with lettering in bronze and its top ornamented with trophies of victory, it shone in the sun, no less than eighty feet high: the gateway to Roman Britain. Brigonius the quarryman wondered how its architect had ensured it would not sink into the soft coastal sand. It must have had deep and massive foundations.

Around the feet of this imposing structure people swarmed, dwarfed. Carpenters erected a stage in the crossroads beneath the arch. There were plenty of soldiers; Brigonius saw legionary pennants, the curling glitter of signal trumpets. It was quite a spectacle.

A decurion approached Severa and beckoned her forward. With some relief Brigonius moved out of the crush of the crowd, and with the women walked towards the stage.

Severa murmured, 'I don't imagine you've been here before, Brigonius. Does it call to something in your blood?'

'I don't understand.'

'It is here that the Romans under Claudius first made their landing in Britain. Of course there was nothing here then, just a bit of beach, no docks—'

Lepidina said, 'And no ugly monument.'

'And,' Severa said, 'it was a landing witnessed by my grandmother, and by your great-grandfather Cunedda. Or so Agrippina always claimed.'

Brigonius was unimpressed. 'Well, there are plenty of Romans swarming here today.'

'An emperor can hardly travel alone. I'm told there are eight thousand troops, and probably as many administrators – clerks and accountants and lawyers – the imperial government travels with his person. And then there are all the cooks and cleaners and doctors and vets, and poets and musicians and architects and actors. The court is a mobile city. No wonder the provincials bleat about the expense! ...'

They found a place amid the crowd gathering before the stage, and prepared to wait.

Severa pressed him, asking, 'Do you ever think of the past, Brigonius? Of the age of Agrippina and Cunedda, of the invasion, those brief days which have shaped our lives ever since? Time heaps up remorselessly. Your northern country is restless still, but it is already sixty years since the last great revolt in the south, when the cities burned. *Sixty years.*'

Brigonius knew about that. His grandparents had been children then, and had survived Boudicca's burning of Camulodunum. Until they died they had been fearful of alarms, of disorder – and of the smell of fire.

Severa said, 'But the invasion was some twenty years before *that.* It is all fading away now, fading into the past. Nobody alive remembers a Britain without the Romans.'

Lepidina seemed bored. 'Why are you going on and on about the dead past, mother?'

Severa said, 'Because of the Prophecy. That's why we're here, isn't it, Brigonius?' She drew a leather satchel from a fold in her tunic. 'In here,' she said, her eyes bright, 'is a single sheet – old-fashioned Latin, scratched onto a bit of parchment. Only sixteen lines. *It's the Prophecy,* Brigonius. The Prophecy I mentioned in my letter. It was written down at the birth of Nectovelin, a cousin of my grandmother, Agrippina.'

She told him something of the history of the Prophecy: how Agrippina and Cunedda had penetrated the house of Claudius himself, how a startling bit of foretelling had come true – and how Claudius afterwards had confiscated the document and placed with the Sibylline oracles. 'My grandmother moved to Rome, and spent many years trying to retrieve the document. She failed – and so did my mother – but at last I found the right person to bribe.'

Lepidina tutted. 'You tell me off about breaking the law with a bit of silver at my neck and you raid the vault of the Sibylline oracles! You're a hypocrite, Claudia Severa.'

'But what is this Prophecy?' Brigonius asked.

'It is nothing less than a sketch of the future – the future of the Romans, and of Britain under them.'

'The future?' He tried to guess dates in his head. 'But it must already be more than a hundred years old.'

'A hundred and twenty-six,' Lepidina said brightly. She fingered the fish pendant at her neck. 'It was written down in the same year as the birth of Jesus of Judea.'

'Who?'

Severa snapped, 'Just the hero of another mystery cult out of the east, another fad for my daughter and other silly children in Rome.'

Brigonius grinned. 'If the Prophecy is so old we are already in the future!'

Severa nodded solemnly. 'But that's the point. Brigonius, *the Prophecy has already started to come true*. The Prophecy is past, present and future, all combined into one document – and through it our families are united across generations.'

Brigonius frowned. 'I'm not sure what you want of me, lady.'

'Listen to what it says.' And she read three lines from the Prophecy:

The trembling skies declare that Rome's great son has come to earth
A little Greek his name will be. Whilst God-as-babe has birth
Roman force will ram the island's neck into a noose of stone ...

Brigonius listened closely. 'What does it mean?'

'Why, I think it's clear enough. Brigonius, the empire has grown huge, with long, unstable borders beyond which barbarians roam restlessly. The new Emperor is concerned to shore up those borders. He travelled to Germany, where he is building long walls of turf. Now here he is in Britain, where he will deal with the northern frontier. He intends to build another of his walls across Britain – in the north, where, I am told, two estuaries converge to make the island narrow. You see? Now, to the best of my knowledge this wall is meant to be of turf, like the German frontier. But I have some associates who hope to persuade him to build it of stone.'

'Stone?' Brigonius felt bewildered. 'All the way across the country? Are even the Romans capable of that?'

'Oh, they're capable of a great many things, if they put their collective mind to it. And if we *can* persuade him to build in stone, then somebody nearby is going to have to provide that stone for him.' She eyed him. 'There will be handsome profits to be made, quarryman Brigonius.'

'But how can you *know* the Emperor will build a wall at all, let alone choose stone over turf?'

She patted the leather packet. 'Because the Prophecy says so. "A noose of stone" – what else could it mean?'

Lepidina seemed sceptical. 'Yes, but what was all that about a "little Greek", a "God-as-babe"?'

119

Severa was impatient. 'Prophecies are always cryptic.'

'You can't just pick out the useful bits, mother! Don't you wonder what the real purpose of the Prophecy is? Assuming it holds any truth at all. You want to use it to make money. Fine. But what was the purpose of God in sending it to us?'

Severa merely shrugged. 'Does it matter?'

Brigonius, though, was impressed by Lepidina's comment. Sometimes she showed surprising depths. He asked, 'Severa – why are you doing this? You have a comfortable life in Rome. Why come all the way to Britain?'

Her face hardened. 'A comfortable life – perhaps. *We* think of ourselves as Roman. Lepidina was born there, as was I, as was my mother. Three generations. But to the true Romans, the old blood, we will always be barbarians. Why, even the Emperor is looked down upon, because his father was born in Iberia! It is only money that breaks through such barriers, money and lots of it that washes away dried-up old blood. Is that motive enough?'

The crowd stirred as men in togas came filing onto the stage – officials of the imperial court, Severa told Brigonius. She pointed some out. 'Those two are important for our purposes. The short, squat fellow is Platorius Nepos.'

'The new governor.'

'Yes, and an old friend of the Emperor's. It is under his control that our wall will be built, if at all. And the skinny chap in the toga is called Primigenius.'

'A slave's name.' First born. But Primigenius, wiry, bald, watchful, did not look like a slave to Brigonius. His face was well-proportioned, perhaps once beautiful, his eyes darkened and cheeks whitened by powder.

Severa murmured, 'He's a freedman but he kept his birth name. Now he runs the Emperor's household – and once, it is said, he warmed his bed. It is through Primigenius that we will obtain access to Nepos, and the Emperor. So if he glances at you, remember to smile. So what do you say, Brigonius? Will you work with me? As far as I can see you have little to lose.' She eyed Lepidina. 'And perhaps a great deal to gain.'

Brigonius was astonished at the implied offer. Could a mother be so cold and calculating as to tout her daughter like this?

But Lepidina was distracted by what was happening on the stage. 'There he is!' she squealed, excited.

A man came striding out onto the stage. The crowd surged forward and roared.

He was tall, vigorous, well-muscled, wearing shining gold armour. His skin looked tanned, and his curling hair and beard were sun-streaked brown. Brigonius judged he was about forty. He glanced over the crowd – and his gaze lit on Brigonius, who with his height stood out from the mob. Thus Brigonius found himself subject to the complex inspection of a man, an emperor, a god – Hadrian.

'He's taller than he looks on the coins,' Lepidina breathed.

IV

Severa arranged an audience with the court. They would meet the new governor, Platorius Nepos, and, with luck, perhaps even the Emperor himself.

'It cost me plenty. Every chancer in the province is trying to get to Hadrian, as you can imagine. And that manipulative snake Primigenius is fiendishly difficult to work with. But I got there in the end. If this comes off, we will have years of profitable business ahead of us – plenty of time for me to pay back my debts.'

'*If*,' Brigonius said. 'You're a gambler, Severa! And if Hadrian decides on turf as he did in Germany?'

'You mustn't think like that, Brigonius. You must be positive – seize this chance – and deal with the consequences later.'

In any event they would have no access to the Emperor until he reached the *colonia* of Camulodunum. And it was going to take many days for the imperial circus to travel that far, Brigonius learned. The whole purpose of the trip was for the people to see Hadrian. There would be stops in the new city of Londinium and elsewhere, so the wealthier citizens of the towns, already heavily taxed in this heavily militarised province, could feel they got their money's worth from the huge expense of this visit.

Rather than wait, Severa decided that she, her daughter and Brigonius would go on ahead. Arriving early at Camulodunum they would have more time to prepare their pitch.

On his journey south Brigonius had travelled fast and light. He rode all the way, changing his horses at roadside inns – *mansiones*, as they were called, stations primarily intended for official despatch riders and the *cursus publicus*, the fast public postal service. But he didn't sleep in the inns. He had a leather tent, in fact a Roman army surplus item he'd purchased at Vindolanda. He didn't like towns; he had been happy to sleep in fields with his own small fire and his horse tethered nearby. Cheaper too.

Going back with two Roman ladies was a different matter. *They* weren't about to sleep in a field; the question never even arose. Severa lavished money to hire a new carriage, slaves and horses. Then, armed with a schematic map of the province, she plotted out a route. From Rutupiae they would travel west through Durovernum and along the south bank of the Tamesis estuary – said to be the route once taken by Claudius's conquering army – and then via smaller towns to Londinium. There they would cross the river by the Romans' new wooden bridge, and head north.

This route would incidentally take them through the homelands of several British nations, including Brigonius's own ancestral people the Catuvellaunians. But these were not marked on Severa's map, which showed only the Romans' new towns, their roads, and the rivers with their new Latin names.

So they set off. They rolled through peaceful farmland. The fields were marked out by hedgerows or stone walls, given over on this summer's day to wheat or barley. Away from the towns, the buildings were mostly round thatched houses; here and there smoke seeped into the sky.

From the start it was an unhappy journey. Lepidina and her mother had already journeyed all the way from Rome, and were frankly tired of travelling. Brigonius had hoped he could at least use the trip to get to know Lepidina a little better. Lepidina did some perfunctory flirting with Brigonius for the first day or two, but soon grew bored and retreated into the back of the carriage, where, curled up among bundles of clothing, she immersed herself in books of poetry.

She showed these to Brigonius. Written out on papyrus scrolls they were poems by somebody known as Ovid. Brigonius found this difficult to read; his Latin wasn't good enough to spot all the allusions and verbal trickeries. But the poetry was racy stuff and he found it embarrassing.

Severa teased him mercilessly. 'You're like all young people. Do you imagine your generation invented sex? ...'

But these intervals of banter were moments in a rather dreary progression.

In the event it wasn't Lepidina whom Brigonius got to know better during the journey but her mother, in the long hours he spent riding with her at the front of the carriage. Alongside Severa, he saw his own landscape through her sharper eyes.

Eighty years after Claudius, Britannia was divided into two distinct parts. The south and east had been pacified, and a civilian government was emerging based on the new towns. But the north and west remained essentially under military control. Thus Brigonius had grown up under an occupying power. The Romans even had different names for the two populations, the *Brittani* of the south and the *Brittones* of the north.

'The country here makes you uncomfortable, doesn't it?' Severa said. 'Home for you is different from all this. The south-east of Britain has more in common with Gaul or Italy than with Britain's own north-west.'

He tried to put his feelings into words. 'At least at home you know who you are. Things are clear. You're Roman or you're Brigantian. Here it's all – muddy.' He said defiantly, 'But even here the touch of the Roman is light.'

She raised her eyebrows.

'Look around you. The farms were here before the road. You can tell from the way the road just cuts through the fields. And the farmers are working the land just as they always did, long before the Romans came. So you see, the Romans have made hardly any difference at all.'

'You think so?' Severa said slyly. 'Look at that.' She pointed to a farmhouse, a complex of whitewashed tile-roofed buildings surrounded by gardens and set amid extensive fields: it was grand, even palatial. 'You could transplant such a house as that to the Mediterranean and it wouldn't look out of place. And what about that?' On a river bank to the east, dimly seen in misty air, a great wheel turned slowly. 'It is a mill,' she said. 'For grinding corn, using the power of flowing water where once human muscle or oxen would have done the job. You can use the wind, too, if you're clever enough. The farmers are even breaking land on hilltops and in river valleys they previously thought not worth working. The population is rising too. I know this is true because the Romans measure such things.'

Brigonius snorted. 'The Romans count us so they can tax us. The farmers only grow more wheat to meet the demands of the soldiers who push us around. And then they have to pay tax on the coin they earn.'

'Yes,' Severa said, a touch impatiently, 'but that's the point. You have to see all of this as a great wheel, Brigonius – like the waterwheel of the mill over there. Once the farmers grew only for themselves. Now they grow a surplus, which they take to the towns to sell. The taxes they pay on their profits are used to develop the towns and to pay the soldiers, who, hungry, must be fed by the farmers' surplus ... Around and around it goes, a wheel driven by a river of money. And everybody benefits, everybody grows prosperous, and everybody is at peace. Why, there have probably never been more people alive in Britain than today. What's wrong with that?'

'But what's the point of it all? The mill-wheel grinds flour for bread. What purpose does your money-wheel serve?'

'Why, it grinds up people. It smashes up petty tribes like your own and bakes the fragments into an empire.'

'It makes everybody the same,' Brigonius said resentfully.

'Yes! And that is the power of it.' Severa dug into her purse and produced a coin, stamped with Hadrian's head. 'Look at this, Brigonius. You could travel along roads just like this one from Britain to Asia, and everywhere you could ask for your daily bread in Latin, and pay for it with this coin. A single language, a single currency, right across a continent. And Britain is part of it! Don't be sentimental, Brigonius! Open your eyes and see the shining future – and embrace it.'

As she made this little speech she touched his hand. Her grip was strong, her flesh oddly cold. Looking at her pale eyes he saw her ambition, and he wondered uneasily just how unsentimental she would prove to be in pursuing her goals.

In the back of the carriage, Lepidina puzzled out a fresh bit of word-play in Ovid's poetry and laughed softly, her voice light as a bird's.

V

Unlike most other British towns Londinium had not been founded on the site of an older settlement. When Claudius came this way there had been nothing at all, Severa said, nothing but the mud huts of a few fisher-folk. Now along the shining river barges and sea-going ships cruised purposefully, and docks sprawled along both north and south banks of the river, with cranes rising like gaunt birds. Beyond a hinterland of warehouses and granaries there were signs of still more impressive buildings under construction.

Using her sketchy map Severa showed him why Londinium had risen. 'You see, the river is tidal, all the way to *this* point, and navigable much further inland. And the city itself is a node of road systems that arrow off across the island north, west, east and south. It is a natural port for trade with Gaul and further afield ...'

It was a port for an imperial province, Brigonius saw, a port for continental trade. Britain did not need Londinium; Britannia did.

After a final overnight stop they approached Camulodunum. It was early in the morning. As they neared the town the road, growing busier, was lined with tombstones, urns half-buried in the ground. Severa told Brigonius that the Romans didn't allow burials within a town's boundary, so cemeteries grew up on the major routes out of town.

The wall of Camulodunum itself became visible, a dark line cutting across rising ground. For miles around the wall, however, Brigonius made out roundhouses, barns and earthworks, most of them abandoned. The Roman town seemed to have been planted on a low hill, overlooking what had once been a much more extensive settlement, now disappearing under the plough.

Outside the town they glimpsed a vast walled structure of bright new stone, too small to be a town, the wrong shape to be a fort. It turned out to be an arena where chariot races were run, under the auspices of priests from the town's temple. Brigonius was amazed at the extravagance. But the arena's upkeep was paid for by the betting on the races, and the eyes of Severa, an instinctive gambler, lit up at the thought.

Severa sent a slave running ahead to prepare for their arrival. As a result they were met on the road by one Flavius Karus, whom Severa introduced as a lawyer with whom she had corresponded over the business of Hadrian's frontier works.

Brigonius and Karus eyed each other suspiciously. Karus was a tall man, as tall as Brigonius, but his belly was heavy and rippled like a sack of water when he walked. His hair was as dark as Brigonius's, though peppered with grey, and he was clean-shaven where Brigonius was bearded. He had donned a toga for the occasion, albeit a bit grubby and splashed with mud at its hem, but he was clearly every bit as British as Brigonius.

Not only that, Brigonius thought, Karus paid rather too much attention to Lepidina. 'So this is the delightful daughter whose company you promised in your letters!'

Lepidina was used to male attention, welcome and unwelcome. But Brigonius thought he saw a gleam of calculation in Severa's eye. He wondered if she used her daughter's charms as a lure to snare fat old fools like Karus as well as youngsters like himself.

The four of them were to walk to Karus's home, inside the walled town; the slaves would follow with the luggage. Karus led the way along the crowded road. The town wall loomed over them: twelve feet high, Karus said with mock pride, not counting the parapets, and eight feet thick. The road passed through an immense double gate. Karus said this had once been a triumphal arch, built to celebrate Claudius's visit here. After Boudicca's disastrous uprising it had been built into the town's stout new walls.

Under the gate Brigonius was stopped by a patrol of soldiers who roughly searched his clothing. The Romans had a law that you couldn't carry a weapon inside any town, and they enforced it, especially where *Brittani* were concerned. Brigonius submitted; he was used to it. The women watched this little exchange, Severa with a jackdaw's fascinated stare, Lepidina rather bewildered. Brigonius imagined they had never seen people of their acquaintance treated this way.

Inside the town narrow streets divided the city into blocks of housing Karus called *insulae*, islands. Every surface was covered with slogans and sketches. To Brigonius the town was cramped and crowded, all straight lines and square angles and a jumble of distracting imagery. It was strange to think that somewhere under all this painted stone and plaster Cunobelin had once held court at the heart of his own empire, a capital now erased from the earth.

Karus's home was in a side-street. It was a tall, skinny sort of building on a square base, its plastered walls gleaming white, roofed by red tiles. At street level the doors were flung wide to reveal a shop, with a broad counter set out with food: meat, pastries, bits of fruit. Still early in the morning, customers crowded the counter, buying their breakfast. The smell of cooked meat made Brigonius's mouth water, but he wondered why all these folk had not simply eaten at home.

Karus led his guests through the shop and to a staircase at the back. It turned out that Karus owned the space on top of the shop, which was, to Brigonius's surprise, like a second house piled up on top of the first. The space up here, small to begin with, was sliced up into smaller rooms by inner partitions. Karus went around lighting wall-mounted oil lamps and candles. The rooms had tiny windows with panes of bluish glass, but it was dark inside the apartment, even on so bright a morning, for the building was in the shadow of others.

Severa and Lepidina made slight noises of appreciation as Karus showed them around. 'It isn't terribly large,' Karus said apologetically. 'But it's all a poor lawyer can afford. You wouldn't believe how expensive land has become close to the town centre.'

Severa said, 'Oh, it's the same everywhere. You should see the apartment blocks in Rome. Some of them are piled so high I swear they would fall over if they didn't lean against each other. But you've made good use of the space, Karus.'

One small corner room was a shrine. The guests inspected Karus's idols and tokens, most of them dedicated to his own household gods. But Brigonius recognised a statue of Fors Fortuna.

Severa said, 'A soldier's god.'

'I'm no soldier,' Karus said, patting his broad belly. 'But most of my clients are. This is still a soldiers' town, Severa. It does no harm to seek the blessing of their goddess.' He led his guests onward.

Brigonius touched the wall. The surface was plastered and painted white, but in places the plaster had chipped away to reveal plaited wood stuffed with mud and straw. He felt increasingly cramped in this small, dark space. It was even worse than the stone-walled forts he had to visit when dealing with the army in the north. Here the thin walls didn't block out the noise from the busy alley outside, or the food smells from the restaurant down below. Not only that, this was Karus's territory, and the fat lawyer seemed to fill the narrow rooms with his talk.

Lepidina took his arm. 'Are you all right? You're like a bear in a cage.'

'I'm fine,' he said stiffly.

128

'No, you're not.'

'It's just – look, it's so different for me.' He waved a hand, trying to find words. 'It's the way all the walls are flat, the edges straight, the corners square. And the space is sliced up for different purposes. You sleep over there, you work over here.'

Severa was interested. 'And is that different from how you live?'

He tried to describe the house he had grown up in and where he still lived, its open round space a map of the cycles of time.

Karus was dismissive. 'Well, polite people don't need to live like animals any more.'

Brigonius bunched his fists, but Severa touched his arm. 'Your grand-father no doubt lived in such a house, lawyer,' she admonished Karus.

Brigonius deliberately relaxed. Karus nodded, which would pass for an apology, and the moment was over.

Lepidina watched this with wide-eyed glee. Brigonius was sure she knew that on a deep level, if the men had come to blows, it would have been over her.

'And another thing,' Brigonius said, determined to keep the initia-tive. 'Where do you cook your food?'

Now Lepidina laughed. 'Nobody cooks for themselves, silly!'

'They don't?'

'You have a lot to learn.' She grabbed his hand and began to pull him to the door. 'Come on. I'm hungry. Let's go see the town.'

'Not me,' Severa said. 'I'm weary, and could do with a nap. You two go and explore.'

Karus said quickly, 'Oh, let's make it three!'

He and Brigonius glared at each other. The women watched them, Lepidina with unconcealed delight, and Severa with calculation.

VI

Lepidina led the two men down the stairs to the counter of the restaurant beneath Karus's home. After being so subdued on the road, she seemed in her element now they were in a town.

'Let's leave my mother plenty of time for her "nap",' she said heavily.

Karus frowned. 'What do you mean?'

'Oh, come on, Karus! You know what a gambler she is. Within the hour she'll be slipping out to find a bookmaker, and arguing about the odds on the next chariot race. She thinks I don't know about it. But I don't say anything, not as long as she keeps winning ... Brigonius, you want to know how we eat? Oh, I have no money. Karus—'

With an elaborate sigh he produced some coins for her, and she turned to the counter.

Brigonius and Karus stood stiffly side by side. Then, as one, they turned to each other.

'Look, Karus—'

'Brigonius, I didn't mean—'

They laughed, broke off, and Karus started again. 'It looks as if we're going to be working together, perhaps for years if all goes well. So we shouldn't let a gorgeous but silly girl lead us both around like two stallions on heat. I mean, it's not to say that I wouldn't – if she chose – to tell you the truth I think I prefer the mother, now I've met her – that proud bust of hers, and the way she walks –' He stumbled to a halt. 'Isn't she marvellous?'

'We should keep love and work apart,' Brigonius said firmly.

'Or at least we can try,' Karus murmured.

Lepidina returned with a handful of food. 'Here,' she said, handing some of it to Brigonius. 'You see? You don't have to cook for yourself, you buy!'

The food turned out to be a patty of ground pork, stuffed in the middle of a slab of bread. The meat was well-cooked and flavoured with onions. Brigonius took a bite. 'Might be better if it was beef.'

Karus said around a mouthful, 'Oh, Romans don't much like beef. Or mutton. Barbarian foods, they say.'

'The soldiers at Vindolanda eat plenty of it.'

'They're probably all provincials themselves.'

Already Brigonius had finished his meal. 'Is that it?'

'I'll buy you more later. Come on, let's go to the forum and do some shopping.' Lepidina took his hand – then, judiciously, Karus's too – and they walked along the street.

The roads were paved, with gutters running down either side; the stonework was good, Brigonius noted. Along with the people animals thronged the streets – chickens, pigs, and many dogs. This was still a town for farmers. Most of the buildings were wattle and daub, like Karus's apartment building, though one or two of the grander houses were built in stone. Most buildings were one-storey private houses, but some had their fronts opened out, like Karus's restaurant, to reveal workshops where pottery was thrown, iron worked, glass poured, cloth woven.

Some of the images on the walls were there to show you what kind of workshop or store this was: cartoon potters turned their wheels, women displayed gaudy jewellery, and the taverns were marked by fat, merry drinkers. Even the brothels had their insignia, stick figures in remarkably inventive postures that Brigonius tried not to stare at. The lettering on the walls sometimes told you who lived here or what they did. Some of it, rougher carvings, was more casual, prayers, insults, curses. And some of it, lauding the Reds, Blues and Yellows, baffled Brigonius altogether. Karus said it was to do with support of the main teams of charioteers in the races. The various factions worshipped their heroes and loathed each other, and rioted on race nights.

Outside one store stood a large pot into which a burly man was noisily pissing; steam rose up from the pot's neck.

Karus watched Brigonius's expression with amusement. 'This is a fuller's; he will use the urine he collects from passers-by to fix his dye. I don't cook in my apartment, and neither do I piss.'

Brigonius grunted, unimpressed. 'And who collects your shit?'

Karus grinned. 'Funny you should ask that.'

They came to a locked door fronting an enclosed hall. Karus produced a low-denomination coin and dropped it into a slot. He pulled levers on the lock mechanism until the coin was swallowed up, and with a satisfying clunk the lock came free.

Karus opened the door to reveal a latrine. Over two rows of holes in the floor people sat on wooden benches, men, women and children alike. Some read letters on bits of wood, others talked, some gambled over dice on the floor between them. One man was bending over to wipe his arse with a bit of sponge on a stick. There was a predictable stink, but it wasn't as bad as Brigonius might have thought – and then he heard a gurgle of water coming from beneath the holes.

'Ah,' he said. 'A stream runs beneath to take the shit away. Cunning.'

Karus shrugged. 'More likely the water is piped here from the river to the north. Public water supply, you see. You'd have to ask an engineer; I'm no expert.'

They walked on. They passed a baths – unfinished, but in use, and quite unmistakable to Brigonius from its musty, boggy smell, just like the soldiers' baths at Vindolanda.

They reached the marketplace. Lepidina, with a squeal of excitement, begged more money from Karus. Soon she was working her way through stalls heaped with jewellery and little bottles of perfume and hair oil. The men walked on.

Once more Brigonius felt overwhelmed. Compared to the rough-and-ready market that had grown up outside the Vindolanda fort there was a bewildering array of goods for sale here: cosmetics of all sorts in little glass jars and bottles, silver and copper pins and brooches, plates and bowls and tiles, stalls heaped with shoes of stitched leather. There were bakers and vendors of broiled meat, and the heat of their ovens turned the air ferociously hot. There were even moneylenders, bankers and lawyers – and many, many bookmakers.

Shoppers thronged. There were plenty of Catuvellaunians, of course. But Brigonius saw Germans and Gauls of the kind the army was full of, and still more exotic types with very pale skin, or very dark, who sold wines and spices for exorbitant prices. They were traders from perhaps far across the empire or even beyond, come here to this corner of Britain to sell their wares. Everyone seemed confident here, happily buying and selling, all of them at home in a place where they knew the rules, all save Brigonius.

And beggars crowded around every stall, silently pleading for change. There were no beggars in Banna; people looked after their own. Brigonius wondered what old Cunobelin would have thought of what had become of his descendants.

More public buildings surrounded the forum. Karus led Brigonius to a great hall whose unfinished walls rose above the heads of the shoppers. They walked through a colonnade of pillars and over a stone floor that was, as yet, unroofed. Brigonius saw that the floor was weather-stained; evidently the building had been in this half-finished state for some time.

'This will be the basilica,' Karus said. 'The great folk of the town will run their local government from here – they will collect the taxes for one thing, and bundle them all off down to Londinium for the procurator to count up.' The construction of the building was proceeding only as the funds became available, so was taking a long time. 'Still, this is the task of our generation. Our fathers set out the town. Now we must build it.'

Brigonius frowned. 'I think I imagined the Emperor would pay for all this.'

Karus pursed his lips. 'Not a bit of it. We enjoy the fruits of Roman civilisation but we must pay for it ourselves. Which we do, of course, gladly. You know, Brigonius, if you're to become a rich man you'll have to learn about how to handle your wealth. To begin with you must *have* wealth – the more the better. From wealth flows power and status; with wealth you are a source of patronage. Second, you mustn't flaunt your wealth. Oh, spend it, yes; make sure people know you have it – but in a restrained way. And you must be sure you invest your wealth in projects for the public good, like this basilica. Paradoxical, isn't it? But Romans are paradoxical folk, in many ways.'

The lawyer seemed to have opened up to Brigonius during this brief walk. 'You know, Brigonius, I'm not much of one for reflection. Live for the day, I say, for yesterday is irrelevant, and tomorrow may never come! But one thing I've enjoyed about Severa's correspondence is her sense of perspective – of history. Just think, a hundred years ago there was no city like this, no building remotely like this roofless basilica, not anywhere in Britain. They've all sprung up like mushrooms. My grandfather was a hunter. He wore moleskins on his feet, stuffed with bird feathers. Now look at me, his grandson! I'm a lawyer. I go to work in an office in a block several storeys high, with windows of glass. I buy my food from vendors, my coins operate locks on latrines – and stamped on every coin is an uplifting message from the Emperor himself. Somehow the Prophecy has enabled Severa to *see* all this, to see these great changes, as if she is standing outside history altogether.'

But Brigonius pulled on his beard, unconvinced. He thought of his northern home, where the people herded their cattle just as they had always done – as indeed the mass of people even in the south still scraped at the soil. This heaped-up wonder of stone and commerce was a fragile, light confection, he thought, built on the extraction of wealth from farmers to whose lives the Roman presence hardly made any difference at all.

'And if it all should end, as fast as it has arisen – what then?'

Karus grinned. 'Then I'd be in trouble. I'm not my grandfather – I couldn't make myself a pair of shoes! But it's not going to end, is it? Severa's Prophecy ensures us of that.'

'Karus, this business of Severa and the stone wall – she is a gambler, you know, just as Lepidina says.'

'I know. But in the game to come the Prophecy is her loaded die, I think.'

They emerged from the incomplete building and walked on past a large semicircular theatre, and came to a broad square paved with stone. And here rose up the grandest building of all. Clad in shining marble it was a temple built in the Roman fashion, with a double colonnade and a terracotta roof. A flight of steps led up to an open interior where Brigonius glimpsed a mighty statue of bronze, many times life-size.

He stood and stared, astounded by the temple's scale. Even its base, a mighty slab of concrete poured into the sandy earth, was stupendous, surely unmatched by anything that had existed in Britain before the Romans.

'This is the Temple of Claudius, built to honour the deified Emperor.' Karus shook his head. 'Astonishing, isn't it? I've grown up with it, but even now it astounds me. In fact it's talked of even in Rome, where they've seen everything.'

Brigonius thought of the wealth and labour this huge structure must have sucked up. 'I'm surprised this could be afforded.'

'Well, perhaps it couldn't,' Karus murmured. 'The Romans don't make you any richer, after all; they just tax you. The Temple always caused great resentment. Boudicca came here and burned it to the ground – along with the veterans and their families who had sheltered inside. When she was put down they built the walls around the town, and the Temple was reconstructed, bigger and better and more expensive than ever. But it was built on ash, and charred pots and burned bones. Makes you think.'

Lepidina came running up. She showed off a new necklace and a comb for her mother's hair, and both men made appreciative noises. 'So what do you think of Camulodunum, Brigonius?'

Brigonius peered up at the Temple's cold, beautiful lines. How could this be a holy place? His ancestors had lived close to the earth, and the divine had been an integral part of an ancient way of life. To them wood was alive, stone was dead. The stone town that was rising here was like a vast tomb.

He looked into Lepidina's excited, sparkling eyes, his feelings deep and confused, regretting that he couldn't share her joy. He merely said, 'It'll look good when it's finished.'

The lawyer turned away. Perhaps Karus detected his true mood.

Lepidina impulsively ruffled Brigonius's beard. 'If you're living in a Roman town you have to look like a Roman. I found a barber in the middle of the forum.'

Brigonius held back. 'Not my beard. You're not taking my beard.'

Lepidina pouted. 'Your hair, then. That mane could do with a good shearing. The barber is good; he knows the latest fashions.'

'How do you know *that*?'

Lepidina held up a coin, imprinted with a picture of the Emperor and his coiffed hair. 'How do you think? Come *on*.' She dragged Brigonius back towards the forum. Like a hound submitting to the feeble pull of a puppy, Brigonius followed.

VII

A day after the arrival of Hadrian's caravan at Camulodunum, Severa and her tame architect were to present their case for a stone wall across the northern boundary of the province. It would be in the course of a grand meal to be hosted by one of Camulodunum's wealthier citizens, Marcus Claudius Verecundus. It took Severa only days to win Verecundus's confidence and set this up. 'She really is a charmer, and so good at getting her foot in the door,' Karus said admiringly. 'Isn't she marvellous?'

Brigonius had no idea what to expect of this occasion. He had met plenty of Romans, but in his line of work, selling his cut stone, he dealt only with soldiers. Hadrian ruled the world, and was worshipped as a god by millions of people; surely nothing about dealing with such a being was going to be normal.

On the day of the meal Brigonius arrived early at Verecundus's home. Planted square in the centre of the town, it was a sprawling complex of buildings. Brigonius wandered, somewhat bemused, awkward in his clean tunic. Other guests circulated, citizens all, mostly dressed in the Roman style. Brigonius exchanged wary nods, but he felt he was making few friends.

The heart of the house was an atrium, an open area flagged by stone but set with beds of flowers. There were benches to sit on, statues and wall carvings to admire, and even a small fountain to gawp at. Brigonius, always fascinated by stonework, architecture and engineering, was impressed to learn that the fountain ran purely from the pressure of the water supplied by the town's public system.

The atrium was enclosed on three sides by a colonnade of slim pillars, and beyond that were the main buildings. Inside, the space was divided up in the usual Roman way into square rooms with different purposes, from reception rooms set out with low couches and tables, offices crammed with scrolls and tablets, and a grand kitchen with a huge hearth over which pots and kettles were suspended on chains. There was even a small bath house, with a boiler under the heated floor.

Slaves stood in every corner, bearing trays of food and drink. All very young, with their hair dyed blond and piled up on their heads, the barefoot slaves shivered in their skimpy clothing.

Given Karus's regular complaints about how expensive land now was in the town, Brigonius deduced that Verecundus's spread was a sign of old wealth; his ancestors must have got here first. And indeed it turned out that Verecundus's grandfather had been a soldier who had come over to Britain in the first wave of Claudius's invasion. On retirement after twenty-five years' service Verecundus's ancestor had chosen to settle here, in a colony of veterans planted as a kind of military reserve in unstable territory. But though Verecundus's house was grand in Brigonius's eyes, it wasn't terribly ostentatious, Karus told him. Perhaps something of Verecundus's austere military ancestry lingered in his blood.

Brigonius was relieved to find the two rooms Severa's party had been allocated. Severa and her daughter were sharing one room, while the other was shared by Brigonius, Karus and Severa's architect, Xander. But there was no space for Brigonius. Xander, a small, fat, fussy Greek, was assembling an elaborate architectural model with the help of a hapless slave who seemed able to do nothing right, and the floor was covered by green-painted plaster hills, blue-ribbon rivers, and toy-like forts and turrets. When Brigonius nearly wiped out a fortress by stepping on it, Xander chased him out in a flurry of Greek.

So Brigonius made his way to the room shared by Severa and her daughter. Furnished with two couches and a variety of low tables and cupboards, the room was strewn with clothes. Severa wasn't there – but Lepidina sat with her back to the door, facing a mirror. Brigonius, holding his breath, stood and watched.

Lepidina had opened her tunic and pushed it back so her shoulders were bare, and her hair was roughly tied up. She was applying cream to her face, scooping it up from a tin jar with her fingers and smoothing it onto her cheeks. With her clothing disarrayed, and her loose-limbed movements as she quietly massaged her flesh, she had an air of abandonment.

Of course she knew he was there. 'You may as well come in, Brigonius, and have a proper look.'

'I'm sorry.'

'Don't be.' She ducked so she could see him in her mirror, and smiled. 'I'm getting myself ready to be seen, after all.' She patted a couch beside her dressing table, and he sat down. 'I suppose all this seems terribly exotic to a rough-hewn barbarian like you. Decadent!'

He glanced over her grooming kit, touching bronze tweezers, nail cleaners and nail files, a toothpick, an ear scoop. This was a kit for travelling; the tools had holes so they could be looped onto a carrying ring. There was a range of pots, but not terribly many: tins of white cream, rouge, powders black as coal, and glass bottles of scent. 'This isn't so much,' he said. 'I've met hairy-arsed Roman soldiers with more stuff.'

'This travel kit was my great-grandmother's, Agrippina's. It is very well made and it still works perfectly well.'

Again she struck him as deeply sensible, under her flighty surface. It only added to her appeal for him.

'Here.' She dug out a little of the white cream and raised her fingers to his face to rub the cream into his cheek. 'How does that feel?'

'It's pleasant.' So it was. The cream was smooth, and cold at first, but soon warmed on his skin, and as she rubbed it in further he felt a powdery, gritty texture. 'What's it made of?'

She shrugged. 'Animal fat, I think. Starch. And some complicated compound of tin.'

'Tin? I thought Roman ladies used lead on their faces.'

'Oh, that's very old-fashioned. Lead's poisonous – didn't you know?'

She continued to rub cream into his cheek, and he relished the warmth of her touch, the close sweetness of her breath on his face. But he pulled back. 'Perhaps that's enough.'

'Oh, but this is just the start. This is a foundation cream which will make my skin glow like a marble statue. Then I'll apply rouge and mascara – this is burned rose petals, see? – to highlight my cheeks and eyes. I will whiten my teeth with powdered pumice, and sprinkle my neck with perfume – this one is my favourite, myrrh mixed with spices.'

He took her hand in his, silencing her. The bones of her fingers felt fragile, like a baby bird's, and her skin was pale against his. Compared to his earthy darkness she was like a ghost, he thought.

She leaned a little closer to him; her face, a perfect oval, filled his vision, and her lips brushed his. 'I bet you don't even shave your chest, do you, Brigantius-Brigonius?'

He hesitated for one heartbeat. If she was toying with him, tormenting a clumsy barbarian, he was about to be humiliated. But it was worth the risk. He slid his hand around her waist. 'Why don't you find out?'

She came at him like a wave breaking, and their mouths locked.

VIII

The formal meal was to be held in the afternoon, from the ninth hour onwards, in Verecundus's largest reception room. This was a very grand, sprawling room that occupied almost the full length of one side of the atrium – 'a veritable basilica', Karus said. Brigonius got there late, but not as late as the Emperor himself, who was out hunting boar.

Brigonius found the room crowded. People lay on couches or strolled with a certain false casualness. The men were as carefully groomed as the women, their faces shaved and their eyebrows plucked. The women wore clothes in an explosion of rich colours, and the men's togas were crisp and shone white. Music played, slaves circulated with trays of food and drink, musicians played lutes and Catuvellaunian pipes, and the conversation bubbled prettily. Oddly, much of the talk seemed to be in Greek. But there was tension under the politeness, and people watched each other with sharp eyes. They were like a flock of hungry birds, Brigonius thought.

And one or two guests were already the worse for wear. One fat, sweating man was rather obviously sliding his hand up the thigh of any slave who passed him, male or female. Brigonius wondered if the Emperor's lateness was a deliberate ploy, so that drink or gluttony could weed out the less worthy of his petitioners.

When Brigonius joined the party Severa's companions were already all here, Severa herself and her daughter, lawyer Karus and the architect Xander, with his model set out on a low table and covered with a sheet. Lepidina seemed cool, composed.

Brigonius sat down, trying to avoid everybody's eyes. He had washed and changed since his tryst with Lepidina, but he was sure the smell of their love must still linger on him.

Sure enough, Karus leaned over. 'Congratulations,' he whispered, slightly drunk.

Brigonius cursed. 'Is it that obvious?'

'Your sheer animal joy is, yes. I congratulate you; she is truly lovely. But have no fear, I won't take her from you, though of course I could. I told you, I only have eyes for the mother ...'

Severa's gaze glittered, and she seemed secretly amused. Severa knew, of course; if Karus had detected it she would have. And Lepidina knew that she knew.

As for Brigonius, all *he* knew was that he was far out of his depth with these complicated women and their games. But Lepidina was worth it.

And beneath all this there was something oceanic in his mood. What he felt for Lepidina was not mere lust, had not been since the moment he met her. There was tenderness too. And now, after their hour together in the morning, was that tenderness becoming love? How vulnerable would he become then to Severa's machinations?

The service began, to Brigonius's relief, and they all had something else to occupy their attention. There was a starter of salad, eggs and oysters from the coast – and snails, big salty beasts brought in from Gaul. Karus, Xander and Severa tucked in. Lepidina ate more sparingly but with every expression of relish.

Brigonius did his best. By the time the first plates were cleared he already felt full, but more plates, more food, quickly followed. There were to be several main courses, he learned, including boar, venison, pork, hare and dormouse; chicken, geese, thrushes and peacocks; more fish and seafood – and finally, in the far future, a dessert of fruit and cakes laden with honey. Even the vegetables were unfamiliar. Lepidina, gently mocking, named such Roman imports as cabbage, broad beans, parsnips, peas and celery. All this was served on fine plates of pottery or silver, and though you ate with your fingers there was a bewildering variety of cutlery: special little forks for pulling oysters out of their shells, knives for scraping meat from bone. Brigonius was continually bewildered at what a wide variety of *things* were available to a well-off Roman.

He kept trying. He sampled what he recognised, but was constantly put off by the peculiar flavours of the sauces. Everything seemed to taste both sour and sweet at the same time, and the Romans doused the lot with a disgusting fish sauce.

Severa glared at him. 'Leave it if you want, but don't pick. You eat like a child.'

'But it's all so appetising,' Brigonius said dryly. He lifted up a dormouse by its tail, poached whole and stuffed with nuts and herbs.

That made Lepidina laugh, but Severa turned away contemptuously.

'And anyhow,' Karus said around a mouthful of minced pork, 'the food isn't the point.' He sighed. 'Though it should be. Food should always be the point. While the Emperor is still away we should review our strategy.'

'Quite right,' Severa said. 'Xander! Come here. Let's go over it one more time ...'

Xander, reluctant to interrupt the meal himself, joined Severa, and they began to discuss empires, borders and walls.

Hadrian had to consider fixing his borders because his empire had reached its natural limits of expansion. In Britain, from Claudius's first foothold at Rutupiae in the far south-east of the island, a wave of military advance had washed over the countryside, leaving behind a network of forts, roads and signalling towers. Brigantia had been the most northern political unit the Romans had been able to deal with diplomatically. But under the Emperor Domitian governor Agricola had gone further, mounting a strong assault on the furthest north, and his ships had sailed all the way around the northern coast. But in a land of mountains, mist and bogs, inhabited by an elusive, fleeting people who never seemed to understand when they were defeated, it had not been a comfortable campaign for the Romans, and Agricola's forces, scattered in garrison forts, were overstretched. When troops were withdrawn from Britain to deal with problems on the Danube the Romans had been forced to fall back to Brigantia.

Elsewhere in the empire similar limits were reached. Domitian's successor Trajan was another expansion-minded soldier-emperor, and he had won swathes of territories in the east of the empire. But towards the end of his life his energies had been consumed by troubles along the empire's long, vulnerable borders, in Mesopotamia, Africa, even in northern Britain once more. And in the east, while he was distracted, the Jews had risen in a savage revolt, that had been put down equally savagely.

This was the complex, unstable situation bequeathed to Hadrian, Trajan's successor in turn, who had served with his mentor in the field.

'You must understand the way these Romans think,' said architect Xander. 'Once the Romans saw no limit to their conquest. Why should they? Especially once their generals started getting rich from it. Expansion pays for more expansion, and on it goes. Why shouldn't it proceed to the ends of the world? But the truth is the Romans can venture no further than the plough ...'

As the Romans had expanded out of their Mediterranean heartland, north and south, east and west, they had taken lands that were already farmed, and which could provide the wealth to make their city rich, and to fuel their further expansion. But Rome could not conquer wastelands. So the empire was like a sea, said Xander, rising to flood the agricultural heart of Europe. But it was dammed in the east by the Parthians, and in the north, west and south its waves broke on shores of forests, deserts and mountains.

Xander was about fifty, with a round, red face and a shock of greying hair. In his ill-fitting toga and with his fingers coated in sawdust from his toy forts, he seemed remarkably unworldly. But Severa listened to him, and Brigonius began to see that the point of view of a Greek, of a race seen as a cultural ancestor of the Romans, was quite different from that of a subjugated people like his own.

Now Xander smiled. 'Like Alexander, the emperors have looked beyond the edge of the world and recoiled, their minds fogged.'

Hadrian, a new emperor forty years old, had formulated a new policy. He was intent on abandoning Trajan's expensively won territories and drawing the empire back into a shell bounded where possible by 'natural frontiers': deserts, rivers. And where necessary such frontiers would be fortified.

As Brigonius thought this over the more it seemed a remarkable ambition, for to succeed Hadrian was going to have to reshape the Roman spirit. No longer expansive conquerors, the Romans would have to turn their empire into a community. Even the army would have to be redesigned, turned from a mobile fighting force to one able to defend fixed frontiers.

'Of course he has his opponents,' Xander muttered. 'There are plenty of generals who would like their turn at the booty-gathering of the past. Critics in the Senate say that to sit behind a wall and jab at your unconquered enemies with a spear isn't the Roman way – but half of them are fools who still dream of the Republic, and scarcely matter. There are some who wonder if, by halting the expansion that has always fuelled Rome's economy, Hadrian isn't committing some drastic, long-term error – although no doubt we'll all be dead before anybody can answer that.'

Karus said, 'Admirably summarised, architect. But as far as we're concerned, Hadrian's dilemma boils down to this. If you're not going to expand then you have to stabilise the frontiers.'

With typical Roman magnificence, Hadrian intended to consolidate his northern provinces' frontiers into a single defensive boundary, a system of forts, walls, banks and ditches that would span Europe, heading west from Asia Minor, following the great continent-draining rivers to pass north of Dacia, Noricum and Lower Germany – and then it would leap across the Ocean to Britain.

'I think it's clear enough where the British boundary is to be,' Karus said. 'To the north of here, in the place where the neck of the country narrows, between the estuaries of the rivers Tinea and Ituna.'

'Very well,' said Severa. 'The question is what will he build there? We can show him all the models and plans we like. But what will convince this man that he must build in stone rather than turf as he did in Germany?'

Karus said, 'The emperors have been building linear defences of one sort or another since the time of Domitian.'

'Oh, we mustn't mention that,' Xander said. 'Every emperor likes to believe he has built the whole world single-handed.'

Brigonius popped a harmless-looking bit of meat into his mouth. 'Well, don't ask me. I doubt if I'll understand anything anyhow. Haven't you noticed – aside from us, everybody here is speaking Greek!'

Karus grunted. 'And an archaic form at that. How pretentious!'

'It's to please the Emperor,' Xander said. 'His own family are from the provinces, you know. Like all those born most humbly he has the highest aspirations, and so has decided he is a devoted admirer of all things Greek.' Brigonius thought this pompous little man spoke of an emperor as if he was an irritating schoolboy.

'Well,' Brigonius said, 'in that case it's a shame the Greeks didn't build walls of stone, for surely Hadrian would copy them.'

Karus slapped his forehead. 'May Jupiter bugger me but they did! Didn't they, Xander? You should know, man!'

Xander, wide-eyed now, nodded. 'Of course, of course.'

Karus grinned and gripped Brigonius's arm. 'My friend, I think you may have just won us the contest.'

Severa's gaze flickered suspiciously between lawyer and architect. 'You two had better be sure you know what you're doing.'

Xander was flustered, but Karus grinned, a lawyer's smile. 'Trust me.'

And now time ran out, whether Severa trusted Karus or not. Trumpets sounded, a clear peal above the babble. All heads turned to see the former slave Primigenius standing at the door, beside a beaming Marcus Claudius Verecundus, the host. Primigenius called, 'Stand for Publius Aelius Hadrianus.'

And the Emperor walked into the room.

Hadrian gave a brief, gracious speech of welcome, then bade everybody sit and continue with the meal. After a decent interval little groups of citizens approached him with their requests, petitions, disputes to be resolved, or paeans of praise. Severa's party waited their turn.

Brigonius watched the Emperor, fascinated. Hadrian sat with his courtiers, talking animatedly, perhaps about the hunt they had just come from. Hadrian, a heavy-set man, wore a toga, but his face was flushed, his thick hair damp from sweat, and his breathing was heavy.

He immediately struck Brigonius as a mass of contradictions. It was clear that he wanted to seem accessible, but his entrance couldn't have been more dramatic if he had rode in on his horse. He aspired to Greek culture, and yet he exuded the primordial thrill of the hunt. He was the richest man in the world, the very quintessence of Rome – and yet he wore a barbarian beard whose magnificence Brigonius envied. His skin was pocked by the scars of some disease: another contradiction, that the most powerful of all should be afflicted by a disease which could strike down the commonest of people.

And though there was none more powerful than Hadrian there was a fearful look in his eyes, an almost hunted look.

'Yes, a complicated man,' Severa whispered, gazing at the Emperor. 'Talking of the future, I think Hadrian fears it – and not just the assassin's blade. He is a scholar who knows that history holds dire warnings for the Romans, for empires have come and gone in the past: even mighty Alexander's realm barely outlived his own death. Take this business of the Jewish rebellion under Trajan – barely heard of in Britain, but a dreadful disaster in the east. The Jews won't become Romans, as we Britons have; it is a clash of minds, a shuddering shock for the Romans. For all Xander sneers at Hadrian's Greekness, I think it is necessary, a matter of policy as much as personality. He embodies the identity of the empire, which is Greek and Roman, and so in the face of the challenge of the Jews he must be more Greek than the Greeks.

'No wonder Hadrian is obsessed by the future even more than by the past. Everywhere he goes he consults astrologers and mystics and soothsayers. And surely a thoughtful man like Hadrian wants to leave a mark on his empire, on history. What else can assure his own worth in the afterlife?'

Karus's eyes glittered as he listened. 'Isn't she marvellous?' he whispered to Brigonius. 'I told you, it's as if she stands outside time itself.'

Lepidina said, 'Poor man.'

Brigonius asked, 'Who?'

'The Emperor. If he really is so tortured. He might draw comfort if he followed the teaching of the Christ. Because then he would understand that cities and empires don't matter. They all pass away, even Rome. But the city of God endures for ever.'

Severa glared at her. 'That Judean renegade promised that *all* would be saved, not just emperors but slaves too. What use is that to anybody? Now shut up about your foolish fad, Lepidina.'

'It's not foolish,' Lepidina shot back. 'If it was, why is our Prophecy connected to it? Even the Emperor Claudius noticed that Nectovelin was born in the same year as the Judean!'

'You never mind the Emperor Claudius. I'm your mother and I'm telling you that our family destiny has nothing to do with some ragged-arsed troublemaker from the east. And what's more—'

'Hush,' Xander said. 'We're being called forward.'

'About time,' Karus muttered. 'I'm bursting with piss.'

The five of them advanced towards the imperial table, Severa, Lepidina, Karus and Brigonius, with a nervous Xander supervising two sweating slaves who carried his model on a slab of wood.

IX

Severa introduced herself and her party. Then she handed the floor to Xander. The little Greek stood fearlessly, Brigonius thought, fearless as only the representative of an older culture could be before a junior, regardless of such incidentals as global power.

Xander spoke in Greek, and Brigonius picked up only a little of what he had to say. He began with a general discourse on the problems of imperial frontiers, with references to historical events all the way back to the wars between the successors of Alexander the Great. Meanwhile his precious model sat on the floor beside him, tantalisingly covered.

Karus had warned Brigonius it would be like this. 'The Romans love speeches,' he said.

Understanding barely one word in four, Brigonius found his attention wandering. Among the soldiers and learned men of the court of the soldier-emperor there were a few women. One of them, beautiful but sullen-looking, must be Hadrian's wife, Sabina, said to have been trapped into a loveless marriage by her great-uncle Trajan to his favoured heir, Hadrian. One older woman was surely the famed Plotina, wife of the dead Trajan. Brigonius wondered what tensions lay beneath the rather cold façade of this imperial family.

Though Hadrian listened, he seemed restless, unfocused, even bored. Brigonius knew that Hadrian thought of himself as a scholar. To him, in an empire which contained Greece and Egypt and Mesopotamia, an empire like a huge museum of civilisations, Britain must seem dull indeed.

For an instant Hadrian's gaze locked on Brigonius himself. Perhaps there was a flicker of recognition in the Emperor's eye; perhaps he remembered him from the speech at Rutupiae. Now he inspected Brigonius more carefully, his neck, his torso, his bare legs.

Brigonius, his blood still hot from the hour he had spent with

146

Lepidina, turned away. Here was something else everybody knew about Hadrian. In Brigantia homosexual affairs weren't unknown, but they were unusual. Among the Romans they were more commonplace – but it wasn't Hadrian's sexuality but his ardour that drew comment. A serious man wasn't supposed to lavish too much energy on his bed-warmers.

And now Brigonius noticed the gaze of Primigenius was on him too, that deadly white face, the black-rimmed eyes, the lips scarlet as a wound. Was it possible this raddled ex-slave was *jealous*? Brigonius suppressed a shudder.

At last Xander got to the point. His slaves whipped aside the cloth that covered his model. The courtiers all leaned forward to see the painted hills, the shining ribbon-rivers and the finely worked forts and turrets. The exquisite detail evoked childlike pleasure in their heavily made-up faces.

Xander described the route he proposed. His mighty Wall would be rooted in the east, at the site of a small fort called Segedunum. It would cross the river Tinea, and then climb to the west following the high ground. Hilltops and a natural escarpment of basalt crags would be incorporated into the new frontier. 'It will seem to all,' Xander pronounced, 'as if the Wall has sprung out of the very rock itself!' Beyond this point would be a further river crossing, and then the Wall would take a less dramatic course through more broken country, finally crossing a plain and approaching its destination at the west coast. The total length would be some seventy-one miles, said the architect, every foot of which would be dominated by a stone curtain fifteen feet high. Not only that, earthworks before the northern face of the Wall would give further protection. The Wall would be punctuated by small fortresses, one every mile, and broken further by turrets, two between each pair of mile-forts, to provide signal points and massing positions. There would be gates in each of the mile-forts so that the Wall could be made as permeable or as closed as local commanders desired.

There could be no doubt that the Wall would be a magnificent piece of engineering, and Brigonius could see that Hadrian and several of his courtiers were immediately taken by Xander, his beautiful model, and his compelling vision. But others raised objections.

The first to speak was Aulus Platorius Nepos, Britain's new governor. He pointed out some of the practicalities of building this monument. Under Hadrian in Britain there were three legions and sixty-five auxiliary units, some fifty-three thousand men in all. All three legions would be devoted to building the Wall – say fifteen thousand men. Nepos swept a hand over the model. 'But all of this must be completed in three years,

147

no more. My question to you is – are you sure of your calculations? Is this feasible in the time with the available manpower?'

Brigonius thought he understood why three years; a governor's term was usually no longer, and Nepos would surely want to see the Wall finished during his tenure. But Xander seemed shocked to hear this time limit; his mouth opened and closed. Recovering, he stood his ground and spoke clearly. 'We Greeks are famous for our arithmetic skills. I can assure you, sir, my calculations are sound.'

The next attack on the proposal came from a legate, the commander of one of the three legions currently stationed in Britain. He spoke of the border control that had already been set up under Trajan, along a line a few miles south of the proposed wall. Here, well-established forts, including Vindolanda, and connected by a good road, already served as a base for a rapid and flexible response to any trouble. Wouldn't it be better to reinforce that existing barrier rather than to start afresh?

Xander was no military man, and he was fortunate that the question got bogged down in discussions among Hadrian's own advisers, who plunged into an evidently ongoing argument about whether a purpose-planned barrier would provide a better long-term solution to the problem of the northern frontier. Hadrian let this discussion run for a while, but no conclusion was reached.

The final objection was raised, diffidently, by an older man, a seasoned soldier who had served in the north. He carefully pointed out that the proposed Wall would cut right through the homeland of the Brigantians. 'Now, the Brigantian nobles, the survivors anyhow, are powerful figures in the local government,' he said. 'They may not take kindly to having their fields sliced in two.'

But nobody among the courtiers took the objections of provincials very seriously.

Hadrian leaned forward, and everybody fell silent. He spoke in convoluted Greek, and Karus translated in whispers for Brigonius. 'He likes the idea. It is a bold statement. But he is a practical man who counts his sesterces. He built a barrier of turf and wood along the Rhine; would that not be adequate here? After all the threat from the northern British is not as severe as that from the Germans beyond the Rhine.'

It was the crucial objection, and Severa stood. Among the courtiers eyebrows were raised at a woman's intervention, but they let her speak. 'A wall of wood and grass will do for a German – but it would never have done for a Greek.' And she spoke of spectacular long walls the Greeks had built centuries ago, connecting places Brigonius had never heard of: from Athens to the Piraeus, and across narrow isthmuses such as at Corinth. 'The Wall will be in the best Greek tradition,' Severa said, 'but in its mile after mile of shining impenetrable stone it will be a truly Roman statement.' Xander who had whispered all this to her, looked pleased.

Hadrian looked impressed.

Karus's eyes were moist. He whispered to Brigonius, 'That mind, that fire – that heaving chest! Isn't she marvellous?'

The Emperor was tiring of business. The courtiers sat back, and to a burst of music a troupe of dancers, jugglers and acrobats exploded into the room.

Nepos approached Xander and clapped him on the back, a bold soldier's gesture that made the little architect flinch. He said in Latin, 'When I was governor of Thrace my province included such a wall, at Gallipoli. Six centuries old, the historians told me, and still standing today.' He turned back to the Emperor. 'You will indeed be building in a grand tradition, Little Greek!'

Hadrian smiled.

But that phrase of Nepos's – 'little Greek' – shocked Severa. '*What* did he call him?'

Nepos had used a Latin word: 'Graeculus', Greekling, Little Greek. 'It's just a nickname from Hadrian's childhood,' Karus said. 'He always had a passion for all things Greek, even then ...'

Severa turned to her daughter, who looked as startled as her mother. 'Rome's great son has come to earth ... A little Greek his name will be ... A little Greek! That's what the prophecy says, mother. Oh, my eyes! It's coming true, it really is ...'

The Emperor and his courtiers continued to chat with fascination over Xander's model, all unaware of the metaphysical shock among those who had proposed it.

And when Brigonius looked up he met the cold eyes of Primigenius. The freedman did not seem happy at this turn of events, not one bit.

X

Once Hadrian had made his decision, things moved quickly.

Governor Nepos insisted that at least some ground be broken, a few stones laid, before Hadrian left the province. And besides, if the ambitious project was to have any chance of being completed within Nepos's three-year governorship, then some progress surely had to be made this year. 'I want to see those stones piling up faster than leaves in autumn,' Nepos declared.

This decree sent Xander into a spin. Brigonius had the uneasy feeling that Xander's toy architecture did not translate quite as coherently as he had given the impression into a real-world project to be built by fifteen thousand hulking legionaries. But an emperor's will was not to be defied. And nor was Severa's: cold as ice, her determination fuelled by the Prophecy, she allowed no room for doubt. Thus they were all committed.

Hadrian planned to advance to the northern legionary fortress of Eburacum to inspect his troops. Once again Severa and her party rode ahead of Hadrian's caravan. Severa would use every hour she could steal to get the project up and running before the Emperor even arrived.

But for Severa's party the journey north was tense and sour. Once they were out of the pacified south, Roman military control was overt. There were no towns here save military outposts. The land was studded with watchtowers and beacons, and churned up by the remains of marching camps. Brigonius had grown up here; it had been his family's home for three generations. As a boy he had even played at the foot of a stern Roman watchtower, erected in Banna before he had been born. But for his companions it was a strange, uneasy landscape, and they barely looked out of the carriages. Xander and Karus kept themselves busy poring over plans of their Wall. Lepidina huddled over her poetry, and even Severa was subdued. In their minds this was the edge of the world, beyond which lay only a chaos that threatened to blow out the orderly lights of civilisation.

Once Brigonius tried to engage Severa and Lepidina in conversation about this. He talked of stories still told around Brigantian fires, of dynasties of bronze and stone, an oral history that went back thousands of years.

Lepidina said, 'I have an aunt who told me that Agrippina, my great-grandmother, told such stories to her daughters—'

Severa cut her off. 'It's all barbarian nonsense. Everybody knows that Britain was colonised by refugees from Troy. That's why Caesar came up against Trojan chariots here. And that is what we are: Trojans, good Mediterranean stock, a few generations removed. I won't discuss it any further.'

The party at last neared Eburacum. The legionary fortress stood on a hilltop on the north bank of a river, its walls square and uncompromising, and a shanty town of traders, soldiers' families and other hangers-on sprawled outside the fort wall and south of the river. Eburacum was one of six military power centres in the province, including the other two legionary fortresses and the three *coloniae*, including Camulodunum. As if to reinforce the permanence of the imperial stranglehold on Brigantia, in the last decade the fortifications of Eburacum had been rebuilt in heavy stone.

They reached a gate in the fortress wall. Here a unit of soldiers under the command of a decurion stopped them and had them dismount so their luggage could be searched.

As they waited at the gate Brigonius at last managed to shepherd Lepidina away from the others. After his hour together with her at Camulodunum, and that lightning-strike of passion, he had barely been able to spend any time alone with the girl.

'You've been quiet for days,' he said.

She pulled a face. 'Are you surprised? This is an awful country, Brigonius.'

'It's just different from what you're used to, that's all. And your ancestors came from Brigantia, remember.' He took her hand; it was warm and soft. 'Lepidina – that hour in Camulodunum, what happened—'

She blurted, 'You're thinking about the future, aren't you? Our future, a future for us together.'

He hesitated, reluctant to ask the next question. 'Aren't you?'

'Yes. Yes, I suppose so,' she said.

He breathed out.

'But standing before all this legionary stone – it seems so unreal, Brigonius. We are so different, our worlds are as far apart as sun and moon. Could you live in a town, even a mudhole like Camulodunum? Or could I live in one of those funny round wooden houses? I want to be with you. I *think* I want it. But how could it possibly be?'

'Then what must we do?'

'Let's give it time, Brigonius. A mere wall takes three years to build. A love takes a lifetime.'

He smiled. 'You do have depths, Lepidina.'

She arched an eyebrow. 'You patronising toad.'

'I wonder if your mother's Prophecy would be any help.'

Lepidina laughed sadly. 'Prophecies deal with trivia like the fall of empires. They say nothing about the important things, like love and the human heart! Look, Brigonius, we don't have to think about this now. If mother succeeds in building her wall, if you sell a thousand cart-loads of stone to the Roman army, then we'll all be rich – ridiculously rich. And one thing I do know about the Roman way is that money changes everything. We'll be able to live as we choose, anywhere we choose. But for now—'

'Yes?'

She kissed him lightly on the lips.

When they got back to the carriage Severa turned on them. 'So you're lovers.'

Lepidina snapped, 'Mother—'

Brigonius raised his hands. 'Claudia Severa, if you're referring to the day of the banquet at Camulodunum—'

'When you screwed her? Not that. What does screwing matter? Animals screw. Humans become lovers. I can see it. You are comfortable in each other's presence. The way you talk, the way you walk. You are fusing. It is obvious.'

Brigonius said carefully, 'Severa, I don't think we know our own hearts. Not yet.'

'Oh, don't you?' Severa leaned forward, and in the gloom under the canopy her face was a mask of bloodless determination. 'Listen to me. Your silly hearts do not matter. What matters is the project. Because the project is our future – the future of our families for generations to come. Remember, both of you, that you are here to serve my purposes. Just keep your mouth shut, Brigonius, do as you're told, and if you must fiddle with my daughter do it out of sight of the Romans.' And with a sneer she turned away.

Brigonius was shocked. Severa had obviously used her daughter as a snare to lure him and his quarry to lend her scheme some plausibility. Now he had crossed some invisible line by getting too close to Lepidina, and she had struck back. There was no room for love in Severa's cold calculations – not even pity.

Lepidina was quietly angry. But it was clear to Brigonius that she had faced such dressing-downs from her mother all her life. Brigonius began to wonder how much Severa was capable of, how far she could go in pursuing her ambitions.

Karus and Xander had of course heard every word of the exchange. Karus, trying to cover the tense silence, rubbed his hands together. 'Well, as for me I could do with a shit, a bath, a drink, and some food, not necessarily in that order.'

Xander snorted. 'For a lawyer you're very crude sometimes.'

'That's the *Brittunculus* in me,' Karus said cheerfully.

Severa extracted a letter from her purse and unfolded it; the bindings of the wooden pages creaked softly. 'I have an invitation from one Ceriala Petilia, the cousin of a friend's friend, who just happens to be the wife of a tribune. She has offered to host us while we are here. A good Roman woman. No more barbarians!'

'Then all we have to do is find her,' Karus said mildly.

Severa glanced about and saw a soldier crossing towards the gate. He was a centurion, as Brigonius could tell from the vine stick he carried. 'You! Come here. I have an assignment for you.' And to Brigonius's astonishment she ordered a centurion of the sixth legion to carry her bags as if he was a common slave. Meekly he obeyed.

'Marvellous,' said Karus, but he sounded uneasy.

XI

'Let me get this straight,' said prefect Tullio. 'You want to build a wall.'
A brisk, bustling man of about forty with a shock of bright red hair, he
was clearly used to command, and he easily dominated his cluttered
office in Eburacum's headquarters building.

Xander, his model set out on the floor of Tullio's office, sat more
nervously, Brigonius thought, than in the presence of the Emperor
himself. 'Yes, a wall,' he insisted.

'Seventy miles long.'

'Seventy-one actually.'

'With three legions.'

'Yes.'

'And you want to do this in three years.'

'Yes.'

Tullio's eyes bulged. 'Are you twisting my cock?' He leaned back and
called through the door. 'Hey, Annius! Get in here and listen to this.
You'll love it.'

Another soldier, evidently one of the prefect's aides, walked casually into the office, polishing a strip of breast-plate armour with a
bit of leather. He was a muscular man whose head was shaped
oddly like a bucket, Brigonius thought, with a narrow chin, protruding teeth, a broad forehead and a mass of black hair. 'What's up,
Tullio?'

Tullio turned back to Xander. 'Go on, friend. Do your routine again.
How many miles? *How* many forts and turrets? ...' As Xander stam-
mered out his plan once more, Tullio and his pal leaned back in fits of
laughter.

To compound Xander's mortification two small boys came running
into the room, squealing. They both had red hair as bright as Tullio's.
They had been playing with short wooden swords, but when they saw
Xander's toy wall with its tiny fortresses and plaster hills they fell on it

154

with delight. Xander, in a fussy panic, tried to keep the boys away, but he only excited them further and made things worse.

Amid this chaos Brigonius glanced around at his companions. Karus looked as if he was having trouble not laughing himself. Severa, however, seemed ready to burst into flame.

Severa had been relatively happy here at Eburacum. Compared to the cities of the south, let alone Rome, it was a coarse, military-tinged place. But the officers of the sixth legion and their wives formed a seamless social circle with ties of patronage, obligation and letter-writing that stretched all the way back to Rome itself – a circle that excluded any British, of course. It was a circle Severa had immediately joined thanks to her friend Ceriala, and so she had restored contact with her own world. But now here she was enduring the goading of this buffoonish barbarian soldier, and her fury was obvious.

The trouble was, if the Wall was ever to get built they had to convince Tullio.

Tullio was prefect of the auxiliary troops stationed at the fort at Vindolanda, just south of the line of the proposed Wall. He was a Batavian, who had begun his career as commander of a unit of troops from that Germanic nation. Tullio had very visibly done well out of his career in the army. Through his service he had become a citizen, and a member of the equestrian class – Rome's highest below that of senator. He had a handsome apartment here in Eburacum. He had even taken a wife, a dark-haired British woman. He was a walking exemplar of the fact that the army was not just a tool for subjugation and control, it was a machine for processing barbarians into serving soldiers, useful veterans and loyal citizens. And as the officers, senatorial-class, were merely working through military postings en route to more glittering career destinations, Tullio was possibly the most experienced soldier at Vindolanda, or indeed in any of the northern postings.

Now Nepos, who as governor was commander-in-chief of the army in Britain, had given this solid man a peculiar commission.

The Wall would be built by the legions, which, descended from Rome's first soldiers, phalanxes of farmer-soldiers from the plains of Latium, remained the core of the army. All three of Britain's legions would send detachments. Legionaries were trained in construction work, and each legion had its own specialist teams of engineers, architects and master builders. There was probably no workforce in the world better suited to such a mighty task.

But once built the new Wall would be manned, not by legionaries, but by auxiliaries. Some auxiliaries were infantry like the legions, but many were specialists: cavalry, slingers, archers. These days many auxiliaries were provincials, co-opted into the army for their special prowess. Auxiliary units were more suited to the rapid-response policing operations of a frontier fortress than the legions, who were trained for set-piece battles in open countryside.

The governor, a practical man, saw the need for a 'foreman' accountable to Nepos himself to oversee the project. As an auxiliary commander Tullio would not command any of the legionary detachments who would build the Wall. But as it was his troops who would use the Wall, Tullio had a vested interest in making it work. And so, wise councils had agreed, Tullio was just the man for the job.

The trouble was, here was this competent, trusted man laughing Xander's precious scheme out of court.

Karus stood grandly. 'Gentlemen, this is an imperial commission. We all have an interest in fulfilling that commission. And you are scarcely being respectful to the lady. Let's have a little gravity, shall we?'

The ploy seemed to work, and Tullio calmed down. 'All right. And you, Butimas, if you swallow that fort you'll be for it!' Tullio aimed a kick at his sons, who fled, laughing at their own jokes. Tullio turned back to Xander. 'Sorry, friend. Try again. Sell me this Wall of yours.'

Trembling a little, Xander restored his increasingly battered model, and turned to a folio of sketches on parchment. 'Here is the Wall itself. Fifteen feet high, ten wide. A foundation of slabs in clay, then two courses of dressed sandstone around a core of clay or cement. In front of the Wall – that is, on the north side, facing the barbarians – you will have a berm eighteen feet wide, and then a ditch, shaped like a V, you see? Twenty-seven feet wide, ten deep, with a drainage channel cut into the bottom.'

'And this thing will cut right across the country, yes?'

'Yes. Local streams will be culverted through the Wall. Over significant river crossings we will need bridges.'

'Bridges, of course,' Tullio said, still mocking.

The aide, Annius, said cheerfully, 'And on top of this you want forts and turrets, I suppose.'

'A fort every mile, with a gate, and two turrets set into the curtain wall between each pair of forts. I have the drawings here ... The Wall will be plastered and painted white.'

'Oh, very nice,' said Annius.

'Such an edifice laid across the neck of the country will be an imposing statement.'

Tullio growled, 'My cock is an imposing statement, but that won't stretch from sea to sea, and neither will this Wall. Look, friend, let me put you out of your misery.' He took a notebook, a fat block of wood, and shook it out into a strip of leaves hinged at their edges. He dipped a pen in ink and briskly began to scribble numbers. 'Seventy-one miles, you say? Ten feet by fifteen? If there are, um, so many feet to the mile ... The point is, friend, I've worked with legionaries. I know how much stone or earth a man can shift in a day ...' He came to a result; he tapped the wood leaf with his pen. 'To haul all that stone from the quarries to the Wall line will add up to about twenty *million* legionary work-days. We'll have fifteen thousand legionaries at most, and each man can manage perhaps two hundred days per year – less this year, as it's June already. And if you divide one number by the other – yes, here we are – you'll find it is going to take you over six years to build this Wall. Not three!'

'But—'

'No buts. Look at the numbers!' Tullio threw his notebook at the architect. 'Oh, it's always possible to shave off a bit. Use only local stone. Push the legionaries that bit harder. Maybe make some use of local labour or slaves, but if they're untrained they won't be useful for much. But none of that will make any real difference. No, I'm saying you simply can't do it, friend.'

Old Xander seemed about to burst into tears.

Severa glared at Tullio. 'I don't know why we're even having this debate. The command for this Wall comes from the Emperor Hadrian himself.'

Tullio sat back and folded his massive arms. 'I don't care whether he's the Emperor of the Romans or the King of the Bog People. You can't build a six-year Wall in three years, love.'

Severa's fury was cold. 'Don't you call me "love", you fur-backed—'

'Severa!' Karus snapped.

Annius was studying the model. 'Tell you what. Why not build it in turf? Just as good at keeping out the hairy lads from the north, and be done in less than half the time.'

'Turf? Turf?' Severa said menacingly. 'Why, you insolent fool, if I had a clod of turf in my hand right now, I would gladly shove it down your throat—'

Brigonius touched her arm. 'Wait,' he whispered. 'I'm a quarryman. I deal with fellows like this all the time. It's all a game. Just give us some time.'

Karus stood hastily. 'Quite right. Let's sleep on it, shall we?' He stood massively over Severa until she allowed herself to be escorted from the room. Then he sat down, blowing out his jowled cheeks with relief.

'Feisty piece, isn't she?' Tullio said.

'You don't know the half of it,' Karus said dryly.

Brigonius faced Tullio. 'Let's get down to business, shall we? You heard her, prefect. This is the Emperor we're dealing with. And the Emperor wants a stone wall.'

Tullio said heavily, 'Listen, black-beard, the Emperor can *want* to build his Wall on the moon, but that doesn't mean it can be done.'

'Then what *can* you do?'

Annius was pulling his lip. In his dull way he seemed the more creative of the two, Brigonius thought, and was at least trying to come up with solutions. 'Tell you what,' he said slowly. 'How about *half* in turf and half stone? You could probably manage that in the time. Then you get the best of all worlds, a complete defensive barrier in three years *and* a nice bit of stonework to impress the boss.'

Brigonius was about to reject this out of hand, but Xander said wearily, 'Four-tenths.'

Brigonius turned to him. 'What?'

'Not half. Four-tenths in turf, the rest stone according to the plan.' He tapped Tullio's notebook. 'That is feasible from the figures, if you are honest in your calculations, prefect. Besides I worked it out for myself earlier.'

Tullio took back the notebook and revised his figures quickly. 'All right. Yes, four-tenths turf, six-tenths stone. Yes, you could do that.'

Xander turned to Brigonius. 'This is the best we can do in the time.'

Karus said darkly, 'And you knew this before we came in here? Why didn't you say something when we put the plan before the Emperor?'

'Because I didn't know we would only have three years,' Xander said. He sounded exhausted. 'Severa didn't let slip that little detail until the audience. What could I do, argue with her before Hadrian himself?'

'It's not so bad,' Annius said cheerfully. 'Everybody goes away happy. And you could always replace your turf with stone later.'

Karus growled, but subsided.

Brigonius glanced around. 'All right,' he said cautiously, not wishing to overstretch the consensus. 'Then the question is, which half will be turf?'

After another hour's discussion, and after a tankard or two of Tullio's coarse German beer, they came a conclusion. From Segedunum at its eastern extremity, the Wall would run west as stone for forty-five miles, and then turf the rest of the way to the western coast. The eastern half of the Wall was closer to local sources of good stone – not least Brigonius's own quarry – and the two soldiers regarded the security situation along this part of the border as more critical, so stone was appropriate for this stretch.

'And besides,' as Tullio pointed out, 'the eastern half is where the

Emperor is. He's going to want to lay a foundation stone, not dig a lump of sod.'

The four of them stood up and shook hands. 'Then we have a plan,' Brigonius said, weary but relieved. 'Now all we've got to do is sell it to the Emperor.'

'That's the easy part,' Karus muttered. 'It's Severa I'm frightened of ...'

XII

The climax of Hadrian's visit to Eburacum was the twenty-fourth of June, a day of religious celebration for soldiers wherever they were posted across the empire. After this Hadrian would ride north and ceremonially install the first foundation stone of the great Wall which would soon divide the island of Britain in two.

Brigonius had been forced to learn a lot about the habits of his sole customer, the Roman army. A soldier's religious life was complicated. To begin with he brought along his own gods. A German here in Britain, for instance, celebrated his feast of Matronalia on the first of March. He would also be expected to pay respect to any local deities. The soldiers seemed to like Brigantia's own Coventina, and thanks to the army's mobility she was gaining adherents even overseas, in Gaul and Germany. But the soldiers' statues of her, crudely made, were alien in the eyes of the Brigantians, who found Coventina in the hills and the streams and in the wind, and did not recognise these busty Romanised cartoons.

The centre of a soldier's religious life, however, was a calendar based on feasts of the traditional Roman deities, principal city days, the anniversaries of the emperors, and dates associated with his unit itself. And of all the feasts on the calendar none was more significant than today, the twenty-fourth of June, the feast of Fors Fortuna, a popular goddess among the troops.

Brigonius had hoped to spend the day in the company of Lepidina. He wasn't sure what Severa's plans would be now, and how much more time he and Lepidina would have together. But as the day's festivities began Lepidina was nowhere to be found.

Then Severa herself peremptorily requisitioned him as an escort. Beside Severa, her face set as hard as Roman concrete, Brigonius found himself trailing the Emperor as he toured the troops.

Accompanied by his courtiers, Hadrian walked slowly from barracks block to training field, and inspected displays of infantry field man-oeuvres and formation riding by cavalry units. It was a festival day, and the imperial party grew raucous on wine and British beer. Brigonius had a policy of staying sober around Romans, but Severa seemed deter-mined to ply him with drink, and he saw no point in defying her. As the ale filled him even her company seemed less than icy.

Hadrian drank his share, but he remained focused on the part he was playing. He was good at detail; Brigonius heard him sympathise with one unit of mixed cavalry and infantry that it was harder for them to put on a spectacular display than for a dedicated cavalry unit with their larger numbers of horse. Each man seemed to grow in his presence, and Brigonius could see why he was so loved by his troops.

It wasn't a bad life, Brigonius was coming to think, to be a soldier of Rome. You received regular pay and reasonable food. You had camara-derie in the barracks, and there was always the civilian town outside your fort, with its shops and inns and brothels and temples, where you might find a little relief, or a companion who could one day become a wife. The barracks could be rife with lice, and the town with diseases. But you could get rid of the lice in the bath house, and if you got sick you could go to the hospital – the army ran the only professional hospitals in the world. You might go through your whole twenty-five-year career with only two or three campaigning seasons, and perhaps without seeing any fighting at all. You were almost certainly better off than the *Brittunculi* or other half-civilised provincials beyond the walls of your fort ... And every so often an emperor came to visit.

Many of the troops had grown beards, in defiance of the usual Roman custom, imitating Hadrian's coin images. This amused Severa. 'Look at them. The Emperor's beard is more famous than he is!'

At noon the Emperor and his retinue, with Brigonius and Severa in tow, retired to the fortress's headquarters. Today the largest reception room in the block had been decked out as a shrine to many gods, and the party settled down to a long afternoon of eating, drinking and fortune-telling. At the inception of his mighty project Hadrian was seeking good auguries. Since dawn his philosophers had been inspecting the sky, looking for unusual clouds and the flight of birds with auspicious patterns. Now animals were put to death on charcoal braziers, entrails were prodded, statues venerated and libations poured, as scholars worked their way through scrolls of prophecies and inter-pretations.

Only the sinister freedman Primigenius sat aloof from it all, as always watching, watching.

With Severa at his side like a gaoler, Brigonius had nothing to do but drink. The chanting of the philosophers and the thickness of the air, cloudy with incense, made him feel as if he were floating out of his body. He tried to strike up conversation with Severa. 'Romans are always superstitious, aren't they?'

'None more than Hadrian,' she said. 'But it's not surprising. He is a soldier who has to come to terms with the prospect of becoming a god after he dies – indeed in Egypt they worship him already. How would that feel, Brigonius? Can you even imagine it? Wouldn't you be fascinated by past and future, if you felt you might some day transcend time itself?'

This kind of philosophising baffled Brigonius at the best of times; now the words flew around in his head. 'Superstitious or not, he's still a soldier. And you can see he still has the touch with his men.' He spotted Prefect Tullio sitting close to Governor Nepos. Tullio was silent, his face like thunder. 'But there's one soldier whose life doesn't seem to have been improved by the Emperor's visit.'

'Oh, things have gone slightly awry for our friend the prefect,' Severa said with silky satisfaction. 'He's still in his post. But he's lost a few of his privileges. His wife and kids have been kicked out of the fortress for a start.'

'Why?'

She inspected her fingers, long, perfectly manicured. 'Because of this solution you cooked up between you and your drinking pals. A Wall that is half stone, half turf.'

Brigonius knew how unhappy she had been with the deal, not least because it violated the terms of her Prophecy. 'Not quite half—'

'Shut up,' she said without emotion. 'I had no choice but to accept it. But it took me some effort to sell it to the Emperor – or, more specifically, the freedman Primigenius. I had to promise some favours.'

He asked uneasily, 'What favours?'

'And even then I found it necessary to shift some of the responsibility. I'm happy to say that it is our oafish Germanic friend Tullio who is taking the blame for fouling up the estimates for the Wall, not me, not Xander.'

Brigonius, his head full of beer fumes and smoke, felt as if he was about to pass out. 'That's unfair on Tullio. He's only trying to do his duty. And you have made an unnecessary enemy. That's a bad habit, Severa.'

'Of course it is unfair, which makes it all the sweeter. That'll teach him to call me "love".'

Something in her tone alarmed Brigonius, but he seemed unable to sit up. 'These favours you promised—'

Her face loomed before his eyes. 'You aren't completely incapable yet, are you, little Briton? The poison I've had dropped in your ale will soon grip you completely, though.'

'Poison?'

'Oh, it won't harm you. It will just be that for a sunset and a sunrise you won't be able to impose your will on your own body.' She ran a fingertip down his chest. 'How awful for you. But never mind, there is somebody else who will be able to make good use of your fine body while you're gone. You've guessed, have you? *You're the favour*, you see, to sweeten the deal you forced me to make. It's not my choice at all, oh no, it's simply a consequence of your own actions. You see that, don't you?'

Suddenly Brigonius remembered the way Hadrian had looked at him. Anger and fear flooded him, but still he couldn't move; he lolled on his couch, a helpless doll, his limbs heavy as logs. 'What have you done – have you promised me to Hadrian?'

Another face loomed over him now: pale skin, black eyes, lips like a wound.

Severa was whispering in his ear. 'Oh, not the Emperor – you aren't pretty or young enough for him – but Primigenius, who wields the power I needed. He has issues with our proposal, you know, for he has his own pet architect he hoped to promote. And then there is simple jealousy, of one bed-warmer for another. Primigenius lusts for you, yet hates you at the same time, for he knows you caught the Emperor's eye, if only briefly. Isn't that a paradox? Won't it add spice to the night you're about to spend together?' She came closer still; he could feel her breath on his ear, smell the spices on her tongue. 'And after he's split you open, o *Brittunculus,* my daughter will never touch you again.'

That red mouth descended towards him, but he couldn't move, couldn't struggle, couldn't even cry out.

XIII

Brigonius rode west towards Banna, along the line of the Wall.

A year after Hadrian's decision, this part of Brigantia had been transformed into a vast construction yard. On this bright late spring morning, from the higher ground Brigonius could see how from horizon to horizon a corridor of broken ground cut across the crags and green-clad hills, mapped out by surveyors' flags and poles, and scarred brown by the ruts of wheels and the prints of feet and hooves. It was a slash through the countryside's green flesh. And all along its length legionaries toiled, hauling and laying stone, maggots in the wound.

In what had been left of last summer, governor Nepos had set his workforce the target of completing three miles of Wall, which had been achieved easily. This year, in the first full season, the three legions working on the Wall were each to complete five more miles.

The mile-forts and turrets came first. The forts were built to a simple rectangular plan, fifty feet wide and sixty deep, with gateways in the north wall and the south. Inside there were small buildings and an oven, and a staircase leading to a viewing platform. The turrets were even simpler, just thatched towers set on bases twenty feet square, each with a hearth and a shelter for the soldiers. The turrets and forts were intended to be part of the fabric of the Wall itself, so they were built with 'wings', stubby extensions on their east and west faces where the curtain wall would be attached.

Such was the speed of construction that in some places the curtain wall was already being built. On a foundation of slabs set in puddled clay, two courses of dressed stone were laid, rows of neat square blocks. Then a core of rubble bonded with clay or mortar was poured in to fill the space between the skin of cut stone. Drains were built under the Wall, and more significant streams were culverted. The completed stone sections were already being plastered and painted white with lime-wash render, and red stripes ran along the line of the wall, picking out the curtain's courses of stonework.

Brigonius, a stone man himself, marvelled at the pace of the work. It wasn't just the hugely efficient transport of stone that impressed him but the Romans' use of concrete. Without a core of concrete the Wall could never have been built so rapidly, or so robustly. Concrete even set hard under water, allowing the construction of firmly founded bridges. If the facing stones were robbed or decayed in the future, the concrete core would stand; the Romans were building for centuries.

The Wall was not meant to be a defensive barrier, in the way that the wall of a fortress was designed to withstand a siege. Its purpose was control. The regularly placed fortified gates would allow the army to control the flow of population through the area – and, indeed, levy tolls from it. The Wall was imposing enough to deter any small-scale raids, but if there were any larger-scale disturbance the legionaries would mass from their bases in the south and ride out through the Wall gates to meet the enemy in set-piece battles in open country. In fact, Brigonius was coming to understand, the Wall was a mere component in a system of deep control, defence and communication that stretched south of here through roads and forts back into the Roman province, and even to the north, where manned outpost forts would be maintained beyond the Wall itself.

But, watching the Wall rise grandly over the crags, Brigonius wondered how much this military theorising mattered compared to the brute physical reality of the Wall. It was a monument to the power of the Roman mind like nothing ever seen before in Britain – or, according to Tullio, in the whole world – and even if it were not manned by a single soldier such a structure would surely deter all but the most fanatical enemies of Rome.

But then, Brigonius reminded himself, despite certain harm done to him, he was not a fanatical enemy of Rome.

Brigonius arrived at his own limestone quarry. This was a great scoop out of the south side of a hillside, not far from the line of the Wall, some miles to the east of Banna. He rode up from the north, so he could stand at the lip of the artificial cliff that had been cut into the crag and view the activities in the pit. Long lines of men snaked from the quarry face to massing points by the carts, lugging stone. They were the men of the sixth legion, mostly drawn from Gaul and Germany but some from further afield. Day after day they hacked into British limestone, roughly cutting the stone blocks and dragging them to the carts to be hauled off to the construction sites.

The speed of the work was remarkable here too. In less than a full season's working the quarry had already been hugely extended, following the seam of rich creamy rock, from the small bite into the turf-covered crag that Brigonius had inherited. The legionaries had a variety of specialist tools that Brigonius coveted, such as heavy hammers, steel-tipped wedges and crowbars, and cranes for lifting heavy blocks. In one part of the quarry a watermill worked a trip-hammer, flailing arms which battered at intransigent rock. He had heard a rumour that in another quarry further along the Wall stone was being cut by a water-driven saw.

But in the end it was brute labour that was getting the job done. Even from here Brigonius could see how the sweat glistened on the backs of the legionaries as they toiled. The Wall would be seventy miles long, and somebody had to cut out every single block of stone, haul it to the Wall line and mortar it in place.

'Brigonius.'

He turned. Here was Matto, his cousin, a stocky man ten years older than Brigonius. Matto was black-bearded, dark-haired, and he wore a heavy woollen coat dyed deep blue-black, so he was a knot of darkness in the middle of a bright summer day. It was hard to imagine a figure more anti-Roman in his style.

'Cousin. You crept up on me.'

Matto grinned, and Brigonius saw yellow-brown quarry dust embedded deep in his pores. 'Just as you sought to creep up on us – eh?'

He was right. It was a trick Brigonius had learned from Tullio the prefect, who was becoming a brusque sort of friend. 'All soldiers are lazy blighters,' Tullio would growl in his thick Germanic-tinged Latin. 'It's in the blood. The only thing to do is to sneak up on them from a direction they don't expect, at a time they don't expect it. The small hours is my favourite time. You should see the whores and catamites run, like pink rats!'

Brigonius asked Matto, 'Am I that predictable?'

'You'll have to find some new spying-points. Here's the latest tally.' Matto handed Brigonius a fold-out notebook of taped-together wood leaves.

Brigonius looked over the figures; at first glance they seemed in order. 'Any problems?'

'None but the Romans,' Matto growled. 'The numbers add up in their neat columns. But they are stealing our stone, cousin.'

'No, they aren't,' Brigonius said patiently. They had had this argument many times before.

'The prices they are paying are ruinous,' Matto insisted.

So they were, even compared to the prices Brigonius had been able to extract from the soldiers at Vindolanda before the coming of Hadrian and his plan. But at least they did pay, when they could have just taken the stone. Brigonius thought he understood. For one thing by paying rather than stealing, even a pittance, the Romans kept their own consciences clean; they might be hypocrites, but they preferred to run their affairs according to the rule of law – that is, *their* law.

And there was a subtler purpose. When he had come to work for Brigonius Matto had had to learn Latin, and to write and tally well enough to keep adequate records. Matto may not have realised it – and Brigonius wasn't going to point it out – but by being forced to deal with the army he was becoming, little by little, literate and numerate, and locked into the Romans' economy.

The Roman army wasn't just a tool of conquest. The largest organisation in the world, boasting three hundred thousand men deployed from the Tinea to the Euphrates, everywhere it worked it used Latin and paid in the imperial coin. The army was a source of Romanness, its walls and forts a stony wave of acculturation.

Anyhow, such was the quantity of stone being extracted to build the Wall that even at the Romans' 'ruinous' prices Brigonius and his family were growing quietly rich.

Matto was recounting a long and complicated anecdote about the behaviour of a particularly obnoxious decurion in the quarry. Brigonius cut him off. 'You're even more sour than usual today, cousin. Something's been twisting your crab-apples. What's up?'

'Everybody's stirred up,' Matto said. 'It's the tax census.'

'Another one?'

'Brigonius, they are actually building their precious Wall right on top of freshly ploughed land. *My* land. Now I'm told I will have to cough up higher taxes to pay for it. And in future to take my cattle from one field to another I will have to pass through a Roman gate and pay a toll!'

'Matto, this is the way things are. Take it to the council if you've a complaint.'

Matto was disgusted. 'What would be the point of that? That bunch sold themselves to the Romans long ago.' Much of the Brigantian nobility had been subsumed into the government of the *civitas*, the Roman administrative region which had taken the name of the old nation. 'Well,' Matto said darkly now, 'there is talk of doing something.'

Brigonius grew impatient. He had to put up with this bluster every time he tried to do business with Matto. 'Like what? What will you do, throw stones at the governor?'

'You would say that,' Matto sneered. 'Some say you're more Roman than the Romans, now.'

Brigonius kept his face closed. 'Then there's no more to be said, is there?' He tapped the record. 'Thanks for this. I'll see you next week.' And he turned back to the spectacle of his quarry and the toiling legionaries. He heard Matto stomp off to his horse.

Brigonius knew he was an easy target for local resentment, because he was much more accessible than a council member. But what twisted him up about such encounters was his memory of what had been done to him a year ago at Eburacum. He had been conscious, helpless but conscious, as Primigenius had used him. When he had at last dared to approach Lepidina again she had recoiled, as if the stink of the freedman still polluted him. He was pretty sure that the harm he had suffered was more grievous than any petty land-grabbing suffered by Matto and his pals.

But the Romans were like the weather, or the passage of time; you couldn't do anything about them, you had to work with them, or slink away and die. That was what Matto couldn't see.

And as for what had befallen him that night it was not the Romans he blamed, not the Emperor, not even the bitter freedman Primigenius. It was the woman who had set the trap into which he had fallen: a Roman but by descent his own countrywoman, Claudia Severa.

In the meantime there was work to be done. He turned his horse's head and set off for Banna.

XIV

Brigonius's birthplace happened to be close to the site where the Wall's western turf construction met the stone eastern sections. Thus as he reached Banna that evening the turf Wall came into view.

If anything it was an even more spectacular sight than the stone Wall, for along its line the legionaries had stripped away the vegetation right down to the pink-white boulder clay beneath. The turfs they cut – and hauled here sometimes from miles away, for good turf was hard to find – were heaped up on a central strip of remnant greenery. The finished curtain wall was fourteen feet high and twenty feet wide at the base, punctuated by turrets of stone or timber, and a rampart of white clay was laid out before the Wall on the northern side. So as Brigonius looked down from the higher ground, the cleared strip of land stood out, a gash in the landscape brilliant white in the sun, with the green-brown line of the Wall itself running along its centre line.

At length he arrived at Banna. To the south of its escarpment the valley still cut deep, and far below the river washed as it always had. But the landscape bore the mark of the Romans. To the north a road set off straight as an arrow, heading for the northern outposts, and the hills where men had once seen the reclining form of a goddess now glimmered with the fires of watchtowers.

Banna itself was now the site of a Roman camp. As he approached Brigonius saw sentries silhouetted against a setting sun, their bare heads and spear tips clearly visible above wooden ramparts. The place bristled with activity, the roughly laid roads that led from east, west and south were full of traffic, and the turf all around had been churned to mud. The camp itself huddled against the escarpment, protected from any threat by a complex of ditches and a palisaded trench to the north, and the cliff to its back.

As he approached the camp's defences Brigonius was passed through a line of sentries. Within was a neat array of the Romans' leather tents.

There were soldiers everywhere, of course, in their leather tunics and trousers, their woollen cloaks, their strapped-up military boots. Even more of them were sporting beards, such was the impression Hadrian had made during his visit last year. The camp was a sketch of the fort that would soon be built here, but it was already functioning, already an operational element in the system of the defence of the province.

Once there had been a Brigantian community here. A Roman watchtower had been built here long before Brigonius was born, a blocky stone pillar that had loomed over his boyhood. The watchtower still stood, but his home had gone, the roundhouses demolished, the defensive ditches filled in. Brigonius wouldn't have recognised the place, save for the essential shape of the landscape.

Brigonius found Tullio sitting in his own tent. Tullio had moved his household and his aides here for the building season; it was a place where he could watch over the progress of both the stone Wall to the east and the turf to the west. Some of his officers were here, including his close adviser the bucket-headed decurion Annius, and also his household slave. Karus and Xander were here, sitting with Lepidina, who looked bored. When Brigonius joined them they were winding down what sounded like a wide-ranging discussion of problems to do with the Wall, a conversation fuelled by wine served by the slave.

As usual Tullio was surrounded by heaps of paperwork. The army's system of assignments was quite complicated, Brigonius had learned, with detachments being sent all over the province, and perhaps only half or two-thirds of the nominal strength of a given unit actually being in its home base at any time. But as a soldier of Rome, in your unit's Acts your duties were recorded daily. It was the army's meticulous record-keeping that enabled the commanders to know exactly not just where each soldier was supposed to be but where he actually was. And to maintain this vast mountain of recording whole teams of clerks were required, an army within the army.

But today the discussion concerned the Wall.

'A fort every mile, two turrets every mile,' Xander said firmly. 'That's the design. That's what we are building.'

'And I'm telling you,' Tullio said, 'that it can't be done. You see, your *design* is all very well. I'm all for *design*. My cock would tumble out of my underpants without *design*. What I'm talking about now is fact, legionaries out there right now putting stones and turf blocks on the ground, one on top of the other. And if you try to follow your every-mile rule rigidly, Xander, you find yourself planting forts at the bottom of a gully where you can't open the gates, or at the top of a crest where if you did open the gates you would fall out.'

'Roman roads run straight,' Karus said, himself faintly mocking. 'Up hill and across valley; everybody knows that. Are you saying you can't build a simple Wall to the same standard?'

Tullio ignored him. 'And it's not just the position of the forts. I'm hearing grumbles from the legionary tribunes who've been up on inspection from Eburacum. If an assault were to come, how are they supposed to deploy through those toy-town gates?'

Xander said stiffly, 'I carefully computed the width and frequency of the gates to ensure—'

Annius said, 'Yes, but the local farmers have to use them too. What are we going to say to the legate of the sixth when he finds himself queuing up behind a flock of sheep?'

The image was so absurd it made Lepidina laugh prettily. Brigonius tried not to look at her.

Brigonius knew that the Wall-building project was actually running to schedule, somewhat to everybody's surprise. But Tullio was genuinely concerned about this issue of the useless mile-forts.

Tullio's slave, a boy aged maybe fourteen, approached Brigonius with a wine cup. Brigonius accepted it and said, 'Thanks.'

The boy looked surprised to be noticed at all. He said, 'Enjoy it, sir,' and resumed his station.

Brigonius watched him go and sipped his drink; it was soldiers' wine, strong, filthy stuff. The boy's tongue was British, Brigantian. His litter-name was Similis. Brigonius wondered what Matto would have thought if he could have seen his cousin now, being served wine by the British slave of a German officer in the pay of the Roman army, as he worked on a Wall which was meant to secure the servitude of the north of Britain for ever.

And he looked at Lepidina. He couldn't help it.

She was sitting quietly, head down, her hands folded around a half-empty cup of blood-red wine. A year under her mother's thumb in northern forts had not been good for this city girl, and there was no sign of the bright spirit she had shown during that first visit to Camulodunum. She was a bird in a cage of stone.

Karus seemed aware of the glum silence between them. As the conversation about the practicalities of mile-forts ran down, the lawyer lumbered across to Lepidina, sat down, and let the slave boy fill his cup. 'So,' he said, 'how's your marvellous mother? I don't see so much of her these days.'

'Nor do I,' Lepidina said. 'She's too busy writing letters to the governor.'

'Yes, I know about those,' Tullio rumbled, looking up from his discussion. 'Full of nothing but good news. She leaves me to tell him the truth, which always looks bad by comparison.' He sighed noisily. 'That wretched woman!'

Karus said, 'She's a difficult friend – but I wouldn't want her as an enemy.'

Xander asked, 'And how is she feeling about her precious Prophecy, now it is failing to come true?'

Lepidina shrugged. Karus glanced uncomfortably at the soldiers. Brigonius knew that to the Romans prophecies, auguries, divinations and the like were seen as sources of power – and, particularly under an emperor obsessed with his own destiny, you had to be careful. But Severa and her family Prophecy had become the talk of the Wall, and much mocked.

Annius said in his chirpy way, 'Funny thing about that Prophecy. It actually says Hadrian would come to Britain and build a Wall, doesn't it?'

'Not quite,' Lepidina said, 'but close enough.'

'I never heard of a prophecy so, so, what's the word? *Specific*. Did you, Tull? Usually it's a business of poking around with leaves and entrails and getting a few portents of doom that could mean anything. This is different. It's not like the gods are setting us their usual puzzles. It's more like a man is speaking to us. It's as if somebody in the future *knew* what was going to happen, wrote it down and sent it back into the past.'

Lepidina said, 'My mother calls him "the Weaver" – or her – the author of the Prophecy.'

'Ah,' Xander said, intrigued. 'But is that possible in any of our philosophies? Do we allow even the gods to know the future – or to change the past?'

Karus said dryly, 'If the legionaries hadn't nailed them all to their sacred trees on Mona it would be interesting to ask a druidh such a question. I know they spoke of a continual exchange of spirits between our world and the Other, but each of our spirits is embedded in time. So I think questions of the existence of the future, or meddling with the past, would be meaningless to them.'

'But in Greece,' said Xander loftily, 'rather more sophisticated notions have been developed.'

'Here we go,' Tullio growled. 'More "sophisticated" horse crap.' He snapped his fingers to have the boy refill their cups.

Xander went on, unperturbed, 'For instance there is the notion of the Eternal Return, in which time is cyclic, and every event is doomed to recur over and again, without limit. This troubled Aristotle, who wondered about causality in a universe in which he existed as much after the fall of Troy as before it. But I suppose you could indeed influence the "past" by ensuring a message about it lasted long enough to reach its recurrence in the "future" ...'

'And what about eternity?' Karus cried, sounding a little drunk. 'I thought you Greeks had plenty to say about that, Xander.'

'And some Romans,' Xander said mildly. 'Eternity: a mode of existence in which all events, past and future, coexist. Lucretius argued that duration is a mere product of the mind, for eternity is the higher reality through which we move, you see, and motion gives the *impression* of change. But of course Lucretius was merely developing older ideas of the Epicureans. And Plato long ago said that our perception of time is a "moving image of eternity", again foreshadowing Lucretius—'

Brigonius struggled to understand this. 'So eternity is like – like what?'

Karus said, 'Brigonius, think of a tapestry. Woven into it are pictures of trees, say, all in their different stages of growth: seeds, saplings, young, mature, old, fallen, decayed away. They are all there all at the same time in the weave, you see. Now, you are an ant running along one thread in the tapestry. And as you run you let your eyes slide over the pictures of the young trees and the old, and you connect them up in your head – and instead of seeing many trees of different ages, you imagine you see only one tree, growing and dying and rotting away. You see? A moving image derived from stasis, passing time derived from eternity.'

Brigonius frowned. 'I think I follow.'

Annius asked, 'So does all this mean that the future can speak to the past?'

Karus laughed. 'If you ask the right question of the right god, perhaps it can! Perhaps time really is a tapestry, its threads all our lives. And somewhere there really is a Weaver, god or man, who sees all, past and future in a glance – and who can, with a few deft plucks, change the pattern of the weave, adjust history, and alter all our lives. But there is always the question of purpose. If the Weaver seeks to perturb history – why, and to what end?'

None of them had an answer to this.

Tullio made an obvious and kindly effort to include Lepidina. 'What of your Christian god, lady? What does He have to say about time and destiny?'

Lepidina said mildly, 'Jesus was God made human. What He had to say to us concerns the way we live our lives. The way we think about each other. He had nothing to say about philosophies of time.'

Karus said, 'Ah, but if I understand your mythology right, Jesus's own life was time-bound, unlike the gods of the past, and it marked a great disjunction in history. He was the God made man, and in His life and His murder He redeemed mankind.'

Xander raised his eyebrows. 'So Jesus is an intervening god, like the gods of Olympus of old. I thought we were done with them! And He was murdered? How?'

'By the Romans,' Lepidina said. 'The governor of Judea had Him put down as a rebel.'

Tullio said gruffly, 'I knew a man, who knew a man, who knew your Christ.'

Lepidina's eyes widened. 'You did?'

'This fellow I'm talking about was a veteran, retired, when I was starting out myself. I was eighteen or so. I met him in Pannonia. And he told me about a veteran he had met when *he* was young, in Africa. This chap had been a centurion, and he was on duty that day in Judea, when your Christ was crucified. The lads showed Him mercy, he said. As He was dying on the cross, one of them gave Him soldiers' wine.' He raised his cup. 'Just like this.'

They sat gravely, reflecting on this.

Karus murmured, '"Whilst God-as-babe has birth ..."'

'From the Prophecy,' Brigonius said.

'Yes. Lepidina, I've often wondered about the meaning of that phrase. Even if you accept that Severa is right that the text of those lines is about Hadrian and the Wall, that phrase doesn't fit. You have always said the Prophecy is bound up with your young faith because of the coincidence of the birth dates of your ancestor and your Christ. I wonder if that line is telling us something of a great conflict to come, between your young god and the old. But if so, what is the Prophecy guiding us to do? What does the Weaver *want*?—'

There was a crash, and a smell of smoke. Tullio dropped his cup of wine and ran out of the tent.

XV

The camp was plunged into chaos. Soldiers were running everywhere, fumbling with weapons and armour, some of them only half-dressed. And from one corner of the camp a plume of smoke was rising.

Xander stared about, bewildered. 'What has happened? What should we do?'

'Stand still,' Brigonius said firmly. He took Lepidina's arm. Her face was closed up and he couldn't tell what she was thinking or feeling. This wasn't the place for her, he told himself angrily. 'Stay with me,' he said. 'The camp is obviously under attack. We're in the safest place, right here. Just let the soldiers do their jobs.'

Karus shook his head, clearly reeling from the wine. 'I'd like to know how they managed to torch the camp. What did they use, a catapult?'

Tullio approached them and glared at Brigonius. 'You. You're a Brigantian. Are you going to give me any trouble?'

'No.'

Tullio pressed him: 'What are you then? On this night when many of your countrymen will have their bellies slit open by Roman stabbing swords, are you a traitor to your kind?'

The question struck at Brigonius's heart. But he said, 'No. But I am no fool either. This isn't the way to deal with the Romans; this can't work.'

'And what is the right way to "deal" with Rome?'

'On your own terms. By skinning you of every sesterce.'

Tullio inspected him closely. 'Very well. Stay close to me or Annius; it's likely to be a long night. And keep these people under control.' Then he turned away, dismissing Brigonius and his party.

A junior officer ran up. 'Sir, we're under attack!'

'Well, I can see that,' Tullio snapped. He drew his stabbing sword and turned to face the north. 'Perhaps those northerners are taking their chance before the Wall is built. Get me a signaller and tell him—'

'Sir.' The officer, no older than twenty-five, was distressed, out of his depth. 'They aren't coming from the north.'

'Then where?'

'From the south, sir. The south!'

Tullio gaped. 'The south? Which side of this cursed Wall are the barbarians supposed to be on? And how did they set fire to my camp?'

'I can answer that, sir.' A tough-looking centurion approached. His face was streaked with ash, and he carried something in his hand, something that dangled and dripped a dark fluid. 'He was *inside* the camp. He had business here; he'd been here before. We'd no reason to suspect him. But he was carrying a bottle of oil which he lit and—'

'Who, man? Who did this?'

The centurion glared at Brigonius. 'This is yours, I believe.' He raised his arm. The thing in his hand was a human head, severed at the neck, from which blood still oozed. The face was obscured by a thick black beard. The centurion dumped the wet thing on the floor.

Brigonius flinched but stood his ground, while Lepidina cowered behind him. 'Matto,' Brigonius breathed. 'Oh, you fool.'

Tullio glared. 'Recriminations later. For now let's get control of the situation. You,' he told the centurion. 'Take charge of what's going on inside the camp. Put that fire out before it does any more damage.' The centurion ran off. 'Annius, you come with me. What are those signallers doing up in that tower, sucking each other off? I need to find out what's happening in the country ...' He stalked off, bristling, angry, competent.

Karus was staring at the severed head. 'I knew this man.'

'He was my cousin,' Brigonius said grimly. 'He worked for me, at the quarry.'

'What was in his mind, Brigonius? He must have known he could not survive a lone attack on a Roman camp.'

'But death didn't matter to him,' Xander said quietly. 'The Romans have encountered such suicide killers before – and know they are hard to deal with. As Tacitus has written, "The man who is prepared to die will always be your master."'

The commands flowing from Tullio soon had their effect. Soldiers swarmed around the camp, preparing weapons and armour. Meanwhile others gathered around the fire. They hauled a cart laden with a heavy tank of water. Two beefy infantrymen began to work a two-handed lever, and water was forced out of a nozzle. The cart was hastily swivelled so that the fire engine's spouting water was aimed at the burning tents.

176

XVI

The light faded, the long day dwindling into night. Brigonius and his party huddled with Tullio's staff in the prefect's tent.

Beyond the camp the country was wild. Brigonius heard shouts, screams, and there was a prevailing stink of smoke. The soldiers prowled around their watch posts, peering out into the dangerous dark.

To Brigonius's surprise, Tullio didn't send his forces out immediately to meet the enemy. During the night the sentries passed only despatch riders. On the old signal tower flags were raised and beacons lit, and across the turbulent countryside more pinpricks of fire lit up in response, as the mass mind of the army channelled and absorbed information about what was happening.

It soon became clear that the uprising had been coordinated. There had been strikes all along the line of the Wall, most of them rash suicide raids. And at the same time there had been a general rising in the countryside, with tax officials and councillors, many of them Brigantian themselves, abused, attacked, their homes ransacked. The most serious rising was to the west of Banna, where a pack of young men had torched the still-incomplete turf wall, kicked in the defensive ditch, and generally made a mess of the Romans' new frontier.

Through the night Tullio sat in his improvised command post, poring over maps and lists of detachment names and numbers on hastily set-out tables. Records, charts, lists, information, information: even as the countryside boiled like a disturbed ant hill, communication, patience, *thinking* was the key to the Roman response. Sitting here Brigonius saw how very wrong Matto had been to resist the Romans' literacy, for it was the army's key weapon. Through words and numbers on paper Roman commanders were able to transmit their commands unambiguously across hundreds of miles, and the bloody lessons of the past were stored without error or distortion, for ever.

While Tullio and his staff worked, the Brigantian slave boy brought them food and more soldiers' wine. Brigonius wondered what was going on in the head of the boy, what he understood of the uprising. Where was his family – north of here, south? But families, even names, were irrelevant, once you were a slave; you had no past, no future, no purpose but that which your master assigned you. Even your children were slaves, and given litter names by your master: 'First-born' (Primigenius) perhaps, or 'Similar', or 'Runt'. But on a night like this, Brigonius thought, even the most docile slave must feel something stirring in his heart.

The long night wore on. Karus drank himself to sleep on a soldier's blanket. Xander, a nervous man surprisingly stoical in the face of a real crisis, wrapped himself in his cloak and sat quietly, eyes wide. Lepidina curled up against Brigonius, and Brigonius welcomed this echo of their brief love, though he knew she wanted no more than comfort. As for himself he could not sleep.

The sun was rising when at last the bugles sang. Brigonius left his companions sleeping, letting Lepidina slide off onto a blanket, and went out to see.

Units of soldiers were forming up, preparing to march out to meet the enemy. Brigonius overheard Tullio and his aides reviewing their information and giving commands to the junior officers. The Romans had delayed their response until they could assemble a sufficient countering force with detachments of the auxiliary units from Banna, other nearby camps, and the forts behind the Wall line. The legionary detachments assigned to Wall construction work were also gathering their weapons, but they were falling back, while other detachments from the legionary fortress at Eburacum, better prepared, were moving forward. The auxiliaries would do the brunt of the fighting while the legions would be kept in reserve, for no large-scale pitched battle was expected ...

And so on. This was how the system was supposed to work. Thanks to its fast communications, detailed record keeping and flexible deployment the army, never numerically strong, was able to deploy rapidly and efficiently, focusing its energies exactly where they were needed most. The army itself was a high technology, Brigonius saw, honed and perfected over centuries of conquest.

Meanwhile the soldiers were individually preparing. Brigonius had worked with Roman soldiers for years. While they could sneer at the *Brittunculi* they had been posted to govern, they had come to seem disarmingly ordinary to him: ordinary fellows doing a job of work, wanting nothing but food, sleep and an occasional shag. But now he saw these men for what they were. In armour that fit like a second skin, wielding weapons with the casual intimacy of a lover's touch, they were barely human at all, he thought; they were slabs of muscles intent only on killing. And as they formed up in their tight disciplined units they seemed more formidable yet. Brigonius's heart felt heavy as he thought of the force that would face them, a rabble of disaffected Brigantian farm-boys stirred up by hotheads like Matto, armed with rusty weapons their grandfathers had been hiding in grain pits since the days of Cartimandua.

XVII

A month after the insurrection had been put down, governor Nepos travelled from Londinium to assess the damage for himself.

Nepos toured the forts and rode the length of the Wall, and spoke to his senior commanders, including Tullio. He returned to Eburacum for a few days to preside over the trials of the suspected ringleaders of the rising. And he announced, in the even-handed way of wiser Romans, that he would consider compensation for farmers who had lost significant chunks of land – always providing they could prove they hadn't taken part in the uprising themselves.

Then he came to Banna, where he ordered a review. Tullio, Annius and their staff were called in, as were senior officers from the forts, a couple of tribunes from each of the three legions, and the architect, Xander, with his sponsor Severa, and Brigonius and other local suppliers.

The meeting was fractious from the start. Nepos demanded of Tullio, 'How could this happen, prefect?'

'We had some failures of intelligence,' Tullio admitted, 'which have been put right. A failure of security too which has been tightened.' Brigonius could testify to that; he had the bruises inflicted by gatekeeping soldiers to prove it. 'But,' Tullio went on, 'we just didn't anticipate the way the attack unfolded. The Wall is designed to deal with attacks from the north, not the south!'

Nepos shook his head. 'I still find it hard to believe. This has implications for everything we are doing here. If this were to happen again—'

'It won't,' Severa said quickly. 'Governor, this was a bit of restlessness by unhappy Brigantian farmers. Once your more lenient policies are accepted—'

Nepos glared at her until she was silent. 'Madam, to my mind we are building for centuries. Perhaps Brigantia will be quiet for a season or two. But in time a new generation of young bulls will rise up who will imagine their grandfathers didn't go far enough – I've seen it all before. We must plan for all contingencies.'

A young man in brightly polished dress uniform stood and took the floor. 'And that isn't all we have to think about.' He bowed to the governor. 'Sir, my name is Galba Iulius Sabinus. I am a tribune of the sixth; my legate at Eburacum sent you his report on the new military dispositions.'

Tullio growled, 'The damn legions didn't deploy.'

'But they might have had to,' Sabinus said with effortless command.

Nepos nodded to the tribune. 'I've seen the report. You may summarise its findings, Iulius Sabinus.'

Sabinus was good-looking, strong-featured, with thick dark hair. Brigonius imagined he might actually be a native Roman – and if he was a tribune he must be of the senatorial class, in the course of a career which might one day lead him to a post like Nepos's own. Brigonius always reminded himself that to men such as Nepos and Sabinus, whatever happened in Britain was but an incident in a long career progression.

'We of the sixth, concerned about the practicality of the Wall even before the uprising, have since mounted a major exercise to test its utility. All this is detailed in the report ...'

The idea of the Wall was that in the event of major disturbances to the north, the legions would deploy from their forts in the rear, march through the gates, and meet the enemy in open battle north of the Wall. When detachments of the sixth had actually tried this they hit problems. First you had to walk a few miles to the Wall itself. Then you had to break formation to make your way to one or other of the gates and file through, and just as Tullio himself had anticipated, legionaries in full battle armour found themselves queuing behind farmers' wagons and herds of sheep. Even on the other side of the Wall you then had to form up again into marching order. During all this time you were terribly vulnerable to attack.

'It just didn't work,' Sabinus said with bold bluntness.

Tullio said, 'In fact it's worse. In some places you have to cross the river to get from the forts to the Wall! The Wall's been my baby, and I hate to say it, but we should pull down the whole wretched thing. We did better under Trajan without a Wall at all.'

Xander stood immediately, plump, anxious, shaking off Severa's restraining hand. 'We must finish what we have started,' he insisted in his heavily accented Latin. 'You can't judge the performance of the

Wall as a system when it is not completed, any more than you can expect a cart to run on only two wheels. When my design is fully realised—'

'It's still not going to work,' Tullio said bluntly. 'Because it will still have the flaws we have identified today. A vulnerability from the south. Inadequate crossing points.'

Sabinus nodded. 'My legate would agree. We have to think too of the longer term implications for the empire as a whole of such a static, frozen frontier. The economic consequences alone—'

Nepos held up a hand to silence him. 'Now your education is showing, Iulius Sabinus,' he said dryly. 'I have only a few years in this chair, and I have to think of the short term, not the long.'

Severa said quickly, 'In the countryside the Wall has already become a highly visible sign of Roman strength. To abandon it now would be a clear sign of weakness. A retreat.' Brigonius saw she was trying to manipulate the soldiers' sensibilities, trying to keep some control of the project.

Nepos sighed. 'Unfortunately I have to agree with you about that, madam. The Emperor would not accept an abandonment. It would harm him back in Rome. The Wall exists, for better or worse. We have to consider where we go from here, not where we would wish to have started from.' He turned again to Xander. 'We will not obliterate your precious monument, architect. But how would you modify it to correct its deficiencies?'

Xander, unfortunately, had retreated into a shell of hurt pride. He all but shouted at the governor, 'The design cannot be modified! It must be expressed!'

Tullio raised an eyebrow, and a ripple of exasperation passed among the Romans in the room, Brigonius thought. *Greeks will be Greeks.*

Sabinus, ambitious, saw his chance. 'If I may, governor? I've taken the liberty of drawing up a few modifications to Xander's design that might accommodate the objections we've heard today.' He held up a scroll. On Nepos's nod of permission, he spread this on a low table before the governor. Brigonius saw it was a rough sketch done in charcoal of the Wall curtain, forts and ditches.

'To begin with,' Sabinus said, 'the vulnerability at the rear. You can see that I've added a further earthwork on the south side.' The cross-section he had sketched showed a ditch some twenty feet wide at the top and ten deep. There were mounds twenty feet across to either side, each set some thirty feet from the lip of the ditch. 'This earthwork will be set back from the Wall to create a protected zone to the Wall's south, an "annexe" if you will, where civilians will be excluded or controlled.

There will of course be controlled crossing points and causeways at the forts.'

Annius nodded, pulling at his lip. 'That would work. I've seen such designs before.' He squinted at the architect. 'And how long will this earthwork be?'

Sabinus said forcefully, 'Why, it must shadow the Wall for its whole length. What use is it otherwise?'

Nepos held up his hand. 'We'll discuss the practical consequences later. I think we all agree that some system such as this will be necessary. Now, Sabinus, concerning your legate's objections about the gates—'

Sabinus directed their attention to another corner of his sketch. 'It is clearly impractical to have the major forts set back from the line of the Wall, and to have crossing points so narrow as the mile-forts. The solution is clear. We must build new forts, each large enough to house an auxiliary unit, along the line of the Wall itself.' He showed a sketch of a fort, the classic rectangular shape lying astride the line of the Wall. 'You can see that half the fort's gates will give directly into the northern area, giving it the equivalent of six mile-fort gates. The unit will be able to deploy immediately from its fort into the north.'

Nepos glanced at Tullio. 'Prefect? Will this do?'

Tullio shrugged. 'The northern walls of the forts will be vulner-able—'

Annius said cheerfully, 'You can fix that. A few pits with stakes would do the job. But this will cut the number of crossing-points in the Wall. The locals will resent it.'

Nepos eyed him. 'The locals just tried to burn the Wall down, soldier. Let them resent.'

Tullio growled, 'Sir, you told me to bring this project in on time, within your governorship. We already had to make compromises – the turf sections for a start. Now to build these new forts – how many, tribune?'

'Twelve,' the Roman said smoothly.

'Twelve, then—'

Sabinus added, 'And I'd advise rebuilding the turf sections in stone while you're at it. A mix of turf and stone in the long run will only invite attacks along the more vulnerable turf section.'

Tullio laughed. 'Yes, let's chuck that in too! Look, governor—'

Nepos said, 'I know, Tullio, I know. Before we accept the inevitability of a rescheduling, is there any way we can speed things up? What if we reduce the width of the stone curtain, for instance? Does it have to be ten feet? What if were eight feet, or six? Wouldn't that do? ...'

They began to talk around such time-saving compromises. Sabinus expertly made himself the centre of the technical discussion, excluding Xander and his sponsor Severa. Xander rolled his eyes in mute horror at this destruction of his vision.

Brigonius was more interested in Severa. As the scope of the project changed before her eyes, she was clearly losing any control over events she might once have had. Not that anybody had any sympathy for her; she had made too many enemies for that. But Brigonius wondered what was going on behind her cold, bitter face.

At last Nepos sat back. 'Well, I think we have a solution, for all but one of our problems: the timescale. Tullio?'

Tullio sighed. 'I don't imagine the Emperor will assign me the Rhine legions to finish the job?'

Nepos smiled. 'You're an honest man. I don't want you to commit yourself until you're ready. But we're talking of years more, aren't we?'

'I'm afraid so, sir.'

Nepos tapped his teeth. 'So whatever the future holds the Wall will no longer be my problem – or my glory. Well.' He stood stiffly. 'I had better begin composing my letter to the Emperor. Good day to you all.'

As he left, the others gathered up their belongings. Everybody was silent, sullen.

But Tullio slapped Brigonius on the back. 'I don't know why you're looking so serious, *Brittunculus*,' he said. 'Seems to me the governor has just ordered an awful lot more of your stone.'

XVIII

It took another month for the final act of the rebellion's aftermath to play itself out.

The execution was to take place outside the camp at Banna. Everybody within half a day's walk of the place was summoned to attend, as were the leaders of the *civitas*.

At the appointed hour Brigonius walked out of the camp. He joined a dismal gathering, a hundred people or so, men, women and children, gathered around the cross on the ground. The August day was unusually warm: it was a Roman heat, Karus said, a heavy heat that flattened your lust and puddled your thinking, the heat of the conquerors.

To Brigonius's surprise, Severa joined him, with Karus. 'I wasn't expecting you two. I didn't know you had a taste for such a spectacle.'

'I certainly don't,' Karus said, his face grey. 'I see it as duty, of a grim sort. It is sometimes my role to argue for the death penalty. I think I should remind myself from time to time what that entails.'

Severa was expressionless, wrapped in a white cloak. 'As for me, I thought I should drain the dregs of a foolish disturbance which did so much damage to my ambitions. I thought that my daughter might be here, however. After all she worships a god who died in such a manner. You'd think she would see this as part of her theological education.'

'You're too hard on the girl,' Karus murmured. 'This isn't the place for her, you know. You're crushing her spirit.'

'I know my own daughter, I think.'

Karus regarded her. 'Once I admired you. I lusted after you – I'm sure you knew it. And your mind astonished me; your gaze pierced centuries. But perhaps your aloofness from history has leached you of your humanity, Severa. Perhaps you have something of the Weaver's manipulative coldness in your heart ...' But his words tailed away, and Severa's glare held only contempt for this man who had been her closest ally.

As for Brigonius, he had nothing to say to Severa. Somehow the company of this vicious, thrusting woman felt appropriate on this awful day.

There was a disturbance. Brigonius turned to see a detail of soldiers dragging a prisoner out of the camp. They towered over him; he was only a boy. Brigonius and his companions had to step back to allow the party through. For a moment the boy's glance met Brigonius's. It was Similis, Tullio's British slave. The boy seemed to recognise Brigonius, who had once thanked him for bringing him a drink. Then the moment was lost, the link between their souls broken.

The soldiers briskly pushed the boy to the ground. They strapped his arms to his cross. Then they laid one foot over the other, and to pin both feet to the cross upright, drove a long iron nail through them. The sound was extraordinary, like a skewer driven into a side of pork. The boy stayed silent; he panted hard, panicky. Brigonius had heard that there was comparatively little pain associated with the nailing, oddly. With a grunting effort the soldiers raised the cross, and pushed its base into a hole in the ground. As the cross was jolted into position, Brigonius thought he heard the flesh in the boy's feet tear. Now the screaming began.

'Oh, have mercy!' Karus said, but it was a whisper, too quiet for the soldiers to hear.

Severa said bleakly, 'Mercy? The suffering is necessary. Not for him and the crime he committed, but for us, so we will not transgress in future.'

'But he didn't commit a crime,' Karus blustered. 'That's what's so monstrously unfair about it!'

The boy's guilt or otherwise didn't matter, Brigonius knew. Severa was right about that. The rebellion had been broken up, its leaders punished. But for the soldiers at Banna one loose thread had remained. Nobody had been found who had supported Matto in his strike at the very heart of their camp, nobody who had ordered him to do it, nobody who had helped him. The soldiers couldn't bear the idea that one individual acting alone could have penetrated so far into a base they thought of as secure. So somebody had to be blamed, a conspiracy concocted. And there, conveniently, was a Brigantian boy serving the prefect himself. Some whispered he had been seen at the gate when Matto arrived, or at the headquarters building before it was torched, or—

'All lies,' Karus moaned. An empathetic man for a lawyer, Brigonius thought; he felt the boy's agony himself. 'All rumours, misunderstandings – a will to see blame where none exists!'

186

Brigonius put a hand on his shoulder. 'For once Severa is right. His suffering is necessary; it is closure. Let's just be grateful it isn't one of us.'

Karus spat on the ground, an uncharacteristically crude gesture. 'Sometimes you are too pragmatic, Brigonius. This may be necessary but it isn't for me.' He stalked off, and Severa, her face unreadable, followed.

Blood dripped steadily from Similis's feet. If he let himself hang from his arms, so sparing his torn feet, he couldn't breathe. But if he tried to raise himself on his feet so he could get some air, the tearing got worse. So he jerked and struggled, shifting his weight from one source of pain to another, his movements minute but agonised.

As the boy fought to stay alive, one by one the crowd drifted away. Brigonius felt he ought to stay, though he wasn't sure why.

When people called him 'pragmatic', he had learned, it was meant as an insult. He didn't think of himself as cowardly, or a traitor to his ancient nation. He could see very clearly how the Romans brought unhappiness to many – and misery or death to those who opposed them. It was just that he couldn't imagine any way of striking at the Romans that would do anybody any good. Surely Matto's futile gesture proved that. But that didn't make him feel any better as he stood here and watched an innocent child die on a cross.

The boy's whimpering quieted and he fell into unconsciousness. As darkness gathered, one of the soldiers who stood at the foot of the cross, taking pity, smashed the boy's legs with the hilt of his sword, and the boy's body slumped further. Unable to support himself, he would surely soon be dead of asphyxiation. But his body would hang there until the crows had his flesh.

Brigonius turned and walked back into the camp.

XIX

The letter from Lepidina was a slip of wood covered in her own rounded, still girlish handwriting. She had returned to Britain from Rome, she said, and would visit the Wall. She said that her mother was coming too – indeed, the purpose of her visit was somehow connected with Severa.

And so Brigonius was going to see Lepidina again. He was shocked to reflect that since the fateful day of the Decision, when before governor Nepos the Wall had been redesigned from end to end, fifteen years had already passed. And Lepidina was no girl now; she was to stay in the fort at Banna with a party led by her husband of fourteen years: Galba Iulius Sabinus, once a pushy young legionary tribune, now a senator.

Brigonius clutched the letter to his heart, wondering what to tell his wife.

On the appointed day he made his way to the fort at Banna. He was passed through the west gate. The double-arched gateway alone, he sometimes thought, was grander than anything seen in Brigantia before the Romans came.

Leaving his horse to be stabled by a slave, he walked along the main drag through the fort, called – as in every Roman fort of this type right across the empire – the *via praetoria*. Banna was no tent city now. Buildings clustered around him like huge bricks: the barracks to either side, and before him the squat blocks of the *praetorium*, Tullio's commander's residence, and the *principia*, the fort's formal headquarters. Beyond that he glimpsed the hospital, and more barracks, stables and workshops. An empty area was laid out with the foundations of two granaries, enough to store a year's supply of grain for a thousand men, which would have raised floors for protection from the elements. But these were yet to be constructed. Progress was always slow, hampered by a lack of local resources. One of the grandest buildings was a drill hall where the soldiers could be trained during the most inclement northern weather; it was a monument of stone big enough to allow javelins to be thrown indoors.

The streets were busy, not just with soldiers but with their slaves, and with local traders and workmen. Pay day had been only a couple of days ago, and the vendors prowled the streets and pushed their heads inside open doors, looking for likely buyers of their wares and services. Enclosed within its walls, self-contained, the fort shut out the untamed countryside around it; it was like an island of Romanness, Brigonius thought, independent of the world outside.

But of the Brigantian settlement that had once stood here not a trace remained. The old Roman watchtower had been demolished, the forest cleared and marshland drained. Even the ancient barrows that had lined the escarpment, the tombs of deep ancestors, had been levelled. This was the place where Brigonius had been born, and the ancestors of Severa and Lepidina; it was here that Nectovelin's birth had long ago been heralded by the strange Prophecy. These days the only Brigantians lived in a shanty-town that had grown around the walls of the fort, just as at Vindolanda. Coventina was banished now.

Brigonius reached the headquarters building. He crossed the broad cloistered courtyard with its well, heading for the central cross-hall, the basilica. These two areas were large enough to hold all the troops in the fort. To the rear of the basilica was a row of offices, at the centre of which was the shrine, the *aedes*, with its statue of Hadrian, the standards of the fort units, and other religious tokens. Two rooms to either side were the offices of the adjutant, the *cornicularius*, and of the *signiferi*, the standard-bearers. The shrine and offices had open fronts with low ironwork screens. This little area was the fort's heart. The *signiferi* were responsible for the crucial issues of the soldiers' pay and savings, and behind the shrine itself was a strongroom containing the fort's cash. Brigonius had watched this being built from the ground up, and indeed had sold the Romans much of the stone they had needed. It was all still so new he could smell the mustiness of fresh plaster.

And today, in the basilica, the fort commander was holding a reception for Sabinus's party. There was little left of the pretty-boy tribune about Sabinus; he had become a tough-looking man of his world, competent and corpulent.

Sabinus was leading this delegation from Rome, representing both the senate and the Emperor's household. It was here to make a regular inspection of the Wall and the situation in the north in general – and, so the rumours went, to deal with a spot of unpleasantness concerning the conduct of Claudia Severa. Brigonius was surprised that Sabinus should have been put in charge of a problem concerning his own mother-in-law. But perhaps this subtle cruelty was characteristic of Rome these days, ruled over by an ageing, detached and increasingly capricious Hadrian.

As if to symbolise the complicated unpleasantness of the imperial court, among the Emperor's representatives was Primigenius. The freedman looked as sharp and wily as ever. But, stick-thin, his head shaven and his sunken face laden with cosmetics, he had not aged well, his beauty long lost. Brigonius was actually introduced to the man, but Primigenius didn't show a flicker of recognition.

And here, of course, was Lepidina with her glowering husband. She looked her age – she was thirty-four now – but she was still heartbreakingly beautiful. Through his sparse correspondence with Severa, Brigonius had been aware of Lepidina's marriage to the Roman. But still he was somehow shocked as, for the first time, he saw Lepidina on the arm of Sabinus. Brigonius understood from whispers that Sabinus's career hadn't progressed quite as well as he had once planned. Perhaps that explained the darkness around his eyes, the lines around a downturned, rather cruel mouth, and an air of patient wistfulness Brigonius sensed about Lepidina.

During the course of the formal occasion Brigonius met her only briefly. There was nothing they could do but exchange pleasantries; Brigonius even found himself asking after her mother's health. But as the evening ended he asked to see her again – just for old time's sake, he said. They agreed to go for a ride together along the Wall the following day. She seemed neither reluctant nor eager, merely polite. And then she was gone, whirled away in the complicated choreography of Roman high society.

That night he could barely sleep. It had been fifteen years, and lying in the dark beside his wife, it seemed that every day of those years hung heavy on his heart.

After the day of the Decision, Claudia Severa had retreated to the sanctuary of the south. Even now Brigonius still had to deal with Severa on matters of business. She had investments in many of the partnerships that had sprung up to serve the needs of the Wall project, including Brigonius's own. He heard rumours that Severa even had a stake in some of the thriving brothels that mushroomed around the Wall forts. She was nothing if not enterprising. But she had lost any real control she had had over the Wall project on the day of the Decision, her final falling from grace in the eyes of the imperial court. And she did not visit again. Brigonius was happy to deal with her only through letters and the dry wordings of lawyers' agreements. He was glad to be shut of Severa.

But when she retreated south she took her daughter with her, and Brigonius had more complex feelings about that. He felt it even more when he heard that while Severa had remained in Britain, Lepidina had gone back to Rome, where she had grown up.

He'd talked this over with Tullio. In one late-night drinking session, as they downed flagons of British beer by the light of the torches that flickered along the Wall curtain, the brusque old Batavian said he understood. 'Of course you miss her. It doesn't matter that you can't have her. You can't have the moon either, but you'd miss its beauty if it were plucked out of the sky, wouldn't you? There are lots of ways to love a woman, Brigonius. You don't need to be waving your cock at them. You can love from afar. I should know.' Tullio's heavy face was a mask of shadows and scars. It was a rare glimpse for Brigonius into the soul of this bluff, competent man, and he wondered how it must have been for Tullio to be taken from his home as a young conscript, transported across the very Ocean, and then to live out his life in such a place as this, so far from home.

Gradually the trauma of that night in the den of Primigenius faded. At last, Brigonius loved again. But he never forgot Lepidina.

And now she was back.

His wife, lying beside him in their bed, was awake too. Cloda, practical and warm, was the daughter of a timber merchant. Her husband had no secrets from her – not even about Lepidina. And so Cloda knew that this spirit of the past had returned to haunt her for a while; and she knew that Lepidina would soon fade into the mists, and she would have Brigonius back again.

XX

Lepidina met him at the fort gate not long after dawn. One of her husband's slaves had prepared horses for them, and a pack of food and wine. It was a bright October morning, only a few days after the autumn equinox, and unseasonably cold; the horses' breaths misted in the air and a thick dew glistened on the ground. But the sun was low, the sky a deep blue, and the light was rich, making the cut stone of the fort walls shine.

And in this setting Lepidina looked wonderful, Brigonius thought helplessly. She wore a sensible leather coat, woollen trousers and heavy sandals. He saw on her neck a medallion he thought he remembered, a fish design done in silver. Her rich strawberry hair, now touched by a little grey, was pulled back from her forehead and tucked under a woollen cap. She didn't seem to be wearing cosmetics, and the natural pink of her skin glowed. She was still beautiful, but it was no longer the beauty of a girl, he thought. This was the wistful autumn beauty of a woman on the cusp of age.

She gazed at him with her deep eyes, and turned away, almost girl-ish. 'You're staring. You always were a fool, Brigantius-Brigonius.' But there was no reproach in her voice.

'I'm sorry. It's just you look so—'

'If you say I look beautiful I'll punch you. I've given birth to three strapping Roman senators-to-be, and a daughter. *She* is beautiful. I'm a mother.'

'Very well. You look Brigantian, then.'

That seemed to touch her. 'I do?'

'You look as if you belong here. As if—'

'As if I belong at your side. Is that what you mean?'

For a moment, as he looked into her eyes, the world expanded around them, and the fort, the horses, the patient slave, even the mighty Wall, receded to leave them alone in a pocket universe of their own.

'It is still you,' he said. 'Inside there. Somehow I can see that.'

'Yes. How much baggage we carry around now! Our sagging bodies, our spouses and children, all our business. And yet *we* are still here.'

He was falling in love with her all over again, he thought, Coventina help him! But the moment passed, and Brigonius tugged on his horse's rein.

They rode along the line of the Wall, to the east of Banna. Their horses were lively, glad to be working their muscles on this cold morning. They were on the south side of the Wall, so the curtain wall was to their left, the defensive earthwork to their right. They rode into a low sun that glimmered from dew on the churned-up turf of the annexed land. In places you could still see where rows of ploughing had been cut off by the line of the Wall – the last relic of some dispossessed farmer.

They came to a rise, and Brigonius pulled up his horse. From here they could see the Wall sweep across the country from the western horizon to the east, the bright red bands painted on the curtain wall shining in the low northern light, the sandstone of the mile-forts' flat faces glowing. The Wall was a man-made thing that cut the natural landscape in two.

And the vista wasn't static, not just a thing of stone and turf, but human too. It was still early but there was already traffic to be seen on the rough causeways leading to the nearest mile-fort, and the smoke from its hearths rose into the crisp air. In one section of the curtain a party of legionaries was busy, with a chime of pick on stone and distant calls like gulls' cries. Even now the Wall was still being built, rebuilt and refurbished, and it always would be.

Lepidina said, 'Do you remember how we drove to Rutupiae, all those years ago? My mother told me that the first thing the legionaries did when they landed there was build a wall across that little coastal island, just a rampart of wood and turf to keep out the local barbarians. And now Roman walls have scraped their way across the length of Britain, all the way here, to become ... *this*. How many miles long – seventy, was it?'

'Nearer eighty now,' Brigonius said. 'Depending on how you measure it – at either terminus it runs into coastal defences which the fleet crews have been building.'

'Old Xander would have been delighted to see it, if he'd lived.'

'Well, perhaps,' Brigonius said doubtfully. 'But look at this.' He led her a little further, to the nearest of the mile-forts. You could clearly see where two wings of thick curtain protruded from the outer walls of the fort, but they were built into a much thinner cross-section of Wall.

'We had to make compromises which Xander would have despised. This mile-fort was already built before the Decision. It was meant to join to a thicker curtain, with those stubby wings. But then we decided to reduce the thickness of the Wall, and so the wings don't fit. There are other messy bits – places where you can see thicker courses of stone overlaid by thinner.'

'I see. It's all rather untidy.'

'That's soldiers for you,' Brigonius said. 'Their work is solid and fast, but it's always functional rather than elegant.'

'Perhaps, but look around you! This is more than a wall, Brigonius. It is like one immense town that stretches eighty miles from coast to coast. I live in Rome itself and have never seen anything like it – I daresay there is nothing like it in all the world. But here it is in Britain, and *you* built it, Brigonius. And even when Rome is gone – oh, don't argue, our Emperor, who rules the wreckage of vanished empires himself, has a profound sense of the mortality of all things – even when the Romans are forgotten this Wall's mighty ruins will strike awe.'

He said impulsively, 'You know, you remind me of your mother.'

She shot him a look of suspicion. 'What do you mean by that?'

He held up his hands. 'Only her best qualities. When we first rode up from Rutupiae together – do you remember? She spoke to me, and it was as if I was seeing my own country through her eyes. So it is now with you.'

She pursed her lips. 'I think you're trying to compliment me.'

He sighed. 'But that woman keeps coming between us, doesn't she?'

'Yes, she does. Shall we ride on?'

They walked their horses further along the line of the Wall, and the sun rose steadily into the sky. Brigonius talked of his wife, his boys; she spoke of her own children who were growing up in such unimaginably different circumstances. And they spoke of old times, of Karus, long retired to Camulodunum – 'I've had enough of history,' he had protested, 'all I want is life!' – and old Tullio, who had completed his twenty-five years in the army, filled a sprawling farm with a brood of red-haired grandchildren, continued to use his own mighty cock as a reference-point in every conversation, and died peacefully in his bed.

They halted on another bit of high ground, overlooking still more of the Wall as it marched on out of sight.

'You told me before that it felt as if I still belonged at your side.'

'You said it for me,' he reminded her gently.

'You thought it, though.'

'That's true.'

'And do you still think so now?'

He said honestly, 'I don't know. Too much has happened.'

'Yes. For us to be together the tapestry of time would have to be unpicked and woven again – wouldn't it? Perhaps if I had stayed in Brigantia all those years ago, rather than leaving with my mother. Or if you had given up all this to come with me to Rome.'

He shrugged. 'What's the point of speculating that way? You can't change history.'

'No. But, Brigonius – *what if you could*? For that is what my mother believes is the meaning of the Prophecy.'

In the intervening years he had all but forgotten Severa's mysterious document. 'That old bit of spookiness. Does it still exist?'

'Yes. And in a way it has been fulfilled, or so my mother believes. There are three lines relevant to our century, she thinks.'

Relevant to our century. Despite the gathering warmth of the day Brigonius shivered. 'Are there words relevant to other centuries, then?'

'Oh, yes,' she said. 'I always did argue with my mother about whether the Prophecy was more than just a tool for her to further her ambitions. Once her plans imploded she started to think about that. And she has decided the Prophecy is a warning from the future, that a Weaver of history has sent it back in order to influence our times – which to him would be the past.'

'And what do you think?'

'I still believe it all has something to do with Christ. Remember, the Prophecy was delivered at the birth of my forefather Nectovelin, who, it happened, was born in the same year as Jesus of Judea. I think the Prophecy actually has some connection to the destiny of Christianity, and this business of conquering provinces and building walls is all incidental. My mother denies this, though; she's nothing if not a loyalist to the gods of Rome. We've always argued about Jesus ... But it's not the future outcome of the Prophecy that concerns me now but its present.'

'What do you mean?'

'The Prophecy is the issue of my mother's supposed sedition. The Emperor's court have always been suspicious of the Prophecy. Now she has been accused of subversion. And where better to investigate the case than here, where the Prophecy originated?'

'So that's why Sabinus was sent here.' They sat for a moment, with the Wall splayed brightly across the countryside around them. Brigonius said sadly, 'You know, here we are talking of mothers and emperors, of walls and prophecies. We aren't talking about *us*.'

'But there isn't really an *us* to talk about, is there?'

'No,' he said hotly. 'But I will always—'

She leaned from her horse and pressed a finger to his lips. 'It's better not said.'

He nodded. 'We should return. The day is advancing.'

'Of course.'

He spurred his horse, and the two of them trotted side by side back to Banna to resume the business of the day, the business of their bifurcated lives.

XXI

Three days later Galba Iulius Sabinus convened what he called a 'necessary meeting' on the matter of Claudia Severa.

Brigonius wanted nothing to do with it. He would have preferred Severa to pass through Brigantia and on again without his ever seeing her. But to his dismay he found he was summoned to the 'meeting' – and at the behest of Severa herself.

The meeting was held in the fort's office of sign-bearers. The little room, cluttered with records of soldiers' pay and savings and other military incidentals, was cramped, awkward. Oil lamps had been set out on the low tables to dispel the gloom of the poky room, and their sooty smoke flavoured the air. Small statues of Antinous, beautiful boy and lover of Hadrian, filled alcoves on the walls.

Brigonius found himself a place on a couch next to the prefect's aides. Severa wasn't here; she was late.

The prefect of Banna, Tullio's successor, was here with some of his aides, as was Primigenius, the shadow-thin freedman. Sabinus was the only man in a toga. He looked as if he never appeared in public without one these days.

Lepidina attended, apparently as reluctantly as Brigonius. She was dressed in what he thought of as her Roman 'uniform' of fine clothes, cosmetics and sculpted hair. The sturdy Brigantian woman he had glimpsed during that morning ride along the Wall might never have existed. She was at Sabinus's side, of course; she belonged there. But she smiled at Brigonius.

As they waited for the accused to show up Brigonius listened to the soldiers gossiping about dice games. The principals in the case, himself and Sabinus, Primigenius and Lepidina, were no more talkative than the many statues of Antinous.

Brigonius understood the game to be played out today. He knew from his own dealings with Roman law that all emperors were suspicious of rival centres of power. That included private enterprises such as his own partnership, the quarry business, whose operations were tightly controlled by contract law, and watched over by the provincial procurator. And this emperor in particular had an obsession with foretelling. In the harshness of his latter reign, consulting prophecies had become a sign of unhealthy ambition; it was said that Hadrian had had one of his own young relatives put to death for such a transgression.

You could see all this as a symptom of the Emperor's own decay, he thought. Just like all these statues of Antinous.

After two decades Hadrian would leave behind much to be admired. He had rebuilt his empire. Brigonius knew farmers who spoke admiringly of another of Hadrian's projects, lesser known than the Wall if no less mighty in scale: after his visit to Britain he had had drained much of the fenland in the east of the island, in the old homeland of the Iceni, opening up hundreds of miles of wholly new land for cultivation.

But as Hadrian had aged his contradictory characteristics had become ever more pronounced. He had always been drawn to the east rather than the west, even though his own family had come from Iberia. In lands where he was already worshipped as a god, perhaps he began to conceive of himself as a monarch as aloof as the pharaohs had once been. Good Romans muttered that this went against the spirit of their enterprising city and its roots in the noisy democracies of Greece. And more practically, if the centre of the empire moved eastward, Brigonius mused, what would become of Britain, its most western extremity?

It had been the death of one of the Emperor's favourites, the beautiful youth called Antinous, which many believed to have been the turning point of his reign. Antinous had drowned in the Nile, during one of Hadrian's trips to Egypt. The death seemed to have unbalanced Hadrian. Suddenly you saw dedications to his lost Antinous appearing everywhere, in frescoes, mosaics and statues, on vases and on coins, in miniatures and in mimes. You couldn't escape his beautiful face even here, in this soldiers' corner of Britain.

It was said that Hadrian, always obsessed by his own death and subsequent immortality, was trying to create a god in the person of Antinous. It was ironic that, as Lepidina had said long ago, if Hadrian had only turned to the one mystery cult he had always rejected – Christianity – he might have found the theological solace that he sought, and on learning of a god made man in Jesus, he might not have needed to soothe his own pain by turning a man into a god.

But none of that justified the savagery of Hadrian's latter years. In the east the Jews had risen again, once more challenging the very identity of the empire, and this supposedly tolerant, inclusive Emperor had put them down every bit as brutally as the conqueror Trajan. This harshness had trickled down into every corner of life – and even here, at the very edge of the empire, it was this harshness that was now to be turned on Claudia Severa.

At last Severa entered the room, and the desultory conversations died.

Sabinus rose and bowed. 'Claudia Severa. Welcome.'

Severa was dressed plainly, in a simple turquoise robe and head scarf. Now in her late fifties she had aged well, Brigonius thought, though her hair, pulled back from her face, was a helmet of silver-grey. But her eyes were just as dead and cold as he remembered.

He was surprised when, without speaking, Severa crossed the room and came to sit beside him.

Brigonius looked into his own heart, and found that on seeing this woman for the first time in sixteen years his anger burned more fiercely than ever. 'Why did you call me, Claudia Severa?'

She raised dyed eyebrows. 'Why did you come?'

'Do you imagine I am your friend?'

'No. I have few friends. But I need someone to support me today. You have no reason to love me, Brigonius, I know that. But I have dealt with you on business matters these last two decades and I know you to be an honest man.' Even now she was arrogant, faintly mocking.

'I would not see even you sit alone in a time of trial, Claudia Severa. But don't read any more into it than that.'

'I wouldn't dream of it.'

Sabinus cleared his throat. 'Perhaps we should start—'

'Start what?' Severa snapped, immediately on the attack. 'Is this a court, Iulius Sabinus?'

Primigenius stood up, cadaver-thin. 'I believe we are all hoping to avoid the necessity of a trial, madam. But there is unpleasantness to be dealt with nevertheless.'

Severa snorted. 'I wonder if you can speak one word truthfully, you snake.'

Sabinus snapped, 'Let's get this over.'

From a table before him Primigenius picked up a battered leather wallet. 'Do you recognise this?' He opened it and withdrew a document. It was a parchment, worn with age. It bore only a few lines, Brigonius could see, written out in an awkward hand.

He did not need Lepidina's gasp to tell him what it was.

Severa asked menacingly, 'How did you get that?' She turned and swept her glare around the room. 'Which of you is the *frumentarius* who rummaged through an old woman's belongings?' There was an uncomfortable silence. The *frumentarii* were one of Hadrian's more unwelcome and un-Roman innovations, a secret police force he used against rivals and enemies.

When nobody answered Sabinus said sternly, 'Madam, what is important now is not how this document was obtained but what it contains.'

'It is a prophecy,' Primigenius said. He paraded it around the room as if displaying it to a court. 'It has been in the lady's family for generations. It was in her possession long before the Emperor came to Britain. And, look here.' He read out the crucial lines, about the little Greek, the noose of stone. 'This lady believed herself in possession of a prophecy which foretold the Emperor's decision to build the Wall. And she resolved she was going to use it to make herself rich.' He pointed an accusing finger at Severa. 'Tell us this document is a forgery, madam, a clumsy fake.'

Brigonius saw that in fact this was a way out for Severa; if she denied the Prophecy was genuine then she would be portrayed as a foolish old woman who merely got lucky, and she might, *might* walk out of here without a severe punishment. But she would not do this; Primigenius evidently knew her and her pride well.

Severa said coolly, 'Get to the point, you ridiculous snake. What is it you are accusing me of?'

'Why, of keeping from the Emperor what is rightfully his,' Primigenius said, as if it were obvious. 'If you believed this document had truly prophetic powers you should have given it up at once. The Emperor's advisers might have made use of it to advance the cause of the empire, and of the Emperor himself. Instead you kept its secret to yourself, didn't you? And you hoped to use it to amass wealth for yourself – wealth that should be the Emperor's.'

Severa turned away from Primigenius, as if in disgust, and addressed Sabinus. 'Son-in-law, you are a senator now. Can you not think for yourself? Can't you see what is happening here? All this business of secrets and lies, of jealousy and theft – it is the paranoia of the Emperor writ large, as if we were all living inside his head!'

Lepidina had her eyes downcast. She had never reminded Brigonius more of the subdued girl of the days of her visit to the north. 'Mother, I don't imagine that insulting the Emperor is going to help your case.'

'What case?' Severa shouted. 'I ask you again, Sabinus – am I on trial here?'

'Enough,' Primigenius said sharply. 'I take it you don't deny the charge I have made against you.' Without giving her a chance to answer he turned to Sabinus. 'Senator, I suggest we cut this short and proceed to the matter of her repentance.'

Severa snapped, 'And what is this *repentance*? More euphemisms?'

Sabinus said heavily, 'Madam, it is this or a full trial. This or the penalty of the state. This or the Emperor's wrath.'

She glared at him, but fell silent. Sabinus nodded to Primigenius.

The freedman produced a wax tablet. 'I have had your finances investigated, Claudia Severa. Thanks to this Prophecy of yours you have made yourself wealthy. I am not vindictive; none of us is. I propose that it will be a sufficient act of redemption for you to pledge all you have earned to the Emperor.'

'All I have earned?'

Primigenius read out a quick summary of his estimation, and then gave a total: 'In excess of one million sesterces.'

There was a startled silence. It was a total, Brigonius knew, equivalent to the property requirement of a senator in Rome.

'Your estimate is excessive,' Severa said.

'Well, you would say that, wouldn't you?' Primigenius tapped his wax tablet with a manicured forefinger. 'But it's all here.'

'Whatever is true,' Sabinus said, 'if you can pay this sum to the imperial treasury, mother-in-law, then no more will be said.'

'I cannot,' she said. 'Even if I had earned all that I could not, for much of it is spent.'

'On luxuries?' Primigenius scoffed.

'On my children,' Severa said.

At that word Lepidina looked up, shocked. Brigonius had thought she was an only child; evidently Lepidina had thought so too. What was this mention of children? ...

Primigenius was closing in for the kill, and his words, delivered steadily, were relentless. 'Then from this moment on you are a debtor, madam. And you can't cover your debts, can you? You know the law. You will have to sell everything you own. But even that will not be enough, will it? *You will have to sell yourself.* You will end your days a slave. For that is the law.'

Lepidina shuddered, and Brigonius knew that if not for her own marriage she would have shared her mother's fate.

But Severa was not defeated yet. 'This has nothing to do with the Emperor, does it? This is all because I out-manoeuvred you over the building of the Wall all those years ago, Primigenius. Have you waited this long for revenge? Do you have a list of victims you score off one by one as the years go by?'

'"Children",' Lepidina said slowly. 'You said "children"'.' She looked up at her mother with grave eyes.

Severa took a breath. 'All right. I have a son. A marriage before your father, Lepidina. He was a fool, a drunkard, he got himself killed in a brawl. The son he left me isn't much better. But he is your half-brother, and he has children of his own. My grandchildren. I support them, Lepidina. And if I can't do that any more—'

Primigenius eyed Lepidina. 'Are these grandchildren pretty? They may fetch a better price than a leathery old boot like you.'

Lepidina said coldly, 'You have always manipulated me. You have used me to further your own ends. Now I learn you have lied to me, all my life.'

Severa said, 'Lepidina, regardless of the past, help me now.'

Lepidina turned away.

Primigenius tutted softly. 'More enemies, Severa. Even among your own blood?'

Severa turned to Brigonius. 'You are a decent man. Help me.'

Brigonius recoiled. But he reminded himself that beneath her hard skin there beat a human heart – and she was Lepidina's mother. He said to the freedman, 'She may hold assets your list does not cover, Primigenius. She has invested in my own partnership, for instance.'

Sabinus leaned forward. 'Perhaps you're unfamiliar with the finer points of Roman law, Brigonius.' He seemed pleased to be able to put this old lover of Lepidina's in his place. 'If one is in debt one cannot sell on shares. So her holding in your partnership, and any others, is worthless to her. Do you understand, Brigonius? Do you have anything else to say?'

Even now Severa was unable to look Brigonius in the eye.

And as Brigonius hesitated Primigenius leered at him. 'Don't let her sell you to me again, *Brittunculus*. Once was enough.'

Brigonius stared at Primigenius and promised himself that he would, some day, somehow, take his own revenge on the freedman. He said, 'You always did make unnecessary enemies, Claudia Severa. It is a character flaw.'

Severa sneered and turned away. Even now she retained her composure. 'Primigenius, you will not win, whatever you do to me. You are a slave, the son of a slave. I am more than that; my family is more. Our future is secured whatever you do to me, for we have the Prophecy.'

The freedman grinned. 'Oh, this old thing?' He held the Prophecy casually, waving it in the air – and he wafted it over the naked flame of a lamp. 'But your grandchildren will have no need of prophecies. As slaves they will never make a decision for themselves again. Besides, in a generation or two your descendants will be illiterate. Whatever is not written down cannot survive.' He began to feed the Prophecy into the flame. 'And the last vestige of this dreadful old curse will be gone for ever.'

Brigonius saw how the burning Prophecy's flame lit up the horrified eyes of Lepidina. And Severa's face showed grief, guilt, and fear – fear of a future now forever unknown.

III

EMPEROR
AD 314–337

I

The gold mine at Dolaucothi was a wilderness of quarries and shafts and crude shacks, its air thick with dust and acrid smoke. It was the sheer extent of the digging that was so overwhelming. The ripped-up ground covered square miles. There must have been thousands of toiling workers here, all of them filthy, bent and dressed in rags, and even more of them tunnelling like moles underground.

Thalius was a man of letters, based in Camulodunum. He had had no idea such places as this existed; the mine, stranded in the untamed country of the west, struck him as a vision of the Christian Hell that not even the most inventive court theologian could have conjured up. And as the mine overseer, a plump little man called Volisios, escorted him through the workings, Thalius was very glad of the scented cloth he pressed over his nose, and of the massive presence of old soldier Tarcho at his side.

But somewhere among the wretches here, Thalius believed, was the boy he had come to find: a slave and the son of slaves, yet a distant cousin of Thalius's, and a boy who might hold the key to past and future.

'This is the only gold mine in all the Britains,' overseer Volisios boasted. 'You can see we work open-cast and by tunnelling underground. That's where the boy is, down in the deep shafts. I'll take you down there in a moment.'

'I can't wait,' growled Tarcho.

Thalius pointed to the wall of a fort, situated on a rise a way away from the churned-up ground of the mine itself. 'You have the army close by, I see.'

'To deter brigands and barbarians,' Volisios said.

'And perhaps to keep your own workers in order?'

Volisios frowned. Aged perhaps forty, some ten years younger than Thalius and Tarcho, he was a small, rotund man with shaven head and plucked eyebrows – an oily man, Thalius thought, slippery. He clearly didn't know what to make of Thalius, and his story of looking for a particular slave boy. Why would one of the curia of one of the most significant towns in all four Britains come to a place like this, if not to spy, sniff around, look for evidence of tax avoidance and other evasions? And so he squirmed and wriggled as he sought to conceal the petty graft Thalius had no doubt existed. Volisios said, 'You must understand that the workers wouldn't be here at all if they weren't scum, or the spawn of scum – and it's the devil's own job to keep them in order.'

Tarcho grunted. 'And it looks as if the devil has had his hands full.' He pointed.

On a ridge close to the fort Thalius saw a row of crosses, each eight or ten feet tall, stark shapes silhouetted in the afternoon light. Rags appeared to be dangling from their frames.

'You can see from the state of those corpses that it's a while since we had any trouble, and just as well for my purse.' Volisios began to talk of the cost of the last petty uprising. Those who ran this mine did so under licence, for Dolaucothi was an imperial estate, and from their profits its managers had to contribute to the upkeep of the fort and its soldiers. 'We even pay for the wood on which the miscreants are crucified,' he grumbled. 'But we get by. I've run this mine for twenty years, as did my father, and his father before him ...'

It was a typical story. Many professions had long been made hereditary, as had Thalius's own position on Camulodunum's curia. People joked that everybody took his father's job nowadays – everybody but the emperors, who killed other people's fathers to take *their* job.

'My father worked this place in the time of the Emperor Carausias,' Volisios went on. 'He kept working right through the time of the Roman Invasion too. That didn't bother him, but he never got over the way the taxes were hiked up afterwards!'

'Carausias was no emperor but a usurper,' Thalius felt compelled to remind him. 'The purpose of the Invasion was to remove him. And of course taxes are higher now. Things have changed since the days of Hadrian, you know.'

Volisios looked confused. 'Who?'

'An emperor from ancient history,' Tarcho said. 'From a hundred years ago!'

'More like two hundred,' Thalius corrected him mildly. He pointed. 'You'll have to take those crosses down. The Emperor has banned crucifixion.'

'He has? Why?'

Tarcho said heavily, 'Why do you think? Because the Christ was executed on a cross.'

Volisios raised barely visible eyebrows at Thalius. 'Everybody is a theologian now, isn't that true?'

'No doubt,' Thalius said, 'those in your charge will be glad to hear the news.'

'Perhaps I won't tell them until I have to;' Volisios said, and he winked. 'Keep the bastards guessing – eh?'

Thalius looked again at the ugly crosses, and thought how strange it was that his own quest to do service to the man who had once died on such a cross had, in such a complicated fashion, brought him to this dismal place.

Volisios glanced up at the sky, where heavy clouds were clustering. 'Now, gentlemen, I think we'd better go underground. Believe me you don't want to be down there when it rains ... Come, come this way. Watch your step, mind.'

He led them across broken ground to the mouth of a tunnel which gaped, black.

II

Thalius descended into the dark, climbing down ladders and staircases roughly cut into bare rock. He was over fifty years old and he felt stiff, awkward; he was unused to physical exertion. Again he was grateful for the presence of Tarcho, who went on below him.

'You'd think they would have some better way of getting important people down here,' Tarcho said. 'A nice wide staircase perhaps. Or a bucket on a rope!'

Volisios called up, 'It's rare anybody comes down if they don't have to.'

Tarcho said, 'If I was younger I'd sling you over my shoulder, Thalius.'

'I'll manage, Tarcho. Just be there to catch me if I fall.'

'I'll throw down the overseer so you'll have a soft landing!'

At last they reached the base of the chain of staircases. As Thalius and Tarcho caught their breaths, Volisios summoned a worker and whispered to him. The man ran off into the dark.

Thalius found himself standing on the rough-cut floor of a cave dug into the ground by the hands of men. There was a sound of running water, a stink of damp, and an unrelenting grind of wood on metal. The only light came from smoky oil lamps fixed to the walls. The place was hot, the smell of smoke strong; he had heard that the miners set fires to break up the rocks.

More shabby workers toiled here. Some of them hauled wooden carts laden with rock fragments; others watched the rest, holding whips and clubs, but the foremen were as grimy as those they controlled. Thalius saw passageways cut into the rock, leading off into a greater darkness. The passages were narrow, some not even tall enough for a man to stand upright, yet workers laboured there too.

That grinding, mechanical noise sharpened. Thalius peered up. In the shadows above his head vast wheels turned.

Volisios spoke with some pride of his family business. 'You can tell we've lots of water to play with here. We're served by two reservoirs. Up on the surface we use it for "hushing", washing off dirt and soil from ore outcrops, and down here to rinse away the bits of broken rock. Of course the deep galleries tend to flood, but we actually use running water to pump them out. See the waterwheels over your head? Their power hauls water from the sump up to the surface.'

Thalius was fascinated by the wheels in the air. He had always been intrigued by technology. 'Once I saw a water-organ playing in an amphitheatre in Gaul. Most remarkable thing I ever saw. Now I feel I'm trapped inside an even bigger machine.'

Tarcho pointed at the galleries. 'Those look awfully tight to me.'

Volisios eyed the old soldier's bulk with a touch of malice. 'Oh, if you were sent to work under me I'd soon thin you down. You find gold in veins in the quartz, and we make the passages no wider than the veins themselves. It's all to do with economy, you see.' He talked about other details of mining processes, in which the extracted ore was crushed and then panned in rocking wooden cradles, leaving tiny particles of gold to be captured by filters made of sheep's wool.

'I hear that in Germany,' Thalius cut in, 'they dig shafts in the ground to bring air to the tunnels. Not here?'

Volisios shrugged. 'It would cost too much.'

'But your miners must die in these holes in the ground.'

'They die anyway,' Volisios said, businesslike. 'You have to balance the cost of cutting the shafts against the cost of the labour.'

Tarcho said, 'Slaves aren't as cheap as they once were.'

'That's true. But convicts are always plentiful,' Volisios said. 'Always plenty more evaders for the tax inspectors to find and shove away down here.'

Thalius turned away. 'I can see why children are so useful to you in those rat runs – even if their little fingers have trouble picking apart the quartz, eh?'

Volisios faced him, cunning and caution in his eyes. 'You're judging me, aren't you? I'm only trying to make a living. This is a place of business, not an orphanage.'

'Perhaps you should bring me the boy now.'

Volisios glanced over his shoulder, and Thalius saw that the man the overseer had summoned earlier was standing in the shadows some way away, waiting. A smaller figure stood beside him, his thin arm held in the man's grip. Volisios snapped his fingers, and the man approached, pulling the boy with him. The boy didn't resist, but his limbs were loose, his head turned away; he was sullen, passive. 'This is the one

211

you're looking for,' Volisios said. 'As far as we can tell, anyhow.'

Thalius felt his heart hammer.

The boy was brought into a pool of lamplight before him. Dressed in a rag, the boy was perhaps twelve, but he was so malnourished and skinny it was hard to tell. His joints were as lumpy as bags of walnuts, and his ribs under his ragged clothing were prominent enough to count. He was filthy, his face streaked with black. But despite that his oval face had a certain beauty, and the strawberry-blond colour of his hair showed through matted dirt.

Tarcho asked Volisios, 'What's his name?'

'Audax,' said the overseer bluntly. A common slave's name. 'He won't know anything about his family,' Volisios warned. 'He'd have been taken from his mother as soon as he was weaned.'

'If only I could see his face more clearly,' Thalius said. He bent to the boy and cupped his chin, meaning to lift his head. But Audax flinched, and Thalius realised that some of the marks around his mouth were bruises, not dirt. Thalius stepped back, uncertain how to proceed.

If Thalius was right about this boy's lineage, he came from a branch of his own family that had been cast into slavery for nearly two centuries.

When he had become interested in the ancestral legend of a lost Prophecy, he had traced the family history back to a bifurcation in the reign of Hadrian, when a brother of his own grandmother many-times-removed, Lepidina, had been sold with his mother (and Lepidina's), a woman called Severa, into slavery. Thalius knew he was fortunate that Lepidina had been spared that fate or he too would have been born a slave – if he had been born at all. Then Thalius had worked forward once more, tracing the fate of slaves and the children of slaves. Romans always kept good records, and even the tallying of slave transactions was surprisingly complete – but then, once the empire's expansion had been halted under Hadrian and the supply of new captives from conquered territories had dried up, slaves had become a commodity worth recording. At last he had followed the thread of lineage here, to this boy, Audax – who, if he was correct, was the very last of the line from that brother of Lepidina's.

If his research was accurate, then if any scrap of the old Prophecy had survived, it would be in the form of this hapless slave boy. But somehow Thalius had never quite worked out what he would do when faced with the boy himself.

'Let me try,' Tarcho said. He lumbered forward massively, and knelt before the boy. He spoke softly, in a variety of tongues; perhaps one of them was a British dialect, the native tongue of Audax's ancestors, and Thalius's. The boy didn't look up, but at least he didn't flinch as he had from Thalius.

Nodding reassuringly, the old soldier took the boy's left hand and then the right, inspecting the palms and nails. He ran his hands along the boy's arms and legs, and brushed through the boy's matted hair – Thalius could see lice squirming – looked into his mouth, and ran a hand over his belly and back. It was a brisk inspection he might give a dog. The boy had evidently been through this sort of thing before and submitted passively.

Then Tarcho turned the boy around and lifted up the rag that served him as a tunic. 'Thalius. I think you'd better come see this.'

Thalius stepped forward. The boy's bare back was a mass of purple-red scarring. Thalius recoiled in disgust and turned on Volisios. 'He has been beaten, and savagely by the looks of it.'

Volisios glared back. 'If he has it's nothing to do with me.'

'No,' Tarcho said firmly. 'Thalius, look again. These are not the marks of a whip. See this circle, the curve here.'

The marks crudely etched into the boy's flesh were letters: Latin letters, roughly arranged in a square array.

P E E O
N E R R
O S R I
A C T A

As they stared, the boy turned his head, a spark of curiosity showing in his eyes for the first time since he had been brought here. Thalius wondered if he even knew he had been carrying around a message inscribed on his back, perhaps all his life.

III

Thalius was profoundly relieved to get back above ground, even if the climb left him winded.

Volisios escorted Thalius and Tarcho to his site office, a mudbrick block a little better appointed than the rest of the shacks here. Tarcho took the boy away to clean him up and inspect him a bit more closely. Thalius was happy to leave the boy in Tarcho's hands. Tarcho was no doctor but he had commanded soldiers in the field, and knew a little basic anatomy and medicine.

While he waited Thalius wanted only to rest, too exhausted even to speak. Respecting this, Volisios served Thalius with some watered-down wine, a rather rough British-grown vintage, and turned to some paperwork.

Thalius reflected on how lucky he was to have Tarcho's support. Tarcho was in his fifties, about the same age as Thalius himself, but a greater contrast between the two men was hard to imagine. Thalius was a man of property and business. He ran a pottery partnership, selling cups and plates to the army. It was a business that had been in the family for generations. He wasn't as rich as he might have been, however, for he had also inherited his father's position on the Camulodunum town council, the curia. His responsibilities for tax collection, upkeep of the town walls and other civic duties were onerous and expensive – which was, of course, why they had been made compulsory and hereditary.

By contrast Tarcho, descended from a long line of soldiers of German origin, was a pillar of a man, calm, solid and stolid, with a ferocious crimson beard now laced with grey. He had served most of his twenty-five years in a garrison on Britain's eastern shore – though some of those years had been accumulated under the reign of Carausias, the notorious usurper. It had been a pragmatic gesture by Constantius Chlorus, leader of the great Roman Invasion of Britain nearly twenty years ago, to have decreed that if soldiers like Tarcho were prepared to

214

switch sides, their service under Carausias would count towards their retirement privileges.

But what was a retired Tarcho to do? He was unmarried. He was too restless to farm, and too scrupulous to serve as some tax collector's hired thug. So he had come to Camulodunum looking for more suitable work, and through friends of friends had run into Thalius, who had been on the look-out for a dependable bodyguard. Thalius had certainly been glad of his company as he had ventured out of the safety of Camulodunum's walls and made this journey to the far west, travelling through one of the four British provinces and into another.

A contrasting pair they might have been, but Tarcho had become a right-hand man to Thalius, a sounding board as much as protective muscle. Both childless bachelors, their company was congenial. And they were united, and divided, by a shared religion: Christianity. On their travels the two of them had had long and interesting debates on the nature of the faith. But then, as Volisios had remarked, everybody was a theologian nowadays.

Tarcho's expressions of his tough creed had actually crystallised for Thalius his own doubts about the new Emperor, and the direction he was taking the faith. It was these doubts, in fact, which had brought Thalius to this mine – and what he hoped to achieve here was but a step towards his own ultimate goal, a confrontation over the direction of Christianity with the Emperor himself.

Christianity was a long-standing passion within Thalius's family, said to go back centuries to Lepidina daughter of Severa, who had lived not long after the death of Christ Himself. Thalius's faith was of an old-fashioned sort, a faith of love and hope, his community united in charitable associations of mutual aid – a faith derived from the teachings of Christ Himself, Thalius liked to believe. Tarcho, though, was a Christian of the new type. Like his Emperor's, Tarcho's was a robust soldier's faith, his god a warrior who had proved His mettle by beating off other deities in battle. It was this metamorphosis of Christianity into a military creed he could no longer recognise that Thalius, gravely concerned, had been forced to reject. But the new direction came from the Emperor himself. What was a man of conscience to do?

When he heard that the Emperor was coming to Britain to do some troop-raising, an idea had struck Thalius, a seed planted in his mind. The Emperor would receive audiences – and so why, then, shouldn't Thalius himself be received, and make his doubts known? Any rational ruler would surely accept the ideas and viewpoints of those he aspired to rule. Why not Thalius?

But as soon as he conceived this thrilling idea he was plagued by doubt. Was he taking himself too seriously? Who was he, a member of a mere provincial curia, to comment on imperial policy?

That was when, casting around for a way forward, it occurred to Thalius to turn to the old family story of the Prophecy, the lost poem of the future. It was a forlorn hope that he might recover it, perhaps, but even in these days of bleed-you-white taxes Thalius was prosperous enough to afford to be able to indulge a fascination for family history. And in a time of such uncertainty, if the Prophecy really did contain a glimpse of the true future it was worth a try to find it. With its authority behind him – always assuming the Prophecy existed, and could be found, and was worth presenting – perhaps he would have an excuse to face an emperor and his court, and the courage to do it.

It was spurious, perhaps, and not even very logical, but it was a plan, a strategy, and he had followed it through this far. And after all it was the family story, passed down from long-dead Lepidina, that the Prophecy actually had something to do with the destiny of Christianity. If that was true – if he could decode it and apply its message, if he could relay its truth to the Emperor himself, Thalius told himself with a kind of breathless anticipation – he might do mankind a great service indeed.

His strength recovering, and as Tarcho had still not come back with the boy, Thalius felt a little restless. He put down his cup and, under Volisios's uneasy stare, prowled around the room.

It was a working office heaped with paperwork. One pile of lawyers' letters was weighted down with a bit of quartz shot through with gold, a pretty stone brought up from the earth no doubt at the cost of much human suffering. There were few personal touches, but there was a small *lararium*, a household shrine, with tokens to gods Thalius didn't recognise. But in among this pagan clutter there was a rough Christian fish symbol, a brooch done in a bit of bronze wire. Such mixings-up of creeds were common. Despite the Emperor's promotion of the faith Christianity wasn't compulsory, paganism not a crime, and Rome's cheerful pantheism was, for now, able to absorb Jesus as just another god.

The most interesting item in the room was a framed set of coins. They had been struck during the reign of Carausias, and showed the usurper's proud profile alongside the legitimate continental emperors he had claimed as his 'brothers', and icons that portrayed him as a fulfilment of Virgilian prophecies of a saviour of Rome.

Volisios was still watching him uneasily.

'So,' Thalius said, 'you were a supporter of Carausias?'

'Never,' Volisios said quickly. 'I just collect the coins. They are already

216

rare, and quite valuable. Just think! The coins of a British emperor. That's all this is, Thalius, a coin collection.'

Thalius had never been one for bear-baiting. 'Oh, you needn't worry, man. I'm no government spy. Though I've no doubt you've plenty of murky secrets – what, a coin hoard? A few sons secreted away to evade the labour levies?'

Volisios shrugged. 'Doesn't everybody try to get away with a little? The taxes these days are too much to bear. And it's all corrupt anyhow.'

'You're right about that,' Thalius said grudgingly. 'Too many are on the take. The Emperor is coming to Britain to raise troops for his war with Licinius.' Licinius ruled the eastern half of a sundered empire. 'But I'm hoping that while he is here he will do something to clean up our civic life.'

'And lower these wretched taxes,' Volisios said.

'Oh, I doubt even the Emperor will be able to manage that,' Thalius said dryly, and he turned back to the coin images of the doomed usurper.

Thalius remembered the rule of Carausias well; he had been in his twenties when Carausias took power. The man had commanded the British fleet, responsible for intercepting Saxon pirates as they sailed across the sea from north Germany. It turned out he was allowing the raiders through, then robbing them as they tried to return home. When the provincial government not unreasonably challenged this policy, Carausias led his troops in rebellion. For a decade he (and later his own usurper) held off the continental Tetrarchy and ruled as emperor in Britain.

It was all very exciting, and Carausias, charismatic and imaginative, had been popular. His island domain was a British Empire sustained by sea power, with a 'Rome' of its own at Londinium, and Thalius, rather thrilled, had wondered if this was a glimpse of the future.

But the hard truth was that for Thalius, at that time a young man assuming his own burdens as part of the curia of Camulodunum, a change of hierarchy at the top of society had made no practical difference. And the fragile rebellion had been decisively crushed when Constantius Chlorus led his massive Invasion of Britain, and reclaimed the island.

Ironically Constantius Chlorus was destined to be the father of another British-based usurper. Constantius had been one of the Tetrarchy, a college of four emperors who ruled jointly – a system optimistically designed to stabilise the imperial succession that was never likely to survive the abdication of its founder, Diocletian. On

217

Constantius's death the British army elevated his son at Eburacum. After a complicated series of political, dynastic and military conflicts, the son had become master of the west, though he still faced his rival in the east. But, of course, as a winner he was no longer regarded as a usurper.

Few of Thalius's friends had studied history as he had, and few knew that poor, charismatic, doomed Carausias had been only the latest of a series of usurpers across the empire. The first British-based usurper had been a governor, African-born Clodius Albinus, who, seventy years after Hadrian, took the British garrison to the continent, only to be destroyed by the emperor Septimius Severus. Severus had split the province in two, so that no governor could ever be so powerful again. A century later Constantius Chlorus had split the provinces again; there were now no less than four Britains. But the years between Severus and Constantius had seen little peace.

Thalius had concluded you could trace all this instability at the top of the empire back to Hadrian and his Wall, completed nearly two centuries in the past.

The Wall itself had proved a durable limit to Rome's ambitions. Though Severus, conqueror of Clodius Albinus, had ventured beyond the Wall, reaching the furthest point of the highlands, his campaign dissipated on the bleak high ground – just as had Agricola's before him. The Romans had never again attempted to conquer the far north.

But there were consequences of the end of expansion. With no new provinces to plunder, the empire's only income was the taxes and levies it raised on its peoples. Meanwhile beyond the static frontiers, even in Caledonia, the barbarians had the chance to form new and more coherent federations, and were becoming an increasing threat.

So while the empire's acquisition of wealth had declined, the cost of defending it was rising – and taxes inevitably rose, generation on generation. The gentry fled their expensive responsibilities in the towns for grand estates in the country, while the poor were driven into evasion, criminality and destitution.

The army was changing too. Posted for ever at static frontiers, the troops understandably became more loyal to their local commanders than to any distant emperor – and generals who had once looked beyond the borders of the empire for glory were now forced to look inward to pursue their ambitions. These centrifugal tendencies spun off one usurper after another, even in Britain. It had taken a new breed of tough, ruthlessly competent soldier-emperors to pull the empire out of a crisis that might have been terminal. But it seemed to Thalius that the character of the empire had been transformed in these trials – and now, under a new emperor, it might be transformed again, even more drastically.

And Thalius, amateur historian, had looked further back in time still. Many of his acquaintances imagined that Constantius's Invasion of Britain two decades ago had been the first Roman assault on the island – as if Britain had always been Roman. But there had been a history, of a sort, even before Claudius's adventure three centuries ago. Thalius had read, fascinated, of British rebels who had sought to throw off the yoke of Rome, calling themselves Brigantian or Iceni or Catuvellaunian – names Thalius had thought only referred to Roman administrative units. He had no idea what the deeper history of these lost nations might have been. He had been astonished to find in his family research that he himself was, at least partly, of Brigantian blood.

Now the British saw themselves as Romans – and if they rebelled, like Carausias, they did so within the system rather than trying to overthrow it. The people of old, his own ancestors, had had minds of a different quality from the modern, Thalius thought. He wondered how much else had been changed, or lost, in the Roman centuries.

There was a noise outside. Volisios's office had small blue-tinted glazed windows; looking out, Thalius saw a band of workers being brought up from a mine shaft and marched off to some rough barracks. As they passed they glared at the overseer's hut. Thalius shivered, despite the heavy irons that bound the slaves' legs and necks.

Volisios stood beside him. 'You don't need to be afraid of them,' he said with faint contempt. 'Most of them have been whipped so hard all their lives that even if you took their chains away they wouldn't raise a hand against you. You have to do it, you know.'

'What?'

'Treat them harshly. I know what you're thinking, that this is a brutal place. But I have to crush my slaves to get every last drop of blood out of them, because the tax men squeeze *me* for profits. It's the way things are.'

'But is this the only way?' Thalius murmured, suddenly appalled by Volisios's bloodless rationalising.

Volisios looked at him blankly. 'Of course it's the only way. This is the way things are. This is the way they have always been, and always will be.'

'Must they, overseer?' Thalius, if unworldly, was an imaginative, deep-thinking man, and it had been a day of vivid impressions for him: the hellish conditions of the mine, the miserable condition of his slave cousin, the mighty churning engines in the mine shaft. Now he plucked a speculation out of the air. 'Consider this. Down there you have men digging out ore, and waterwheels pumping out the shafts. What if you installed more waterwheels, and used *them* to dig out your ore?'

'Impossible,' Volisios said immediately.

'Not to an engineer ingenious enough to make a water-powered organ, surely. *What if the mine could mine itself*, as an amphitheatre organ plays without human hands? Can't you see it? With such a source of wealth, isn't it possible that the empire could grow rich again, rich and strong – and nobody would have to suffer for it?'

Volisios frowned. 'Are you a fan of gadgets, then, Thalius? I myself have always been drawn more to *episteme* than to *techne* – true, deep knowledge rather than to low cunning and trickery.'

Thalius was irritated by this Greek-quoting snobbery. 'Must we be so limited in our thinking? I'm more interested in a single waterwheel than a thousand long-dead Greek philosophers!'

'Well, that's up to you.'

'Yes, but what if—?'

'Besides, what would we do with all the slaves? Free them? They would butcher us in a heartbeat.' And, laughing, Volisios turned away.

Thalius peered out of the window, listening to the grinding noise of the giant machines deep underground and the groans of human misery, and his rudimentary vision of a technological future evaporated.

At last Tarcho brought in the boy.

IV

Audax had been washed, that pale hair cut and brushed, and he was dressed in a fresh tunic. He was probably as clean and presentable as he had ever been in his life, Thalius reflected. But he was nothing but skin and bones, and there were marks, like the bruising around his mouth, that no amount of water would wash away. But Audax clung to Tarcho's hand, and Thalius saw that Tarcho was finding a way to win his trust.

It struck Thalius that he had not yet heard the boy speak, not one word.

'Apart from that scarring on his back his health is reasonable,' Tarcho said now. 'Nothing a bit of sunshine and some decent food wouldn't cure.' He said more cautiously, 'He has some bruising around the thighs, however. His mouth and throat are damaged, and—'

'Enough,' Thalius snapped.

Tarcho said to the overseer, 'I know what goes on in these places. A pretty boy like this will be traded for a morsel of food.'

Volisios said, 'What did you expect? But things are more complicated than you probably understand, soldier. The men, trapped in the dark and the damp, turn to each other for comfort, for there is nothing else. Why, some of our longer-lasting workers have "marriages" that have fared better than my own! This boy may have been hurt, but he's just as likely to have been treated with kindness.' But he didn't look at the boy as he said this, or ask him to confirm or deny it.

Thalius asked carefully, 'And the marks on his back?'

Tarcho nodded to the boy. Audax turned around and lifted up his tunic, exposing skinny legs, flat buttocks, and a back covered with livid scars. But now the dirt was off Thalius could clearly see the shapes of the letters, sixteen of them, in their square grid:

Tarcho scratched his head. 'And is this what you came looking for?'

'It must be.'

'The boy has no memory of having received this tattoo.'

'I'm not surprised,' Thalius said. 'See how the letters are stretched, distorted? He must have received these markings when he was very small, an infant perhaps. As he has grown the marks have grown with him. Perhaps the marks were copied from his own father at his birth, and his father before him ...' Thalius imagined it: a slave painfully pricking out letters into the raw skin of his child, perhaps with a bit of quartz from the gold seams, and rubbing in dirt or vegetable dye.

It had been the curse of Severa's sentence to slavery that her grandchildren would not even be literate. So with the Prophecy burned, its words would be lost after a generation, two, three. But evidently, Thalius thought, excited, somebody had come up with a way of preserving at least some of the text, inscribed into the very bodies of children. Thalius had read something of Severa, his remote grandmother of so many generations ago; perhaps it was that hard woman herself who had come up with this way of saving the Prophecy in blood and pain.

Volisios had become a lot less respectful since Thalius had admitted he was no government inspector. 'So you have what you wanted. What will you do with the boy? Throw him back down into the pit? Or would you like him to warm your own bed first?'

'You disgust me,' Thalius snapped.

But Tarcho said, 'Actually he has a point, Thalius. Slaves are expensive, you know .'

'He is blood,' Thalius said. 'Distant blood, but blood. I won't leave him here to be raped to death. Name your price, overseer.'

Volisios nodded and, business-like, reached for a wooden note block and a pen.

The boy watched all this, wide-eyed; surely he hadn't understood a word.

Tarcho studied the tattoo again. 'But what does it mean?'

'I don't know. Not yet. It's clearly some kind of acrostic.'

'A what? Never mind. And where will this quest of yours lead us next?'

'To Rutupiae.'

'The east coast? What for? Who will be there?'

Thalius said simply, 'Constantine.'

V

It would take many days for Thalius, Tarcho and Audax to travel from Dolaucothi in the west of Britain all the way to Rutupiae in the extreme east, where Thalius intended to gain an audience with the Emperor. With the boy in Tarcho's care they set off, the three of them in Thalius's cart.

Once they had crossed the Sabrina river they passed out of what Tarcho called 'soldier country', where wild men of the hills chased flocks of ragged sheep between the walls of Roman forts, to the more settled lands of the south and east. The cart rolled along busy, well-maintained roads through farmland – rather a lot of it abandoned.

On the way to Durovernum Cantiacorum and Rutupiae they stopped in towns, including a night in Londinium. All the towns looked the same, with their basilicas and their forums, their baths and their townhouses: all miniature models of faraway Rome itself. But many of the public buildings had seen better days. Shabby old basilicas had been turned into granaries or stock sheds or arms dumps, and sometimes you could see fire damage nobody had bothered to fix. Even in Londinium there was a monumental basilica only half finished and apparently abandoned; entwined by vines and carpeted by grass and weeds it seemed to be turning into a ruin before it had even been completed. And a new wall ran along the north side of the river, cutting through the wharves and dock facilities that had once served the grand cross-provincial trade routes. People, over-taxed, just didn't put their money into civic developments the way they once had. Most wouldn't even pay to keep the public sewers working, or to clear away rubbish. As a result, the towns stank.

And all the towns had walls: massive thick barricades with cores of rubble and concrete and imposing facing stones. Thalius knew all about fortifications like this; even at Camulodunum, always a walled

223

town, the cost of the renovations of the town's defences had fallen heavily on the curia.

Times had changed since the days when the towns had been planned. The country was a lot more dangerous now, as organised bands of barbarian raiders came breaking through the northern Wall, or sailing across the Ocean. There were plenty of home-grown brigands too. From top to bottom, with everyone tied to their jobs from birth, society was static. But when your farm failed, when the taxes and levies got so tough your land wasn't economical to cultivate any more, you had nowhere to go. Many farmers had just slunk off into the night, to become part of a growing underclass of poachers and bandits living beyond the law.

The towns were like hedgehogs, Thalius thought, their old, shabby buildings huddling behind massive walls that had taken generations to pay for and build, bristling nervously in a dangerous, depopulating countryside. Thalius knew enough history to see how strange this would have seemed to a citizen of Hadrian's time. The towns were no longer centres of commerce and culture; they were like fortified prisons for a trapped population.

But in all the towns there were a few grand new houses, rising up out of the rubble of older developments. In an age when the tax system was squeezing everybody tight, it was still possible to get rich, if you were a landowner buying up the failed properties of the marginalised, or a government stooge on the make.

As they rode, Thalius watched the boy.

He wondered how much Audax understood of what was happening to him. The boy spoke only when asked a direct question, and even then in a guttural, vocabulary-poor British tongue that even Tarcho had difficulty understanding. Surely it had sunk in that Thalius had saved him from the mine, that Thalius was his distant relative. But the boy seemed distrustful, perhaps because Thalius had been so obviously interested in the message he carried, not in *him*.

The boy's head seemed to be a jumble. Certainly Audax had no idea who the Emperor was. Why should he? The brutes with whips who had run his life in the mine had had far more power over him than Constantine, even the power of life and death. He hadn't even seen the cycles of daylight for much of his young life, and in open spaces, crossing abandoned fields or moorland, he would cower, as if longing for the safe enclosure of the grimy walls that had confined him.

Audax stuck to Tarcho, though. The big soldier in turn was careful never to raise his voice to the boy. Thalius thought that with Tarcho's support there might be hope for the boy yet; he was still young, and had time. And as for Tarcho he seemed to be developing a duty of care towards this helpless, half-formed child. What did that say about Tarcho? That he should have had children, Thalius thought.

And it was this fragile boy Thalius was going to present to an emperor, he thought, his nervousness growing the closer they got to Rutupiae.

He had a way in, of sorts. When he had heard Constantine was returning to Britain he had written to a friend of a friend of a friend in the imperial court, one Ulpius Cornelius, pulling in favours in the Roman way, to request an audience during the Emperor's stay. Constantine had begun his career as a soldier, and as a consequence many of his advisors were soldiers. Cornelius was no exception; he had once been a senior army officer, and now served as a prefect under Constantine, one of the inner circle who ran the empire.

Somewhat to Thalius's surprise, this Ulpius Cornelius had responded to Thalius's letter with a note inviting him to come to the court at Rutupiae, soon after Constantine's landing. And so here was Thalius travelling to confront an emperor – not for himself, not even for the good of the empire, but for Christ.

But what was he going to say to Constantine? Distracted by his own deep thinking, and by a gathering dread of his meeting with the Emperor, Thalius failed to puzzle out the Prophecy-acrostic on poor Audax's hide, its dense pattern of letters mocking his ageing mind.

VI

As Thalius and his companions neared Rutupiae they crawled along a road crowded with carts, horses and pedestrians, with officials and civilians, rich and poor, here on business or for a once-in-a-lifetime chance to see an emperor in the flesh.

Thalius's heart lifted as it always did when they first glimpsed the Ocean, glimmering in the east. There was something magnificently primal about the Ocean, something you couldn't tame, even to the extent that you could tame the land by slicing it up into farms and studding it with cities. It was odd for a town-dweller like Thalius to feel that way, perhaps, a man whose whole life depended absolutely on the continuance of order, but there it was.

Of course even the Ocean had changed. Once the Ocean had been thought of fondly by the British as a great moat, mightier than any of Hadrian's works, which excluded the barbarians who caused such havoc in Gaul and Roman Germany. But now the Ocean was less a barrier to brigands than a highway for them to travel over.

Thalius had read that there were reasons for these 'Saxons' from north Germany to make the hazardous journey to Britain. Their narrow coastal homelands had been squeezed between vast movements of peoples from further east in the mysterious heart of Asia, and the Ocean itself which, year on year, rose inexorably higher. Thus the world was changing, reshaped by vast forces of population movements and even shifts in the tides that not even an emperor could command.

In response to this threat Rutupiae, once an open town, had become a fortress.

The fort itself was surrounded by an immense system of double ditches, and the streaming crowd had to cram itself onto a narrow causeway that approached the east gate. Ahead, thick walls with angular towers glowered down. The walls were built in the solid Roman fashion, with slave-worked concrete so strong it was said it would withstand the sea-coast weather for ever. But embedded in the walls Thalius identified fragments of broken columns, bits of statuary, even what looked like soldiers' tombstones, all smashed and reused. Thalius wondered how many people here today knew that Claudius's invasion force had once landed here, or mused on the irony that a triumphal arch commemorating that epochal landing had been demolished to build a fortress intended to repel new invaders. This was a grim age, an age of closure and huddling, not a time for grand gestures.

Still, regardless of its complicated history, today the fort was hosting Constantine himself, the Emperor of all the western provinces, ruler of half the known world. And on the Ocean beyond the shoulder of the fort walls Thalius glimpsed the purple sails of the ships that must have brought the Emperor and his retinue here. Thalius felt excitement grow inside him, a thrill he had barely known since he had been a child younger than Audax, waiting for the chariot races to begin in the circus outside Camulodunum.

As they passed through the fort's west gate, Thalius and his party found themselves working through an access system mediated by officials from the local towns, the provincial government, the diocese of Britannia, even the prefecture of Gaul, and from the imperial court itself. All these officials, taking the chance to make a profit out of the Emperor's visit, seemed to expect to have a coin or two stuffed in their hands for the favour of passing you through. The process was watched over by hard-faced members of the Emperor's own German bodyguard – not the Praetorians, Constantine had run down those overpaid emperor-makers – who were not averse to a few hand-outs themselves. Tarcho grumbled as he handed over yet more coins from the heavy purse he carried.

But Thalius found it impossible to be sour, despite the queuing and the petty corruption. You couldn't ignore the eagerness and anxiety, the hopes and dreams of the supplicants, for today Rome was here, on this windy British shore.

At last, thanks to his note from Ulpius Cornelius, Thalius found himself part of a crowd of petitioners drawn up before a stage, hastily erected just off the road inside the fort's western gate – a stage on which Constantine himself sat, advisers and guards at his shoulders, patiently listening to complaints and pleas.

If Thalius had expected to see a soldier on that wooden throne, he was disappointed. Constantine was a big-boned, strong-looking man in his early forties, but he wore his hair down to his shoulders, so luxuriantly blond Thalius was sure it had to be false. He was dressed in a long, flowing robe of what looked like silk, embroidered with flowery designs done in gold. Even his shoes were studded with gems. And though Thalius thought he detected a soldier's bluff amiability in Constantine's not unhandsome face, to approach him you had to go down on your knees and press your head to the floor.

He muttered, 'Why, he's not like a Roman at all. He looks like something out of Egypt or Persia. Augustus would have been horrified.'

Tarcho growled, 'He looks like what he is – the Emperor. Do you expect him to dress like a latrine cleaner? He has to put on a show. And he's a good lad, this one.' He cupped his hands and called out, 'Good on you, Constantine!'

Thalius knew that Constantine had always been popular among the British troops. After all it was they who in Eburacum, on the death of his father Constantius Chlorus, had elevated thirty-five-year-old Flavius Valerius Constantinus as the new 'Augustus', one of the college of emperors, and then had fought under him when Constantine had achieved his greatest victory so far in dislodging a rival, Maxentius, to become sole ruler in the west.

And he had won with the help of the Christian God, Constantine declared. On the night before the decisive battle outside Rome, he had a dream that the Christian God came to him. In the morning he had his troops chalk crosses on their shields. That victory had cemented God into his life, and his empire, for good.

The fruits of Constantine's conversion were visible before Thalius now. The Emperor's mother Helena travelled with him; once a concubine, she was becoming a kind of pilgrim with a mission to travel across the empire to Judea in search of relics of Christ Himself. And there were bishops among the Emperor's retinue, on the stage with him, almost as grandly dressed as he was, Thalius observed with disgust, men of wealth and power a world away from the vision of the carpenter's Son. There were cynics who muttered that it only took a mote of dust in the eye to enable anybody to see a cross in the sky, and Constantine's 'conversion' may have owed a lot to the manipulation of events by the wily bishops in his court.

And some Christians of the old school, including Thalius himself, were deeply troubled that it was a warrior deity that was being cemented into the machinery of state, not the gentler God of Christ's own teachings.

At last Thalius, his heart thumping, was beckoned forward towards Constantine's dais – but his way was blocked by the man whose response had brought him so far.

Ulpius Cornelius, aged perhaps forty, wore a purple-edged toga. He was tall, angular, thin, his hair black and swept back, his mouth small and down-turned, his prominent nose ideal for looking down on people. Before him Thalius felt poor and shabby, a low-class provincial. If Constantine looked like an eastern potentate Cornelius was every bit the classic Roman – and therefore out of place in Constantine's court.

Cornelius, consulting a list, looked Thalius over keenly. 'So you are the prophet,' he began bluntly.

'I wouldn't call myself that,' Thalius said, embarrassed and disconcerted. 'It is a legend of my family that—'

'But in your letter you did speak of a prophecy. Of specific warnings of an uncertain future, of momentous events unfolding in our lifetimes – events that might deflect the course of history forever. Yes?' His Latin was so pure it sounded strangulated.

'Sir, I am a Christian. I am here because of my concerns over the future of men's souls, not—'

'Yes, yes. But I am what is now referred to as a "pagan", what I would call a defender of Roman tradition. I have precious little interest in your slaves' cult. It is not your anguished proclamations of faith that caught my eye, citizen, but your claims about this Prophecy. I researched your family in the libraries in Rome and Alexandria. I even traced a mention in the biographies of the Emperor Claudius himself. Imagine that! And there is indeed something about a Prophecy there ... But you say the Prophecy is lost.'

'Not entirely,' Thalius said.

Cornelius raised one plucked eyebrow. Thalius was urged to say more, but he felt Tarcho touch his arm, and he stayed silent. Cornelius seemed to notice this interplay, and looked at Tarcho with new interest. He stepped closer to Thalius and spoke more quietly. 'Listen to me. Things are changing. The empire is not as our grandfathers would have recognised it, and soon it will change again, one way or another. The question is how it will change. If your Prophecy has any validity at all it may be a very powerful weapon in this time of great historical flux.'

Thalius heard only one word. '"Weapon"?'

Cornelius studied him. 'In your muddled way you want to deal with Constantine, don't you? You want to alter the course he has set himself on.'

'I'm not sure I'd put it like that—'

'You'll find you're not alone. There are many of us who have reservations about the Emperor, reservations which have nothing to do with Christ but with the traditions of Rome – and their survival, and the survival of city and empire, into the future. Do you see?'

'I think so. But I—'

'And,' Cornelius said almost wistfully, 'is it true that your Prophecy speaks of freedom? Was that truly the subject of the enigmatic final lines of which Claudius wrote? Was the unknown seer writing of a return to the freedoms of the Republic, the lifting of the heavy hand of the Caesars?'

'I wouldn't know,' Thalius said.

'Well, now I've met you I can see you aren't ready to meet the Emperor today. I will arrange another audience. In the meantime perhaps we will find time to talk. Now go.' He turned away.

Thalius, dismissed, felt crushingly disappointed he would not after all confront Constantine today; but already the processes of the court were moving on.

Tarcho snorted. 'These Romans and their foretelling – always have been a superstitious bunch!'

'But I didn't come here to conspire against Constantine.'

'Didn't you? Perhaps that stuck-up Roman saw your soul better than you see it yourself.' He pulled Thalius's sleeve. 'Let's get out of here. We've already lost our place in the line, and it doesn't do to hang around an emperor's court.'

Thalius let himself be led away. Tarcho held Audax firmly by the hand. The boy, wide-eyed, hadn't spoken through the entire exchange.

VII

Thalius, with Tarcho and Audax, joined the imperial procession from Rutupiae. The Emperor rode in a gaudily adorned litter, with his bishops flocking like exotic birds. Thalius grumbled, 'The Christ rode into Jerusalem on an ass. How He would have been appalled by the sight of those strutting fools!' Tarcho, who seemed to think of Christ and God the Father as something like a centurion and his commander, was only confused by this remark.

Constantine would visit the four provincial capitals, including the overarching diocesan capital at Londinium, and he would call at all the principal military bases, including Eburacum and the Wall forts in the north. The Emperor had many objectives. He wanted to firm up the new provincial government arrangements his father had left him, and to bed in army reforms begun by Diocletian and continued by his father. Constantine also intended that his visit would spark off a wider programme of refurbishment and renewal of the four provinces' shabby public facilities and military infrastructure.

But everybody knew that Constantine's main purpose was to detach units of British troops for his coming conflict with Licinius, Emperor of the east: he was here to take from the island, not to give. Constantine was popular in Britain, but there would be much resistance to his stripping troops from the diocese in a time of uncertainty. Constantine was wily enough to understand this. So he had come here in person, to dazzle and reassure even while he bled the island's garrisons.

After Londinium Constantine proceeded towards Camulodunum. But his route took a long detour to the north, so he could visit the fen country, an enormous quilt of farmland in the east conjured out of the sea by a vast system of dykes, canals, drainage ditches and roads – all paid for by the local people and maintained by labour levies and slaves. In older countryside the farms and settlements had grown out of communities and cultivation patterns that had been here for centuries before a Roman ever visited Britain, and so they were more disorderly, ancient, stubbornly chaotic. Here, though, the new land had been a blank canvas for the Roman planners to set down the orderly patterns they preferred, and in this utterly flat, wholly manufactured landscape the roads and dykes ran arrow-straight for mile after mile. Thalius thought that this geometric fenland was the quintessence of the obsessively disciplined Roman mind.

The reclamation wasn't perfect, however. In places Thalius saw farmers dismally scraping at soggy ground, and some farms had been abandoned to flooding altogether. If is was true that in Germany the Ocean was rising perhaps it was true here too.

During this progression one member of the imperial court deigned to join Thalius and his companions: Ulpius Cornelius. His preliminary excuse was to show Thalius a letter he had been carrying, on a folded-over slip of wood.

Thalius scanned it quickly. It was from one Claudia Brigonia Aurelia, a widow of Eburacum – and it concerned prophecies about Constantine. Thalius handed it back hastily, chilled.

Cornelius seemed to enjoy his discomfiture. 'Aurelia's family, it seems, has its own legends about prophecies and emperors. Was some ancestor of hers tangled up in the complicated stories you have told me?'

'How does she know about me?'

'Through me,' Cornelius said smugly. 'I'm a thorough man, Thalius. I told you I confirmed the existence of your Prophecy through hints in the archives. But in following it up I drew extensively on contacts in Britain. And it happened that I caught the attention of this lady Aurelia, and sparked her interest.'

'"Sparked her interest"? What does that mean, Cornelius? What does she want?'

'Why, I've no idea, not specifically. But, like you – and me – it seems she has concerns about the direction in which the Emperor is taking us all.' He grinned coldly. 'I don't think she had ever heard of you, Thalius. And yet it seems you have another member of your conspiratorial cabal.'

As from the beginning of his dealings with Cornelius, Thalius had the feeling that events were spinning out of his control. 'I don't have a conspiracy, and I don't want a cabal!'

'Then the Emperor has nothing to fear,' Cornelius said smoothly. 'And nor do you.'

It seemed to Thalius that what Cornelius really wanted of him was an ear in which to pour complaints about his own grievances. Not that those grievances weren't extensive, for somebody of Cornelius's patrician background. 'Constantine's butchery of authority and tradition has reached all the way to the heart of imperial government,' Cornelius complained, 'in fact, into his own court ...'

Constantine had created a whole new layer of aristocracy, called the 'Order of Imperial Companions'. His council, the *consistorium*, was drawn from this group. Many of the Companions were the gaudy bishops who made Thalius so uncomfortable. And by establishing the Companions Constantine had excluded the old senatorial and equestrian classes. Cornelius's family, senators since republican days, had been largely disenfranchised, and Cornelius's own position in court was precarious.

Cornelius fumed. 'Not only has Constantine violated centuries of tradition, he has casually upturned checks and balances within an imperial system that has been evolving since the days of Augustus ...' But Thalius was sure that Cornelius's concerns were not about the welfare of the empire but his own ambitions.

And it struck Thalius that Cornelius, for all his sophistication and power, was so obsessed with court intrigues and his own ambitions that he simply could not see the deeper truths of his age. After all, within Thalius's own lifetime the empire had nearly collapsed altogether. You could complain about Constantine's reforms, as Thalius did himself, but was it possible that the Emperor actually had no real choice in how he acted, if he was to hold the empire together?

CITY OF LIMERICK PUBLIC LIBRARY

VIII

The caravan at last approached the bristling walls of Camulodunum. The lead carriages came to a gate in the west wall which had once, curiously, been a triumphal arch before being incorporated into the wall, and was now mostly blocked up. Here the caravan broke up.

Thalius, happy to see the back of Ulpius Cornelius for a while, led his own companions to the townhouse he owned just a short walk from the forum. It had actually been some months since Thalius had been back to the city. Even though he had grown up here, and his affairs were closely bound up with the city, he much preferred his country estate half a day's ride out of town. Now, as he walked through a grubby, decayed town crowded with hawkers, chancers, beggars and prostitutes all drawn to the tawdry gleam of a soldier-emperor's court, Thalius was reminded why.

The grand old Temple of Claudius still stood, however, rising out of a sea of vacant lots, rotting houses, tatty public buildings and filth-strewn streets. As they passed the colonnade Thalius peered inside to see the great statue of the wily old fox, lit up by candles and lamps, his arm still raised in victory as it had been for three hundred years. But a small Christian chapel had been set up within this temple to a long-dead emperor, whose exploits had been forgotten by almost everybody who passed by this way.

Thalius was relieved to reach his own modest but well-maintained townhouse. He was too old for travelling, he thought, too old to be dealing with complicated and poisonous individuals like Ulpius Cornelius. At least within the walls of his house he could be in control of things for a while, and find some peace.

So he was dismayed to find he had a visitor, waiting for him in the living room. Sitting beneath his most expensive tapestry, a scene of a colonnaded courtyard under a bright Mediterranean sun, she was sipping watered-down wine served to her by the elderly freedman Thalius employed as a housekeeper.

She stood as Thalius approached. She was a woman of about sixty, Thalius judged, well-dressed and poised. Her cheekbones were high, her chin well-defined. Her complexion was dark, and she wore her grey-streaked black hair swept back from her face. She was unafraid of showing her age, then. She was immediately intimidating, with something of Ulpius Cornelius's air of cold command.

And she was remarkably attractive. Despite her age, there was something sensual about her, even animal, and she seemed to use the fumes of her scents as a weapon to confuse him.

Thalius, still grimy from the road, felt inadequate in his own home. He was weakened by the helpless attraction he felt for her, which she must perceive, and had no doubt calculated to inspire. Suddenly his life had become even more complicated, he thought tiredly.

'I think you know who I am, sir.' Her voice was husky.

'You must be Claudia Brigonia Aurelia. Your correspondence with Ulpius Cornelius—'

'What a helpful man he is.' She gazed at Audax, her eyes rheumy but bright. 'And this must be the mysterious slave boy.' She reached out a bony hand.

Audax cowered behind the massive form of Tarcho.

'You're frightening him.'

She looked puzzled. 'Cornelius warned me about your sentimentality. You're a Christian, aren't you? A faith of soldiers and slaves, so they say.'

'Madam, what is it you want here?'

'Why, the same thing you do, I believe. To know the future.' And she eyed the cringing boy as if wishing she could simply flay him and take his marked hide away with her.

Thalius sent the boy off with Tarcho, and ordered the housekeeper to bring more wine and plates of light food. As social routines cut in, Aurelia calmed. But she watched Thalius constantly, as an owl watches a mouse.

She told him something of herself. Born and raised in Eburacum, she had been widowed young. She had inherited her husband's business interests, and had run them herself ever since, evidently not needing the shadow of a man to win herself a place in society. Her husband's interests were an old family business of quarries in the north country, which supplied stone to army installations, including the Wall itself. And it was in the north country that the paths of their families had once crossed, she said.

'It's all family legend,' she purred. 'Tittle-tattle. But the legend is that my husband's remote grandfather, one Brigonius, was the lover of *your* remote grandmother, Lepidina. But they never married, and had no offspring.'

'And this was when?'

'Two centuries ago. At the time of the famous visit of Emperor Hadrian,' she said, sipping her wine. 'And that is how the Prophecy of Nectovelin entered the mythology of my family. I grew up fascinated by the tale. A Prophecy all one's own. Think of the power! So when I came across Ulpius Cornelius and his not-very-discreet inquiries I was fascinated.' She glanced somewhat dismissively at his expensive tapestry. 'It was a thread, I thought, a loose thread in time's tapestry that I couldn't resist tugging. And when I did it led me to you, and here we are.'

'You talk about power,' Thalius said uneasily. 'The power to do what?'

'To see where our charismatic soldier-emperor is leading us. And,' she said more coldly, 'the power to do something about it.'

Thalius flinched, but he forced himself to believe that there were no spies from the imperial court in his own home. 'What is it you don't like about Constantine?'

'That's simply answered,' she said. 'I don't like his taxes.' And, just as Cornelius had complained long and loud about Constantine's policies at the heart of the imperial government, so now Aurelia railed about the effect of the Emperor's decrees on her own position.

'You don't appear bankrupt,' Thalius broke in gently.

'No, but I soon will be at this rate! Thalius, I know you're a man of business, and in a curia, as I am. What an onerous chore it is – don't you think? Why, do you know that some criminals and evaders have actually had curia responsibilities thrust upon them as a punishment? And if you default you are beaten up by the governor's thugs. I know it happens, I've seen it! It's not surprising everybody is getting out of town if they can – as you do, Thalius, and don't deny it.'

Thalius sighed. 'I pay my dues,' he said. So he did, but he knew that what she said was true. The worst tax by common consent was the *chrysargyron*, the 'gold-and-silver' levy imposed on manufacturers and merchants, from owners of the great pottery factories right down to the humblest cobbler. Like farmers of marginal lands, small merchants were being squeezed 'until their bones cracked', Aurelia said. 'In fact literally! You must have seen it, Thalius. How the collectors summon the people from the town and country to the forum – how even children are forced to give evidence against their parents.'

'I have seen such things,' Thalius said stoically. He was well aware too of the shocking corruption that was rife in every level of the system, making it even more of a burden.

She put down her wine cup and leaned forward, her face intent. 'You have already decided I am a selfish old woman who is solely concerned about the contents of her own purse. Don't bother denying it, it's plain enough on your face. But I hope you'll see that my imagination goes beyond my own welfare. I believe that Constantine's taxes will, in the long run, lead to the ruin of us all, and I don't exaggerate. And if the system falls, I fall with it. So I'm concerned. Call it enlightened self-interest.'

It was a hard argument to refute, and Thalius had heard it rehearsed many times before. But just as in his talks with Cornelius he wondered if Aurelia had ever considered that the Emperor, crushed by rising military costs and with no other revenue sources, might have no other choice but to tax his citizens until they bled white. 'Is there any other way?'

'There may be. Do you know how my husband died? Of course you don't. He fought with Carausias. And *his* father fought under Postumus, the Gallic Emperor, twenty-five years before Carausias. Twice in living memory these islands have broken from Rome. *Why not again?* Why must Britain pay for Rome? Why must we pay for the upkeep of the Emperor's court – you've seen it, Thalius – and his bureaucracy and his extravagances and his building programme, his endless churches, churches, churches? And now there are rumours that Constantine is planning to build a new capital even farther away, in the east some-where. Why should we pay for *that*? That's what I'm asking.'

'And so,' he said carefully, 'would you oppose Constantine?'

'Ah,' she said. She smiled and leaned back languidly, quite unrea-sonably erotic. 'That's the question – and that's where your Prophecy comes in. I'm no gambler, Thalius.'

'You will oppose Constantine if you think you are sure to win. You want the reassurance of the Prophecy.'

'Isn't that your own game plan? And,' she added earnestly, 'is it true that your Prophecy speaks of freedom? Was this unknown seer, the Weaver of time's tapestry, promising the liberation of the western provinces from Constantine's oppression?'

Thalius recalled Cornelius, whose dream of freedom was the freedom to be a traditional Roman; for this British woman it was the freedom to be loose of the centre, to be British-Roman, not Roman. But surely these were fantasies imposed on tantalising phrases in a document that was, after all, lost.

'I wouldn't know about freedom,' he said dryly. 'Or the Weaver's intentions. Even the name "Weaver" is only a word that has come down from my own ancestor, as it has to you, a fragment of speculation. We know nothing about him, or her, if he even exists.'

She leaned forward. 'Well, now we understand each other, won't you bring me your slave with the tattooed hide?'

Thalius was hugely reluctant. Ever since he had met Cornelius he felt he had been taking one step after another along a very dangerous path indeed. And yet what choice did he have about it, even now?

He turned to his housekeeper, and called for the boy.

IX

Two days later in the afternoon, Thalius invited Cornelius and Aurelia
to his townhouse in Camulodunum. Thalius had arranged for his triclinium, his dining room, to be stocked with food, wine and water,
so they need not be disturbed by service. He insisted his guests leave
their attendants outside; he sent them off to the kitchen where they
would be fed and watered. And he strictly ordered his housekeeper to
keep everybody out of the room until he, Thalius, gave instructions
otherwise – and that was to include the housekeeper himself.

Cornelius mocked him. 'Oh, Thalius! You are a conspirator after
all!'

'No, I am not,' Thalius said coolly. 'But this is an age of spies. I want
nobody in the room with us who I don't know and trust.'

Aurelia smiled coldly. 'But you don't know us – and if you trust us
you are a fool.'

'But we are already locked together in complicity,' Thalius said. 'You
will not betray me for to do so would be to betray yourself. Enlightened
self-interest – was that your phrase, madam?'

Cornelius said, 'And the boy, the slave on whom the destiny of an
empire pivots?'

'I have sent him to the kitchen with Tarcho – and, incidentally, I
have instructed Tarcho to guard the boy as he has guarded me these
last eight years.'

Aurelia said, 'Why have you invited us, Thalius? What do you want
to achieve today? Have you thought it through that far?'

Cornelius rumbled, 'I doubt if any of us has.'

Thalius said, 'We appear to have a common interest. We may uncover
a common goal. Let's leave it at that for now.'

That seemed to satisfy them. For a while, in the closed and locked
room, sipping diluted wine, they were silent.

Claudia Brigonia Aurelia lay on her couch. She seemed effortlessly in control, utterly superior. Thalius was sure that the soft crossing of her ankles, the way the drapery of her dress fell about her hips and thighs and hung away from her breasts – none of it was accidental but the product of a lifetime of self-training. With such simple tools she must effortlessly dominate the men around her, even now she was growing old. He thought too of what she had told him of an unrequited love affair between their ancestors, centuries ago. Was it possible that such unsatisfied lusts could send echoes down the generations? But that was a very un-Christian thought, he decided.

Aside from her sexuality he sensed she was a natural snob, and had the manner to go with it; before her judgemental gaze he felt unreasonably ill at ease in his own home. Though her family was no better off than Thalius's, she did have an ancestry she could trace back to the Claudian conquest, the date at which British history began – but she spoke of legends of royal blood even before that. Perhaps her ancestor was a princess of Troy, for the British race was supposed to have been founded by Trojans, who, fleeing the war with the Greeks, had brought the chariots that had met Caesar. It was only as an adult that Thalius had come to challenge this imported Mediterranean legend – and to wonder what true history had been lost, what old remembered wisdom dissipated, when the ancient British nations had been obliterated by Rome.

While Aurelia sat, Cornelius carried a brimming cup of wine and walked around the *triclinium*, looking at the frescoes and the tapestry. *He* didn't seem distracted by Aurelia's charms. Perhaps, Thalius wondered, as many of Constantine's eastern-tinged courtiers were rumoured to be, Cornelius preferred to pluck his fruit from a different tree.

Thalius lumbered to his feet, picked up a jug of wine and refreshed their cups. 'In the absence of a servant I must remember my duties as a host. You're taken by that fresco, Ulpius Cornelius?'

This particular painting showed a portrait of Christ at the time of His mission, a smooth-faced man of thirty or so, His hand raised in blessing. The figure was surrounded by symbols: the *chi-rho*, a sunburst behind Christ's head, and a small acrostic in a lower corner.

'It's done well enough,' Cornelius said, rather patronisingly. 'But Christ was a fisherman in Judea, wasn't he?'

'Actually a carpenter.'

'And a rabble-rouser. He would never have worn a toga!'

Thalius smiled. 'That's what the pattern-book showed, and my artist didn't have the confidence to deviate from the design.'

'Interesting symbolism.' Cornelius tapped the *chi-rho* with a fingernail. 'I've seen this before.'

Aurelia languidly uncurled from her couch and joined them. 'It's called the Christogram. The first two letters in Christ's name in Greek, superimposed – you see?'

'I have seen this scrawled on temple walls. Even in Rome.'

Thalius said, 'A relic of the days of persecution. Such symbols as this united a community under pressure.'

'But now Christians are under pressure no more,' Cornelius said. 'And your Christogram has become a symbol of pride, yes?'

Aurelia said, 'Ah, but the Christogram is more than that. Look again, Cornelius. Haven't you seen figures rather like this in other contexts?'

Cornelius stepped back and tipped his head. 'Do you know, I have. In Egypt, I think. It is rather like the *ankh*, an ancient mystic symbol – surely much more ancient than Christianity!'

Aurelia murmured, 'As a girl I learned to write Greek. This is also rather like a sign you make when editing a passage of writing – *chi-rho* for *chreston*, which means good.'

'One symbol with many meanings, then,' Cornelius said.

'But that's intentional,' Aurelia said. 'You can scrawl a *chi-rho* on your wall; a Christian will see the Christogram, a pagan will see an Egyptian good-luck sign. It appeals to everybody and offends nobody. The Emperor's advisers are wily to encourage it.

'Constantine is a Christian. Everybody knows that. And he wishes to establish Christianity as the empire's core religion. But almost everybody else of influence – like you, Cornelius! – remains pagan. Most of the army too, despite Constantine being one of its own. Constantine, and the bishops who manipulate him, is proceeding subtly, through tools such as this clever little symbol. But, like the rain beating on your tiles, Cornelius, each drop brings you pagans closer to the day when the roof falls in.'

Thalius said, 'You seem to have thought deeply about this, madam.'

'Emperors make the weather,' she murmured. 'It is best to pay them attention. Besides I am fascinated by the sheer machination of it all.'

Cornelius said, 'Machination, yes. And there are plenty who doubt Constantine's sincerity about his conversion in the first place. How is it even possible for a good pagan to become Christian?'

'Oh, I believe he is sincere,' Aurelia said. 'And as for how he was converted, you can see it painted up here on dear Thalius's wall.'

Cornelius looked again. 'You mean the sunburst around Christ's head?'

Aurelia said, 'Constantine grew up as a *protégé* of Apollo. And some years ago he hailed the sun god, Sol Invictus, as his tutelary god. Some would identify Apollo with the sun, and others identify the sun with your Christ, Thalius: Jesus is *sol justitiae*, the sun of justice. So you see there is a progression, logical in its way, through an overlapping identity of deities, from Apollo, via the sun, to Christ. But it will be quite a challenge for the biographers to make sense of all this one day.'

Thalius felt irritated at this smug analysis. 'All this theological trickery has nothing to do with the true nature of Christ and His message.'

Aurelia just laughed.

Cornelius turned to Thalius. 'It is a little difficult to understand, good Thalius, what it is you object to about an emperor adopting your own long-marginalised faith.'

'But the faith of Constantine isn't necessarily mine,' Thalius said unhappily. 'Constantine's warrior God has nothing to do with Christ and His teachings. And the Church he is creating is a mirror of the man and his empire: centralised, autocratic, intolerant, ruthless. That is why true Christians are appalled. Many of us are turning away – becoming ascetic, hermits and monks, retreating into the wilderness.'

Cornelius winked at Aurelia. 'What a loss to society!'

'Be nice, Cornelius,' murmured Aurelia.

'Frankly, Thalius,' Cornelius said, 'the fate of your derivative little sect is of little interest to me compared to the use Constantine evidently plans to make of it.'

Aurelia was interested. 'And that use is?'

'Isn't it obvious? Constantine is turning the empire into a monarchy. He will be a king as supreme and unchallenged as the rulers of ancient Persia and Egypt. And he wants to draw on the unity of Christianity to cement all that in place; he imposes this alien cult on us in order to control us all.'

Aurelia said, 'You asked Thalius what he objected to in an emperor who adopted his own faith. Now I ask you, Ulpius Cornelius: what is wrong with an emperor whose goal is to unify the empire? Isn't that better than the bloody chaos of our youth?'

'Not if it is done the wrong way,' Cornelius said. 'Not if it means abandoning everything that made Rome strong in the first place. For if he does that, even if he succeeds in the short term, in the long run only ruin will ensue.'

Aurelia tutted, mocking him. 'And I had you down as a rational man, Ulpius Cornelius. Are you superstitious like Thalius here? Do you fear that if you turn your back on Rome's old gods they will punish you?'

Cornelius reddened, and Thalius saw there must be some truth in the charge. But the courtier said, 'I talk of political realities, madam. Of a system that has worked for centuries. There has always been room for another god or two in our infinitely flexible pantheon! And that way nobody, from Germany to Africa, from Britain to Asia Minor, need be excluded from the consciousness of empire. It is not its army that made Rome strong but its inclusivity.'

'But that is because Rome's gods are so like its subjects' gods,' Aurelia said. 'The Romans were farmers, as our ancestors were, Thalius. And farmers, rooted to their land, have gods of specific places. So the gods can happily coexist – each to his own scrap of land. The Jews, though, were nomads. And their god, who became Christ's God, was a god of no-place, or perhaps of all places, an infinite god of the sky. But there is only one sky, and in such a scheme there can be only one god. Now the Romans are accepting this sole nomadic god as their own. There will be a fight to the death, Cornelius, a battle between the old farmers' gods and the new sky god. There cannot be room for both. Now there will only be exclusivity, and intolerance.'

Cornelius pursed his lips, and Thalius saw his deep dislike of being analysed in this way by a provincial woman, however valid the points she made. 'Well, madam, you are here too. What is your objection to Constantine?'

Aurelia was unperturbed. Thalius imagined she dealt with bullying men like Cornelius in the course of her working life all the time. 'It's simple. My concern isn't for the fate of empires, still less for the immortal souls of humanity, but for Britain.' She railed about Constantine's excessive taxes, and repeated the rumours she had heard that Constantine had plans to move the capital of the empire permanently to the east. 'Somewhere in Greece, it is said, or Asia Minor, or even Africa. Do you know anything about this?'

The courtier pulled his lip. 'There are always rumours. And there are practical issues involved, not least the defeat of Licinius first. But, yes, there is such talk. Rome will always be the heart of the empire. But Rome isn't terribly convenient as a capital: it is far from the frontier provinces, like Britain, where the energies of the empire have to be concentrated. It is overcrowded, cluttered, difficult in the summer—'

'And,' Aurelia said laconically, 'it is full of potential opponents of the Emperor, from the ever-hungry mob to old families like yours, Cornelius.'

'I won't deny that. Here is the bald truth. The eastern provinces are far richer than the west. Isn't it sensible to place the capital at the economic core of the empire?'

Aurelia said, 'Only if you want the rest to wither away and die, neglected.'

'Well – so here we are, the Christian, the pagan and the ambitious provincial, all united in believing that *something must be done*. But nothing is going to happen unless we manage to decode the slave child's puzzle-tattoo – eh?'

'There is that, yes,' Thalius said gloomily.

Aurelia sighed and settled back on her couch. 'I've been working on it and have got nowhere, I'm afraid.'

Cornelius said, 'These acrostics are a Christian game, are they not? Like this one on the wall.' He pointed to a cryptogram carefully painted in a corner of the Christ portrait:

```
R O T A S
O P E R A
T E N E T
A R E P O
S A T O R
```

Thalius said, 'The fresco painter added it.'

Cornelius bent to see. 'Very clever. Reads the same up and down, forward and back. But so what? *The sower Arepo guides the wheels carefully.* What is this, some reference to a holy life? Oh, I do hate word puzzles!'

'Perhaps, but there is more in it than that,' Aurelia said. She unfolded herself from her couch, dipped a delicate fingertip in the black of an extinguished candle, knelt down by the acrostic, and with her blackened finger wrote lightly on the wall. 'Do you mind, Thalius? I am sure it will brush off. You see, you can rearrange the letters in the form of a cross, like this.'

```
                P
                A
                T
                E
                R
P A T E R N O S T E R
                O
                S
                T
                E
                R
```

Cornelius studied the result. 'A cross for Christ – eh? And it reads *Our Father* both ways.'

'The first words of the Lord's Prayer,' Thalius said.

Cornelius frowned. 'But you haven't used all the letters.' He compared the cross to the original acrostic, and dabbed his own blackened fingers to pair up the letters in each.

Thalius groaned, 'My housekeeper will disembowel me for this mess!'

Cornelius sat back. 'You made a mistake, Aurelia! You have two As and two Os left over.'

'There's no mistake,' Aurelia said. 'It's yet another layer of meaning, Cornelius, at least for a Christian. A and O, or Alpha and Omega: this symbolises the "beginning and the end" in the Christian revelation ...' Her eyes defocused. 'Oh.'

Thalius took her arm, mildly alarmed. 'Madam, are you all right?'

'No. Yes! I think I have it.'

'Have what?'

'The key to your slave's puzzle, Thalius – and perhaps the key to all our destinies.' She stood up. 'You must take me to the boy – now!'

X

Thalius led the way to the kitchen, where Tarcho was looking after the boy. He was greeted at the door by the warm smell of cooking bread. Inside, Tarcho was pounding vegetables with a mortar and pestle. Audax, standing close by, watched, fascinated. On a whim, Thalius paused, and his guests waited behind him, curious.

Thalius heard Audax say to Tarcho, 'You didn't squash beets when you were a soldier.' He was proving a fast learner, but his Latin was still rudimentary, uncertain, his accent strong, his abused throat gravelly.

'Oh, I did, and more. Soldiers do everything for themselves.'

'Soldiers fight.'

'Well, not all the time! And in between fighting we do other things. We build forts and lay roads and build bridges.'

'And squash beets.'

'We squash beets *and* lay roads.'

'Do you work in mines?'

'Sometimes.'

Audax pulled a face. 'Why would you work in a mine?'

'Well, you have to, if you're ordered to.'

'A soldier is like a slave, then. You have to do what you're told.'

Tarcho faced the boy. 'No. Never like that. A soldier is free in a way a slave never can be. It's a good life.'

'Why is it so good?'

'Because the emperors need us. The whole of the empire, all of it, the cities and the walls and the forts, is like one vast farmyard designed to feed the army. Why? Because without us it would all collapse in a day. Have you heard of an emperor called Severus?'

'Who?'

'Came to Britain to put down a rising.'

'Carausias?'

'No, long before him. While he was here Severus took the whole of Britain, far to the north of the Wall, then his sons gave it away again. Long story. Anyhow Severus had to sort out a mess, and it was the army that sorted it for him, and Severus knew it. "Feed the soldiers," he told his sons, "and let the rest rot." Or words to that effect. Dead a hundred years, but he was right. And every emperor since has followed his advice.'

'Should I join the army, Tarcho?'

Tarcho looked at the boy, surprised. 'Well, you'd have to be bought out of your slavery ... Is that what you want? You'd have to fight for Rome, you know.'

'That wouldn't make me Roman.'

'No, true. But if you aren't Roman, what are you?'

'What I always was. Brigantian.'

So, Thalius heard, fascinated, under the surface of Britannia the old nations survived, if only in the memory of slaves.

Audax said now, 'I want to be like you. I've got the muscles. Look.' He held up an arm, pitifully thin, and bent it to show a bicep like a walnut.

Tarcho grinned, and in a brief and uncharacteristic moment of tenderness, hugged the boy against his own massive chest.

'Sweet to watch them,' Aurelia whispered. 'Like seeing an eight-year-old care for a three-year-old.'

Cornelius murmured, 'I suggest we get on with our business, Thalius.'

Thalius took a breath. 'Very well.' He coughed loudly to announce his presence and walked into the kitchen.

Tarcho stood, surprised, dropping the mortar and pestle. Audax hid behind Tarcho. The kitchen staff were startled, and Thalius waved a hand at them, shooing them out.

Tarcho stepped forward. 'Sir, is there something I can do for you?'

Thalius sighed. 'Not you but your charge, I'm afraid. Audax! Step forward now.'

The slave obeyed without thinking, his head bowed. Tarcho stayed a step behind him.

Thalius bent and whispered, 'I'm sorry about this, lad. You must show your back again. But it won't be for long, and I promise you won't be hurt. Is that all right?'

The boy didn't reply. For all Tarcho's good will the boy's spirit remained a flicker.

Thalius straightened up. 'Turn around and lift your tunic. You know what to do.'

The boy leaned forward to expose the grid of letters he had borne all his life but never seen:

P E E O
N E R R
O S R I
A C T A

Cornelius, bending stiffly, inspected the boy. 'Tell me again where this thing came from, Thalius?'

Thalius shrugged. 'I have only legends, passed down for generations. The original Prophecy was a poem, sixteen lines long. It was burned at Hadrian's orders. But it contained an acrostic – the first letter of each line, perhaps making up the core of the Prophecy's message – that was remembered and passed on. And then, at some later time, it was encoded into this grid form.'

'Then this mass of scars is all that is left of your famous Prophecy.' Cornelius peered, pointing to the letters with his finger. 'Well, if it's an acrostic it's cleverer than the one on your wall, Thalius. That one made sense whether you read it up or down, back or forth. This one doesn't make sense any which way!'

'But I think it does,' Aurelia said. Tension shaped her aged, vulpine face, and Thalius wondered how he could ever have found her attractive. She said, 'It is how I visualised it, but now I can see it – here, see the A and O in the lower left, upper right corners. Alpha and omega – remember? This is an acrostic compiled by and for Christians, just like the *Pater Noster*.'

But how could that be? Thalius wondered, chilled. For if the old legends were correct the acrostic came from a poem written down in the year of the birth of Christ, when there *were* no Christians.

Cornelius said, 'But there is another A, another O – never mind! Can you decipher this jumble?'

'With the start and end points of the A and O, I think I can, yes.'

'Then do it, woman!'

Aurelia paused, staring at the scar for a long breath. Suddenly, quite uncharacteristically, she seemed hesitant. 'First we must be sure we *want* to know.' She turned away from the boy. 'You Romans have a word for such a moment as this, Cornelius: *discrimen*, a crucial, life-shaping decision, a choice that might lead to triumph or catastrophe. Even if I can read the Prophecy, should we follow its advice? Constantine's elevation may be the most significant event ever to have occurred in Britannia. Rome is the world's greatest power, and decisions made by emperors cause history to shudder. And now we propose to deflect an emperor from his mighty path. History's Weaver may want this, but do we? *Are we sure?* Cornelius?'

Cornelius considered. 'If left unchecked this emperor will dissipate the very strengths that have made Rome strong. Rome must rediscover itself – and if Constantine is the man to lead that revival I will be happy. But he must be shown the way. And you, madam?'

'I am concerned for Britain. We are being taxed to death. And if the heart of the empire is moved east, the west could wither. Yes, he must be deflected before his course is set. I'm sure. And you, Thalius? Will you follow the Prophecy?'

Thalius, heart thumping, tried to think it through.

The others forever took a partial view, it seemed to him. The fact was the world was a different place from the arena in which Rome had achieved its first dazzling successes. Now there was no room to expand, and from the heart of Asia whole peoples were on the march, fleeing drought and famine.

The Romans were not technical innovators, but, Thalius believed, they were social innovators. They had already put themselves through one vast transformation, when the pressures of running their huge acquisitions had become too great for the fraught political processes of a republic, and the emperors had been hatched. Now in response to the pressures of a new age, Constantine was attempting a still more drastic metamorphosis as he tried to weld a conglomeration of differently developed provinces into a single nation, tightly controlled under one man's authority, and bound together by the theological cement of Christianity. It seemed to Thalius that Constantine might be hailed by future generations as truly great, as a genius of his kind.

But what of Christianity? If, in preserving Rome, the Church was corrupted or destroyed, Thalius concluded sadly, the loss to mankind would be greater even than if Rome fell. So what was to be done?

He closed his eyes in brief prayer, seeking guidance. If only Constantine could see the effect of his policies on his subjects, perhaps he could use consent, not force, to unite the empire around a new set of goals to meet the challenges of the age – rebuild the empire as a truly Christian nation – and all fifty, sixty million of its citizens could move forward together. A letter, he thought: yes, a letter signed by a spectrum of concerned but good-hearted individuals – a letter backed by the mysterious authority of the Prophecy – that might encourage the Emperor to clarify his own thinking on many issues. Perhaps it could be circulated to other concerned groups. A petition, then. Standing there, eyes closed, he imagined how he might draft the first paragraph

249

– he would need advice on the honorific to be used when addressing a modern emperor—

'Falling asleep, Thalius?' Cornelius's voice was sardonic.

Thalius's eyes snapped open.

Aurelia was watching him, her face impassive. 'What are you thinking, Thalius?'

Irritated, defensive, he said, 'I am thinking that even Constantine's actions are trivial compared to the greater forces that shape our age. I am thinking that perhaps we are simply distracting ourselves from the uncertainty of the future with a word game.'

'Perhaps that's so,' Cornelius said, apparently not offended. 'And perhaps we aren't as shallow as you seem to believe, Thalius. Whatever you say we are faced with a decision. *What will you do?*'

Thalius, embarrassed by his outburst, took a deep breath. 'I am with you.' He glanced at Aurelia. 'Read the Prophecy.'

Aurelia stepped towards the boy, who, with the dogged, choice-free patience of a born slave, continued to wait, back bent, tunic pulled over his head. With surprising tenderness Aurelia touched his shoulder. 'I'm sorry, child. It will be over in a moment.' And with one manicured fingertip she began to trace the acrostic.

P E E O
N E R R
O S R I
A C T A

'From A to O, alpha to omega – bottom left to upper right, for by your tradition God is always to be found on the right hand side, am I correct, Thalius? This is a path to God, then, the true route for the pious. But it is a long and tangled path. How do we proceed? I believe these diagonal letters are a clue: C, O, and then up to the N ... C-O-N referring to Constantine perhaps? And then I suppose we follow the diagonal back down again – S, T – and then to the corner – A, and work our way back up the long diagonal ...'

Thalius held his breath as the trail of her finger, working back and forth along the diagonals of the square, picked out words:

A * CONSTARE * PERIRE * O

'From alpha to omega,' he read. 'To stand firm. To die.'

Cornelius straightened up and snorted. 'Is that it? It's not even a sentence. A nice motto for you pious types, I suppose. *Hold true in death and you will be led to God.* Fine. But it's no use to us, is it?'

Aurelia said, 'Look again, you fool. There are layers of meaning. Can

250

you not see it? *Constare* – Constantine – *perire* ...'

And in that moment Thalius saw the meaning of the message. The scrap of text was three hundred years old, yet it was quite specific, and it went to the heart of his own modern dilemma like an arrow from a bow.

If the true Church was to survive, Constantine had to die.

The slave boy was beginning to tremble.

XI

After Audax was sold to Thalius, he had been brought all the way across the country to the coast at a place called Rutupiae. Then he was taken through an immense city and across a huge river, through mile after mile of a green land of farms and canals and ditches, and at last to another city, Camulodunum. Now he was bundled into Thalius's cart once again to be hauled off to what Tarcho called 'the Wall'.

Tarcho tried to explain where he was going, with maps sketched in the dirt with sticks. Audax didn't understand what a map was in the first place, and north, south, east and west were all the same to him.

And he didn't want to leave Thalius's house in Camulodunum, because of the food. He had been fed in the kitchen, with the slaves and servants, and sometimes Tarcho joined him. It was better food than he had had in his life. Sometimes he was given so much that he stopped being hungry, so much food *he couldn't finish it*. Tarcho promised that Audax would never go hungry, he could always share Tarcho's bread.

But whether he understood or not, of course, whether he wanted to go or not, he had no choice about making the journey.

And now they had new people to travel with, and that was another problem for Audax. The lady Aurelia rode with them, and sometimes Ulpius Cornelius too. The three of them, Thalius, Cornelius and Aurelia, would huddle in the back of the cart, whispering.

Audax, utterly dependent on their goodwill, was acutely sensitive to their moods. Thalius, overweight, fussy, clumsy, was a good man. Audax couldn't imagine him harming anybody on purpose. But he was vague. When he turned his attention on you, you could bask in his kindness, but then he would turn away, his head full of thinking, and he would forget you even existed. Thalius was all right, but he wasn't to be relied on.

As for Aurelia, she was an old woman with the body of a girl. Caked

252

in creams, she trailed a cloud of stinks that made Audax's nose itch. She hadn't been unkind to him, that time when she had touched the tattoo on his back. But to her Audax was just a slave, no more than a bit of furniture, and just as easily disposed of. Audax understood this very well.

It was an attitude Ulpius Cornelius shared too. But sometimes Cornelius looked at Audax with a searching stare. Perhaps Cornelius was a 'dirty man', as the boys in the mine had called the men, slaves and overseers alike, who had used them. Perhaps he was working out how he could get Audax alone, or dreaming of what he would do if he could. But he made no approach to Audax. Tarcho was careful not to let Audax out of his sight.

All this discomfort was dwarfed by a deeper dread.

Audax had spent almost all his life in the mines, shut up in the dark. Before Thalius and Tarcho came he had had only broken memories of the wider world, relics of when he was very small. Now he was stuck out in the open, and he hated the vast pulsing of day and night. It seemed unnatural, somehow out of control.

Thalius ambitiously tried to explain to Audax the difference between 'finitude' and 'infinity'. Audax's deep confusion came from a life spent in the enclosed and finite, and now he was stranded in a world of openness without end. Audax dimly grasped these ideas. But he thought it just went to show that Thalius had never been a slave. Slaves understood infinity, even if they had no words for it, for slaves faced a lifetime of labour, of an utter lack of choice, without end. Servitude was infinity.

The one element in this huge open world of the outside that he felt drawn to was the sun. When the sky was clear the warmth of that great lamp in the sky sank deep into his bones and drew up his blood. Thalius gently explained to him that it was the sun that gave life to all things on earth, and that some people worshipped it as a god. Some believed it was a form of Thalius's own god, the Christ, who had also been a man. The sun reminded Audax of Tarcho, in his strength, his warmth, his patience. Audax imagined Thalius's Christ as a huge bearded soldier in the sky who smelled of sour German cabbage.

They stayed a couple of nights at a place called Eburacum. This was a city of massive walls and towers strung along a riverfront, looking down on the civilian town that huddled around it. A huge building loomed out of the centre of the town, visible for miles around. It was the Roman military headquarters, Tarcho said.

Founded as a legionary headquarters Eburacum had always been an important place. One emperor had died here: Severus, a century ago, after his campaigns in the Highlands, and after making Eburacum capital of one of his two British provinces. Since then the fortress and its walls had been rebuilt, massively. And another emperor had been created here, in Constantine, who had been proclaimed in that imposing headquarters building. Now Eburacum was the base of the military commander of the north, the Duke of the Britains.

But Thalius didn't like the place. 'With its aloofness and arrogance and monumental military architecture,' he said, 'it prefigures in stone the haughtiness of the absolute monarchy of the future.' Audax didn't think even Tarcho knew what he was talking about.

Travelling further north still they passed through more hilly country. The sky was huge and full of immense clouds. Somehow Audax found this wilder, more rugged landscape less intimidating than the crowded hills of the south. Thalius gently pointed out that this country was Brigantia, Audax's home. But none of Audax's ancestors had seen home for generations.

Tarcho grew more animated. He pointed out forts and camps and watchtowers that were part of a 'deep defence system', he said, reaching far back into the countryside south of the line of the Wall itself. And the land was studded by big blocks of greenery at the crowns of the hills and in the valleys. They were managed forests, planted especially to provide the Wall with timber for its baths and ovens. While the Wall was here to defend the country from the savages in the north, the country had to feed the Wall. Audax began to think of the Wall as a great ravenous beast, sucking the blood from a cowering land.

They arrived at last at a place called Banna, where there was a fort.

Before it reached the fort itself the road snaked through a patch of farmland owned by the fort – the 'soldiers' meadow', Tarcho called it – and the party crossed over a ditch clogged with weeds and stinking rubbish.

Then they passed through a kind of town, sprawling east and west along the road outside the fort walls. The roads were more like sheep tracks than Roman roads. The place was noisy, smelly, crowded. Some of the buildings were quite smart and built to square plans, but the rest were just shacks. Many of them had open fronts, and Audax peered into shops where metal was worked or cuts of meat were piled high. There were soldiers, dressed in military belts or bits of armour like Tarcho's. But there were plenty of women, and children ran everywhere, getting in the way of the horses. Audax liked it better than Camulodunum. It seemed a cheerful place. But Tarcho hurried him past the soldiers' taverns, gambling dens and brothels.

At last they approached a stone wall. This was the fort itself. The buildings of the scrubby town outside lapped right up to the wall. At the fort gate they had to pay a charge, and the carriage was searched for weapons.

Inside the fort Audax was overwhelmed by a stink of blood and smoke and piss. Tarcho told him it was always like this; the soldiers used their own urine to cure leather for their armour and harness gear. Though Aurelia and Cornelius pressed bits of perfumed cloth to their noses, Tarcho opened his chest and sniffed in the foul air through his big, black, snot-crusted nostrils. 'Home! Nothing like it.'

The buildings, of stone, mudbrick and wood, were a bit more orderly than outside, the narrow cobbled streets between them straighter. But you could see the buildings were old and much repaired. Audax thought two big buildings with two storeys and sparkling tiled roofs must be palaces. Tarcho said they were granaries, where the soldiers stored enough grain to feed them for weeks, in case the barbarians ever attacked. There were more soldiers, including a few who lounged at their posts on the walls. The troops here were a thousand-strong cohort of Dacian origin, Tarcho said, called 'Hadrian's Own'. But nowadays most of the soldiers, locally recruited, were British, not Dacian.

Aurelia, her cloak over her arm to keep it off the muddy ground, looked around at the shabby fort with disdain. 'So this is what has become of the mighty Roman legions!'

'There were never any legions posted here, madam,' Tarcho said. 'In fact strictly speaking there are no more legions nowadays ...'

She shuddered. 'By Jupiter I wish I'd never come here. If this is all that stands between me and the barbarian hordes of the Highlands I'll never sleep soundly again.'

The party split up. Thalius, Aurelia and Cornelius were taken to the fort commander's quarters, a grand old stone building. Tarcho took Audax to a much smaller house of mudbrick and thatch, one of a block. The house belonged to a soldier, an old family friend of Tarcho's, and it was no barracks, as in former times, but a home. Tarcho's friend lived here with his wife, two young sons and a whole pack of eager dogs. Audax didn't know what to make of the noisy bedlam, and the dogs, used to control the slaves in the mine, terrified him. But Tarcho had a quiet word with the soldier's wife, and she made a fuss of Audax and fed him bread and beef, and Tarcho showed him her husband's curving Dacian sword, a *falx*, and he began to feel better.

That night, in a small cot in the corner of a room he and Tarcho shared with the soldiers' sons, Audax slept well. He felt safe, encased by the walls of the house, and then by the walls of the fort, all of it watched over by soldiers like Tarcho. He thought that Thalius would have said it was a cosy piece of finitude sliced out of an infinite and troubling world.

He was woken in the dark, by a big hand gently shaking his shoulder. Unthinkingly he turned limp, imagining he was back in the mine. If you fought the dirty men they made it worse for you. But he was still in Banna, and it was Tarcho.

'Come on. Get dressed. I've something to show you.'

Outside the house the fort was a pool of shadows. The only sound was the coughing of a soldier on sentry duty somewhere on the fort walls. The sky was a deep blue-grey, a warning of the dawn, and the light reflected from dew on the cobbles.

Tarcho led Audax to a watchtower on the wall, and showed him a ladder. 'Take care,' Tarcho whispered. But Audax was used to ladders in the pitch dark, and climbed up more easily than Tarcho himself.

They arrived on the narrow platform at the top of the tower, alone. Up here the air was fresh, crisp with dew, and the customary piss-stink was dissipated by the green smell of growing grass.

Audax looked out over the countryside. The fort was on an escarpment, and looking south he could see how the land fell away to a deeply cut valley where a river gurgled. A steamy stink rose up; the fort's bath house had been built down there near the water.

And when he looked east and west, Audax at last saw the Wall itself, built into the outer shell of the fort, striding in great straight-line segments across the country. Where the gathering light in the east caught the curtain's southern face, the pale stone shone. Buildings and forts studded its length, and Audax could see hearth smoke rising, as if it was one gigantic house.

It was centuries old, Tarcho said proudly. 'My own great-great-great-something-grandfather worked on it. He was called Tullio. I know his name, you see, because it is written on stones set in the Wall itself. He came from Germany. And his sons and grandsons have served on the Wall ever since. Here is the Wall, all patched up, still serving its purpose eight, nine, ten generations later, after most of its builders' names have been forgotten. What men they must have been in those days, that their vision still shapes our age today! What heroes! And one of them was my grandfather.'

Audax found it impossible to imagine that men had ever built this thing, this Wall. He might as well have been told that men had dug out the valley to the south, or spun the clouds that caught the dawn light overhead.

'Did anybody live here before the Wall?'

'Why, I don't know. Nobody important, just a few hairy-backs. Two hundred years! Think of that.'

Lights sparked along the dark line of the wall, splashes of yellow fire flickering and dying.

Audax was alarmed. 'What's that? Is it an attack?'

'No. They are signal beacons. The watch is changing. All along the Wall soldiers are standing down, and they light their beacons to tell their mates that all is well, all is well ...'

They stayed on the watchtower until the sun had risen. Then they descended into the fort and joined the day's growing bustle.

XII

A week after Thalius's own arrival at Banna, Constantine and his entourage arrived – or some of them; many had stayed behind at Eburacum.

Constantine immediately ordered a review of the fort's troops. This took place on a bright, fresh morning, and Thalius and his companions watched from the comfort of a pavilion as guests of Cornelius.

The soldiers in their centuries drew up in good order outside the fort walls. The centuries' standard-bearers held aloft the emblems of their units, and each held a *labarum*. A new military standard said to be of Constantine's own devising, this was a long spear covered in gold, with a transverse bar to give it the shape of the Christian cross. At the summit of the cross was a wreath of gold and precious stones, containing a finely worked *chi-rho* Christogram.

The troops made a respectable sight, even though Thalius could see their armour and weaponry were scuffed and much repaired – it was said that some of these bits of kit had been handed down from father to son for generations. Not only that, in the light of day the walls of the fort itself looked frankly dilapidated. The fort and its units had been here for centuries, slowly subsiding into the cold northern mud, while the boundary between the soldiers and the civilian population from which they were recruited grew ever more blurred.

One of Constantine's projects was to cement reforms of the army begun under Diocletian, reforms which reflected the military reality of the age. The old distinction between legions and auxiliary units was abandoned. Now the army was divided between a mobile field force, and static units of border troops, like the units here at Banna. There was a new military hierarchy, of dukes and counts – like the Duke of the Britains stationed at Eburacum, and a Count of the Saxon Shore who controlled coastal forts like Rutupiae. Once the governors had been commanders-in-chief of their provinces' armies, but now the dukes and counts were independent of the governors – indeed their remit generally spanned more than one province. This was another example of the emperors' continuing strategy to fragment power and so limit the challenge of any one rival.

Thalius understood the military logic, he believed. You held off the barbarians at the border, and if they did get through you allowed them to penetrate deep into a fortified country, while bringing your mobile forces to bear. Even the walled towns were a part of the system, in a sense. But it was in the nature of stasis to decay, and frontier units like this tended to lose their shape and discipline. Thalius had heard lurid rumours of corruption, of commanding officers drawing pay for long-dead soldiers. It was just as well that the Emperor had come by to give the place a sprucing-up.

And this was a big day for these soldiers, a chance to break up the lifelong tedium of frontier duty with a display before the Emperor himself. Everybody knew that Constantine was here looking for units he could detach for his looming war with Licinius, Emperor of the east. Having grown up at their fort, with families of their own and roots generations deep, many of the soldiers here probably couldn't even imagine how it would be to serve under an emperor on a long campaign in a foreign land. But they were still Roman soldiers, and beneath those hand-me-down armour plates, hearts must have been beating with anticipation.

At last the Emperor himself rode by, a burly, powerful man, accompanied by his generals and aides. They all wore expensive, brightly coloured parade armour, including elaborate helmets with carved carapaces and bejewelled masks. The soldiers stood proud before their Emperor's inspection.

Cornelius, ever the traditionalist, murmured a commentary in Thalius's ear. 'Quite a mixture of symbolism – don't you think? Here you have a Roman army with its roots, let us not forget, in the citizen-farmer communities of Latium. But see the Emperor and his cronies in their fancy parade armour. I've heard travellers to Egypt and Persia say that the more centralised the society the more you see the flaunting of such symbols of rank ...'

Aurelia hissed, 'Oh, do shut up, Cornelius, you bore. It's less than an hour before our audience with the Emperor.'

'Since I arranged the audience,' Cornelius said stiffly, 'I'm well aware of it.'

'Is the boy ready?'

Thalius glanced across at Tarcho and Audax, who sat in the pavilion a few rows behind the others. The old soldier was looking reasonably smart in his own polished armour, though he obviously longed to be out on the field with the troops. Audax had been washed, dressed in a smart new tunic, his hair trimmed and combed. He still looked thin and pale, though, much younger than his years – he was still the sun-starved worm Thalius had found in Dolaucothi. And yet he was the key to everything.

'He's ready,' Thalius said to Aurelia.

'All right,' Cornelius said. 'Let's go over it one more time. I will lead you in, Thalius, with the boy. I've managed to interest the Emperor in the Prophecy etched on the boy's back. He is fascinated by such things, in his credulous soldier's way. Then I will call you forward, madam—'

Thalius said, 'And with Aurelia's help I will show him how to read the acrostic.'

'A prophecy of his own murder,' Cornelius said with a cold grin, just softly enough not to be overheard, loudly enough to make Thalius fear that he had been.

'Then I will present our testament.' Thalius tapped his tunic, within which he had tucked the ten pages of parchment on which he had written out a fair copy of the final agreed text: *Honest Advice Humbly Offered by Concerned Citizens.*

Now they were so close he felt his confidence growing stronger. It was an extraordinary thing they were attempting, to change an emperor's mind in such a profound way, and Thalius had barely slept for the last two nights. But though the Emperor feared no human, he did fear God, and perhaps he would take the Prophecy as the warning they intended, and be receptive to the logic of their missive.

Then he noticed Cornelius and Aurelia sharing a look he could not read. It reminded Thalius he was not in control of this situation. His confidence evaporated like dew, and a dread of possibilities he could not envisage gnawed at his stomach.

XIII

Being presented to the Emperor didn't feel like an honour to Audax.

It felt like the time he had been hauled up before overseer Volisios because he had cut his hand in a tired fall in a quartz seam, making himself useless for days. It had never even occurred to him to try to explain that he had been kept without sleep for two nights by a gang of dirty men. After yelling at him for a while the overseer had shown him the row of crosses where the bird-pecked remnants of slaves dangled, Audax's destination if he made any more mistakes, and then had handed him over to a burly brute for a whipping.

That was how this felt today, as Thalius and Aurelia led him into the elaborate shrine-like room where the Emperor sat on his throne. The room was filled with light that dazzled from the Emperor's clothes and jewelled crown. Audax recognised some of the people with the Emperor. On his right hand side was Helen, his mother, almost as fancily dressed as her son. To the Emperor's left was Cornelius, his eyes on Audax but murmuring to the Emperor. And beyond them were hard-eyed soldiers, their hands on the hilts of their stabbing swords, watching every movement.

He was brought to within a pace of the Emperor, close enough to touch him. Constantine was terrifying. Audax thought he could feel heat radiating from him. He had spent a lifetime suppressing the instinct to resist, but Audax couldn't help but pull back. But then Constantine caught his eye and smiled at him. Suddenly he seemed human, and Audax's dread subsided, just a little.

Thalius and Aurelia, he nervously, she with smooth confidence, began to describe Audax's scarring and how it had come about. Audax could understand a little of their Latin talk, of a family history, a rich woman who sold her descendants into slavery ... Constantine listened with an expression of faint boredom. Audax imagined him listening to hundreds of people every day, each of them with a story they needed him to hear.

Then came the revelation of the scar itself. Aurelia turned the boy around and had him lift his tunic over his head. Audax waited, his head swathed in his tunic, smelling his own sweat, hearing the muffled voices of the adults as they discussed the one thing about him that made him interesting to them. An acrostic ... Christian elements, the alpha and the omega ... encrypted words. He felt a warm, heavy finger tracing across his back, perhaps the Emperor's own, and his gruff voice teasing out the words: *Constare, perire.*

The boy was straightened up, his tunic flopped down, and he was turned around to face the Emperor. Audax saw that one of the guards had drawn his sword. Everybody understood the true meaning of the two words. Suddenly the tension in the room was enormous, and Audax, at its focus, was very afraid.

It was Helena who spoke next. *Are you threatening my son? Is he to die today?*

Thalius spoke rapidly, clearly terrified; he hadn't anticipated this reaction. *Nobody will die ... Not a threat ... We bring you the Prophecy in good faith, we did not make it ... We hope you will take it as guidance for a better future for all of us ... We bring you a letter ...* He fumbled beneath his toga for his document, and the guards glared at him even more intently.

And while they were distracted Audax discovered a knife in his hand, a fine, polished blade. It had been put there by Aurelia. As he looked down on the blade, her cold fingers closed around Audax's hand, and the knife.

And she pushed Audax, stretching his arm, and the blade was thrust forward. Audax saw all this as if watching from outside his own body. It had been beaten into him across a lifetime that when an adult pulled you around you didn't resist, not so much as a muscle. So it was his hand that held the knife, but Aurelia's strength that shoved it through layers of cloth, a briefly resisting skin, and then into a wet warmth beyond.

Even as the knife pierced the Emperor's chest, Aurelia screamed, 'No! The slave is a rogue! Help me hold him back, oh help me!' When the knife was embedded to its hilt, Aurelia fell back with a cry.

For a heartbeat all was still. Audax and Constantine were locked together, the knife hilt still in the slave's hand, the blade in the Emperor's chest. Constantine's mouth gaped, with strings of spittle stretched between his lips. Audax's hand felt small, pressed against the huge warmth of the Emperor's body.

Then there was pandemonium. Helena screamed, the soldiers yelled and drew their weapons, and Thalius and Aurelia were both grabbed and held. But nobody dared touch the Emperor himself, or the boy.

Constantine raised his hand, and everything stopped.

The Emperor was breathing slowly, carefully, and he kept his eyes locked on Audax. 'Don't move,' he said in Brigantian.

Audax was surprised enough to speak. 'You know Brigantian.'

Perhaps his arm moved, just a tiny bit, as he spoke. Constantine gasped, and his huge body shuddered, as if he was a puppet controlled by the boy, and the knife.

Constantine said breathlessly, 'I was a soldier here, serving under my father, for many years. This was my home. I learned British. What is your name? Nobody thought to tell me.'

'Audax, sir.'

'Audax. All right, Audax, listen to me carefully. There are two very important things that I must tell you. The first is that I know that it wasn't your fault. I saw the woman push you – what is her name?'

'Aurelia.'

'Yes. I saw it. So whatever happens today, if I live or die, you won't be punished. Do you believe me?'

Audax thought it over. 'No,' he said.

Constantine gritted his teeth. 'I wish my advisors were half as honest. I am the Emperor, Audax. If I make a promise it is kept. So believe me.'

'What is the second important thing?'

'The second thing is that as a soldier I learned a lot about the human body. Mostly by cutting holes in other people. And I know that if you move that knife, even a little bit, you will puncture the vessels of my heart and I will surely die. If you do not move it, I might yet live. Do you understand now why I asked you to stand still?'

'Yes,' said Audax.

Yes, he understood. But his arm, held out straight, was tiring, and the blood was seeping out of the Emperor's robes, bright crimson, and soaking his hand in slippery warmth. He did move, just minutely, no matter how hard he tried to keep still. He couldn't help it. And with every jerky motion he felt the Emperor shudder and twist in response. It was the way Audax had seen crucified slaves jerk and twitch, tiny motions as they tried to relieve the pain in their chests and feet. And just as Audax had learned to recognise mortal fear in the faces of the crucified, so he saw fear on Constantine's greying face now, beneath the clamp of calm.

The Emperor said, 'Can you see the man behind me? The tall man with the spectacles – I mean the bits of glass on his nose? He is my physician – a Greek, and a very good one. He is called Philip. If you want you can let Philip take the knife from you, then I will live. Or you could choose to twist the knife and I will die.'

Audax heard Aurelia yell, 'Kill him, slave! Kill the monster—' Then her voice was muffled, perhaps by a soldier's heavy hand.

Audax stayed still, his arm aching.

The Emperor said, 'Why do you think that woman wants me dead?'

'The words on my back say you will die.'

'All right. But what do you think, Audax? Do you think your choice should depend on a prophecy? Look at me. What do you see?'

Audax considered the man before him: heavy-set, powerful. He reminded Audax of Tarcho. 'A soldier,' he said.

'Yes. Good. That is what I am above all, and always will be.'

'I want to be a soldier,' Audax said.

Constantine nodded, just a little. 'Then I promise you shall be – if you choose to let me live. But it is your choice, Audax. Quite a thing, isn't it? Here we are, Emperor and slave, the highest and the lowest, the top and the bottom. And yet because of a simple knife, at this moment it is you who holds more power than anybody else in the world – you, at whose every tremble all history shudders.'

'It is true,' Thalius whispered. 'It is true! The unravelling of a Prophecy three centuries old – the fate of the whole world to come – all of it boils down to this moment, a knife in the hand of a slave!' But Tarcho hushed him roughly.

Constantine whispered, his voice growing weaker, his face greyer, 'The world is a complicated place, Audax. The future is unknown. And yet we must make choices even so. What do you think such choices should be based on? Words burned into your back, or the judgement of a man like me?'

Audax felt detached from the world, as if he was going to faint. His arm, outstretched, was so stiff, his blood-soaked fingers so numb, that he could barely feel the knife any more, and he didn't know if he was keeping still or not.

And as the world turned to grey, he thought he saw the walls of the room break down, like a collapsed wall in the mine, revealing corridors leading off to misty destinations. Dimly he discerned that the Emperor was telling the truth, and so was Thalius, that momentous events affecting the lives of people for generations unborn depended on what he did in the next few heartbeats. Who was he to trust, then – who or what?

If Constantine had been Tarcho he would not have hesitated – Tarcho, the only person in his life save perhaps his dimly remembered mother who had ever been truly kind to him. And yet Constantine was enough like Tarcho that he found he trusted him. People were real, Audax thought. People and their characters and their judgements. That was all that mattered in the world. Words, prophecies, were nothing.

'Call your doctor,' he said.

Constantine's eyes did not move, but his expression softened. 'Philip. Come here. As slowly as you like, sir ...'

Nobody dared move until the Greek doctor had taken the knife from Audax's hand, and then slowly extracted it from the Emperor's chest. Audax, released, fell back, his head ringing, and that strange sense of detachment evaporated, and the room closed up to become just a room once more.

After that there was an explosion of movement, a flashing of blades. Tarcho grabbed Thalius and Audax and pulled them out of the mêlée.

XIV

In the autumn of the year that Constantine died, Thalius arranged to meet Audax before the steps of the Temple of Claudius in Camulodunum.

He fretted how he would even find Audax. After all, twenty-three years had elapsed since that extraordinary audience with the Emperor. And besides, he dreaded leaving home. It was a market day, this bright autumn morning, and the town would be full of farmers and their wives and brats, their dogs and sheep and cattle, and the traders, prostitutes and petty thieves who preyed on them. Some days Camulodunum was more like a vast cattle pen than a town, he thought grumpily. At the exceptional age of seventy-five years old, Thalius found it increasingly difficult to get around, and on days like this he preferred simply to hole up in his townhouse.

But he had no choice, for this was the only day Audax could meet him. The boy had had to travel all the way from his posting in far Constantinople, using up most of his leave on the complicated journey across the western empire, and even then he was required to spend most of his time in Londinium, at the headquarters of the diocese of the four Britains. Well, if Audax was prepared to come so far, Thalius could pluck up the courage to step out of his own front door to greet him.

And after all, they were both here for old Tarcho.

The mêlée before the Temple was just as difficult as Thalius had feared. Vendors had set up stalls on the steps and even inside the colonnade itself. They filled the air with the stench of broiling meat, and sold clothes, bits of cheap jewellery, second-hand pottery, little miniatures of the divine Helena – endless bits of tat. There was hardly an item here that was new, hardly anything that hadn't been manufactured within a mile of this very spot.

Thalius could see a lot of barter going on, rather than cash sales

– half a chicken for a pretty bit of jade, a scrip promising a day's labour on a thatched roof in return for a much-used, much-repaired amphora. Those who did have cash hoarded it, out of sight of the tax collectors, but Thalius was aware that the collectors and their spies were probably circulating through the marketplace even now. In an age when even the army was prepared to accept payments in kind, a black market didn't stay black for long. The market was a vastly unpleasant place to Thalius, making him feel like a mouse among a swarm of mice feeding off each other's garbage.

The people around him were unpleasant too. Almost all of them younger than him – well, he had been used to that for years – and they were coarse, uncivil, disrespectful to each other and worse to old duffers like Thalius. It was an age of selfishness, he thought, an age of ill manners. And it was all because of Constantine. Poor, foolish, long-dead Aurelia had been right, in her narrow way. The burden of excessive taxation, the huge and still growing gulf between rich and poor, had coarsened society at every level. But what other way was there?

Here, though, amid all the rubbish, was a table piled high with books. There were scrolls, heaps of wood slips, even some densely inscribed wax tablets. Thalius began to rummage; it was a relief simply to be handling books. But none was mint, and some didn't even look complete. And very many of them were utterly uninteresting (to him) treatises on various aspects of the Christian faith.

There was an awful lot of this stuff around. After Constantine's imposition of Christianity his bishops and theologians, drunk on sudden power and money, indulged in ferocious infighting over heresies and counter-heresies. People were addled by intriguing theological complexities, and nowadays read only the Bible and commentaries on it – if they read anything at all. And as the numbers of the illiterate grew, and as the literate retreated into mysticism, nobody *thought* any more, nobody questioned, nobody remembered that things had ever been different from the way they were now.

But Thalius quickly identified a Tacitus, a Pliny, a Cicero, relics of an age when people could still think, and argue, and write.

He looked into the gloom of the covered stall behind the table. A youth sat on a stool, chewing on some herb, watching a girl on the next stall with a lascivious leer. Thalius snapped his fingers. 'You!'

The boy's head swivelled to face him. 'You're talking to me?'

'Not by choice, but it does seem you're the purveyor of these books. What is their provenance?'

The boy scowled. 'What?'

Thalius sighed. 'Are you selling these books? Where did they come from?'

'House breakage,' said the boy. 'Prices as marked.' His Latin was coarse, simplified. He was perhaps sixteen, with a hard, surly expression. Thalius wasn't frightened of him, but he was somehow disturbed. Here was a boy who had grown up almost outside society as Thalius had known it, with no compulsion to obey the rules of civilised discourse. What a resource for the future of Britain and the empire!

Thalius ran a finger over the scrolls. They were probably the debris of a minor tragedy, no doubt once owned by some member of the curia, more or less like himself, who had failed to maintain his balance in the endless cliff-top walk that was civil life these days.

But there were some interesting titles. One was a story called *The True History* by a Syrian-Greek called Lucian. Thalius had read it as a boy, and had since sought out other tales of fantastic voyages to strange corners of the world, or beyond the earth altogether – not myths, which always seemed a little hollow to him, but notions of what might actually be possible. But he had learned to keep his interest in these speculations quiet. Literary snobs always claimed that such tales were for adolescent boys, that the authors were running out of plots, and characterisation was sacrificed for the sake of ideas. It did Thalius no good to protest that the ideas were the whole point. With regret he replaced the Lucian; he already owned a better copy, though not one he kept on display.

As he browsed he was aware of a younger man beside him, also pushing through the heaps of scrolls. He jostled Thalius, to his intense irritation, as he tried to study the books.

The boy behind the counter took an interest in Thalius. 'If you're serious about buying, you might want to see this.' He dug around under the table and produced a scroll even more dog-eared than the rest. Thalius, his eyes rheumy but still sharp, saw that it was a memoir by the Emperor Claudius. 'Talks about his time here in Camulodunum. This is his Temple,' he said, casually jerking his thumb over his shoulder.

'I know whose Temple it is!' snapped Thalius.

The boy was expressionless. 'Good souvenir then.'

Thalius knew it was true that such an item was indeed difficult to find outside the great libraries of the Mediterranean cities – and even harder since Constantine had moved his capital hundreds of miles east. And he supposed the price would reflect its rarity. 'Let me see it. Is it complete, good condition? What generation copy is it?' Books nowadays were as tatty as everything else; you always had to check. He reached out for the scroll. The boy held it up before his chest. Grumbling at his lack of consideration, Thalius leaned forward over the table.

And as he was off balance the young man next to him punched him in the belly, and there was an explosion of quite unreasonable pain, while a hand rummaged inside his tunic.

Another hand, much stronger, grabbed him by a fistful of cloth at the back of the neck. 'Thalius. Are you all right?'

For two, three long breaths Thalius felt his heart racing, and his vision greyed. But he did not fall. Gradually the pain in his punched belly receded. He looked up.

A man stood before him, in his thirties perhaps, tall, well-built, his hair bright strawberry-blond. He was a soldier, as you could tell from the elaborate military brooch at his shoulder, and his expensive-looking belt. He held up his hands. He was holding two items: the Claudian memoir, and Thalius's leather purse. 'Those two rascals were hunting in a pack.' He tossed the purse to Thalius, who caught it clumsily. 'I'm afraid I had my hands full and had to let them go.'

Thalius glanced around. The shoppers thronged oblivious; there was no sign of the robbers. 'The shame of it,' he growled. 'To use books as a lure for thievery and violence! What is the world coming to?'

'I rather think you're owed this, don't you?' The man handed Thalius the Claudian scroll.

Thalius took it uneasily. 'I long to read it,' he said. 'But how shall I pay?'

The soldier laughed. 'The same old Thalius – honest through and through, but so unworldly you're concerned about paying the men who just tried to rob you! Forget it, Thalius. Take the book – they won't be back for it, it was probably stolen anyhow, and it will only rot otherwise.'

Thalius nodded. 'If there is no right course of action—' He looked up. 'But how do you know my name?'

The soldier smiled. 'You really haven't changed, dear Thalius. When I arrived here I knew that to find you I only had to follow the smell of musty old books.'

'Audax.'

XV

Tears embarrassingly pricked Thalius's eyes. 'I'm such a fool. I was somehow expecting the boy. Why, how you have changed! I really wouldn't recognise this great tree of a man as having grown from the wretched sapling I found in that gold mine, all those years ago.'

But Audax's face clouded a little, and Thalius understood there were layers of memory probably best left undisturbed.

He went on hurriedly, 'Besides, you know, with my head full of books I had quite forgotten that I was here to look for you. I'm like that nowadays, I'm afraid. And now here you are caring for me, as poor Tarcho looked out for me all those years.'

'It's been a long time.'

'And how is your wife?'

'Melissa is well. We have a townhouse in Constantinople – smaller than yours, Thalius, but it suits us well.' He said cautiously, 'Things seem to be better out there. In the east. There are lots of small farmers who own their own land. It's not like here where you have whole swathes of the country owned by a few super-rich. You don't have the same—' He waved a hand, his soldier's inarticulacy betraying him.

'Gross inequality?' Thalius finished for him sadly. 'I know, Audax, it is ruining us all, that and the decline of education ... But you have sons. Tarcho told me all about them. Your letters always thrilled Tarcho.'

Audax smiled. 'I called the older boy Tarcho – another soldier I think! But the younger has brains rather than brawn. He's more like you, Thalius. We are family after all. I'm glad I named him after you.'

Thalius was thrilled. 'It would be wonderful if you lived closer, so I could get to know him – tutor him a little, perhaps.'

'My place has always been at the Emperor's side.'

'I understand.'

'Anyhow I'm here now – here for the first Tarcho ...'

'Yes. Poor Tarcho! Come. Walk with me.'

They moved away from the book stall and, with Audax's broad shoulders and military insignia easily clearing a way, they walked up the stairs, through the colonnade and into the Temple. It was a relief for Thalius to reach the comparative calm beneath the Temple's roof, but it was painful to walk.

Audax touched Thalius's arm, offering support. 'How do you feel?'

Thalius gasped, 'As if that thug buried his arm in me up to the elbow.'

'If you feel you need a doctor—'

'I'd rather walk with you, old friend.'

Audax glanced around at the Temple. 'I haven't been here since I was a child, and then I was too young, or bewildered, to make sense of it. Surprisingly grand, isn't it?'

'You mean for a run-down province like this one? Well, so it is, but it's lasting the years well.' Though there was some rubbish strewn on the floor, and the dead leaves of the summer just ended, the grand old monument wasn't in terribly bad shape. You could see where money was being spent on it by those townsfolk like Thalius himself still civic-minded enough to care: repairs to the roof tiles, refurbishment of frost-cracked pillars. 'But it has been rededicated to Christ, as well as to the divine Claudius.' Thalius pointed out a *labarum* propped up in one corner, the emblem of a soldier-Christian.

'It is still standing,' Audax said, 'which is more than can be said for many pagan temples these days.'

Since that fateful and last visit to Britain all those years ago, Constantine had pressed ahead steadily with his programme of converting his empire to Christ. He had played a long and patient game, but as the power of pagans in the ruling classes and the army had steadily diminished, he had at last felt able to proclaim Christianity as the empire's prime religion – and to command a reformation. The wealth of the pagan temples was turned over to the Church, and the imperial treasury.

Audax rubbed a clean-shaven chin. 'I was involved in some of that. As money-making schemes go that was a good one, even for an emperor who always had a nose for cash like a dog for a bone.'

Thalius laughed, but winced at the pain. 'That's cynical for a soldier of the Emperor's bodyguard!'

Audax shrugged. 'You can be realistic and loyal at the same time, can't you?'

'True. As was Tarcho, always.'

'I'm not surprised the Temple of Claudius has survived. Even Constantine could hardly order the stripping of shrines to his own deified predecessors – especially as he is to be made a god himself.'

Thalius gaped. 'You're joking! After a lifetime of promulgating Christianity? Well, it will be a popular move here. They always loved Constantine in Camulodunum. Soldiers' town, you know. And that mother of his – they are thinking of adopting her as a patron saint!'

'Well, I know one thing for sure. Tarcho was a good Christian, of his kind. And he would never wish to be buried here.'

'No indeed,' Thalius said. 'Come, let's visit him.'

They crossed the temple floor, threaded their way down the steps through the crowded market stalls, and made their way along the city's principal street. Once an axis of the invaders' fort of Claudian times, it was rubbish-strewn, its gutters clogged with dirt.

And as they walked, they spoke of the aftermath of the night of Aurelia's attempted assassination of the Emperor, the night that had entwined their fates for ever.

Constantine himself survived. His Greek doctor said that though his wound was deep, the narrow blade had fortuitously missed any major organs. Aurelia herself, who had hidden her fanaticism from Thalius until the moment of the attack, was cut down immediately by the blades of the Emperor's guards, and that was the end of her. Tarcho shielded Thalius and Audax from the guards, but they had all been taken into custody as the search for complicity began. The worthy missive Thalius had haplessly carried might have been enough, in the fevered atmosphere of a paranoid court, to see him executed. Thalius always believed it was Tarcho himself who saved him, by arguing forcefully with his military accusers for Thalius's naiveté and innocence – not to put too fine a point on it, his stupidity.

As for Audax, he could have been executed with no questions being asked at all – or at the minimum tortured, for under Roman law slave testimony was *only* valid if extracted under torture. But if Tarcho had saved Thalius it was Constantine himself who saved Audax. In those moments when they had been joined in an embrace of life and death, the Emperor had seen something he liked in the slave, and he had pledged to protect him. When the fuss had died down Thalius hastily granted the boy his freedom and gave him into the care of Tarcho, who he judged was likely to do a much better job of keeping the boy safe than Thalius himself ever could.

As for the other principal in the drama, Ulpius Cornelius had made noises about the betrayal of his trust, receded into the shadows of the court, and Thalius had never seen him again. And he never knew if Cornelius had been complicit in the attempted assassination – if Thalius was the only dupe.

Tarcho had made good the Emperor's promise that Audax would have the chance to try life as a soldier. At the age of sixteen he was enlisted into the frontier garrison at Banna. He immediately flourished under the healthy food, medical supervision and training regime of the army; by the time he was eighteen he had shed the last shadow of the pale-as-a-ghost slave boy Thalius had dug up from the mine.

But he had rapidly proved too effective to be wasted in the stasis of a frontier post. On a letter of recommendation from Banna's commander, Audax was transferred away to the field army units in Gaul. Thalius saw him only rarely after that.

Audax was too young to fight in Constantine's first serious engagement with Licinius, Emperor of the east. It was a partial victory for Constantine; Licinius ceded territory but survived. The showdown came ten years after Constantine's visit to Britain, and by now Audax was old enough to serve.

'It was magnificent, Thalius,' he said now. 'They say it was the largest war for a century – there were perhaps a hundred and fifty thousand men on each side, and it raged across Europe and Asia for a year before Constantine's final victory near Byzantium ...'

Audax forbore from telling Thalius any war stories, and the older man was glad of it. The civil war had been another terrible internal grinding-up of resources that could surely have been better deployed against external enemies, like the Franks and the Alamanna, new barbarian federations on the Rhine border, and the Goths on the Danube, and the revived Persians in the east. Even while Constantine fought Licinius, Visigoths had taken the chance to cross the Danube, and Constantine found himself at war along a front three hundred miles long.

After Constantine's victory over Licinius he called for Audax to join his own personal bodyguard, the *scholae palatinae*. 'You saved my life once already,' he said in Brigantian, on greeting the boy. 'So I believe I can trust you to do it again!'

So it was that Audax followed Constantine on the next great adventure of his reign – the move to the east. Again Aurelia had been right, and decade-old rumours were proved true. The site Constantine chose was Byzantium, a minor Greek city in Asia Minor – the place where he had won his final victory over Licinius. The new city was inaugurated only two years after that victory, and after some frantic rebuilding was dedicated four years after that.

'The new capital must be a marvellous place.'

'Not really,' Audax said candidly. 'It was thrown up quickly. Some of the new buildings are pretty shoddy, and it has attracted a scruffy class of people, I can tell you. It does have a forum and a senate of its own, and a dole of free grain, just like Rome. But it isn't Rome yet!'

'Ah, but it will grow.' And, Thalius thought sadly, soon the empire's wealth would flow from the east, from trade routes to India and beyond, and nobody would care about the western provinces with their poverty and long, vulnerable land borders: it was just as Aurelia had feared. But he said none of this to Audax. 'It is the epicentre of empire, and will be for a thousand years. And it was founded in our lifetimes, Audax. Think of that!'

The young man's eyes shone. 'I do miss you, Thalius. You always did fill me with a sense of wonder.'

Thalius, moved, took his arm. 'Then we must write. That way perhaps my fancy will enrich your life as your strength and courage have always enriched mine.'

They reached, at last, a small church. One of several in Camulodunum, it was modest, a boxy building on a rectangular plan. But it was neatly built of stone reused from some expensive ruin, and a wooden cross rose up above its tiled roof.

'Towards the end of his life, this is where Tarcho came to worship,' Thalius said. 'In fact this church grew out of a soldiers' chapel – there was once a mithraeum here, I think.'

Audax seemed briefly unable to speak. Then he said gruffly, 'And he is buried here?'

'Inside the church. His grave isn't marked.'

'It's a fitting place for a soldier.'

'Yes. The time was right for him to go, perhaps. He was always an admirer of Constantine, you know. A "good lad", he would say. He enjoyed reports of the preparations for a campaign against Persia. The dream of Alexander revived again, Tarcho said! I think it pleased Tarcho, in a way, to die in the same year as such a man.' He prompted gently, 'But Tarcho gone, and Constantine too – what next, do you think, Audax?'

'Things may be a little difficult,' Audax said with grim understatement. 'The campaign against Persia was controversial even in the Emperor's court. The east has always defeated the Romans if they push too far. And then there is the succession. Constantine's three sons have spent their youth fighting like puppies in a sack. I fear blood will be spilled before one of them emerges as top dog.'

Thalius sighed. 'And more strength bled from the body of the empire, while our enemies watch and wait. Audax, you must be careful.'

'I will be,' Audax said. 'I'm thinking of a change of posting, away from the court.'

'Then you're wise. You know, sometimes I am glad I am no longer young – sometimes it seems a comfort I won't see much more of the drama. But perhaps every old man thinks the world is decaying as fast as his body.'

'You mustn't think like that.'

'One must be realistic,' Thalius admonished him. 'But, Audax ...' He asked cautiously, 'What of the Prophecy?'

Audax's face hardened. 'I suppose I have to thank it for saving my life. I'd have surely died in that hole in the ground if you hadn't come to find me, and it. But when I joined the army I had the tattoo burned off my back.'

Thalius winced. 'But the scarring—'

'I'd rather wear that than the hateful thing which preceded it. Thalius, do you still believe the true purpose of the Prophecy was to change the destiny of the Church?'

That took Thalius aback. He had spoken with nobody about such matters since the day of the attempted assassination. 'So you have been thinking this through.'

'Look, I'm no philosopher,' Audax said. 'But I had that thing tattooed to my back since birth, and, on long campaigns, there was plenty of time to puzzle about its meaning. The way I see it is this: the Prophecy was a message, and *somebody sent it*. Now, whether it was God or demon, or even a wizard—'

'The Weaver,' Thalius said softly. 'And if Constantine had been killed, Christianity might not have been incorporated into the empire, and the capital might not have been moved east. History would have been changed – the history of the whole world, for all time.'

'Yes. Well, whoever sent back the Prophecy had a purpose. The question is, what could that purpose be? Christian symbols were written into that acrostic, the A and the O. Could it really be that the sender was trying to deflect Constantine's adoption of Christianity?'

Thalius said, 'It is what I believed at the time, I think – though others made their own interpretations of the Prophecy, and its lost promises of "freedom". Perhaps the Weaver wanted what I always wanted – strange thought! Certainly Constantine has remade the Church, and the results have been just as I feared. The bishops have taken to chastising those who won't follow the official line. The persecuted turned persecutor! Oh, I believe that thanks to Constantine the Church will live for ever. It is just that it is not *my* Church.'

Audax grunted. 'So if the intention of the author of the Prophecy was to "save" the Church, he or she failed.'

'Really? Perhaps you just don't want to believe, Audax, that all of the future hung on your choices in those few terrible heartbeats when you held that knife – but it did, you know. And consider this.' He shivered, an inchoate dread stealing over him. 'If history has been changed around us, Audax, if we are now living in the *wrong* history – *how would we know?*'

Audax had no answer.

'Will you tell your son about the Prophecy?'

'No.'

'You must,' Thalius said firmly. 'Ours is a remarkable family with a remarkable story. You would be depriving him of his past, his identity otherwise. Here,' he said impulsively, and he handed Audax the scroll of Claudius's memoir. 'You take this. Keep it for when he's older. Claudius was bound up with the Prophecy too, and perhaps it will help little Tarcho fill in the blanks in the story. If he's as clever as you say, he may end up understanding far more of this strange business than I, than any of us, ever did. I never even saw the Prophecy itself,' he recalled wistfully, 'not even the few lines which might have described the great upheaval of our own lives ...'

Audax hesitated, then took the book. 'Very well, Thalius. I'll make sure he understands it is from you.' He looked around a cloudy sky, seeking the angle of the sun. 'Thalius, I must go. My duties – I have people to see here on behalf of the imperial heirs.'

'I understand,' Thalius said.

Audax stepped away, returning to the crowded street. 'I hope I'll see you again before I leave.'

'You know where I am – I never go far these days!'

But Audax was already lost in the crowd. Thalius, alone, empty-handed, felt his bruised belly twinge again. Moving cautiously he turned away and headed for home.

EPILOGUE
AD 418

I

Isolde hated the idea of travelling to Britain with her father.

For one thing Isolde, nineteen years old, didn't know anybody in Rome who had even been as far as Gaul, much of which was in the hands of *foederati*, German 'allies' of the empire. All Isolde's friends knew about Britain was that giants had built a mighty Wall across the neck of the island to keep out capering monsters.

Nonsense, said Nennius, her father, predictably. You could tell when he got really angry because a pink flush spread all the way up his round cheeks to the shaven patch at the top of his head. Britain was just a place, its inhabitants just people, not monsters – and there *was* a Wall, but it had been built by Romans, not giants. Why, it was less than a decade since the British Revolution, when 'ragged-arsed rebels' had refused to pay their taxes. Britain had been detached from the empire many times before, and would no doubt be rejoined to the mother state when time and resources permitted.

'And anyhow,' he told her with a certain malicious glee, 'we're off to visit a cousin of mine, who lives *on* the famous Wall. We share a grandfather, cousin Tarcho and I, a slave who became a soldier called Audax, who was at the heart of the Prophecy story. And do you know how I happen to have a cousin there? *Because you and I are British ourselves*, daughter – a couple of generations removed, but British all the same ...'

Nennius's latest scheme was all to do with a Prophecy, he said, a Prophecy lost and now partially found again, a Prophecy made but never fulfilled – a Prophecy that might have shaped the world. The key to reconstructing this puzzle, he believed, and perhaps even to recovering the Prophecy itself, lay in Britain. And so because of this old man's legend Isolde must travel beyond the empire itself.

Isolde had learned long ago that it did her no good to argue. Her whole life had been shaped by her father's ambitions, and so it was now. But as they crossed a Gaul in which you heard nothing spoken but German, and as they took to the sea in the leather-sailed boat of a blond Saxon trader with bad teeth, she felt terribly vulnerable. She was a pregnant woman accompanied only by an absent-minded old man. Not only that, her stomach churned with every tip and rock of the boat. The trader offered her a remedy, a cold tea of German herbs, but Nennius forbade her even to try it.

She tried to tell herself she was safe with her father, but she had never believed that even as a small child. He simply didn't pay enough attention to you to make you safe.

Isolde's mother had died young, and even as a young girl she had seen how unworldly Nennius was. Respected thinker and monk he might be, famous for his friendship with the great theologian Pelagius, but there were mornings when he couldn't put his own trousers on the right way round. In fact Isolde grew up thinking of herself as the adult in their relationship.

Isolde had briefly escaped when she married a young man called Coponius, of ancient Roman stock. But his good looks had belied a sickly nature. Only a month after Isolde found out she was pregnant he had been carried off by a nasty little plague, one of a series that had nibbled at the population of Rome in recent years. So Isolde had had no choice but to return home to her father, a widow at nineteen, and carrying a child. Nennius was not uncaring; Isolde knew her father loved her. But with his head forever filled with one dream or another – and now stuffed with his determination to make this extraordinary journey across the known world – there was no room for Isolde.

The boat landed at a place called Rutupiae, where a grim-looking fort loomed over a good natural harbour. The fort had seen better days. Its elaborate earthworks were clogged with rubbish, and the facing stones of its massive walls were crumbling away under the assault of the caustic sea breeze. In places they looked as if they had been robbed, quarried out.

Nennius was excited, for it was here, he claimed, that Roman invaders had, centuries ago, first set foot on the island. The only Roman from such incomprehensibly ancient history Isolde had ever heard of was Julius Caesar, and when it turned out not to have been him who had conquered Britain, she lost interest.

Anyhow there were no emperors here now, and the place swarmed with Saxons. Living in clusters of small wooden buildings outside the fort's earthworks these Germans handled the sparse trade from the continent. They used this old fort, built to repel their own piratical

280

ancestors, as a storage depot, and just as in Gaul the only tongues you heard were Germanic.

Isolde and her father found a small timber-built church set on the fort's north-west corner. It had a pretty baptismal font, made of reused red Roman tile. They said prayers of thanks for their safe passage this far. Then they returned to the small wharf and stood together uncertainly while the trader unloaded his boat.

The Saxons looked extraordinary to Isolde. Many of them were blond and blue-eyed. The men shaved the front of their heads and let the hair grow at the back, an effect that made their faces look long, like a wolf's. There were plenty of kids running around the wooden-hut settlement. Perhaps their fathers had been pirates, but these were clearly immigrants and had no plans to go anywhere. But every adult wore a knife at the waist; even some of the older children carried weapons.

Isolde was relieved when a young monk came pushing through the throng to greet them. He dressed as Nennius did, in a plain robe of heavy brown cloth, tied off with a belt of rope. He was young, perhaps not much older than Isolde. But his tonsure, severely cut, looked rather old-fashioned to Isolde, though she was no expert on monkish modes. His name was Damon, he said. 'I bring greetings from the bishop of Camulodunum, and I come to escort you there.'

'Oh, how kind, how thoughtful,' Nennius burbled. 'The exchange of letters I have already enjoyed with Bishop Ambrosius has been delightful, and I am sure the gift of his hospitality will be most welcome ...'

Damon guided them to a carriage, crude but covered and serviceable. He had a man with him, a rough-looking servant too surly to be a slave; he hauled the visitors' baggage from the wharf to the cart. Damon went on, 'The bishop asked me to stress that the honour is all his. Any friend of Pelagius is welcome in his palace.'

Nennius nodded. 'Britain has become something of a refuge for we Pelagians, I fear. But then Pelagius was born here; he is one of our own.'

Damon said cautiously, 'Perhaps you haven't heard the most recent news.'

'About Pelagius's excommunication by Pope Zosimus? Quite a victim for Augustine and his crew!'

'Bishop Ambrosius comforts us that truth and goodness will prevail in the end,' Damon said mellifluously.

They walked to the carriage as they talked. Isolde felt tired, bloodless, even a little giddy, but her father was oblivious to her, of course, and so was Damon, the young monk, and nobody helped her.

The Saxons, going about their own business, ignored them as they passed. The shoulder straps of the women's gowns were fixed with brooches, they had sleeve-clasps around their cuffs, and around their waists they wore belts from which dangled odd metal good-luck charms like large keys. Isolde thought the style was rather attractive, and the quality of the metalwork looked good. She wondered if they would stop at any markets where she could do some shopping.

II

It would take two days' travel to reach Camulodunum. The three of
them set off in Damon's carriage, with the servant walking silently,
leading the horses.

To get out of the harbour area they had to pay a toll, in Roman
coin, to a fat, hairy Saxon. Isolde wondered who the toll was being
paid to, and the young monk explained that the governments of
the four provinces of Britain still functioned, and still collected taxes
– though nothing on the scale of 'the old days', as he called them,
before the British Revolution and the expulsion of the diocesan tax collectors, a revolt that had occurred when he, Damon, had been about
fifteen.

Beyond the harbour, it wasn't an easy journey. The road they travelled was one of the first Roman roads ever built in Britain, her father
proclaimed. That might be so, but that must make it very old, and it
was so tatty! You could see where cobbles had been prised out, the
holes never filled in, and so the road was full of potholes that shook
Isolde painfully. Once the servant had to calm the shying horses. He
said curtly that there was a body lying in the clogged drainage ditch;
flies rising from the decaying corpse had spooked the animals. Isolde
looked away and tried to breathe shallowly.

The country itself was quiet. It was a landscape of farms, of stone-
walled fields and small wooden buildings. There were even some grand
farmhouses, tile-roofed, enclosed by bristling walls. But many of these
were evidently empty, shut up or even burned out, and many of the
fields were clearly abandoned, their rain-eroded furrows strangled by
weeds. It was rare that Isolde saw anybody working the land.

Nennius remarked on this to Damon.

'It's the Saxons,' said the young monk. 'Too many of them around
here. So people are packing up and going off to the towns, or to live
with relatives further west or north, or in Gaul. Even the rich have

sold up, if they can, and cleared out.' He murmured, 'The Saxons are pagans, you know. They don't mix with us.'

Isolde wondered what tensions were concealed behind those simple phrases.

They came upon Camulodunum in the evening. The city itself sat within massive walls; it looked more like a vast fortress than a town.

And in the rolling fields outside the town and beside the river there were more Saxons – many, many of them, warriors with their horses and wives and children, camped out in tents or in clusters of small wooden huts, some of them set up in the bowl of a disused circus. The travellers picked their way uneasily through this loose camp, along the old Roman road. It was almost as if the Saxons were besieging the city. Damon reassured them there was nothing to fear; the Saxons were mercenaries and had been hired by the townsfolk for their protection. Isolde had no doubt that these fierce-looking warriors would be useful to have on your side. But she wondered what might happen if the money to pay them ever ran out.

They entered the city through the west gate. It was a big double archway that had been almost blocked up by chunks of stone, so that only one person could pass at a time. A soldier in very worn armour stood here collecting more tolls, this time on behalf of the curia, the town council.

Isolde was glad to enter the town, just to get away from the desolate and depopulated British landscape. But this was not Rome. The town within its walls was a bowl of rubble, a shattered townscape of derelict houses, weed-choked gardens and silted-up ditches. The baths were shut down, the theatre was a rubble-filled rubbish tip, and even the main road was ankle-deep in filth. There were none of the public buildings she would have expected in a town this size, or if they existed they were being used for something else. There were some grand houses here, but many of them were abandoned, and as they walked by Isolde saw cooking-fires set up on tessellated floors.

Damon said that in the darkest days of barbarian incursions and banditry, the army had moved its weapons workshops and depots and stock pens within the protection of the town walls. So the town had become a fortress once more, as it had been centuries ago at the beginning of its life. Now the Roman army had gone away, of course, but Saxons and other mercenaries still used the infrastructure it had left behind.

Amid the roofless shells, heaps of building rubble and lakes of sewage, there were functioning offices, however, where the town council or the provincial government still collected taxes, organised work levies and administered justice. And Camulodunum seemed to be full of churches, small but solidly built of reused stone and tile, rising out of the general rubbish like mushrooms from compost. 'There are more churches than people,' Nennius joked wistfully.

Damon picked his way along the rubbish-strewn road quite cheerfully. All this was normal to him. To Isolde and Nennius, though, the whole place stank like the vast garbage heap it was. And there were so few people that Isolde felt like a child creeping through a huge house abandoned by adults.

The bishop's palace was one of the grander buildings. It was a townhouse about thirty years old, built in something like a classical style, with separate blocks set out around an atrium. Isolde learned it had once been owned by a diocesan tax official.

Bishop Ambrosius himself was here to greet them. With receding silver hair, richly dressed in a ground-length purple robe, he was about Nennius's age, but he looked as if he could still throw a healthy punch. When he took her hands Isolde felt reassured for the first time since she and Nennius had left Rome.

After days on the road they were all hot, dirty, hungry, and the stench of the city lingered even here. There was no bath house, but the house had underfloor heating and hot water, and after an hour of pampering herself with her scents and creams Isolde felt almost human. She joined her host and his guests in a large, well-appointed triclinium.

The meal they were served relied heavily on meat, mostly mutton and pork, but there were olive oils and dates and a rather good fish oil, imports from the continent which, the bishop said, were a luxury these days. No wine, though, and Ambrosius apologised for serving them watery British beer, but it was strong enough to warm Isolde's blood.

Her father, as usual, seemed to have forgotten she was here, and made no effort to include her in the conversation, and nor did Damon. But the bishop was gracious to her, and his servant, another young monk, was attentive to her needs. In the light of the low fire, as the aches of the journey were soothed away, Isolde was content to let the talk wash over her.

Ambrosius and Nennius were churchmen of a similar age, both in their late fifties, one from the heart of the empire, the other from its now-amputated limb, and they had lived through tumultuous times. And, like all men of their age, Isolde thought fondly, they believed the world was in decline, from a Golden Age a few decades before. Born a generation after Constantine, now known as 'the Great', they spoke reverently of the first Christian emperor, whose reign had been an interval of comparative peace.

But all over the known world the weather was bad. Even within the empire the great crops of wheat and millet which fed the large urban populations began to fail. Among the barbarians, as famine descended, pulses of refugees washed out of the heart of Asia, driving others before them, to press ever more relentlessly on the borders of the empire.

Constantine himself had stabilised the border by allowing barbarian peoples to establish new homelands inside the empire's borders – vast numbers of them, for instance no less than three hundred thousand Sarmatians. This policy of 'federation' brought peace for a while, but there was much muttering about whether the empire could absorb such huge influxes.

There was trouble with the barbarians in Britain too. When Ambrosius was a boy of five, there was a 'Barbarian Conspiracy', a major invasion from several directions at once: by the Picts across the Wall, the Scots and Irish and Saxons from across the Ocean. For a whole year order was lost. Ambrosius and his family, he said, huddled inside the town walls as the children told each other blood-curdling tales of the baby-eating foreign savages who roamed the countryside.

Meanwhile after Constantine's death fratricidal war between his three competing sons brought renewed turmoil at the heart of the empire. Britain threw up usurpers, such as one Magnentius, who had killed one of the sons, only to be defeated by another, at Mursa in Pannonia. The empire once more became an arena of conflict between strong men and their armies. Then, when Constantine's treaties were repudiated by one barbarian group, the Visigoths, decades of simmering conflict finally led to battle at Adrianopolis – a battle the Romans lost, at a terrible cost.

Times had changed, and a weakened empire could no longer afford such bloodletting, and after Mursa and Adrianopolis the Roman army had never been able to recover its strength. The emperors employed barbarian federates in their armies, and still more alien peoples settled within the borders – following Constantine's precedent, but now the process was all but uncontrolled. Thus the army was barbarised, and the empire was hollowed out by foreign polities.

The British felt increasingly exposed, and its elite and officer corps threw up one usurper after another – roughly one a generation, as young rebels dreamed they could do better than their fathers. And as soon as he took power each of them headed overseas, taking yet more troops with him from the British garrison. One, grandly named Magnus Maximus – 'the Great, the Greatest' – killed another emperor, and had the dubious honour of being the first western ruler to order the execution of a Christian heretic.

But the troops stripped from the British garrison by each failed rebellion, and indeed by each officially ordered transfer to reinforce the centre, were never returned. Without the army to enforce collection the taxation system began to break down. People hoarded their coins in the hope of better times, and a barter economy sprang up. But as demand dwindled there was much destitution, and Ambrosius, by now a young priest, found himself ministering to the starving poor.

Then, one New Year's Eve, a vast horde of Alans, Suebi and Vandals crossed the frozen Rhine, and pushed their way into Gaul and Iberia.

Britain was cut off. Now no money was coming from the central treasuries to pay the remaining British troops. The imperial standard still flew over the forts and towns, but there was little left of the Roman army beneath it. After a succession of bloody, panicky coups a low-born general who styled himself 'Constantine III' put together yet another ragged army, and just like his predecessors immediately crossed to the continent. Constantine was the last throw of the dice, the last British attempt to save Britannia.

As Constantine's campaign on foreign fields descended towards defeat, another turning point was reached. This time it wasn't the officer corps or the ruling elite in the cities who rose up but the comparatively poor and lowly. What was the point of being taxed white by a centre which was better at producing usurpers than keeping out the barbarians? The revolt, once it broke out, spread like wildfire. The tax collectors were expelled from their offices and plush townhouses, and then the Christian poor turned on the still-pagan rich. The diocesan government collapsed. The middle-ranking officials in the towns and the four provincial governments decided to join the rebels, and legitimised and organised the revolt.

This 'British Revolution' was less than ten years old, and Isolde thought she detected pride about it in the calm voice of this churchman. Not that things were perfect. The four provincial governments had started to develop independent armies, mostly made up of Germanic mercenaries. But civilisation had been saved until the day came, as it must, when Britain was reunited once more with the centre of the Roman world of which it had always been part.

'And it was a blow for freedom,' Nennius said, enthused, eager for revolution in a way, Isolde thought a little sourly, only a comfortably plump old man far removed from the action could be. 'Isn't that a deep tradition in Britain? Why, you could say it informs the work of Pelagius himself.'

'Ah, but never let Augustine hear you say that ...'

Isolde had met Pelagius herself once, as a little girl. About ten years older than her father, born in Britain, he was not a cleric, but he had developed forceful views about the direction of the Roman church, which he saw as corrupted, immoral and slothful. And he took great exception to the teachings of Augustine, a bishop from Africa, who argued that human beings were born fundamentally flawed, and that human actions depended on the will of God. Pelagius insisted that humans were essentially good, and were responsible for their own moral advancement.

'But a church of free men and women cannot be controlled by the centre, and so it won't do for an imperial cult,' Nennius said gloomily. 'Perhaps in future the Roman church will deal with all Pelagians as it has with Pelagius himself ...Think of it, Ambrosius! Excommunicated for proclaiming that mankind enjoys free will! What is the world coming to? Where is our church going?'

'The question is, where are *you* going, my friend?' Ambrosius asked with gentle humour, pouring more beer. 'Are you still determined to find your cousin on the Wall? It won't be an easy journey.'

'No. But as I told you in my letters it is a dream of freedom that draws me there. Pelagius would approve! A dream, or rather a hint, a tantalising hint of a better future ...' And he began to speak of family legend and of fragmentary prophecies, of emperors and of history.

But the evening was ending for Isolde. Exhausted by travelling, heavy with food and drink, and with the baby slumbering softly within her, she made her excuses and left for her bed. The old men talked on softly, as young Damon, huddled by the fire, listened as attentively as a puppy before its master.

III

For Isolde the journey north to the Wall was a long and brutal haul along the spine of this dismal island. Following poor roads they passed through town after shabby walled town, and they had to pay more tolls as they crossed invisible provincial boundaries.

Isolde was so immersed in the oceanic aches of her own body she barely noticed the change in the character of the country as they headed north, from the rolling chalk hills of the south with their abandoned farms and fortified country houses, to the more rugged north with its bristling forts. But the further north you went the fewer Saxons you saw. Perhaps the people in the north had found other ways to look after themselves.

They arrived at last at the line of the Wall. Though the paintwork was faded, and in places you could see where damage had been roughly repaired, the Wall was still intact and very impressive, its powerful lines cutting across the neck of the countryside.

And the Wall was manned. Nennius turned westward, planning to travel to a fort called Banna. They soon reached what Nennius called a mile-fort, built around a gate that was roughly blocked with stones. Two grubby soldiers in woollen tunics flagged them down, to extract still more tolls. According to the soldiers the whole line of the Wall was under the command of the 'Duke of the Britains'. The soldiers gave them a chit scribbled on a wood slip, so they wouldn't have to pay any further tolls.

Isolde found the Wall and its soldiers, even the process of paying the toll, reassuringly familiar. Sooner this semblance of the Roman way than relying for your protection on the bands of blond-haired barbarian thugs like in the south. But no standard was erected over the mile-fort's eroded stones; no eagles flew here.

They continued westward, passing more mile-forts and watchtowers, and arrived at Banna. The fort sprawled on an impressive escarpment, and to the south a river with shining gravel banks curled through woodland. The northern wall of the fort was built into the line of the Wall itself. There were houses and other buildings outside the walls of the fort, but they looked abandoned, their roofs missing, walls of mud subsiding back into the earth.

They passed through a gateway in the eastern wall. The soldiers on duty let them pass with a brisk inspection of the chit from the mile-fort, and a letter of passage Nennius carried from his cousin Tarcho, the commander here. The fort was crowded and busy, with men, women and children going about their business. The civilian settlement out-side might have been abandoned, but the people hadn't gone away, they had just moved inside the fort's walls. And the soldiers were still here, evidently.

Isolde recognised a granary, its floor raised for ventilation, a second granary which looked abandoned, and blocky buildings which might be the fort's headquarters. Some of the buildings were quite impressive, large and stone-built. But many were derelict, their roofs collapsed, their walls robbed of stone.

Nennius was excited to be here. Once their remote ancestors had lived here, he said. He knew that because his grandfather, Audax, had told him that the famous Prophecy had actually been created here at Banna. But there was no sign of that lost primeval home in this decaying fort, and even Nennius's nostalgic enthusiasm soon faded.

To Isolde's surprise, they were led to the intact granary. As they walked inside Isolde realised that it had been converted into a hall, its interior divided up by wooden partitions. But there was still an agricultural smell about the place, Isolde thought, the dry tang of the grain that had once been piled up here to feed hundreds of long-dead soldiers.

They were greeted by Tarcho, Nennius's cousin and commander of Banna, and by his wife, Maria. Evidently about the same age as Nennius, in his fifties, Tarcho was a big, slightly plump man with a bristling moustache, and his hair was a pale strawberry-blond laced with grey. He wore the insignia of a Roman soldier, including a handsome officer's belt, but also a shoulder-brooch and a belt heavy with knives, like a Saxon. His wife, too, a plump ball of energy and bustle, wore silver sleeve-clasps, Isolde noticed with faint envy. The Saxons hadn't come this far in great numbers, but their fashions had, it seemed.

Nennius greeted Tarcho eagerly. For him the end of a long quest was nearing. For Isolde, though, it was just another day of her pregnancy, and a long, hard day at that.

Maria saw this and immediately took Isolde under her wing. 'Oh, my dear, I know exactly how you are feeling. I should, I had five of my own, all boys, all of them as fat as their father, and look at *him*. Come,' she said, taking Isolde's arm, 'let's see if we can make you comfortable in this soldiers' hovel ...' She led Isolde to a small private room with a couch and pillows, and brought her hot water in a bowl. Her palm was rough, her grip strong, her skin dry, a worker's hand. 'I know you're far from home,' Maria said, 'and you must be frightened. But your father and my husband are cousins, so you're with family, aren't you? And believe me you're better off here than anywhere else. The soldiers always did have the best doctors. You'll be in good hands, I promise.'

'Thank you,' Isolde said sincerely. It was a huge relief not to be totally dependent on her father.

It was already late afternoon. She lay on her cot and slept a while, to gather her strength before the evening meal.

That evening Isolde was the last to join the group. They were in the largest room in the granary-hall, set out like a Roman *triclinium* with couches around a small central table. Nennius was holding forth about politics in Rome. He had a small leather satchel on the table before him. Isolde knew it contained documents about the purpose of his quest – to retrieve the Prophecy, as he called it, lost so long ago.

Her belly feeling heavier than ever, Isolde levered herself down onto a couch. The light from lamps and candles was cheerful enough, and the food, meat, bread and stewed vegetables, was warming and palatable, if it lacked spices for Isolde's taste.

This corner of the old granary was walled on two sides by unplastered stone through which holes had been roughly knocked to make windows. It was a working room, an office of sorts, with desks heaped with scrolls and tablets. Christian symbols could be seen in the clutter on the desks – a bronze fish, a *chi-rho* medallion. And the papers on Tarcho's desk were weighted by a stone statue, a reclining woman painted crudely in blue, the colour of the Virgin Mary. Isolde learned later it was a much older piece, a Roman soldier's carving of a local goddess called Coventina of whom nobody remembered anything but her name, now repainted as Christ's mother.

But despite these hints of civilisation, of religion and literacy, there was something brutal about the place, Isolde thought. Uncivilised. Armour and weaponry hung from the walls, along with the heads of animals: deer, a fox, a wolf. There was even the outstretched wingspan of a buzzard, evidently brought down by a soldier's arrow.

Tarcho, knives glinting at his belt, seemed in his element here. To Isolde's eyes he seemed more barbarian than Roman, and there was something in his hard, calculating expression she didn't like.

Maria prompted Tarcho: 'So you and Nennius share the same grand-father.'

Tarcho spoke around a mouthful of dripping meat. 'His name was Audax. He was born a slave but died a soldier. He named his son Tarcho, after the soldier who took him in and cared for him. *That* Tarcho was my father, and he named me for himself.'

'Ah, yes,' Nennius said, 'but Audax came from an old family who hadn't always been slaves. He was evidently a clever man, and that hereditary intellect seems to have been passed down to his second son, who was my father, called Thalius after another of his patrons. Thalius moved to Rome where I was born, as was my daughter. I'm sure old Audax would have been proud to see you in command of a place like this, Tarcho.'

Tarcho shrugged. 'Ten years ago I was a serving soldier in the Roman army. Then the British Revolution came. Farm boys in turmoil,' he said dismissively. 'We didn't really know what was going on up here. We just kept the peace along our stretch of the Wall. But there was no more pay ...'

Without pay, some of the soldiers stationed on the Wall drifted away from their posts, some turned mercenary, others resorted to brigandage and robbery – and others, Tarcho said, had gone off to Gaul with their service records in their packs, wistfully hoping to get their back pay. But most of the Wall troops, born and bred where their forefathers had served for generations, just stayed put. This was home; where were they to go?

'When the dust settled we got new orders from the Duke.'

Isolde asked, 'The Duke?'

'The Duke of the Britains.' The military commander who, under the emperors, had been in command of the Wall and the northern forts that supported it. 'He was no longer receiving orders from the diocese, or indeed from the prefect in Gaul, or the Emperor.'

The Duke of the Britains, suddenly finding himself free of his chain of command, took control. The troops would continue to function as army units, he ordered; they would continue to protect and police the population. But without central pay it was up to the local people, the farmers, to supply the fort, paying in kind in foodstuffs, materials, animals, labour.

'There was some grumbling,' Tarcho said honestly. 'But then the Picts came. One night they tried to sneak over the Wall, as bold as you please. Well, my men dug out their Roman armour and weapons, and we formed up and sent those brutes packing. After that the farmers were happy enough to cough up, and they turned out to cheer the

Duke when he stayed at Banna a few months back ...'

Isolde cynically wondered what choice the farmers had but to pay up. This Duke of the Britains, a Roman commander, seemed to be setting himself up as a warlord of a very old type, with the Wall his seat of power. No wonder this granary had the trappings of a barbarian chief's hall. Still, perhaps the locals were glad of some order and protection, for any was better than none. And perhaps to many of them, toiling at their land, it made no difference who called himself their lord from one day to the next.

She noticed Tarcho made no mention of the provincial government at Eburacum, nominally still in control of this area. Evidently, ten years after the British Revolution, the political situation had still to sort itself out.

'Ah,' Nennius said, 'but *need it have been this way*? Need the great tide of empire have drawn back from Britain?'

Tarcho frowned. 'I don't know what you mean.'

'Pelagius preaches of free will,' Nennius said. 'Each of us is free to shape his or her destiny. The future is unfixed – it depends on the decisions we make – *and so the past too was malleable*, dependent on human actions.' He smiled. 'There is a passage in Livy, written before the time of Augustus, in which he speculates what might have happened if Alexander had lived on, rather than die so young. Suppose he had turned his attentions *west*, rather than dissipate his strength in the endless deserts of the east?'

'He'd have come up against Rome, even then,' Maria said.

'Yes – a young but vigorous Rome which would have defeated him – so said the good Roman Livy! The history which seems so fixed to us is actually a fragile tapestry whose weave depended on human whim. And that's my point. If the decisions of the emperors had been made differently perhaps the eagle would still fly over Britain even now.'

'I don't see how,' Tarcho said reasonably.

'Then take one example,' Nennius said. '*What if this Wall had never been built?* What if the Emperor Hadrian had decided that rather than fix the border here he would complete the conquest of the whole island of Britain, all the way to the north, and devote a legion or two to keeping it? For it was tried, you know, several times, from the age of Claudius himself, and by the Emperor Severus, and later Constantius Chlorus led a force to the far north.'

'But the land up there is poor and the people are ugly savages who live in bogs,' Tarcho said practically. 'What use would it have been? Better to draw a line here.'

'In the short term, perhaps. But we are living with the long-term consequences of Hadrian's decision, Tarcho. And what do we find? Secure beyond a frontier fixed in stone, the barbarians have organised, federated, found capable leaders, and now break through the Wall to crush us. But if Hadrian had taken the land of the Caledonians *they would be Roman by now*, and Britain would be secure, at least internally. Think of it – a whole island to serve as a garrison for western Europe. Couldn't Gaul and Spain then have been defended when the Franks and the Goths came?'

'Yes, well, if you want to know what I think,' Maria said suddenly, 'we all got into this mess because of the way Constantine barbarised the empire. That's my view. That's why Gaul is full of Franks and Spain is full of Goths and the south of Britain is full of Saxons. I know, I've been down there. They care nothing for our ways and they're only out for themselves. And now, who is strong enough to throw them out? Nobody, that's who.'

Tarcho grunted. 'I see what you're driving at about Hadrian, Nennius. But she's right. If it's decisions and their dire consequences you want to talk about it's Constantine you have to consider. After all he did move his capital to Constantinople, taking all the money with it.'

'Then there's another possibility,' Nennius said. 'Suppose Constantine, instead of moving his capital to the east, had moved it *west* – to Gaul, even to Britain itself, where he was after all elevated. Imagine the empire run from Londinium or Eburacum! Why not? Britain was stable, relatively, and rich too: its corn and metals supplied the armies on the Rhine and the Danube for generations. That is why Britain has been the seat of one usurper after another, including Constantine himself. And with the British garrison behind them, and the focus of the emperors here rather than in the greasy fleshpots of the east, isn't it possible the empire could have been saved?'

Londinium as the capital of the Roman empire! The thought was so breathtaking it silenced them for a moment – and Isolde knew it wasn't such a terribly implausible idea. After all many of the usurpers of the last few decades before the final British Revolution had tried to set up a separatist empire of the western provinces.

'But I don't see what difference any of this talking makes,' Maria said now. 'Maybe things could have been different if somebody had done this instead of that – but so what? What's done is done. The past may have been malleable for those who lived in it, Nennius, but to us it is surely fixed.'

'Ah, but is it?' Nennius asked. 'Have you read what Augustine has said of eternity – in between his diatribes against Pelagius, that is? God is eternal, not time-bound as we are. He is *supreme above time* – I think that was the phrase. And to Him past, present and future coexist in one timeless moment. And if that is so, isn't it possible that God could intervene in the past as well as in the future?'

Tarcho pulled his moustache. 'Ah. I think I see where you're going with this, cousin.'

Nennius nodded. 'This is why I came here. We must talk of the Prophecy of Nectovelin.' And he pulled parchments from the leather case on the table before him.

IV

Nennius sketched the history of the Prophecy: how it had been uttered by Nectovelin's mother during his birth, how it appeared to predict events that occurred during the reigns of Claudius, Hadrian and Constantine. A trace of it had survived, as tattoos on the skin of generations of slaves, all the way down to Audax himself. But apart from that it had been lost to history – perhaps.

'I have this,' Nennius said, brandishing one of his documents, a dog-eared scroll. 'It is a memoir of the Emperor Claudius, who, it seems, actually saw the Prophecy for himself. This book was my father's, in fact, given to him by Audax, and he left it to me on his death. The Prophecy as Claudius describes it had sixteen lines, and though he doesn't reproduce it here – he seems to assume his readers would have it available – he summarises most of it well enough to reconstruct.

'This story of the Prophecy has fascinated me ever since I was a boy and heard it at my grandfather's knee. It is about emperors, you see, three emperors of Rome who would come to Britain. And it contains a crucial passage on Constantine. From my reading – and what my grandfather told me of the events of his own youth – it implored the reader to kill the Emperor! I believe that the assassination of Constantine was the *purpose* of the Prophecy. All the rest of it, predictions about Claudius's invasion and the building of the Wall, were included only as proof of the Prophecy's authenticity. They were there to make those who owned the Prophecy in Constantine's day take its mandate seriously.

'But these are only guesses. How I long to know more! I have written down my own reconstruction of the piece – here, somewhere ...' He scrambled in his bag, producing more bits of parchment. 'But the last few lines are not recoverable from Claudius's memoir, for he seems uninterested in them. He describes them only as "maunderings on freedom and the rights of peoples".'

Maria said, 'You spoke of God having the power to rewrite the past. Are you suggesting God himself ordered our family to kill an emperor?'

Nennius struggled to reply. 'Surely not God – but if God has such powers, who's to say that humans won't be able to emulate Him some day? *What if it was a man,* a man or woman of our time – or even of our own future – who, through the power of prayer, reached back to meddle with the past through the Prophecy? The family legend is of a Weaver, who stands outside the tapestry of time and can pluck at the courses of our lives as if they were mere thread.'

Tarcho said, 'And if he did, this Weaver – what was the point? Why murder Constantine?'

'To save Christianity,' Nennius said briskly. 'That was clearly the meaning our grandfather and his companions extracted from the surviving acrostic. If Constantine had died then, he could not have corrupted Christianity into an arm of the state – and it would not have become as intolerant as it has. There would have been no persecution of one Christian by another, no hounding of a thinker like Pelagius.'

Tarcho nodded. 'So Christians of the future tried to have Constantine killed, and their faith restored to a lost purity. Is that what you're getting at?'

'Yes,' Nennius said. 'Well, perhaps. I don't know! I am reconstructing events of centuries ago, and the mysterious motives of figures behind them, without even having available the primary evidence, the Prophecy itself.'

Tarcho frowned. 'It all sounds a bit devilish to me.'

Maria mused, 'But if you had such power, if you could deflect history – why use it that way? The Church is surviving even where the empire isn't – like here, in Britain. It's like a suit of clothes worn over the body of the empire, still standing even though the skeleton within has rotted away. If I could change history, I wouldn't worry about the Church, for the Church is robust enough to withstand the meddling of a thousand Constantines. I think I would find a way to hurry up the day when Britain returns to Rome.'

Nennius nodded sagely. 'Of course. Britain has always been part of the Roman world. It is only a matter of time—'

Tarcho snapped, 'No. It's different now. Rome is the last of a line of antique empires that go back to Alexander. But the world has changed, and Rome has had its day. If the Caesars ever do come back they won't be welcomed.' He eyed Nennius. 'You know, you should stay here, cousin. Here in Brigantia. Our family has been many things, soldiers, stonemasons and scholars. But at heart we have always been Brigantians.'

Nennius frowned. 'But Aeneas of Troy came to Britain and—'

Tarcho waved a hand. 'Forget that garbage. Here in the north, we haven't forgotten who we are. Our grandfather Audax grew up a slave, yet he remembered he was a Brigantian. And now the Romans have gone we're in a position to restore Brigantia to her old power. Think of that. Why not an empire of the Brigantians this time – and with us at the top? Why, we could take on the Caesars themselves.' His eyes gleamed.

Isolde wondered what the Duke of the Britains and the Eburacum government would have to say about such an ambition. And Nennius looked confused. Isolde knew that exiled Britons in Rome boasted that they were descended from Trojans who had fled the Greek siege, and that such groupings as 'Brigantians' were just artificial labels, imposed by the Romans for their administrative usefulness.

Was the future to resemble the past, then? Would Rome return, as Maria seemed to hope? Or, if they ever existed, could Tarcho's old erased nations really be reborn? And what of all the Saxons milling around in the south? They weren't going to disappear. She had a feeling that the future would be much more complicated than either Maria or Tarcho imagined, or hoped for – complicated, and bloodier—

That was when she felt the first contraction. She bit her lip and bent forward, clutching her belly.

Maria leaned forward. 'Isolde! Are you all right?'

Typically, Nennius didn't even notice his daughter's difficulty, and nor did Tarcho. 'We must talk of my purpose here,' Nennius said. 'My grandfather told me about the Prophecy. He had decided our family must remember the truth about itself. But the Prophecy, of course, was lost. *Or was it?*

'I simply couldn't believe no copy exists! Claudius hints of a copy placed among the ancient Sibylline oracles. I looked there – but Stilicho, Honorius's Vandal general, had the oracles destroyed decades ago.'

'And so,' Tarcho said, 'you wrote to me.'

Nennius sat up on his couch, intent. 'I know what meticulous record-keepers you army types have always been, Tarcho. It was here that the Prophecy's original was, supposedly, destroyed. But, I wondered, couldn't a copy of it have survived *here*, deep in some old vault? Wouldn't the tidy, indeed superstitious, mind of a soldier have ensured that much? And so I wrote to you, and asked you to search in advance of my visit – and, well, here I am. Come now, cousin, stop teasing me! Tell me if you found what I asked you to look for.'

Another contraction. Through her pain, Isolde clung to Maria at her side. Maria murmured comforting words.

Tarcho, evidently growing bored, shrugged. He reached inside his tunic and drew out a battered slip of wood. 'You were right. Somebody did make a copy, from memory at least – a pagan, probably, too superstitious to risk offending the gods by destroying their words; you're right about that too. Here.' He flipped it to Nennius. 'Probably all a forgery anyhow, or a hoax.'

Nennius grabbed the slip and unfolded it tenderly.

Another surge of pain, and there was liquid between Isolde's thighs. Now she did cry out. Maria, with calm competence, felt between Isolde's legs. 'Your waters have broken. Oh, by Jesus, I think I can feel its head.'

'It can't be. It's too early,' Isolde gasped.

Maria rolled up her sleeves and made Isolde lie down on the couch. 'They make their own time, dear.' She turned to a waiting servant. 'You, fetch my sister. And get some clean water and cloths.'

The servant hurried from the room.

Even now Nennius was more concerned about his precious Prophecy than about his daughter. He read, '"Ah child! Bound in time's tapestry, and yet you are born free / Come, let me sing to you of what there is and what will be" ... Sixteen lines – the alpha-omega acrostic – it's all here – oh, Tarcho, I think it's genuine all right! And here are the lines about Claudius, and Hadrian – the "little Greek", hah, I knew what it meant, I was nearly right in my reconstruction. This reference to a "God-as-babe" must refer to the birth of Christianity, for the faith was finding its feet in Hadrian's time.

'Oh, and here are the lines that must refer to Constantine. "Emerging first in Brigantia, exalted later then in Rome! / Prostrate before a slavish god, at last he is revealed divine, / Embrace imperial will make dead marble of the Church's shrine" ... Yes, yes! Wasn't Constantine proclaimed at Eburacum? Wasn't Christianity always called a cult of slaves? Didn't he have himself deified after his death, despite his conversion to Christ? And a church turned into dead marble – yes, surely that refers to Constantine's institutionalising of the faith. It speaks the truth! I knew it. I knew it all along, that the Prophecy was real, that it was truthful. If only Thalius and his plotters could have seen this document in full! How might history have been deflected?'

Isolde barely heard any of this. Her world contracted to the inside of her head, the heaving of her lungs, and the pulsing contractions of her belly.

Maria murmured in her ear, 'Don't worry, love. We'll fetch the army doctor. He's the son of a doctor too. I told you you're in good hands ...'

Somehow Isolde found the words slippery, wriggling from her grasp like fish in a stream. What were words beside the bloody reality of pain? But even as ocean-deep agony washed down her body, she felt impelled to speak. She turned her head, opened her mouth – but the words that poured from her lips were harsh and unrecognisable, even to her. She tried again, but only more alien words came.

Tarcho turned, curious now. 'What's she saying?'

'I don't know.' Maria frowned, concerned. 'It isn't Latin – is it? Or any British tongue.'

'I think it's German,' Tarcho said. 'Saxon maybe. Or Angle-ish. Why would a girl like that learn to speak Saxon?'

But I never have, Isolde thought, locked inside her own head. She tried again to speak but more of the repetitive gibberish, this Saxon, poured from her mouth.

'I know what this means,' Maria breathed, her face flushed. 'It's happening again.'

Tarcho asked, 'What is?'

'The Prophecy! You heard how Nennius described it. This is just as at the birth of Nectovelin – oh, get a stylus, you fool, and write it down!'

Tarcho stared. Then he disappeared from Isolde's view.

Isolde longed for her father to come to her, but he was still poring over his document. 'And the Prophecy's final lines – at last!—'

The pain intensified even further. Maria yelled, 'It's coming!'

Nennius read, ' "Remember this: We hold these truths self-evident to be—"'

'The baby's head – I can see it'

Even now, even as she pulsed with pain, Isolde helplessly gabbled Saxon.

'Why is she speaking Saxon?' Tarcho growled. 'The future is Brigantian, not Saxon!'

'That may not be up to you,' Maria said. 'Now shut up, you fool, and help me.'

' "I say to you that all men are created equal, free / Rights inalienable assuréd by the Maker's attribute / Endowed with Life and Liberty and Happiness's pursuit ..." ' Nennius sounded baffled. 'Life, liberty and the pursuit of happiness? What does it mean? If these are the words of the Weaver, what dream of his is this? Oh, what does it mean?'

The pain squeezed Isolde like a vast fist, and her baby fell into Maria's arms.

CITY OF LIMERICK 51220 300 PUBLIC LIBRARY

Afterword

I'm deeply grateful to Adam Roberts for his expert assistance with the Prophecy of Nectovelin, and for an invaluable reading of the book at manuscript stage. I'm also grateful to my agent Robert Kirby and editor Simon Spanton for even more than usually wise suggestions regarding the concept of this project.

As new archaeological evidence comes to light and written evidence re-evaluated, our understanding of Britannia is changing all the time. See for instance Alan Bowman's *Life and Letters on the Roman Frontier* (British Museum Press, 2003) on the remarkable 'Vindolanda letters', a mass of correspondence some of which was discovered as recently as the 1990s. A comprehensive recent reference is *A Companion to Roman Britain* ed. Malcolm Todd (Blackwell, 2004). I used the *Companion* as my guide in my choice among variant spellings of names. The best map of Roman Britain remains the Ordnance Survey's *Historical Map and Guide* (fifth edition) which I used as reference for variously spelled place names not mentioned in Todd's *Companion*. (For clarity I have not used pre-invasion versions of Latinised place names: Camulodunon for Camulodunum, for instance.)

A good if somewhat dated reference on the Claudian invasion is *The Roman Invasion of Britain* by Graham Webster (Routledge, 1993). A good reference on the life of Constantine is Michael Grant's *The Emperor Constantine* (Weidenfeld and Nicolson, 1993). New interpretations of Britannia's fall include Ken Dark's *Britain and the End of the Roman Empire* (Tempus, 2000) and Neil Faulkner's *The Decline and Fall of Roman Britain* (Tempus, 2000).

Regarding places, a recent reference on Richborough (Rutupiae) is Stephen Johnson's *Richborough and Reculver* (English Heritage, 1997), and on York (Eburacum) Patrick Ottaway's *Roman York* (Tempus, 2004). A magnificent new statue outside York Minster, on the site of the headquarters of the Roman fortress, commemorates Constantine's elevation there. A recent reference on Colchester (Camulodunum) is Philip Crummy's *City of Victory* (Colchester Archaeological Trust, 1997). The circus at Colchester is a recent discovery, not yet published at time of writing. A recent reference on Birdoswald (Banna) is *Birdoswald Roman Fort* by Tony Wilmott (Tempus, 2001), and the standard reference on the Wall is *Hadrian's Wall* by David Breeze and Brian Dobson (Penguin, 2000). But there is no substitute for visiting these wonderful places.

Any errors or inaccuracies are of course my sole responsibility.

Stephen Baxter
Northumberland
June 2005